The Little Blue and White House

About the Author

Jan worked at the University of Nottingham until taking early retirement to pursue her passion for writing. With an over-active imagination and a love of storytelling she wrote her first novel. Jan lives in the East Midlands with her husband and crazy cocker spaniel, and has three gorgeous grandchildren.

The Little Blue and White House

Jan S Clark

Copyright © 2024 Jan S Clark

The moral right of the author has been asserted.

Apart from any fair dealing for the purposes of research or private study, or criticism or review, as permitted under the Copyright, Designs and Patents Act 1988, this publication may only be reproduced, stored or transmitted, in any form or by any means, with the prior permission in writing of the publishers, or in the case of reprographic reproduction in accordance with the terms of licences issued by the Copyright Licensing Agency. Enquiries concerning reproduction outside those terms should be sent to the publishers.

This is a work of fiction. Names, characters, businesses, places, events and incidents are either the products of the author's imagination or used in a fictitious manner. Any resemblance to actual persons, living or dead, or actual events is purely coincidental.

Troubador Publishing Ltd
Unit E2 Airfield Business Park,
Harrison Road, Market Harborough,
Leicestershire. LE16 7UL
Tel: 0116 2792299
Email: books@troubador.co.uk
Web: www.troubador.co.uk

ISBN 978 1836280 156

British Library Cataloguing in Publication Data.
A catalogue record for this book is available from the British Library.

Printed and bound in Great Britain by 4edge Limited
Typeset in 11pt Minion Pro by Troubador Publishing Ltd, Leicester, UK

To my wonderful family, for always believing in me
and for your endless encouragement.
And to Kerry Maria Clark, forever in our hearts
1973–2002

Chapter One

Suitcase unpacked, Keri leaned on the balcony railing taking in the spectacular views across the cove. She could now unwind and soak in the atmosphere of this little gem of an island. Clinging to the coast, the village itself was surrounded by lush green hills with rugged mountains beyond, fragrant with lemon trees and an abundance of olive groves. The narrow road winding down into the bay had paths branching off on either side leading to a handful of villas.

Mesmerised by the clear blue waters of the Mediterranean lapping gently over the pebbles and swirling amongst the seashells at the water's edge, she took a deep breath and knew instinctively that Galazios Bay was everything she had been searching for.

To the south of the bay she caught sight of two figures on the breakwater. The smaller one was a young girl in a yellow dress, the taller of the two, a slender woman with long dark hair wearing black trousers and a pale camisole. As the girl dropped pebbles into the water her excited cries travelled like music through the air. Keri poured herself a glass of wine and settled down in the wicker chair on the balcony to watch the sunset unfold.

'Annys! Not too close to the edge please,' Maria called to her daughter.

'Mummy, look at the little fish, they're all squirmy,' cried Annys.

'Do you think they can see us?'

'They can probably see our shadows. If you stay very still they might come closer.' Maria replied as Annys knelt down and dipped her fingers gently into the crystal-clear water.

'One touched me!' she squealed with delight.

Maria watched her daughter with enchantment, the concentration on her face as she softly swirled the water. Her small inquisitive fingers caressed the water in a pattern resembling a figure of eight. What joy Annys had brought to her life, she thought. Thankfully she would never remember that dreadful night almost two years ago when her father had been taken by a merciless stormy sea, a tragedy that would change Maria's life forever.

Maria looked up to see Helenka waving from the terrace of the taverna. A short, plump, cheery woman in her early fifties with greying hair and big brown eyes; a colourful character, always the centre of attention.

'Look, there's Helenka!' Maria said. 'Should we go and see the pups?'

'Yes please! Will I be able to hold them?' asked Annys.

'I'm sure you will my darling,' she replied.

Helenka busied herself in the taverna, checking the menus were in order, making sure the napkin container was full, smoothing down the green and red checked tablecloths with the white plastic clips on each side to hold them in place should there be a breeze. Not much chance of a breeze tonight she thought. It had been a particularly hot day in Galazios Bay and without doubt would be a very humid evening. She lit the small oil burning lanterns on each table, even though all the tables would not be occupied as Sunday evenings were always fairly quiet, unlike the previous evening when the whole restaurant had been bursting at the seams, with music and dancing until the early hours.

'Helenka! Helenka! I've been stroking the little fish. One came right up to me and nibbled my finger!' Annys pointed her finger upwards for Helenka to get a closer look.

'Hold it still then, let me see,' said Helenka bending down and with as much enthusiasm as Annys. 'Did it tickle?'

'Yes, but not as much as when the pups lick my hand,' replied Annys with a chuckle. 'Can I see them now?'

'Of course you can,' replied Helenka taking Annys' hand and guiding her through the maze of tables to the back of the taverna, and up the narrow path past her little whitewashed house. Maria followed greeting Theo on the way and pouring some cold drinks.

'*Kalispera* Maria!' said Theo reaching out and taking her hand in his. 'How are you on this fine evening?'

'Very well thanks Theo, and you?' replied Maria.

'Alright thank you. I must say though I'm looking forward to a quieter evening tonight. Has Annys gone through to the pups?'

'Yes, she's so excited. Helenka's asked her to name them all,' she said continuing on her way.

Dear Theo, she thought. What a character! And with more energy than a man half his age!

The property was nearly 150 years old. It had been extended in the 1960s by Helenka's parents so that they could open up the taverna in the front section which led down to the beach. Helenka only vaguely remembered the house where she grew up with her parents, her memories now tied up in the old black and white photographs which adorned the walls of the taverna – the taverna that her father had named Ellas. Helenka had a happy childhood. As an only child she grew up with the bustle of life in the busy restaurant and learnt at an early age the demands of running such an establishment. To begin with she took on small tasks, such as filling up the condiments and folding napkins in a particular way, which was quite a skill in itself for a ten year old. She would sweep the veranda where the sand had blown up from the beach and run errands for her papa. The older she got came bigger responsibilities, clearing plates away, handing menus out and taking the orders for desserts. Helenka loved talking to the customers and helping them choose their sweet, describing each dessert in detail, much to the customers delight. It was in these early days that the seeds had been planted for her future in the family business.

To the side of the house, behind the taverna, was a little courtyard brimming with terracotta pots of different shapes and sizes, containing a variety of plants chosen for their hardiness in such a dry climate. In the corner stood a small round wrought iron table with a colourful mosaic pattern embossed on the top and four matching chairs. At the far end of the terrace a wooden gate led to a grassed area with an old stone outbuilding, this being the home of Kimba and her pups.

As Annys got closer she could hear them yapping, and peeped over the wooden stable door, the top half of which was wide open and fastened back to the wall to let the light through. She stretched over to stroke Kimba who was first to greet her, shortly followed by all five pups jumping around eagerly. Helenka unbolted the lower door and they scampered out clumsily tumbling over each other heading for the grass. Keeping a watchful eye, Kimba, a six year old Meliteo Kinidio with a black shiny coat, light brown patches, and a smattering of pure white fur down her chest, wandered over to where she was standing and nuzzled her head into her arms. Helenka had brought her to Ellas when she was just a few weeks old from Iona Petros who lived in one of the villas high up in the hillside. She had known Iona for many years and was upset to hear that her dog, Sheeba, the mother of Kimba, had recently passed away. On a recent visit Iona had been so taken with the pups that she decided there and then to have one of the bitches from the litter saying that it would be a welcome companion for her. The rest of the litter had been found homes too. Annys had chosen one of the females. Helenka's two friends, sisters from a craft shop in the next village, were having the two males and Helenka had decided to keep the last of the bitches.

Maria joined them in the garden with three iced drinks, balancing them precariously as the pups weaved in and out of her feet.

'Oh thank you Maria,' said Helenka taking one of the drinks. 'I'm ready for this!'

'Can I give them names now?' asked Annys.

'Yes, of course you can,' Helenka replied sipping the cool orange juice. 'Have you chosen names for all five of them?'

'Yes I have. This one is going to be called Tasha, because it is my favourite name, and she is coming to live with us.' Annys announced putting Tasha carefully back onto the ground. She then reached across to pick up the next one declaring its name would be Sophie. 'And that one over there with the white tail is Kayle,' she said proudly pointing across to where Kayle was running around in circles.

'They are lovely names Annys!' exclaimed Helenka. 'And what are you going to call the two boys?'

'Prince and Zeppo.' Annys declared clarifying which one was which.

Keri watched the sun disappear below the horizon. Finishing her glass of wine, she got up out of the chair and made her way over to lean on the railing again. Cobalt blue striped pots with vibrant orange and yellow marigolds adorned the left side of the balcony creating some privacy from the vehicles travelling down the hillside into the village, whilst adding a splash of colour against the backdrop of the apartment's whitewashed walls. As she moved her blonde wavy hair away from her face she thought of the colourful sunsets back home in Ireland. The Ireland she left nearly a year ago.

The evening before she began her travels through Europe Keri remembered the astonishing sunset on the western coast of Ireland. She had just finished an evening meal with her parents and was enjoying a stroll around the garden with them, chatting excitedly about her upcoming journey.

Earlier in the day they had shared with her the stories of their travels. She had heard them so many times before but was still enthralled. It had been a warm day with a few light showers in the afternoon followed by a glorious rainbow. The early evening had been particularly balmy and as the sun went down over the Galtee Mountains the sky was the most breath-taking combination of oranges imaginable.

Keri subconsciously twirled her necklace around her fingers; a handcrafted piece of jewellery made during her travels. She'd had the long silver chain for a while and was searching for a silver Celtic style pendant set with a cerulean blue stone. Upon visiting a craft fare whilst staying in France she had found the perfect companion for the chain, and to her delight had also come across some tiny matching gemstones to create a pair of earrings to compliment the necklace. Keri had a fascination for handcrafting her own jewellery from an early age and would make gifts for her family and friends.

Picking up the empty wine glass from the table, she turned to go back inside the apartment. Muffled voices could be heard drifting up from the path running alongside the taverna. Keri glanced over her shoulder. It was the little girl in the yellow dress and the woman with the long dark hair. She smiled to herself and closed the balcony doors behind her.

Maria and Annys turned to wave to Helenka. They walked together hand in hand along the winding footpath by the side of the taverna leading down to the sea. There was a wooden boardwalk stretching from one end of Galazios Bay to the other. Maria's house was at the far end of the bay. They reached the beach and turned left onto the boardwalk.

As they walked along, the scent from the trees was soft and sweet. It took Maria back to the evenings she shared with Demetrius where they would walk hand in hand dreaming about their future. Demetrius and Maria had grown up together; they played as toddlers; went to school in the next village, and upon leaving school were inseparable. In their late teens Demetrius and Maria told their respective families of their intention to spend the rest of their lives together. Their parents had been friends for many years and were thrilled with this news. At the age of 21 they married and set up home together in the little blue and white house at the end of the bay. The house belonged to Maria's grandparents who had passed away some years before. Demetrius and Maria restored and decorated their new home beautifully both inside and out, with the help of their family and friends.

Maria glanced down at the wooden walkway. Carved into one of the pieces of wood were Demetrius' initials. All the villagers who had helped build the boardwalk had their initials engraved into some of the timbers which were then placed along the length of the walkway. The idea of a pathway along the edge of the beach had been brought up in many conversations over the years. Helenka and Dino's eldest son, Yannis, had suggested putting forward an application to the local authority for its construction. After many negotiations and visits, an agreement was reached that the local council would supply all the materials but the design and building work would be done by the villagers. The whole village came together for the project; plans were drawn up, materials were supplied, delivered and stored on the piece of land Dino owned on the lower slopes of the hillside. It was here that the men of the village worked together to create the walkway, each bringing to the project their own thoughts and ideas. During this time the rest of the community made sure they had a constant supply of refreshments. Copious amounts of Mythos beer and Metaxa brandy, which the men affectionately called the nectar of the Gods, were commonplace amongst the group. The comradery of the men laughing and singing together could be heard throughout the village; some days there was more drinking and socialising done than actual work. They would animatedly discuss political issues and how they would put the world to rights; and there was always time for friends to come together for a game of *tavli*, backgammon. Frequent visits from various people during the day offering mezes, from olives and feta to a whole assortment of local dishes, were welcomed with open arms. They revelled in all the attention received.

As Maria and Annys approached the end of the boardwalk and turned onto the cobbled path that led towards the side gate, Maria looked at her watch, a present from Demetrius for their first wedding anniversary. This evening they were a little later returning home than usual, Maria thought, as they entered the house through the door that led straight into the kitchen. She switched on the light, put her keys on the table and went to fill the kettle while Annys went through to the living room. Maria loved this room; it was cosy with a couple of two-seater settees covered with red throws and a collection of orange, yellow and dark blue hand-made scatter cushions. The walls were painted in a very pale shade of yellow and decorated with a smattering of pictures, family photographs and portraits. In one corner of the room was a small brass lamp that was placed on a crafted oak coffee table. Underneath the lamp were Maria's two favourite photographs in silver frames: one taken on their wedding day and the other a photo of Demetrius and Annys playing on the beach two and a half years ago. At the far end of the room a patio door led onto the terrace which overlooked the sea and the spectacular views across the bay.

'Annys, could you open the shutters please? We'll sit outside for a while.' Maria called from the kitchen as she poured herself a camomile and limeflower tea, preferring the delicate taste of camomile to the stronger herbal flavours. 'I'll be through in a minute.'

'Okay mummy,' replied Annys. 'I'll get a book and we can sit outside to read it.'

Maria walked through the living room and out onto the terrace with her cup of tea and a glass of milk for Annys, who had retrieved a book from the shelf and was skipping along behind her. Maria placed the drinks on the round blue table and sat down on one of the four wooden and wicker chairs. Annys dragged one of the other chairs over to sit beside her and climbed up, book in hand.

'I'm going to ask Mrs Kashiotis if I can paint a picture of the pups tomorrow. She said we could paint something we saw at the weekend,' said Annys.

'What a great idea, that would make a lovely picture,' replied Maria. 'We could put it on the kitchen wall with the others.'

A collection of Annys' artwork adorned the kitchen walls. Only last week she had returned from pre-school with two rather large, dried pasta and rice collages, one in the shape of a sunflower for Maria, and the other a rather wonky tree for Helenka.

Mrs Kashiotis was an elderly lady who taught at the local school in Lefko Bay and had been there for many years. The school only had two classes, one being pre-school children and the other five to seven year olds. Mrs Kashiotis generally taught the younger children. As far as anyone could recollect she had always lived in the bay and had been part of the school for well over forty years, watching the generations come and go. The school building itself was long and narrow, formerly a row of four fisherman's cottages, with extensions added on over the years and a small playground to the rear.

As the last page of the book was turned over Annys stifled a yawn, rubbing her tired eyes. It had been a long hot day and she knew that as soon as Annys' head touched the pillow she would fall fast asleep.

'Go on up, I'll come and tuck you in soon,' Maria said clearing the table.

'Have you seen Max?' asked Annys as she squeezed the book back onto its shelf. Max was Annys' teddy bear, a present on her first birthday from *yiayia and pappous* Aetos, Maria's parents.

'He's on the chair in the kitchen. I'll bring him up in a minute.'

Maria dried her hands, and climbed the narrow staircase to the first floor, past her bedroom and along the landing to Annys' room, where her bedside light was casting pink shadows. She was nearly asleep. Maria carefully lifted her arm up and laid Max at the side of her, covering them up with the pretty pink duvet. She bent down to kiss her daughter.

'Goodnight darling, God bless,' she whispered.

'Night-night mummy, love you,' replied a sleepy Annys.

Maria closed the bedroom door and made her way back downstairs.

Helenka poured Theo a well-deserved nightcap. It had been a fairly quiet evening at Ellas. He placed a bowl of bar snacks on the table and sat down. Helenka joined him with the drinks. Theo had been a chef at the taverna for many years; originally employed by Helenka's parents. He initially worked in the evenings and occasionally during the daytime, but over the last few years preferred to just do evening shifts, which suited Helenka. The lunchtimes were covered by herself, Maria and Mark, with Helenka doing most of the cooking. Maria helped in the kitchen and took the customers' orders when they were busy. Mark would wait on the tables, organise the refreshments and run the bar area. The arrangement worked very well.

Mark was a bit of a free spirit who enjoyed the simple things in life. He wandered into Ellas for some casual work three years ago and had been there ever since. The customers loved him.

'*Yamas* Theo!' said Helenka as she raised her glass to his.

'*Yamas!*' replied Theo wiping his brow with his chewing gum white handkerchief. 'It's been a very warm evening again.'

'It certainly has! I've just watered the plants in the courtyard and settled Kimba and the pups in for the night.'

Theo and Helenka sat together sipping their drinks in the moonlight. They had been friends for a long while, comfortable in each other's company. She slipped off her sandals and stretched out her weary legs.

'Tell me, did you see a young woman on the balcony

of one of George's apartments tonight?' remarked Theo curiously.

'Yes, I did notice someone up there earlier.' Helenka replied. 'I must say that from just a quick glimpse she reminded me of someone; but I can't quite put my finger on whom…'

Chapter Two

Maria was hypnotised with the blanket of stars twinkling in the midnight blue sky, feeling she could almost reach out and touch them. The shallow water trickled softly over the rocks below the terrace and the silvery moonlight shimmered on the ripples of the sea. In the harbour the silhouettes of colourful fishing boats swayed back and forth. She still expected Demetrius to sail into the bay on The Crimson Tide, the fishing boat he shared with Dino. She sighed, lost in her thoughts. Tomorrow would have been their eighth wedding anniversary.

The wedding had been quite a celebration with the whole village involved in some way or another. Galazios Bay was transformed with gold and silver streamers glistening in the sunlight. White and gold ribbons fluttered in the trees and garlands of white balloons shaped into arches formed a pathway along the main route through the village leading to the chapel on the edge of Lefko Bay.

Maria woke early to the sound of birdsong outside her bedroom window. The Aetos family home was spread over three stories, an ivory coloured house with rich blue window shutters, perched halfway up the hillside amidst lemon groves above Galazios Bay. To the front was a magnificent terrace on two levels overlooking the whole bay with black wrought iron railings around the perimeter and a spiral staircase to one side leading to the upper level where grapevines growing over a pergola created natural shade from the hot Mediterranean sun.

She opened the balcony shutters and fastened each one back to the metal catches on the wall, the brightness of the early morning sun lit up the whole room. As she turned around her eyes were drawn to the beautiful white Italian satin wedding dress on the mannequin in the corner. On the dressing table lay the tiara and hair jewels and draped over a stand the veil with thousands of tiny hand sewn crystals replicating the intricate pattern on her dress.

Maria got dressed and made her way downstairs to the kitchen where her mama and papa were preparing breakfast. Papa was singing his favourite song with great animation as he peeled and sliced the fruit.

'*Kalimera!*' her mama greeted as she wiped her hands on her apron. 'Did you sleep well darling?'

'Oh yes mama, wonderful!' she replied joyfully. 'I can't believe today has finally arrived. My head's in a whirl!'

'It's going to be such a lovely day! Come and get some breakfast. What would you like to drink?'

'Tea please,' she replied picking up the jug of milk and pouring it into the cups. 'And just a small bowl of muesli.'

Maria's papa danced over to the table and placed the fresh bowl of fruit in the middle. He bent down to kiss the top of this daughter's head.

'*Kalimera* papa!' she said smiling up at him.

'*Kalimera* Maria on this your special day!' he crooned.

'The fruit salad looks delicious!' she said pouring milk onto her cereal.

'It's the best way to start the day,' he declared as he sat down and spooned some into his bowl, covering it in rich creamy Greek yogurt. 'What time's Lela coming?'

'She should be here about 9:30. She's having her hair done in the salon first. Spiros is bringing her here and then he's going to collect the flowers,' she replied reaching out for a bowlful too.

Lela was Maria's best friend; they had grown up together. After leaving school she had trained as a hairdresser and beautician. She was thrilled to be matron of honour. Maria, her mama and Lela had spent the last few weeks trying out different hairstyles, nail colours and makeup for the big day, usually accompanied by a glass of wine or two.

After breakfast Maria helped mama clear the dishes away and headed upstairs for a shower. Lela had left specific instructions that Maria must wash her hair no later than 8:30 so that it would be ready for her to style when she arrived. Lela was a stickler for organising everything with military precision. Out of the two girls she was the bossy one, Maria on the other hand was very laid back: two totally different characters but one great friendship.

As she stepped into the shower she could hear papa serenading mama in the garden. She hoped her and Demetrius would be as happy after so many years.

Spiros reversed his taxi down the narrow driveway, Lela turned to wave.

'See you later, drive carefully!' she called 'I want the flowers here in one piece and don't stop chatting on the way!'

'Okay! Okay!' he shouted back waving his arms animatedly as he disappeared from view. Spiros knew every bend and twist of the hillside like the back of his hand having lived in the area all his life and driving through the mountainous roads for over thirty years.

Lela positioned the mirror at the back of Maria's head so she could see what her hair looked like from all angles. She had created a very pretty style, loosely tussled and pulled back softly from her face with a sparkling crystal comb, and ringlets to the side. There was a light knock at the bedroom door. Lela reached over to open it.

'Here we are girls!' said mama as she placed a small tray with three glasses of freshly squeezed orange juice onto the table in the corner.

'Oh Maria, your hair looks beautiful,' she exclaimed. 'Lela… it's just perfect!'

'Thank you mama Aetos,' Lela replied feeling rather pleased with herself. 'Are you ready to have your nails done now?'

'Go on mama,' said Maria as she took a glass from the tray and admired her hair in the mirror. 'I'll have mine done after yours. Lela wouldn't let me move a muscle whilst she was doing my hair so I'm going to stretch my legs for a while.'

'Yes okay, then we'll go downstairs for some lunch. I've got some salad, cheeses and fresh olive bread ready. Papa's put a bottle of champagne on ice and Spiros should be back soon with the flowers so we can all have lunch together.'

Maria walked over to the balcony and stood for a while watching the boats in the bay. In less than four hours she would be Mrs Maria Triantis.

Spiros handed the flowers to papa who placed them onto the cool marble floor in the dining area. The bridal bouquet was a cascade of pale pink and soft ivory roses entwined with light green foliage and a twisted cream silk bow on the handle. The dainty oval posy for Lela was in the same colours with small wispy stems of maidenhair fern threaded throughout. There were cream buttonholes for the groom, best man, papas and the ushers, and corsages for the ladies. Spiros had already dropped the flowers for the reception off at Helenka and Dino's taverna before coming up to the house.

The pre-wedding lunch was a lively affair in the Aetos household with Maria, mama, papa, Lela and Spiros all talking excitedly and sipping the chilled champagne. Papa made a toast, his third one to count!

'*Yamas*! Be happy Maria! May you and Demetrius have a long and happy life together,' he said as he raised his glass again.

'*Yamas*!' everyone cried in harmony together.

It was early afternoon. Spiros had gone home to get changed, and mama and papa were getting ready too. Lela helped Maria step carefully into her dress fastening the tiny silk buttons all the way up the back. A tweak of the hair and a bit more lacquer. Now for the final touch: The veil. Perfection!

The short journey to the church for Maria and papa was in a horse drawn carriage decorated with white and gold ribbons. Lela and mama had started walking to the chapel some time earlier with guests joining them along the way. By the time they arrived there was quite a procession, with local musicians gathered outside playing a selection of well-known long established tunes. As the carriage pulled up, Dino, in his role as best man, opened the door. Maria smiled lovingly across at Demetrius who was standing in the doorway of the chapel with his parents. Mama held Maria's bouquet whilst papa outstretched his hand for his daughter, who descended gracefully from the carriage while Lela smoothed out any creases in Maria's dress and adjusted her veil.

The ceremony itself was a traditional Greek Orthodox wedding with some time-honoured personal touches. All the close family members stood at the front, Maria's on the left and Demetrius' on the right. To the side of the alter was an ornate table with two large decorated candles, the wedding rings, the crowns, a goblet of red wine and the New Testament. The first part of the ceremony was the betrothal; the rings were blessed by the Priest and exchanged between Maria and Demetrius three times. He then placed on their heads the two flowered crowns joined together with white ribbon. They took three sips of wine symbolising the marriage of Cana and the beginning of their life together, after which the Priest led them around the sacramental table, a symbol of eternity, whilst the congregation sang three short hymns. After carefully removing the crowns he pronounced them man and wife. A final prayer, then came Maria's favourite part, the stamping on toes.

'Who is going to be the head of the family?' the Priest asked Maria and Demetrius.

With the swiftest of moves Maria stamped on Demetrius' toes much to the amusement of the congregation.

'Looks like Maria then!' he declared with a grin.

Once outside the chapel, the photographs were taken, after which friends and family formed two lines facing each other creating a pathway leading from the door to the gate for the wedding party to pass through. Demetrius helped his new bride into the carriage. He sat down beside her, looked adoringly into her eyes, took her hands in his and placed a lingering kiss on her lips.

'Maria Triantis... I love you so much!' he whispered into her ear. 'Today you have made me the happiest man alive.'

The chauffeur presented them each with a glass of champagne before travelling slowly to the reception. The guests followed in cars and on foot to Ellas, whilst the musicians continued to play along the way. Arriving at the reception everyone made their way to the tables, laden with bottles of wine, ouzo, water and soft drinks, whilst Maria and Demetrius had more photos taken.

Dino stood on one of the chairs, tapped his knife against his already half empty wine glass. 'Please raise your glasses and welcome the bride and groom – Maria and Demetrius Triantis!' he announced above the merriment.

They entered the room and the band began to play their favourite music, the guests stood up cheering and clapping to welcome them. Helenka took Maria's hand and led them towards the wedding table decorated with fresh flowers and a scattering of gold and silver confetti. A meze of tempting starters was served, the platters of bite-sized food being an integral part of the fabric of Greek life; a tradition dating back to ancient times. With the drinks flowing freely, they tucked into the colourful salads, seafood platters, cheeses, fresh bread, tzatziki and taramasalata.

'Can I have your attention ladies and gentlemen?' the tall thin band member called into his microphone. 'Mr and Mrs

Triantis, please make your way to the dance floor for the first dance of the evening.'

Everyone started to applaud and stamp their feet as the bride and groom moved through the maze of tables to the dance floor. As they danced closely together Maria could feel their hearts beating as one; cameras were flashing all around them wanting that perfect picture of the happy couple. Before long they had been joined on the dance floor by their parents, closely followed by the other guests.

'Let's liven things up a bit should we!' the tall frontman bellowed above the music. 'Can you all make two circles, a smaller one in the middle and a bigger one on the outside… now hold hands and here we go!'

The band started to play Zorba the Greek on their bouzoukis, the whole room were up on their feet; with the exception of one old woman from the village who sat towards the back of the room knowing her dancing days were well and truly over, but quite happy to watch the other guests as she sipped from a long glass of ouzo. The two circles moved slowly in opposite directions in time with the music, quickening the pace as the dance went on. The children had broken away from the main circle to create their own dance at the side of the room and were thoroughly enjoying themselves.

The exhilarated guests made their way back to their seats and the main course was served. Most people had opted for the moussaka with béchamel sauce. Others chose the grilled chicken breast with artichokes in white wine or a fillet of salmon served on a spinach base. Everyone was eating, drinking and full of lively conversation throughout the meal.

Maria looked out towards the sea. The late afternoon sun was sparkling on the horizon; people had started to move away from the tables and were spilling out onto the boardwalk and the seashore. Most of the youngsters were paddling in the shallow waters at the front of the taverna.

The newlyweds threaded their way through the room thanking guests for coming, for their generous gifts and good wishes. Upon reaching the front of the veranda Maria stepped out of her shoes, steadying herself on Demetrius' strong arm, and walked down the steps onto the soft sand below. Demetrius bent down to pick up her shoes. He was a handsome man with thick shiny dark hair scraped back from his face revealing his rugged bone-structure, brown mysterious eyes, and a deep bronzed skin. They strolled together hand in hand along the water's edge enjoying a quiet moment with just each other for company. Maria loved to feel the grains of sand between her toes. She bent down to pick up a shell in a delicate pink shade with an alabaster rim. Her fascination for seashells and pebbles had started from being a young girl, when her parents would bring her down to the beach and she would spend hours collecting shells of all shapes and sizes; washing them, polishing them, and sometimes even managing to turn them into jewellery. Her mother was particularly proud of the jewellery box covered in small coral-coloured shells made for her one Christmas, to this day it still had pride of place on the dressing table in her bedroom.

'My present to you Demetrius,' Maria said smiling cheekily as she placed the shell into his masculine hands. 'When you look at this you'll always remember this moment.'

'I'll treasure it forever. It will be a token of our love,' he replied. 'I too have a present for you. Close your eyes and turn around.'

Maria covered her eyes and turned to face the sea. She could feel his fingers lightly caressing the nape of her neck sending a shiver all the way down her spine. He carefully placed the delicate necklace around her neck.

'Open your eyes darling,' he whispered.

'Oh Demetrius… it's beautiful,' she said looking down at the silver heart shaped locket with a tiny Austrian crystal set in the centre. He wrapped his arms tenderly around her as the sun disappeared on the skyline leaving a hazy pink glow in the sky. Maria turned slowly and gazed into Demetrius' eyes lifting her arms around his neck. Moving back slightly he steadied himself against one of the trees along the shore, his arms reaching around her waist as he pulled her closely towards him. Lost in their own private world.

They made their way back to the taverna. White twinkle lights decorating the trees throughout Galazios Bay glistened in the waning early evening light. The sound of joyous celebrations from Ellas drifted through the air. Maria squeezed Demetrius' hand tightly. She would remember this moment forever.

The evening celebrations were just as jubilant, perhaps even more so, almost certainly due to the amount of alcohol consumed during the afternoon.

A group of dancers from Lefko Bay dressed in Greek national costume gave a magnificent performance to include the infamous handkerchief dance, followed by the traditional plate smashing to represent good luck and happiness for the bride and groom.

The evening drew to a close. The exuberance of the day now a wonderful memory as the pace slowed to a more relaxed one with couples shuffling dreamily around the floor together.

Maria shivered, startled from her thoughts by the screeching of fireworks on a neighbouring island where a fiesta was taking place. Vibrant reds, blues and golds burst into the night sky. She put her hand into her pocket and took out the pink shell she had given to Demetrius eight years ago. How she wished with all her heart he was sitting beside her on their terrace.

Chapter Three

Keri stepped onto the balcony, coffee in hand, feeling the warmth of the early morning sunshine all around her. She felt refreshed. The first good night's sleep she'd had in such a long time. Looking around Galazios Bay she realised why her parents were drawn to this beautiful place. It was almost as if there was something magical about it and she couldn't wait to explore. Finishing her drink, she went into the bedroom to get dressed. A quiet day had been planned. A walk around the village and a spot of lunch in that lovely beachfront taverna would be the order of the day, she thought.

Keri chose a floral green and pink cotton dress; the sort of dress you might wear to a typically English garden party at the height of the summer. She opened her jewellery box and picked out a light green necklace with matching bracelet complimenting the colours in the dress. Brushing her shoulder length blonde wavy hair, she decided to tie it up securing it with a pastel green hair band. Her look complete and a quick glance in the mirror told her this was the perfect choice for spending a morning wandering around the village. She smiled to herself, picked up her handbag, sunglasses and keys from the sideboard and made her way out of the apartment walking down the stone steps to the street below. Turning to the right she admired the window display in George's craft shop underneath her apartment. George and his wife Anna had owned the property for a number of years, and they had divided it into four sections. To the left on the ground floor they had created a small craft shop selling everything from handmade ceramic ornaments to an array of leather goods. They had made their home to the right of the adjoining shop. There were two apartments on the first floor; both tastefully decorated with stunning views across the bay. Anna had a flair for interior design which was reflected in the apartments, their home, and the displays in the craft shop.

Across the road, the adorable taverna with the red and green tablecloths was coming to life. How inviting it looked she thought. Yes, it would be lunch there today.

'Good morning George.' Keri called as she entered the shop.

'*Kalimera* Keri. How are you? Are you settling in?' he asked as he came into view from behind the wooden counter in the corner.

'Yes thanks,' Keri replied. 'You have a lovely apartment, the décor and furnishings are beautiful, and the views are simply perfect! Last night you asked me to let you know how long I would be staying. If the apartment is available, I'd like to stay for one month initially please.'

'No problem. It's free until the end of September. Just pay me on a weekly basis in case you change your mind,' said George as he shook Keri's hand.

'That's great thanks.'

'What are your plans for the day?'

'Not much really. I'm just going to wander around the village and probably have some lunch in the taverna opposite.'

'A good choice if I may say so. I've known Helenka and her family for many years. She'll make you very welcome,' he replied walking towards the door with her and wedging it open with an ornate doorstop hoping to let a little breeze flow through. Keri continued on her way.

As George turned to go back into the shop, he caught sight of Helenka.

'*Kalimera* Helenka!' he shouted across to her.

'Oh! *Kalimera* George. Sorry, I was miles away. How are you?'

'Not bad thanks. I'll pop across later,' he replied.

'Okay, see you then,' she answered and carried on setting the tables, placing some freshly cut flowers on each one.

The colourful wind chimes hanging from the ceiling of the shop swayed gently. George looked at his watch, 10 o'clock. He went into the little room at the back, filled the kettle and switched it on. Anna would be back from the bakery soon with fresh pastries to have with their coffee.

Just a short walk along the road Keri admired another craft shop much smaller than Georges. Once inside it was like an Aladdin's cave with surprises around every corner. As she moved slowly through the narrow aisles her senses came alive with the heady aromas of jasmine and sandalwood. There were pretty handmade bags of lavender displayed on a wooden stand. The fragrance brought childhood memories flooding back of visits to her grandmother who would hang pouches of lavender in her wardrobe and always had sprigs placed around the house. On another shelf there was a collection of joss sticks with every fragrance imaginable, from subtle vanillas to spicy musks, along with a small selection of hand-carved wooden holders. Keri chose an assortment of joss sticks and a holder. She paid for the goods and made her way across the road and down a narrow path leading to the beach.

With the sun glistening on the sea she took off her sandals and sat on the edge of the boardwalk feeling the warm sand between her toes taking in the beautiful vista before her. To the far north of the bay, she noticed an adorable blue and white house sitting on the edge of the rocks with a terrace overlooking the sea. She could see a woman and a young girl on the terrace. Perhaps it was the same people she'd seen last night walking along the breakwater. Imagine living in this wonderful place, waking up every morning to the sound of the waves gently washing over the shore. Brightly painted fishing boats rising and falling softly with the rhythm of the sea captivated her. She gazed to the right and saw a boat yard and what looked like a fishing hire shop with a small jetty running into the sea. She could see two men launching a small motorboat. One jumped aboard whilst the other pushed the boat further into the sea watching it for a while as it moved steadily through the labyrinth of boats that were moored nearby, then made his way back to the wharf. Her eyes followed him as he went about his work, brushing the yard vigorously, his muscular arms moving ropes and fishing equipment from one side of the jetty to the other. He straightened up, leaned the brush against a wall and ran his fingers through his dark brown hair taking something out of his pocket to tie it back with, then continued sweeping the yard.

Sitting for a while longer Keri took in the fabulous views around the bay. She glanced across to the boat yard again. The man was just disappearing into the building and out of sight. She stood up, straightened her dress, brushed the sand off her feet and put her sandals back on. A different pathway was taken back to the main road amongst a profusion of fig trees, which sheltered her from the hot midday sun. Once back at the road she continued in the same direction, strolling past a block of apartments, some more craft shops and a small supermarket where she bought a bottle of chilled water to quench her thirst. Keri noticed a dusty track leading down to the boat yard. Beyond this, weaving up into the hillside was a group of outbuildings; one looked like a makeshift art studio with canvases drying outside in the sunshine. To the rear of the building was a large piece of overgrown land. Reaching the signpost for Lefko Bay she turned and headed back towards the village centre looking upwards at the vast green hillside with its houses dotted throughout the sloping landscape.

Helenka chatted with an elderly couple as she served them a seafood platter and some olive bread. Turning to go back into the kitchen she noticed a young woman in a green and pink dress looking at the menu on the wall at the entrance to Ellas. Her face looked vaguely familiar.

Keri walked into the taverna and sat down at one of the tables overlooking the sea, with some natural shade from the grapevines above. She glanced around taking in the pleasant surroundings, the neatly laid tables with their checked tablecloths and fresh flowers, smiling at the couple nearby as they enjoyed their seafood platter.

'*Kalispera*! Welcome to Ellas,' said the friendly owner as she offered the menu to Keri. 'Can I get you a drink whilst you look through the menu?'

'Good afternoon,' replied Keri in a delicate Irish accent which seemed to be disappearing ever so slightly the longer she spent away from her homeland. 'I'll have a sparkling mineral water please.'

She browsed through the menu and chose tuna fish in pita bread with a Greek side-salad. Minutes later Helenka returned with a tall glass of water garnished with a slice of lemon and took Keri's order. Whilst waiting for her lunch to arrive she sipped the cool drink and remembered what her parents had told her about Helenka and her family. Promises made all those years ago to keep in touch but as both their lives moved on they had not kept in contact with each other as often as they would have liked. Keri's parents treasured the precious memories and still had a handful of photographs, one in particular that Keri had been given before her travels: A lovely family photo of Helenka, her husband Dino and a very young Yannis which had been taken on the wooden steps of the taverna they loved so much.

Helenka walked over to Keri with her food placing it in front of her. How different this woman looked from the young happy-go-lucky one in the photograph, she thought. It was almost as if something had taken the sparkle out of her eyes.

A light pat on her shoulder brought Keri back from her daydreams. It was George.

'Oh hello George,' she smiled as she thanked Helenka.

'I see you've met my good friend,' he said reaching out to kiss Helenka's hand.

'Good friend am I now. Yesterday I was the apple of his eye!'

'Looks like you've already met my pretty little Irish girl,' he said with a wink. 'Keri's staying in the apartment above the shop for a while.'

'Welcome my dear. I'm sure you'll enjoy your stay in Galazios Bay.'

'Thank you. I had a walk around the village this morning. It's such a beautiful place and the people I met were just so friendly.'

'Yes, you'll find that. It's a very close-knit community. Everyone knows everyone else's business, and if they don't they'll make a point of finding it out. A word of warning for you though Keri, George is a bit of a one, he's an eye for the ladies. I don't know how Anna's put up with him all these years!'

'Get away! She loves me. It's my boyish charm!'

'You'd better get going, she'll be wondering where you are and sending out a search party!'

'More to the point she'll be wondering where her lunch is!' George chortled.

'We'll leave you to have your lunch in peace Keri. If there's anything you want just let me know,' smiled Helenka as she took George's arm and led him into the kitchen to collect his and Anna's lunch. Keri returned her smile. Yes, she thought, she could feel quite at home here.

Maria turned to wave to her parents as she made her way steadily along the winding lane and down the hillside into the village with a basket full of lemons and limes for Helenka. For many years Maria's papa had supplied Ellas and a handful of local tavernas with fresh produce from the small orchard behind their house. Maria had spent the morning with her parents picking fruit and tidying the garden. They had enjoyed lunch together and she was now on her way to collect Annys from pre-school, dropping the basket of fruit off with Helenka first.

At the bottom of the hill she crossed the road and looked over towards the beach. Couples were relaxing in the sunshine and strolling hand in hand along the water's edge. Families playing on the sand, building sandcastles with moats around them; children filling their buckets with seawater and rushing back to pour what was left in them into the moat. It seemed like only yesterday Demetrius and Annys had built their sandcastles decorating them with shells and pebbles. In the evenings they would watch the sea gently wash over their creations. Demetrius telling Annys that they could build another sandcastle the next day. Annys thinking that the sea God, as she called him, took their sandcastles because they were the best ones on the beach. When Demetrius died Annys innocently told Maria that the reason the sea God had taken daddy, uncle Dino, Milos and Nikolas was because they were his favourite fishermen and he wanted to look after them forever. Out of the mouths of babes, Maria thought.

She walked down the pathway to the side of Ellas as Helenka came bustling up to take the basket from her.

'*Kalispera* my darling,' she greeted with a warm smile.

'*Kalispera* Helenka,' she replied as she swept a long piece of hair away from her eyes. 'I'm glad to give you the basket. It didn't feel that heavy when I left mama and papas.'

'Come and sit down. I'll get you a nice cool drink. You on your way to collect Annys?'

'I am. I hope you don't mind but she wanted to see the pups again this afternoon, so I said we'd call in on the way back home if that's alright?'

'That'll be lovely Maria. I bet she'd like an ice cream. I'll have her favourite ready for when you get back.'

Helenka walked over to the bar and poured a glass of lemonade for Maria filling it up with crushed ice. Maria chose a table in the shade and sat down watching the boats moored around the bay, their reflections shimmering on the surface with the gentle rise and fall of the tide rippling underneath, slowly turning them around in circles.

'There you go Maria; this will cool you down a bit!' said Helenka as she put the drink on the table. 'How are mama and papa today?'

'Thanks Helenka,' she replied gratefully as she lifted up the glass to her lips. 'Mmmm… they're good. We spent the morning in the garden. Papa was keeping himself busy tidying the orchard and I helped mama with the pruning and cutting back the shrubs. Not quite the way I thought I'd be spending my wedding anniversary, but it kept me occupied.'

'Yes, it's been fairly quiet in here today, unlike eight years ago… now that was some celebration wasn't it!'

She pulled up a chair and they talked easily together. Two people sharing their happiest times and memories, brought even closer together with the tragedy of losing their loved ones. For Maria every time she looked at Annys, Demetrius lived on. For Helenka in her boys, Yannis and Manos, Dino lived on.

'The flowers look lovely,' Maria remarked as she leaned forward to smell them.

'Pale pink and soft ivory roses. They're beautiful aren't they?'

'Thank you Helenka. They certainly are.'

Keri finished her lunch, dabbed her mouth on the serviette and sipped the last drop of mineral water as Helenka walked up to her table.

'Did you enjoy your lunch my dear?' asked Helenka as she reached over for the empty plate. Would you like the dessert menu?'

'It was lovely thank you. I'm much too full for a dessert but I wouldn't mind another water please?'

'Yes of course,' Helenka replied disappearing into the kitchen with the empty plate.

Keri looked around the taverna, her eyes resting on the photographs on the walls. They looked like they had been taken many years ago. Perhaps they were Helenka's parents.

Helenka walked over to Keri with the glass of water.

'What beautiful photographs.' Keri remarked. 'Are they your family?'

'Yes, most of them are of my parents, grandparents, and great-grandparents. The taverna has been passed down through the generations in one form or another. The story is that it started out as a couple of fisherman's cottages built by my great-grandfather and his brothers who were the first men to fish in these waters,' she said pointing to one of the older blurry photographs. As you can see the building has altered quite a lot over the years.'

'How fascinating,' replied Keri. 'It's a magnificent place. The whole bay has got such a lovely feel about it. I've done a lot of travelling over the last year or so and I have never seen such a beautiful spot. It almost feels kind of magical.'

'Thank you Keri. I've always lived here and can't imagine living anywhere else.'

She finished her drink and walked over to Helenka to pay for the meal.

'Thanks Keri,' she said giving her the change. 'Hope to see you again soon.'

'Oh you will. I'm sure you'll be seeing a lot more of me,' she replied with a warm smile walking towards the entrance, passing Maria, realising it was the woman with the little girl who lived in the pretty blue and white house at the end of the bay. Maria gave a fleeting glance and smiled at Keri who said a quick hello as she strolled out of the taverna and across the road to George's apartments.

'Thanks for the drink Helenka. I really needed it," said Maria getting up and pushing the chair back under the table. 'See you later with Annys.'

'*Adio* Maria,' she said waving her on her way.

Whilst Maria walked along the sandy pavement on the winding road leading to Lefko Bay she wondered what Annys had done at pre-school today. On approaching the school she could see Annys in the doorway with a rather large painting in her hand. Mrs Kashiotis waved to Maria as she ran towards her excitedly.

'Mummy! Mummy!' she squealed. 'Look what I've done. A picture of the pups. Tasha is the big one at the front and the others are on the grass behind her,' she said proudly. 'Can we go to see Helenka? I want to show her my painting.'

'Of course we can darling. I'm sure she'll love it too! She's getting a special ice-cream ready for you.'

They walked together holding hands with Annys chatting away excitedly about her day. As they came to the brow of the hill between the two bays Annys saw Manos working in the boatyard and shouted over to him. He immediately stopped what he was doing as she ran over and crouched down to look at the picture she was waving in front of him.

'Wow!' he exclaimed. 'What a great painting! You've used some lovely colours.'

'It seems we have a budding artist on our hands Manos,' said Maria as she joined them.

'Keep up the good work Annys and I'll be displaying your artwork in my studio before long.'

'Yippee! I'll do my next painting for you Manos,' she cried with excitement. 'We're going to see the pups now and Helenka's got an ice-cream for me.'

'What's your favourite flavour?' he asked. 'Mine's strawberry.'

'Chocolate's the best one!' she cried. With lots of chocolate sauce on top.'

Manos stood up. Annys turned around and ran down to the sea collecting some pebbles on the way. She dropped them into the water one by one.

'How are you today Maria?' Manos asked. 'When I spoke to mama this morning she reminded me that it was your anniversary.'

'I'm not too bad,' she replied as Manos put his arms around her shoulders. 'It just feels a bit of a strange day. I'm a bit…well…kind of lost really.'

Arms linked; they strolled down the slipway to Annys who was happily playing by the water's edge. Maria had always been able to talk openly to Manos, unlike his older brother, Yannis. The brothers were nothing alike. Yannis could be quite abrupt, bordering obnoxious, was extremely ambitious and wasn't happy unless he got his own way. Manos, on the other hand, had such a caring, thoughtful nature, a very laid-back character, friendly and compassionate, always willing to lend a helping hand. Manos, the shorter of the two brothers, was never without a smile. His thick dark brown hair rested easily on his broad shoulders and his warm hazel eyes were like coffee with swirls of cream. Yannis wore his brown hair short and had distant, almost troubled piercing brown eyes. He held a prestigious job in the City. In contrast Manos was more than happy with his modest quieter lifestyle spent in the boatyard and his art studio. How different the brothers were.

Manos asked Annys to collect some flat pebbles. She did so and shared them with him. He bent down and began to skim some of them along the tranquil surface of the water making them glide gracefully. Annys squealed with delight. He then patiently taught her how to skim pebbles across the water. After a number of disastrous throws it all came together and in no time at all Annys had learnt the art of skimming.

Helenka scooped some vanilla ice-cream into a sundae glass, poured some chocolate sauce into it and a generous helping of chocolate ice-cream topped off with a flake and more sauce. She spotted Annys happily skipping down the road. Helenka walked over to the table at the side of the entrance to the kitchen and placed the ice-cream, spoon, and serviette down. Annys rushed over to Helenka and hugged her tightly.

'*Kalispera* Annys!' Helenka said rocking her side to side. 'How was school?'

'It was good, but not as good as this ice-cream!' laughed Annys as she spooned it into her mouth quickly. 'Mrs Kashiotis let us paint whatever we wanted today. I've painted the pups,' she declared pointing to the painting Maria had placed on the table.

'What a beautiful picture. Who's the pup at the front?' Helenka asked.

'That's Tasha of course!' replied Annys in such a way as to assume Helenka should have known this already.

Maria came out of the kitchen with two coffees, offering one to Helenka and told her how they'd met Manos on the way back from school. Annys joined in the conversation explaining with great enthusiasm how he had taught her to skim pebbles across the water. She scraped the spoon round the sundae glass to make sure every little bit had gone, licked her lips and wiped the ice-cream from around her mouth on the napkin.

'Did you enjoy that darling?' asked Helenka.

'Yeah, it was scrummy!' Can I go and see the pups now?' she asked.

'Yes, that's fine as long as it's okay with your mama,' Helenka replied.

Annys looked across to Maria fluttering her eyelashes cheekily.

'That's fine, go on then, remember to be gentle though,' added Maria.

She climbed off the chair and ran to the back of the taverna through the side door and along the narrow path to Helenka's little house. Once at the side of the building she could hear the pups scurrying around. Through the courtyard she weaved in and out of the terracotta pots full of plants and flowers to the bottom of the terrace and through the wooden gate shouting to Kimba who was already peeping over the stable door wagging her tail excitedly. The pups scurried around Kimba's paws, jumping and stretching, clambering over each other to see who their visitor was. Annys stroked Kimba's head tenderly and on her tiptoes reached over to unbolt the stable door. Out spilled the pups tumbling over each other. She knelt down on the grass and played with them whilst an ever watchful Kimba rolled around in the warm afternoon sunshine.

Maria asked Helenka about the girl with the fair hair who was in the taverna earlier that afternoon in the pink and green dress.

'Her name's Keri. George introduced her as his pretty little Irish girl. She's staying in one of his apartments above the shop. I don't know how long for. She seemed a very nice girl and was intrigued by the old photos on the walls.'

'Wonder if she's on holiday or just passing through?'

'She mentioned that she'd done a lot of travelling over the last year.'

They finished their coffees, and both got up from the table. Maria picked up Annys' painting and followed Helenka through to the garden. She knelt down on the grass and patted her knees. Kimba ambled up and nuzzled her head into Maria's lap. Annys was rolling around with the pups giggling, screwing her face up as they licked it. The white tailed mischievous one stopped, looked up and realised he had another playmate. Bounding towards Maria, ears flapping, he leapt full pelt into her arms; not quite having worked out where his brakes were yet. Moments later she was bombarded with another four pups all wanting her attention. Annys skipped over clapping joyfully at the spectacle.

Closing the garden gate behind them they walked up the path to the main road. Annys clutched her picture and turned around to wave goodbye to Helenka. As they strolled along the main road holding hands Maria glanced up to George's apartments to see Keri sitting on the balcony with her feet up reading a book looking very relaxed.

Chapter Four

The evening in Ellas was quiet. Theo had his usual nightcap with Helenka, then left the taverna walking steadily up the winding path at the back of George's apartments to his little house in the hillside. He looked up. The clear evening sky was covered with an abundance of gleaming stars lighting his way through the thick olive groves.

Helenka stared out to sea as she cleared their glasses away. The moonlight danced on the water forming silvery shimmers across its surface. It was at this time of night when everywhere was quiet that she found the most difficult with friends and customers long gone. She remembered the many conversations with Dino well into the early hours, sitting together discussing the events of the day, sharing their thoughts and ideas for the future. Sadness crept over her like a wave. During the day she had learnt to put on a façade, disguising her true feelings. To the outside world she was bubbly and cheerful and played the part very well. How she wished she could just sit with Dino for one more day, listening to his soothing voice, breathing in his musky aroma, and running her fingers through his soft jet black hair. But alas, she thought sorrowfully, these things she would never take pleasure in again. She could still hear him calling goodbye to her on that fateful morning. She began to weep. Her tears were not only for Dino and the boys who lost their lives, but also for herself…

'Bye my love. See you later,' Dino called as he pulled the door to behind him on his way to the boatyard.

'*Adio* my Dino. God Bless,' she replied as she'd always done for nearly 30 years.

He made his way along the boardwalk. The sun was breaking on the horizon and the sea particularly calm. Sensing someone behind him he looked over his shoulder to see Demetrius. He acknowledged him with a friendly wave and slowed his pace.

'*Kalimera* Dino,' whispered Demetrius putting his hand up to his face to protect the early morning light from his delicate eyes. Perhaps too much ouzo the previous night might be to blame. 'Do you remember much?' he asked.

'No, not really,' replied Dino squinting behind a pair of sunglasses. 'Some music… some ouzo… some dancing…'

'Arrggh! It's all coming back to me now,' recalled Demetrius.

'It must have been too much dancing!' chipped in Dino.

'Nothing to do with the ouzo then?' Demetrius said with a cheeky grin.

'No, I wouldn't have thought so,' he chortled shaking his head.

It had been Theo's 60th birthday. He didn't want a fuss, just a small get together with friends. Of course, with the ouzo flowing it soon turned into an occasion with half the villagers there and Demetrius, Dino, Theo, and Spiros performing their party-piece handkerchief dance. All in all it soon became a very memorable evening, leaving the partygoers a bit worse for wear the next morning.

They reached the boatyard. Milos and Nikolas were already there. The kettle was on, and they were discussing how the younger generation could handle their booze better than the oldies. Looking at the state Dino and Demetrius were in as they walked towards them perhaps there was some truth in it. After finishing their mugs of very welcome coffee they prepared to launch the boat. The four men had worked alongside each other for a number of years now, and it all came together like clockwork – even with the hangovers, and there had been many of them! The shipping forecast had been checked. It was going to be a changeable day; hot and sunny in the morning, turning cloudier with a south-westerly breeze in the afternoon. A few kilometres to the east of where they would be fishing the forecast was not so good, with storms brewing up early afternoon but dying out before reaching their area.

Galazios Bay disappeared from view as they sailed their red and blue fishing boat, The Crimson Tide, due south towards the Cretan Straits. The sky; an interesting medley of pinks. The zephyr; a light warm westerly wind. As they travelled further south the familiar outlines of coves and bays grew smaller, with the houses clinging onto the side of the cliffs vanishing one by one until they were just mere dots on the horizon.

Demetrius and Dino had been the best of friends for over ten years despite the twenty year age difference. When they decided to go halves buying The Crimson Tide, Maria and Helenka were thrilled since they had been using an old leaky fishing boat which spent more time being repaired in the boatyard than out at sea earning them a living. The Crimson Tide was a much larger fishing vessel, so they put the word out to find a couple of local young fishermen to work with them.

When Milos and Nikolas left school without a single qualification between them they drifted from one job to another until Milos found work as a handyman in Lefko Bay, and Nikolas took on some shifts in a bar at weekends and worked in the local supermarket during the week. Neither were afraid of hard work. Nikolas heard that Dino was looking for two men to work with them and approached him one afternoon. He had met Nikolas a few times and was impressed with his enthusiasm and energy and asked him to come along to the boatyard with Milos the next day. Even though neither of them had any experience in the fishing trade they were eager and quick to learn the ropes. Before long all four men had formed a good solid working relationship.

Dino poured a coffee from the flask and sat down on one of the upturned crates.

'Can't you take the pace old man? teased Milos as he walked over to him, taking a bottle of water from the cool box.

'Hey! I can drink you under the table any day young whippersnapper!'

'Is this a private party or can anyone join in?' butt in Nikolas. 'You feeling okay Dino? You're looking a bit green around the gills. Must be all that dancing eh!'

'You're like a bloody double act! Now piss off and let me have forty winks!'

Leaving Dino to have his nap, Milos grabbed another water from the bag and tossed it over to Demetrius. Ever since they'd all been working together, once they'd settled down in the waters where they were fishing for the day, they would take it in turns to each have an hour or so break, a luxury that Dino and Demetrius hadn't previously enjoyed. Within minutes Dino invariably lost himself.

Upon waking he felt the swell of the sea had changed. He stretched and stood up, steadying himself on the side of the boat. Perhaps he was imagining it but something was definitely not quite right. Often these waters were a bit on the choppy side but today things seemed different; the sea was billowing and the air turbulent. He stumbled over to Demetrius who had decided to draw in the fishing nets. Dino helped him haul them in whilst the boys started to prepare The Crimson Tide for its return. In the distance the thunder rumbled.

Within what seemed like only minutes the sea had become confused with angry waves whipping up around them tossing the red and blue boat into the air. They struggled to steer it, perilously isolated, as the waters raged on with unpredictability.

'Mayday! Mayday!' cried Nikolas over the radio. 'Mayday! Mayday!' But there was no reply. 'Mayday! Mayday! Please come in! Over!' Nothing except a faint crackling could be heard. 'Can anyone out there hear me? It's The Crimson Tide... Come in! Come in! Over!' he called into the microphone pinpointing their position.

With the weather worsening rapidly and all radio contact seemingly lost, Milos reached for the flares in the hope that a cargo ship in the vicinity might pick up they were in trouble. The sky churned into a threatening murky black. The sea lashed by the ferocious winds, was driven into mountainous heaps, and crashed against the sides of the fishing boat.

Unforgiving stormy seas pounded the boat relentlessly. The men were exhausted. The wind sucked up the sea and spat it out into steep tormented funnels dragging the susceptible boat around violently and breaking the wooden vessel in two, like one would snap a cocktail stick. The men were whipped into oblivion. They fought the mighty power of the atrocities of the sea… and lost… as many had done before them.

A piteous silence now rested all around. A scene of deprivation where The Crimson Tide had once been. An inky black darkness, now still, motionless. The sea ebbing and flowing – like a metronome keeping the rhythm, a peaceful place, a quiet place, where nothing or no-one can intrude. Shadows of people lost before them. And now Dino and Demetrius, Nikolas and Milos… ghosts of the merciless sea.

Following Dino's tragic death, Helenka had the arduous task of dividing his estate between their two sons. Apart from the taverna, which she had inherited from her parents, Dino's other assets were the boatyard, a small collection of neglected outbuildings and a substantial piece of land to the side which snaked up into the surrounding hillside. After a lot of discussion with her sons, and a number of sleepless nights, it was agreed that the boatyard would go to Manos. His wish was to renovate the outbuildings to make an art studio so that he could concentrate more on his paintings. Yannis had never shown any interest in the boatyard or outbuildings but was more than happy to have ownership of the piece of land to the side, thinking he might look into building himself a villa on the higher slope, and perhaps a handful of small apartments on the lower level nearer to the village which he could then rent out. All in all, everyone seemed quite happy with these arrangements.

Manos loved his art studio. He was happy in his work, whether he was in the boatyard renting out the half a dozen small motorboats to holidaymakers or absorbed in his painting. He would spend the mornings in the boatyard maintaining and servicing the boats, touching up any paintwork and keeping the paperwork up to date. His afternoons were spent painting in his art studio. Some bystanders would talk to him whilst he worked, others just stood transfixed in peaceful serenity. He had learnt to display his artwork on the wall outside his studio catching the trade of passers-by and had often been asked by holidaymakers if he could paint their portrait or a caricature and was more than happy to oblige.

He took a step backwards to admire his latest work and added some gentle brushstrokes to the cerulean sky. The light of the mid-morning sun brought out the varying shades of blues used to create the feeling of a hot summer's day. At the top of the painting a darker blue sky fading downwards to more delicate hues enhancing the brilliant whites of the crooked stone buildings with their dark blue doors and window frames. To the forefront of the painting a crazy-paved patio area with terracotta pots brimming with vibrant orange and yellow blossoming plants, a spectacular display of colour against the whitewashed walls. To the left, a small blue wooden patio table with two chairs and a bowl of succulent fruit positioned in the centre. A stone archway led down to a twisting path of uneven steps with the sea beyond. He stepped back again and nodded. Pleased with the panorama he had created before him he carefully removed the canvas from the easel and leaned it against the studio wall. He whistled contentedly as he cleaned his pallets and brushes in the deep sink at the rear of the building. His eyes were drawn towards the trees by the sound of the birds chirruping loudly. Something had stirred them from their restful state. Coming into view he saw Felix, the local tabby cat, a bit of a mischievous rogue by all accounts, padding along slowly watching his prey high up in the trees willing them to come down so he could show them who was boss. It had become a bit of a game between him and the birds as to who would gain ultimate supremacy. Ambling lazily into the studio he made his way over to Manos who put the cloth and brushes aside on the bench and bent down to scoop him up into his arms, playfully chastising him, telling him that the birds were very clever and were never going to come down from their safe haven to take their chance with such a scamp. He purred shrewdly.

Helenka looked up from her newspaper and saw Spiros' taxi travelling down the road. He had taken a group of four Italian friends back to their holiday apartment on the far side of the island, after they had enjoyed an unhurried lunch at Ellas. The taverna had been highly recommended to them by the owner of the apartments, who happened to be a distant cousin of Spiros. He parked the car and got out. Helenka went over to the bar and poured two iced frappes. Pulling up a chair he took one of the coffees from her. She sat down again folding the newspaper and placing it on the edge of the table. Helenka noticed that Spiros seemed a little preoccupied, nervously turning his rosary beads around in his clammy left hand. Mark approached the table with a small platter of tapas, a couple of plates, forks and serviettes, exchanged pleasantries and returned to the kitchen.

Spiros pushed his glasses up onto the bridge of his nose. They had a habit of slipping down every so often, especially when he was worried or anxious. How could he tell Helenka what he had seen today? He knew how underhanded Yannis could be, and a gut-feeling told him that he was up to no good. He always trusted his first instincts and felt uncomfortable about the Frenchman he had picked up from the airport earlier and whom Yannis had welcomed with open arms. Beads of perspiration trickled down his weathered face. Reaching into his trouser pocket he pulled out an off-white handkerchief to mop his brow.

'Is something on your mind?' Helenka asked.

'No. What makes you think that?' he replied.

'You just seem a little lost in your thoughts... a bit distant. Is something bothering you Spiros? If you don't tell me we can't put it right and you know you can tell me anything,' she said light-heartedly. 'How does the saying go? A problem shared is a problem halved.'

'I'm alright... nothing's wrong. Stop fussing woman! If there's anything wrong you'll be the first to know. I'm just a bit hot, that's all. The heat doesn't usually get to me but today it's been a bit too much,' he explained deciding that he'd shelter her a little from what he saw but would drop into the conversation that he'd met Yannis in the City. He had a lot of admiration for Helenka and didn't want to worry her unnecessarily. Perhaps he was imagining it, but something just didn't sit right. Could it be the extreme heat over the last few days playing tricks with his mind and making him look a bit too deeply into things?

Mark took off his black apron and hung it up on the metal hook behind the kitchen door. He walked out of the kitchen and through the taverna rolling up his white cotton shirt sleeves gesturing to Helenka that he'd see her in the morning and waving goodbye to Spiros who raised his arm in response.

'I've had quite a busy day so far. I'm hoping it'll quieten down a little now. I had a couple of airport runs at the crack of dawn and it's been non-stop ever since,' he told Helenka trying to justify himself. 'As I was leaving the airport for the second time I was hailed by a rather discourteous Frenchman wanting a lift into the City. If I'd have known how impolite he was I wouldn't even have given him the time of day, let alone a ride in my taxi!' he babbled. 'I always chat to my passengers… always have done… always will do! In all the years I've been driving I've never had such a rude customer, wouldn't engage with me at all other than saying he was a hotel developer here on business!'

'He doesn't sound very pleasant,' sympathised Helenka.

'Oh, and I saw Yannis in the City this morning,' he said wiping his brow again. 'He looked as busy as ever, rushing around.'

'I'm always telling him to slow down and take things a little easier but he's so head-strong and takes no notice.'

Spiros was deep in thought once again. How can I tell her about the Frenchman and Yannis? How her son had extended such a warm welcome to the stranger and how uncomfortable he looked upon realising that the taxi his business associate had just got out of belonged to Spiros. Yes, he felt somewhat troubled.

Chapter Five

Mark walked up the steep lane to his apartment. With his shift at the taverna done the rest of the afternoon lay before him. A familiar rustling noise was coming from the bushes at the side of the path. It was Felix. Mark had got used to the cat's quirky antics. Felix could sense the time he would be walking up the hill and play a game of hide and seek in the bushes; the only problem being that he couldn't stay still in one place long enough to create any surprise. Weaving in and out of Mark's legs he purred with contentment. They were similar in many ways. Both loved to roam around, were happy with the simple things in life, very much free spirits and so incredibly easy to get along with.

It was Mark who had named the stray tabby cat found wandering around the village two years earlier. He was reminiscent of the cat from his childhood in England who was called Felix. Mark had taken him under his wing in much the same way that Helenka had looked after him in those early days after his arrival in the bay. She was looking for some help in the taverna and he was looking for a part-time job for the summer months. Helenka knew Mark and his family very well as they had regularly holidayed in the village and intuition told her that he would be perfect for the job.

Mark's family were from Ashbourne, a quaint market town in the Derbyshire Dales, the heart of England. His parents had lived in the town since the early 1970s, both coming from nearby villages and deciding to set up home there, buying an elegant Victorian house shortly after their marriage. It had come a long way from the dilapidated building which they had lovingly restored and was now a stylish three-story property. The front door was in the middle of two very large bay windows, a heavy stylish black door with polished ornate brass fittings. On the step at each side of the entrance were two tall bay trees in large square black planters. They were in the antique trade and had converted the right side of the property for the business making their home on the remaining ground floor and the two floors above. The window display always looked spectacular from the roadside; a lot of care went into designing it to draw the attention of the passer-by and captivate them into entering the shop. The long decorative hallway had a separate entrance which led directly into the shop with its assortment of antiques. As soon as the customer walked in they felt they were entering a different era, working their way through the array of curios in all shapes and sizes, a wonderful display of collector's items from eighteenth century vases to colourful 1970s kitsch knick knacks. Their customers were seldom disappointed.

Mark loved to help out in the shop after school and at weekends. His favourite job was setting out the window display and he was particularly fond of the hand-crafted wooden painted rocking horse which had been bought for him when he was just a small child, which now adorned the bay window looking out onto the street below. The rocking horse was not for sale, unlike everything else in the shop. A collection of pristine Victorian dolls on a Welsh dresser waited patiently for someone to give them a home. Trinkets full of rustic charm and small ornaments filled the shelves. In a corner, at the back, stood an elegant grandfather clock in immaculate condition, chiming on the hour, every hour, without fail. It had been in the shop for over ten years and would now seem unusually quiet without it ticking rhythmically in the background. A stylish mahogany dining table and six chairs was positioned in the centre of the room with a silver service tea set on a tray and a pair of silver Corinthian column candelabras to each side. It was on this table where Felix had had his unfortunate incident. He had always roamed freely around both the house and shop weaving in and out stealthily, but one particular hot summer's day a butterfly fluttered through an open window and his eagle eye spotted her. With the swiftest of moves he leapt onto one of the dining chairs taking a swipe at her missing by a hair's-breadth but upsetting an old Japanese tea set which crashed to the floor shattering into dozens of pieces. From that moment onwards Felix was banished from the shop.

Behind the table stood a tall glass cabinet packed with memorabilia from two World Wars along with mementos spanning three centuries. Coloured glass perfume bottles in all shapes and sizes gleamed as the sun's rays shone through the window. Scattered throughout an abundance of 1950s and 1960s trinkets and costume jewellery, not of great monetary value but more the choice of someone wanting to collect such items from a particular era. Over the years Mark's parents had learnt to tell the difference between an antique enthusiast and a browser who had just strolled into the shop. They could spot a professional dealer by the way they handled and scrutinised the items. Some even had little handbooks, taking them out discreetly now and then as they wandered around.

The door at the end of the hallway led to their private quarters. To the rear was the dining kitchen with its beautiful cast iron aga, the centrepiece of the room. Much entertainment had taken place in this room over the years. Mark would often arrive home from school to the smell of home-baked bread and cakes, and it was here he sat with his mother at the large pine table to do his homework. After Felix was exiled from the shop he decided to set up home in the dining area and spent a lot of time curled up on one of the chairs watching the comings and goings throughout the day, knowing there would always be someone around to fuss him.

To the front of the house on the left hand side was an elegant lounge decorated in rich greens and reds with a luxurious deep red leather Chesterfield suite. In front of the open fireplace stood an ornate Victorian fireguard. A mahogany mantelpiece surrounded the fireplace matching the rest of the antique furniture in the room. A beautifully crafted writing bureau was positioned in the bay window which showed the intricate carvings when the light bounced off it in a certain way. A framed photograph had pride of place in the centre of the mantelpiece. It was taken during one of their many holidays to Galazios Bay when Mark was a young boy. Posing for the picture were Mark and his parents, Helenka, Dino and their two boys, taken on the steps leading down to the beach at the front of the taverna.

He opened the door to his apartment and scooped Felix up who purred contentedly knowing he'd get a saucer of milk, as he did every afternoon when Mark returned from work. Felix knew he had the best of both worlds. At the taverna he could roam around being fussed by the customers, apart from the occasional one who would shoo him away! Helenka always had some food for him in the early morning and during the evening; even with the arrival of the pups he still knew he was the most important one around and would strut along the wall at the back of the taverna tormenting Kimba and her brood whenever the mood took him.

Mark flung the balcony doors open and placed Felix's milk on the veranda, going back inside to pour himself a cold drink to enjoy in the afternoon sunshine. He slid down in his chair, put his feet up on the balcony railing and before long with the warmth of the sun on his face, his eyes heavy, he dozed off. Felix settled down on the floor at the side of him watching the birds in the trees, soon he too was fast asleep, dreaming of the day when he would show the birds who was boss!

Yannis and the Frenchman, Christophe, a tall thin man with short light brown hair and piercing green eyes, left the restaurant in the City and returned to Yannis' office a short walk away. Christophe loosened the neck of his shirt, a well-travelled businessman who always wore a suit and tie, but perhaps in hindsight should have prepared his wardrobe a little more carefully for this particular trip, especially with the extremely high temperatures that had been raging in the islands over the past few days. As Yannis opened the door to the building the coolness from the air conditioning in the reception welcomed them. Taking the lift to the top floor where his small insurance investment company was, they stepped out and into the offices opposite. The view of the City was of rooftops, very noisy and dusty with the traffic below but from here he ran his little empire. He proudly showed Christophe around the suite of three offices explaining that he had built the business up over the last five years.

'Is it always this hot in here?' enquired Christophe petulantly.

'Not usually. I'm afraid the air conditioning is on the blink at the moment. Can I get you a coffee before we look at the plans?'

'Yes. Black. No sugar,' he answered abruptly.

Christophe looked around the office, disappointed with what he saw, feeling he might be wasting his time in this little Greek backwater, worlds away from his business suite in Jersey. It was the last time he did any favours for acquaintances, no matter how enthusiastic they were! Christophe felt irritated. His eyes scanned over the plans for the hotel, they weren't drawn up to the standard he was used to. Finishing their drinks they arranged to meet the next afternoon to discuss the project.

Back in his hotel room he thought about Yannis and his plans. Christophe had never known how hard it was to start with such humble beginnings. As an only child his business was inherited from his parents who were both killed in France when he was young; his father a wealthy businessman; his mother a barrister. With thriving property investments and businesses throughout France, including Paris and La Rochelle on the west coast of France, where he moored his luxury yacht, he was a well-known and highly respected member of the elite. St Helier, the capital of Jersey, was where he had made his home, and where he escaped to whenever he wasn't working or sailing around the Mediterranean.

Opening his flight bag, he reached for the bottle of malt whisky bought from the duty free shop at the airport, poured himself a generous glass and sat on the chair nearest to the window. Being used to a more temperate climate he was glad the hotel room had a modern air conditioning system. Recalling his brief look at the plans earlier he felt Yannis was getting out of his depth with his big ideas for the hotel development. He could see that his ambitions would lead him nowhere without the proper management and expertise behind him, which of course, he had plenty of. But did he want to get involved? Was Yannis strong enough to take on the challenge?

Reaching for the bottle and pouring another whisky he thought of the last trip on his yacht with friends travelling down the Portuguese coast with a stopover at Lisbon, through the Gibraltar Straits and hugging the eastern coast of Spain, before spending a few days in the millionaires' playground that was The South of France, with his crew of six pampering to their every need. It was on this trip that the little Greek island had been mentioned as an up-and-coming holiday destination and ripe for investment. One of his acquaintances had contacts on the island and had heard that a local businessman was looking for financial backing to develop a hotel complex on his land in a prime location, and he thought that with Christophe's experience and driving ambition he would be just the right man for the job. After copious amounts of wine had been consumed the two shook hands on it and Christophe said he would fly over to see if a deal could be done.

Looking out across the crowded rooftops he wondered whether Yannis had ever been on a yacht. How different his life must be here on this little Greek island. But there was something about Yannis he liked. He had drive and enthusiasm in abundance. Everyone had to start somewhere after all. This could be the big break Yannis needed. He decided there and then to give this guy a chance. What harm could it possibly do?

Manos locked his studio door, took a quick look around the boatyard and started walking towards Ellas. Earlier he'd stood all his canvases against the wall inside, except one. They had dried so quickly in the heat of the afternoon. Tomorrow he would take them in his pick-up to the weekly craft market in Lefko Bay, usually managing to sell a few to both tourists and locals alike. A friend had a small ceramics business in the area, so he'd drop the paintings off early in the morning as usual before returning to open the boatyard. At the market they shared a craft stall which worked well, with the paintings filling the wall space and the ceramics displayed on the table area.

'*Yassou* mama!' called Manos as he neared the taverna. She turned and shouted over to him.

'Manos! *Kalispera* to you too!' she replied as her eyes rested on the canvas in his hand. He lifted it up to show her.

'It's beautiful Manos! Just beautiful! When did you finish it?'

'Earlier this afternoon. I'm really pleased with the colour palette.'

'I could almost reach into it and take a piece of fruit from the table. Oh Manos!' she exclaimed. 'I'm so proud of you!'

'I'll put it on the wall over here mama,' he remarked walking over to the whitewashed wall.

'I'm sure it won't be there very long… someone will snap it up before you've even finished hanging it!' replied Helenka as she went to get a couple of cold drinks from the bar.

He positioned it on a picture hook already in place on the stone wall and took a card out of his pocket with his name, phone number and price on and placed it underneath the painting. At least once a week he brought one of his paintings down to the taverna to display. He noticed that another couple had gone. Helenka returned with the drinks. He turned around to take the cold beer from her and commented on how quickly they were selling.

'I know!' replied Helenka. 'All the customers are admiring them. Can you let me have some more of those cards, because folk keep asking me for them, some have even mentioned wanting to place orders.'

'Business is booming! It's really taking off,' Manos said gleefully. 'I'll be needing a bigger studio soon. I'm taking a dozen or so up to the market in the morning. Last time over half of them went. I can't keep up with demand!'

Helenka watched Manos as he finished his beer, his eyes vibrant and energetic; thinking how much he looked like Dino in his younger days. He had come such a long way in such a short space of time. She might suggest he look at taking on some help in the boatyard leaving him more time to concentrate on his artwork.

Theo walked into the taverna and across to where Helenka and Manos were sitting greeting them warmly.

'*Kalispera* my friends!' he said 'How are you both?

'Good thanks!' she replied 'Come and look at this painting Manos has just finished.'

'Blimey mate, it's brilliant!' Theo declared. 'It's not gonna stay there long!'

'I was just saying exactly the same!' Helenka added. 'I know you've painted lots of canvases but this one is something else!'

'Okay the pair of you, you're embarrassing me now. Look! You've got some more customers coming in. They've come for a bit of food not to hear you two going on about paintings, if they wanted to hear all that they've had gone to an art gallery!' he joked.

Helenka greeted her customers, showing them to their table and collecting a couple of menus on the way before taking a drinks order from them. As she walked over to the bar she mentioned to Manos that George wanted to have a word with him sometime.

'Okay mama, I'll pop across now. Do you know what he wanted?'

'No, sorry I don't… but I am intrigued,' she replied taking the drinks over to the customers.

'You're always intrigued!' he replied with a glint in his eye. 'See you soon.'

As he crossed the road his eyes were drawn to one of the apartments above George's shop. The balcony doors were open and fastened back and he could see a young woman talking on the phone, blonde hair cascading over her shoulders. Walking into the shop he called out to George, who appeared at the end of one of the aisles.

'*Kalispera* Manos. I've been wanting to ask you something.'

'Go on George,' he replied curiously. 'I'm all ears.'

'We've been looking to stock a new line in giftware and were thinking of selling prints of the local area and small canvases, and were wondering if you'd be interested in supplying them? We don't need an answer straight away… will you think about it though?'

'No need to think about it George. I'd be only too pleased to.'

'That's brilliant, thank you!' he replied reaching out to shake his hand.

'Thank you George! It's just what I needed. I'm trying to expand the business, and this will be perfect. Should I pop across sometime tomorrow with a few samples?'

'That would be good. Anytime to suit you Manos. Anna will be really pleased. She's been pestering me to ask you for ages. I didn't like to bother you as you always seem so busy.'

'No, that's fine, I'm glad you asked. Can I leave you some business cards too?'

'Of course you can.'

'Anyway, I must be getting back over the road and give mama the good news. I've just put another painting on the wall in Ellas – she was joking it wouldn't be there long!'

'It won't be if Anna sees it!' George said glancing over his shoulder to make sure his wife wasn't within earshot.

Keri disconnected the call and thought about the conversation. She spoke to her parents at least once a week and kept in touch in between with numerous WhatsApp messages and photos. She could picture her mother sitting on the wooden bench on the patio area watching the sun set over the mountains and could almost smell the sweet scent of the lavender as it wafted through the air on the delicate evening breeze. She imagined her father watering the plants in the borders, the perfumed roses with their dark green leaves standing majestically in rows framing the edges of the garden, and the hanging baskets with their colourful display.

Switching off the light in the apartment she made her way across the road to Ellas looking forward to her evening meal. As she approached the table her eyes were drawn to a new painting on the wall, and she commented to Helenka how breathtaking it was. She proudly explained that her son Manos had painted it. Keri was captivated.

As Manos made his way back to Ellas he glanced back over his shoulder and noticed that the apartment above George's shop was now in darkness. Once back at the taverna he joked with Helenka that there must be some kind of conspiracy as everyone wanted to buy his paintings! A vaguely familiar face caught the corner of his eye.

'Mama, who's the girl with the blonde hair sitting at the far end looking at the new painting?' he whispered.

Looking across discreetly to where Manos was gesturing she replied, 'That's Keri. She's from Ireland and staying in one of George's apartments – such a lovely girl. Seems to be another admirer of your artwork!'

Manos told Helenka about George's offer. She was over the moon and decided that now was the time to talk to him about her idea of some help in the boatyard. She went on to explain that if he still managed it, looked after the boat rentals, and did the book-keeping, but got someone in to do general labouring and cleaning the boats between customers, this would free up more time to spend in his studio.

'Well, it's turning into quite an evening!' he exclaimed.

'What do you think Manos? Do you reckon it could work?'

'It's a really good idea. We could certainly afford someone part time. I'll put the word out tomorrow when I'm in Lefko Bay. There are plenty of youngsters who would jump at the chance. I've been thinking about it myself lately with the sales going up. It's as if you can read my mind mama!' he said planting a kiss on the top of Helenka's head.

Unbeknown to Helenka and Manos, Keri had spotted this show of affection and tears prickled in her eyes. Seeing the scene before her made her realise that she was missing her family more than she thought. Could it be she felt this way because she was coming to the end of her journey, she pondered?

Manos stood on the smooth wooden boardwalk, hypnotised by the bronze grains of sand being drawn back and forth slowly, methodically before him. The full moon high in the sky kept watch over the bay like a guardian angel. How pleased his papa would be knowing that finally the studio was no longer a dream but a reality. Papa would always encourage him when he was younger with his *'gift from the Gods'* as he liked to call it. Oh, how he missed his papa, and would have loved to share this moment with him.

The flame from the candle flickered in the middle of the table. Keri finished her glass of wine and got up to take a closer look at the newly hung painting. As the evening had drawn on the silvery moonlight had cast its magical glow onto the picture. Touching it gently with delicate fingertips she could feel texture of the oils on the canvas. A voice nearby brought her back from her reverie.

'Hello… you must be Keri?'

She spun around to see the man she had been watching in the boatyard, his warm hazel eyes sparkling, and his dark brown hair tousled around his muscular neck. Her heart skipped a beat.

'Sorry if I startled you. I'm Manos, Helenka's son.'

'Pleased to meet you,' she said shyly proffering her hand. 'I was just admiring your artwork… Helenka told me you painted it.'

'Thank you so much,' he replied modestly. 'Can I get you another glass of wine?'

'Oh, yes please, that would be lovely,' she replied.

Manos walked over to the bar and was quickly joined by Helenka.

'I see you've met Keri,' she said softly with a glint in her eye and disappeared into the kitchen.

As he walked over to Keri, he was struck by her natural beauty, the soft glow from the moon lighting up her face like a porcelain doll. She reached over and took the drink from him, thanking him warmly. He smiled and made his way back to the bar clearing some tables of empty glasses as he went.

It had been a quiet evening in the taverna. Keri watched Helenka straightening the chairs at each table and decided she better make a move. Standing up and stretching her legs she walked over to Helenka.

'I'd better get off now,' she said.

'Did you enjoy your meal my dear?' she asked.

'It was lovely thank you. Could I just ask you something Helenka?'

'Yes. What is it?' she replied.

'I was wondering if I could buy one of the paintings – the one I was looking at earlier. I haven't been able to take my eyes off it all evening. It's beautiful. And I should hate to come back another day to find it gone.'

'Of course you can. If you want I'll get Manos to drop it off for you tomorrow.'

'That would be great, if you don't mind,' replied Keri smiling as she reached into her handbag for her purse to pay for her meal and her newly acquired piece of artwork.

Keri left the taverna that evening with an air of excitement, turning to wave to Helenka as she carefully placed a sold sign on the painting.

Chapter Six

Spiros maneuvered his car through the familiar tracks snaking down the hillside and into the village. On the brow of the hill approaching Lefko Bay he saw in his peripheral vision a car parked at the top of the wasteland behind Manos' boatyard, and two figures in the distance disappearing from view as he travelled further away.

With the early morning sunshine glistening on the azure sea it was undoubtedly a great location for a hotel, albeit a little on the small side, Christophe thought as he tried to visualise how it could work with the land being so very steep. It would certainly lend itself to cascading balconies offering uninterrupted views over the sea. Perhaps a pool at the top with a bar and restaurant in the middle and a reception on the ground floor with a side entrance. His trained eye estimated no more than twelve bedrooms; maybe with the outbuildings gone and the boatyard out of the way, another half a dozen with direct access onto the beach.

From the top of the hill Yannis pointed out the shops, bars and tavernas in Lefko Bay and how it was a much larger village than Galazios Bay. Since arriving Christophe sensed Yannis was a little edgy, constantly looking around as if he didn't want to be spotted, so he thought he'd test the water.

'My initial thoughts are that it could work, but only if those outbuildings and boatyard over there were gone, giving it direct access onto the beach.'

'We can't use the area around the boatyard!' Yannis said a little too quickly.

'Why?' asked Christophe.

'It's only this area here,' he said pointing out the boundary of the land again.

'For it to be successful the property would need to extend all the way down to the beach. I'm sure the owner will sell for the right price!'

'I don't think so. It's the only boatyard in the bay and they'll not give it up,' he said with absolute certainty.

'How do you know that?' Christophe pushed. 'Money talks. Anyone will sell for the right price. I'll put some figures together.'

Taking one last look around he headed back to the car. Without the boatyard the land was just too small and the financial return once it was developed would be much too low.

Manos stepped out of the workshop shielding his eyes from the bright sunlight. Hearing voices in the distance and realising one of them was Yannis, he waved, but he didn't appear to see him. He shouted up to his brother, but still nothing. Christophe turned to look as Yannis continued walking towards the car without even a backward glance which Christophe thought a bit strange.

They got into the car and Christophe questioned why he didn't acknowledge the man in the boatyard. Yannis replied saying he didn't hear anything. He went on to ask how he had acquired the land, to learn that it was inherited it from his father. As they drove back down the hillside and through the village Christophe thought he saw a woman waving to them at the front of a restaurant, once again it appeared that Yannis had turned a blind eye.

Back in the hotel Christophe thought about his visit to Galazios Bay and the overgrown strip of land, not to mention Yannis' rather peculiar behaviour. He could only assume that no-one else knew about the proposed plans, and decided to visit the bay again, this time under his own steam.

There was a knock on the apartment door. As Keri walked across the room to answer it she ran her fingers through her hair teasing the blonde curls forward. Opening the door she found Manos standing there looking bronzed in navy shorts, a white t-shirt and his shoulder length hair pushed back over his ears exposing his rugged features. Her heart skipped a beat.

'Hello Manos. Come on in,' she said moving aside from the doorway.

'Mama asked me to bring this across to you,' he said resting the painting on the floor against the wall.

'That's great, thanks very much. Can I get you a coffee?'

'That would be lovely,' he replied following her into the small kitchenette. 'Milk, no sugar, please.'

She filled the kettle and took two cups from the cupboard. Leaning against one of the units she asked how long he had been painting.

'Since I was small really. Mama and papa always encouraged me. Most of the kids went down to the sea after school but I was quite happy to sit on the boardwalk with a sketchpad.'

'You've got a great talent…'

'Stop! Stop!' he interrupted laughing. 'You sound just like mama.'

'As soon as I saw the painting in the taverna I just knew I had to have it,' she said smiling.

'And may I say madam, you have such wonderful taste,' he joked.

Keri poured the water into the cups, stirred in the milk, and offered one to Manos.

'Let's sit on the balcony, there's usually a bit of a breeze about this time,' she suggested.

He followed her outside and they sat together for a while chatting like old friends.

'What are you doing for lunch?' Manos asked.

'I hadn't any plans. Why?'

'Would you like to have lunch with me? My treat. I can thank you properly then for buying the painting.'

'There's no need to do that. But, yes, I'd love to have lunch with you, thanks,' replied Keri fidgeting with her necklace.

'There's a nice little taverna on the road into Lefko Bay.'

'Oh yes, I think I know which one you mean. I saw it yesterday when I was walking through the village. Is it the one on the brow of the hill with the yellow window shutters?'

'Yes, that's it. I often pop in for a take-away if we're busy in the boatyard.'

'I'll get my handbag and keys. Do you buy lunch for all

your customers?' Keri quipped as she picked her mobile up from the coffee table and popped it into her bag.

'Only the special ones!' he replied with a wink.

Keri blushed and locked the door behind her.

As they walked along the dusty pavement Keri talked about her travels and how she had ended up in the bay. Manos listened with much interest as she explained that her parents visited the bay when they were younger, and she grew up with enchanting stories about the people and their lives, always planning to finish her travels through Europe in this wonderful place.

Upon reaching the taverna she turned to admire the view. With the gentle fragrance creeping through the air from the lemon trees her senses came to life. The paved area between the two bays was a profusion of colour. Lefko Bay was much larger than its neighbour with a handful of small hotels, an abundance of bars and tavernas, two supermarkets and gift shops lining the streets. The bay was geared towards tourism and well-known for its beautiful stretch of golden sandy beach. During the summer months a bustling resort with families spending their days playing on the beach; small children paddling in the sea whilst teenagers enjoyed the water sports and the thrill of the paraglider as it lifted them up into the sky like a bird in flight soaring through the silent world above.

Café bars lined the edge of the beach catering for countless tourists passing through each day wanting a quick snack and drink before hitting the beach again. Row upon row of sun loungers and parasols stretched from one end to the other, with the sweet scent of coconut oil and sun cream wafting through the air. At one side, a quaint marina with colourful yachts, their masts chinking rhythmically with the sway of the sea. To the other end, a weathered rocky outcrop covered in dark green seaweed washed up onto the rocks by the movement of the tide. At the foot of the cliff foam frothed over the golden sand gently lifting the pebbles and embedding them into patterns along the water's edge.

At nightfall, the cove is alive with music and dancing into the early hours. Tall bamboo oil torches light the trail down to the beach where the mouth-watering smells from the barbecues entice. In the hillside, the old town with its maze of twisting lanes lit by ornate streetlamps takes your eyes to the focal point of the village: St Dionysios Church. Across from the church is one of the oldest buildings in the village, the post office, next door to the school, formerly a row of fisherman's cottages.

The Town Hall sits impressively with its cornucopia of fragrant white jasmine spilling over the huge hanging baskets and lilac bougainvillea cascading down the walls framing the windows and central doorway. It is at the front of the Town Hall the weekly market is held and has been for the last few hundred years, captivating young and old alike. Passing through the market isn't just for the tourist but more a social event for the locals on a mission to get hold of all sorts of things they had no intention of buying and a chance to bump into family and friends along the way. A weekly social event not to be missed. At the crack of dawn every Wednesday faint rumbling noises can be heard as the old wooden stalls are dragged across the cobbles. Generations of families have held the same stall in the market square for many years, and it has become quite a tradition for the children to grow up watching their parents, grandparents and even great grandparents spend each Wednesday in the village square selling their wares, listening to tales of mystical folklore and enchantment from days gone by.

As they left the taverna Keri decided to take a leisurely walk back through the village and Manos made his way to the boatyard stealing another peek at her as she strolled down the road in the warm sunshine. Walking towards Ellas she spotted Helenka standing in the doorway fanning herself with a folded serviette.

'Hello Helenka!' she called out.

'*Kalispera* Keri. How are you?'

'Good thanks,' she replied crossing over the road. 'I've just had lunch with Manos. He brought the painting across to me this morning and took me out for lunch as a thank you; I told him there was no need, but he insisted. We had a lovely meal at the taverna on the hill between the bays.'

'Oh yes, Mrs Antoniou's place. She's been there ever since I can remember and makes the best *eliopsomo*, olive bread, on the island. 'Why don't you come in for a drink Keri? It's on the house.'

'Everyone's treating me today, thank you Helenka. I'd love to,' she replied following her into the cool shade of the taverna.

It was quietening down after the lunchtime rush; not that you could really call it a rush, more a laid back affair in the pleasant milieu that was known to everyone as Ellas. Keri took the glass from Helenka, and they both sat down at one of the side tables so that she could keep an eye on her customers.

'Manos was telling me he's always loved painting,' said Keri sipping her drink.

'Yes, since he was a very young lad really. Yannis, his brother, was the boisterous one always running about getting himself into trouble, but Manos was the quiet one, happy to watch the world go by; like chalk and cheese they were, in fact, they still are. Just excuse me a minute my dear whilst I see to this customer,' she said getting up and walking over to a young couple who had attracted her attention.

Keri's thoughts drifted to what the place would have looked like all those years ago when her parents were here. She remembered the old photograph in her handbag and took it out briefly. There were three people smiling back at her. The stories her parents had shared with her so many times over the years came flooding back.

'When you arrive on the island make sure you spend some time in the Bay of Keri,' she remembered her mammy telling her. 'It's the first bay as you travel from the port.'

'To the north of the port that is…' interrupted her daddy, bringing the map over to show her exactly where it was.

She listened intently as her parents recalled their journey around the island and how they ended up in the Bay of Keri.

'We found a lovely hotel on the beach front called Athena,' said her mammy. 'I wonder if it's still there. It was in the middle of the bay, we stayed there for a couple of weeks. After all the travelling it was nice to relax and take time out to reflect on all the places we'd visited on our journey.'

'Can you remember the fabulous sunsets from the cliff and the beautiful little taverna teetering on the edge, where we drank ouzo until the early hours and strolled back down into the town?' her daddy recalled.

'Oh yes! And how we danced through the streets on the way back to the hotel. Do you remember the vase?'

'The vase?' asked an inquisitive Keri.

'Yes, the vase!' chuckled mammy. 'We were walking back from an evening out and decided to have a nightcap in a bar near the hotel and I happened to say how much I liked a bright orange and lime green porcelain vase on a shelf behind the bar. We finished our drinks, were just leaving and your daddy turned around saying he'd forgotten something and would catch me up in a minute.'

'That's right,' he recalled continuing with the story. 'I went back and asked the barman if I could buy the vase as my wife had been admiring it and we couldn't find one like it anywhere. With that, he turned around lifted it carefully off the shelf, and said I could have it for the bargain price of 5,000 drachma. The deal was done!'

'The next minute your daddy came running down the road in a rather drunken stupor waving the vase in the air declaring his love for me…much to the amusement of a few onlookers!'

'Oh daddy, what are you like!' Keri exclaimed. 'Where is it now?'

'Well, when we woke the next morning and saw the vase on the coffee table, we both looked at each other and burst out laughing. In the cold, sober light of day, it was rather hideous!'

'So there's a lesson to be learnt there – if you've had too much ouzo don't go buying vases from strangers!' he sniggered.

'How did you get it home?' asked Keri with amusement.

'We didn't. When we stayed in Galazios Bay and got to know Helenka and Dino quite well, we were chatting one night and told them about it and she joked that you could never have too many vases, so when we left to come back to Ireland we gave it to them as a keepsake. I wonder if they've still got it?' considered her mammy.

Helenka rejoined Keri noticing a faraway look in her eye. It niggled her that the girl reminded her of someone from way back…who on earth was it? The chair scraped across the tiled floor as she pulled it towards the table bringing Keri out of her musing.

'All sorted. They've been pondering what to have for dessert for a while. I'm not one to rush anyone,' said Helenka. 'Are you alright my dear? You look miles away.'

'Yes, I'm fine thanks,' Keri replied in her soft Irish tones.

She looked at this kind woman smiling back at her warmly and knew instantly that she could talk to her about anything. Perhaps that's why her mammy got on so well with her all those years ago. Keri always planned to keep everything close to her and not make any emotional attachments during her travels, but something was happening in this little paradise that made her feel quite different, and for the first time since leaving Ireland she felt ready to share her feelings. Everyone in the village had welcomed her with open arms, especially Helenka. She began to feel quite emotional.

'I was just thinking about my family back home in Ireland. I find I'm thinking about them more and more just lately. I've been away for so long you'd think I'd have got used to it by now,' she said reaching into her pocket for a tissue.

'You're bound to still get homesick from time to time, it's only natural when you're travelling around. I know I'm no substitute for your family but if you ever want someone to talk to I'm here for you…I'm a good listener you know,' she said touching Keri's hand lightly.

'Thank you Helenka, that means such a lot to me.'

They sat together companionably in the warmth of the afternoon sun. Keri explained how she had ended up in the bay and Helenka told her all about the islands history. She got up and went over to the bar to get some more drinks. On her return Keri decided to show her the photo that she had carried with her on her travels and began to explain about her parent's travels years ago and how they too had ended their journey on this lovely island, in fact, right here in Galazios Bay. She took the photograph out of her bag offering it to Helenka. Gently taking it from her hand she saw some very familiar faces smiling back at her; Dino, Yannis and herself. It seemed a world away. Keri explained how her parents had given it to her when they knew she'd be coming to the island.

Helenka listened, hanging onto Keri's every word.

'All through my childhood and teenage years I've heard so many stories of the bay and the people who live here. I just knew I had to come and see it all for myself. They asked that when I got to Galazios Bay I look you up. I feel I know you all so well already. As soon as I arrived I instantly felt I belonged here, like part of me had come home. It was such a strange feeling, quite overwhelming in fact.'

Helenka stared at the old, faded photograph in her hand and the memories came flooding back. Keri's voice paled into the background as she remembered the moment it was taken, as if it were only yesterday.

'...and when I spoke to mammy on the phone the other evening she said to give you and Dino her love.'

'Oh!' exclaimed Helenka hearing Dino's name. It was at that moment it suddenly dawned on her that they didn't know Dino had passed away.

'Sorry Helenka, I'm babbling on. It's just such a relief to tell you everything. I wasn't sure how you'd react because mammy said you had all kind of drifted apart over the last few years.'

'My dear Keri.' Helenka said. 'I know now why you looked so familiar when we first met. You are your mother's double, not just in looks but everything about you! You've brought such happy memories back to me. I often think about them. We exchanged letters, Christmas cards and photos for many years. Your parents were so young and carefree and a breath of fresh air...always so happy walking through the village hand in hand. They loved playing with Yannis on the beach. He'd be about five years old at the time. They'd buy him ice-creams and sweets. Dino and I always said they'd make great parents.'

Keri was fascinated. It was lovely to hear the stories so familiar to her but from such a different perspective.

'...then shortly after they left for Ireland we received a letter with the good news that they were expecting a baby! They were going to name the baby after the Bay of Keri, and the rest of course is history.'

'Yes, I've heard that story many times!' laughed Keri.

Helenka placed the photo gently on the table.

'Let me show you something,' she said walking over to the bar and reaching up to the top shelf on the back wall of the taverna. She carefully lifted down a colourful porcelain vase and brought it over to Keri.

'Did they ever tell you the story of the vase?'

'Yes!' exclaimed Keri, 'Is that the one?'

'It most certainly is. I've cherished it all these years! They gave it to us after I said you could never have too many vases. It was a standing joke for many years – we even sent them a photo of it in case they were missing it!' Helenka laughed.

Keri noticed she had a sparkle back in her eyes, just like the woman in the photograph. They talked for what seemed like hours. Helenka explained about the tragedy that had taken the life of her beloved Dino, Demetrius and two more young men. Keri listened attentively as Helenka reminisced knowing how upset her parents would be when they heard the sad news.

Helenka picked up the photo and looked at it again before handing it back to Keri. She took her hand saying how happy she was to hear about the family and what they had been doing over the last few years. At that moment Maria walked into the taverna with a beautiful bunch of fresh flowers. Helenka got up to greet her, kissing her on both cheeks, taking the flowers from her and bringing them up to her nose to take in their delicate perfume. Maria smiled at Keri and said hello, returning the compliment she asked Maria if she would like to join them.

'Thank you, I would like that,' Maria replied as Helenka introduced them properly.

'I'll just pop these into a vase,' she said winking at Keri, who carefully passed the vase to her without hesitation.

'Are you enjoying your time in the bay?' asked Maria warmly.

'Oh yes thank you, very much so. It's such a beautiful place.'

Helenka put the vase of flowers on the sideboard gently coaxing them into place before rejoining the girls with a jug of welcome ice-cool lemon squash, pleased to see the two of them getting on so well.

Chapter Seven

As the sun disappeared from the horizon, its golden rays danced lightly on the sea. Manos walked steadily along the boardwalk picking up pebbles and skimming them, breaking the rhythmic pattern of the waves. Climbing the wooden steps of the veranda at Ellas he was greeted by his brother.

'*Yassou* Manos. Good to see you,' said Yannis.

'*Yassou* Yannis,' replied Manos. 'How are you keeping? I saw you this morning up on the hillside. I shouted up to you. Didn't you hear me?'

'No!' he answered bluntly.

'That's strange!' said Manos equally brusque making his way past Yannis into the kitchen. 'Your friend turned to take a look!'

Manos greeted Helenka who was busy preparing a selection of salads. She wiped her hands on her apron.

'*Kalispera* Manos!' she said reaching up to kiss him on each cheek.

'*Kalispera* mama!' he said squeezing her shoulders gently.

'I'll put these salads in the fridge. Yannis has just arrived. Would you get some drinks please and I'll be with you both in a minute?'

Helenka made her way over to her sons, changing the music in the CD player to a more suitable one for the early evening.

'I thought I saw you driving through the village this morning,' said Helenka to Yannis.

'Yes, so did I!' chipped in Manos.

'Did you?' replied Yannis.

'Well, I thought it was your car. Perhaps I was mistaken,' replied mama.

'You weren't mistaken at all, was she Yannis? I saw you on the land at the top of the hill with a guy in a suit.'

Thinking quickly on his feet and without batting an eyelid he told them he was looking into having a villa built on the patch of land and was with his architect but didn't want to say anything until the plans had been drawn up. He thought he'd quite like to move back to the bay.

'Why are you thinking of building now? You've never been interested before. You couldn't wait to move to the City, now you can't wait to come back. Seems a bit strange to me!' challenged Manos.

'Can't a man change his mind?' Yannis snapped.

'Come on boys! It would be lovely to have you back, we hardly see you nowadays. Will you be moving back permanently? What about your business in the City?

'Mama, slow down! It's only an idea at the moment.'

'I hoped you'd come back to the bay and settle down here, the City's no place to put down roots.'

'Put down roots!' exclaimed Manos.

'Papa would be so proud; a successful business, and having your own villa built in the bay.'

'Oh come on mama, he's got no intention of settling down here! Am I right Yannis?'

'Well, it's only at the planning stage, there's a long way to go. You don't realise what's involved!'

'No, I don't suppose I would, not being businessman of the year!'

'Stop it! That's enough!' cried Helenka. 'Why do you two constantly bicker the minute you're together?'

'Yannis won't be building a home for himself on papa's land. He doesn't do anything unless there's a profit to be made!'

'That's not true Manos! I'll prove you wrong!'

'Yes. You normally do don't you!'

'Stop it! Stop it this minute! she screamed.

'Sorry mama. I'll see you later,' said Manos as he turned to walk down the wooden steps.

She called after him, but he was soon gone, making his way along the beach, and resting on some rocks at the end of the breakwater, head in his hands in utter frustration.

'Why are you so hard on your brother Yannis?' asked Helenka.

'Come on mama. He's always interfering in my business. Just because he's happy with his life here he thinks everyone else should be.'

'He only wants the best for you. We don't see much of you now and sometimes you seem a bit distant and distracted, and you know we'd love you to come back to the bay. Manos might not show it, but he does miss you, we all do.'

'Well he's got a funny way of showing it mama!'

He finished his drink, said goodbye to Helenka and walked back to his car. After waving him off she turned to look at her youngest son in the distance and watched him for a while throwing pebbles carelessly into the sea. How completely different her two sons were. It concerned her that they seemed to be growing further apart. Perhaps it would bring them closer together if Yannis did build his villa.

The early morning stream of sunlight shone through the slats of the wooden shutters forcing Keri to open her eyes for a brief moment before drifting off to sleep again and back into the same dream, reliving her travels…

The four of them could just about distinguish the port of Roscoff in the distance. They had been sailing on the overnight ferry from Cork to Brittany which had taken nearly twenty hours and wasn't the smoothest journey. With storms throughout the night, the ship had been pitching and rolling for the most part and all four girls were feeling a little green around the gills. They reached the port with the smell of seaweed penetrating their nostrils along with the malodorous diesel fumes spewing out as the ship docked.

'What great travellers we're going to make if before we even step foot on French soil we feel so ill!' commented a rather pasty looking Carol, usually a bright cheery girl, but not so this morning.

'Touche Christopher Columbus!' added Julie bending down to pick up her rucksack.

'I'm glad to be on dry land,' declared a pallid Emma.

A bit of sea sickness wouldn't keep these girls down

for long though with excitement in the air as they stepped off the ferry to start their adventure through Europe! Less than an hour later they got off the bus in the pretty village of Carantec. Emma took the map out again turning it this way and that to get her bearings.

'I think we need to turn left at the island over there,' she said pointing to a mini roundabout. 'And then straight down the hill towards the beach. It should be on the left-hand side.'

'You mean... *tournez à gauche à l'île...et puis directement en bas de la colline vers la plage...du côté de main gauche...*' chipped in Keri studying her handy little phrase book.

'Alright smart-arse!' laughed Emma as they all broke into fits of laughter.

At the bottom of the hill they walked through the gates of the holiday park and followed the pathway covered either side in colourful flower beds leading them to the reception. The four friends dropped their heavy rucksacks onto the floor in the lobby. Emma and Keri went to the reception desk to check in for the weeks holiday they had booked to begin their travels through France and Italy. Their route through Europe had been planned with precision and they had all secured various summer jobs en route.

'This must be it!' said Carol who was slightly in front of the group with the keys, site plan in her hand.

'I think you're right. Oh isn't it lovely!' declared Emma.

The caravan was on a slight incline overlooking the pool with its waterslides and lazy river. There were three bedrooms, two shower rooms and a well-equipped kitchen, which had been pointed out by Carol whose parents ran a hotel and restaurant back home in Ireland. She had spent most of her childhood helping her father in the kitchen and had done a two-year catering course at college, so they certainly wouldn't go hungry.

They chose their bedrooms with the toss of a coin! Two would be sharing the large twin room; the others a small double each. In a very short time they had unpacked, showered, and were sitting on the sun terrace with a glass of wine. Carol, being in catering, had of course had the foresight to pop into the supermarket on the walk from reception to pick up some provisions to keep them going; wine being the priority. From their vantage point they watched families splashing around in the pool and floating along the lazy river in large rubber rings. Holidaymakers dotted around the patio area sun-drenched and motionless soaking up the early afternoon rays, while the gentle tip-taping of the ping pong ball on table tennis bats could be heard coming from the bar at the bottom of the hill. The four friends chattered easily as they relaxed in the sunshine outside the caravan planning their next move.

'Who fancies a swim?" asked a rather hot Emma.

'Brilliant idea!' said Julie stretching her long legs and going inside to get her towel.

The other two girls got up wearily. Keri rubbed her tired eyes and reached for her sunglasses. Perhaps a swim would perk her up a bit. In no time at all they were on their way to the pool leaving their towels and books at the poolside. After lolling around in the red-hot afternoon sun it was refreshing to feel the coolness of the water on their sweltering skin. Julie and Keri headed for the lazy river, grabbing a rubber ring each. Julie managed to lose hold of hers halfway round, off into the air it shot leaving her bobbing around in the swirling water, with both of them in hysterics. Carol carried on swimming in the main pool whilst Emma went back to the terrace to dry off in the sunshine and read her book.

As the sun went down the girls got ready for their first evening in the village. Earlier in the day they'd spotted a pretty little restaurant in the square and decided they would go out for a special *"beginning of their great adventure"* meal. The rest of the week would be done on a budget with barbecues and Carol at the helm!

For their first evening in France they pushed the boat out spending the evening tucking into plentiful French tapas and drinking copious amounts of wine, soaking in the atmosphere with music and Bretagne dancers spilling from the bistros all around the village square.

The evening drew to a close and the high-spirited friends danced their way back to the caravan park weaving in and out of the labyrinth of narrow streets. During the latter part of the evening it had become very humid and sticky, but this didn't detract the girls from their *joie de vivre* and all agreed it had been a fabulous start to their holiday.

With groggy heads the next morning they woke one by one, searching out the painkillers, Julie vowing to never touch another drink as long as she lived!

'Ouch! What hit me?' asked an unsteady Emma, shuffling barefoot from the bedroom to the kitchen, her hands shielding her eyes, opening the fridge and reaching for a bottle of water. 'The last thing I remember is walking back from the village.'

'I think we all had too much sun yesterday,' stated Keri matter of factly as she stood in the doorway.

'That'll be it; the sun will do it every time!' murmured Carol.

'It doesn't look like we'll be soaking up the rays today. Did the thunder wake you?' added Keri.

'No, it was the thumping inside my head that woke me!' replied Emma quietly.

Standing in the open doorway of the caravan, Keri pulled up the collar of her polo shirt. Rain started pelting down from the murky sky with clouds hanging heavily. A rumble of thunder could be heard in the distance as the lightning flashes pierced the skyline. Seconds later an enormous crash sounded above the caravan. Hailstones bombarded the roof, and one final crack overhead made her jump back from the door.

Keri jolted awake! *What on earth was that? Was it a dream?* she thought rubbing her eyes. Laying there for a moment gathering her thoughts she listened to the noises drifting up from the street. Stretching her arms high above her head and giving a long yawn she swung her legs out of bed feeling the coolness of the smooth marble floor on the soles of her feet. Walking over to the balcony she pushed the doors open wide, letting the refreshing breeze flow through and watched the activities on the street below. A lorry caught her attention, a delivery to George's shop. The rear doors were slammed hard shut again with quite a bang!

'*That was it!*' she said out loud. It was the same noise she had heard in her dream. The same noise that had startled her. Gazing at the early morning comings and goings of the village she smiled to herself remembering fondly her time in France – the beginning of her incredible journey.

Chapter Eight

In the little blue and white house at the end of the bay Annys was getting ready for pre-school as Maria washed the breakfast pots.

'Are you nearly ready? Don't forget your sunhat, it's going to be hot today.'

'Got it. Can we go and see the pups on the way to school?'

'Not today darling or we'll be late.'

'Oh mummy…please…'

'No Annys.'

'Why?'

'Like I said, we'll be late.'

'We'll only be quick. We won't be late,' she persisted.

'No Annys!' Now come along and get your shoes on.'

'No! I won't!

'Annys!'

'Don't want to!'

'That's enough young lady! Come here now!'

She sauntered up to Maria head bowed down. 'Please… just for a few minutes,' she pleaded scrunching her toes up and pushing them into the shoes.

'What part of no don't you understand? Stop squeezing your toes and put your feet in properly. If you behave yourself we'll go after school.'

'Okay!' she answered back sulkily as she raced out of the door.

Keri locked up and made her way down the steps turning into George's shop to say good morning to them. After a quick chat with Anna, as George had gone to see a supplier, she emerged into the bright sunshine lifting her glasses from her head to shield her eyes and started walking towards Lefko Bay.

'Keri! Hiya!' shouted Maria as she and her daughter crossed over the road.

'Oh, good morning Maria,' she said cheerily. 'And this must be Annys. I've heard such a lot about you.'

'Annys, this is Keri. Say hello.'

'*Kalimera* Keri,' she said shyly – not the same little girl who was screaming and shouting only minutes before.

'*Kalimera* to you too.'

'We're just off to pre-school in the next village.'

'I hear there's a market on today. I'm heading that way too.'

'Yes, that's right. Would you like to walk with us?'

'That would be lovely, thank you.'

As they headed for Lefko Bay Maria told Keri about the Wednesday market and how she always had a wander through after dropping Annys off, asking Keri if she would like to join her. They then spent the morning soaking in the atmosphere of market day, weaving in and out of the stalls, breathing in the mellow aroma of incense drifting through the air and talking about everything under the sun. Moving slowly through the cobbled streets strumming his slightly out-of-tune guitar was the local minstrel, a regular at all the markets on the island, performing songs whose lyrics told stories of far-off lands, always attracting quite a crowd and somehow managing to make a living out of it. Local farmers with their baskets of succulent fruit and fresh vegetables picked at daybreak, and folk from the mountainous villages with their homemade wines and olive oils, selling their wares. Keri was drawn to a stall with tapestries in luxuriously deep colours.

'Look at these Maria. Aren't they beautiful?'

'Oh yes, they're gorgeous. The lady who makes them is in her nineties and her granddaughter frames them. Her husband makes leather moccasins and bags. I bought this one from him a couple of years ago and it's still as good as new,' she said lifting her handbag up for Keri to see.

On a corner under the shade of a rambling fig tree was a small jewellery display. Keri picked up a silver ring with a tanzanite stone set at such an angle that the sunlight bounced off it creating a profusion of blues and purples.

'Wow! Look at this Maria.'

'It's stunning. What kind of stone is it?' she asked captivated, holding it up to the light, fascinated by its flashes of blues and violets.

Keri explained how it had been crafted from a piece of tanzanite. 'Look at how the light reflects off its edges. It's one of the most beautiful gemstones on the planet. It's quite unique you know. I never expected in my wildest dreams to come across it here.' Her eyes lit up like a child's in a sweetshop. 'It's mined in the foothills of Mount Kilimanjaro – the only place in the world – how amazing is that!

'You seem to know a lot about it Keri.'

'Yes, I once made something very similar at college. I based it on one of the first displays of tanzanite jewellery at Tiffany's in New York in the 1960s and won first prize for my design. I could only use a tiny slither of the gemstone, but it still looked incredible.'

Keri replaced the ring carefully and thanked the woman for letting her look at it. The girls carried on moving slowly through the busy market passing by stalls selling pottery, glassware and raffia souvenirs – the sort of mementos taken home as a reminder of a holiday. The market reached up into the little backstreets like an octopus stretching its tendrils. It was certainly the place to be on a Wednesday morning Keri thought. So different to the quiet village square she had visited only a couple of days before where old men sat in small groups smoking, drinking coffee, passing worry beads through their fingers and watching the world go by; and the old women were happy to sit on hard chairs in their doorways, sewing or lacemaking, watching small children playing nearby and dogs lazing around in the hot sunshine.

The Town Hall clock chimed echoing throughout the village; two hours had already passed. The inviting smell of food made her realise how hungry she was. Stallholders were shouting passers-by to come and sample their foods, from international cuisine to traditional Greek dishes tantalising the taste buds. The girls succumbed to offers of tasters taking their hunger pangs away for a while. They'd already decided to have lunch together before fetching Annys from pre-school and made their way towards a café bar on the edge of the market. Some paintings caught Keri's eye with the style looking very familiar. Maria explained that it was where Manos displayed some of his artwork, on his friend Alex's stall.

'I just love the style of his paintings!' exclaimed Keri. 'I was having dinner in Helenka's taverna the other night and was mesmerised by one of them. I knew if I didn't have it I'd regret it so bought it there and then. I don't know how I'm going to get it home though. I didn't think that far ahead! Helenka must think I'm quite mad just staring at the painting all evening. She's so lovely. She even got Manos to deliver it personally to me, and he took me to lunch as a thank you. Does he do that for all his customers? He'll never make any money if that's the case!'

'Only the pretty Irish ones!' replied Maria roguishly.

'George keeps calling me that!' she laughed.

'I know. He told us all about you. You should know there's no secrets in the bay. No seriously, I've seen how Manos looks at you, steeling a peek when you're walking along the beach; dropping into Helenka's when you happen to be there. I've grown up with him, he's like my little brother. If anyone knows him, I do. And I tell you he's got a soft spot for you!'

'Well, he is rather gorgeous isn't he?' said Keri with a twinkle in her eye. 'Can I ask you something? It's a bit of a strange question, but I was wondering, has he got a partner?'

'No, he's had a few admirers but nothing very serious.'

'I suppose he must be so busy with the boatyard and his artwork that he's not got much time left for anything else.'

'Oh I don't know. I think it's just that the right girl hasn't come along yet…but I've got a feeling that's all about to change!' said Maria linking arms with Keri and dragging her away from the stall towards the café. Come on. Time for lunch!'

The girls chose a table on the paved area outside the café and ordered lunch. Keri told Maria about the phone call the previous evening from Julie, one of her travelling companions, who had just got engaged and was planning an engagement party and wanted to time it for when she returned to Ireland. She went on to explain about the dream she had last night and that she thought it was perhaps the phone call that prompted it.

'Tell me about some of the places you've visited,' said Maria.

'I don't want to bore you,' she replied.

'Oh don't worry, you won't. I'll stop you when you do!' she said with a smile.

'Okay, here goes…'

And with that Keri began to tell her about her friends and their journey from Carantec, down the coast of Western France to the Vendee region. This was where Julie had met her fiancé, Mark. The girls were playing boules in one of the villages. They had been standing on a grass verge watching some locals having a game and were invited to join them. Always up for a challenge they agreed. By lunchtime they had drawn quite a crowd including a handful of guys from Ireland who cheered them on with immense enthusiasm! When they had finished the game they thanked their hosts and started walking towards a nearby café. The Irish lads asked if they could join them and introduced themselves properly. They spent the afternoon in a local bar and learnt that they were on a back-packing holiday through France. They spent the next few days travelling around the local area, and that is when love blossomed for Julie and Mark. The boys had lined up summer jobs in a French ski resort, and this would be their last stop before returning home to Ireland as they were all due to start university at the end of September.

Maria was wrapped up with it all. 'Go on…' she urged Keri.

'Are you sure you're not bored yet?'

'No, it's really interesting,' she replied taking a sip from her drink and checking her watch to make sure they weren't running late to collect Annys. No, plenty of time.

Keri continued with her story explaining that after nearly six weeks on the west coast they travelled across the Limousin region staying in youth hostels and working farms along the way. The money earned from grape-picking in the vineyards helped boost their funds and they were even able to take a hot-air balloon trip. She recalled the glorious chateaus and magnificent castles; the rivers that wrapped themselves around the hills and lakes that looked like small iridescent puddles scattered around the countryside beneath them. As they travelled through Auvergne on the way to Provence and the Cote d'Azur, Julie met up with Mark a few times. It was great seeing them together. They were made for each other and spent half the time locked away in their own little world planning where and when they would next meet up. Sometimes Mark would bring the other guys with him, and we'd all go out and hit the town.

One particular week the girls hired bikes and went cycling every day, suffering with terrible saddle soreness by the end of it. All the fresh air and exercise though gave them incredible appetites and they always found plenty of room to polish off the home cooked evening meals prepared by the lady whose farmhouse they were staying in.

In Provence they rented a gite in the heart of the

countryside set amongst a vast expanse of lavender fields. Row upon row of lavender swaying in the breeze, its delicate scent filling the air, oceans of soft flower heads brimming with a purple haze. She went on to describe how she had always had a passion for art, and it was when they visited this area that she understood why artists like Cezanne and Van Gogh were so passionate about the South of France. It was like stepping into one of Cezanne's paintings. While they were staying at the gite it was Keri's birthday. She'd never spent a birthday away from her family, so the girls hatched a plan to secretly arrange for her parents to spend the week in a small bed and breakfast just down the road from where they were staying. They all had a fabulous time and to this day she never knew how they had managed to keep it secret from her, especially Carol, who apparently was bursting to tell.

As they moved further south the landscape changed dramatically. Left behind were the rolling green hills and pastures for the elegance and sophistication of the Cote d'Azur. They stayed in an apartment in the old town of Nice, a tall thin coral colour building with not a level floorboard to its name, which after a drink or two you couldn't tell whether it was you or the floorboards that were wonky. The windows had green rickety wooden shutters and on the wall outside, a black wrought iron streetlamp was suspended high above the narrow cobblestoned lane below. All around were tiny boutiques displaying Provencal fabrics, and patisseries on every corner guiding you to the picturesque harbour.

Maria was captivated. 'It sounds fantastic! What a great time you must have all had! Is it as beautiful as you see in the magazines?'

'It's over and above everything I could have imagined. I think Nice was my favourite place.'

Keri was happy to continue sharing her memories with Maria. They ordered another drink and settled back down.

'By day Nice is a cultural City with a rich artistic heritage,' she began remembering the harbour with its million-pound luxurious yachts costing an obscene amount moored up in rows against the old harbour walls, dwarfing the twisted buildings huddled together shoulder to shoulder as if vying for the best position at the water's edge. 'We loved wandering through the shopping area in central Nice bustling with people soaking up the vibrant atmosphere. A plaza called Place Messina with its spectacular fountain displays was always a crowd pleaser. In the early mornings flower stalls were dotted along the tree-lined avenues, emitting their sweet fragrance into the air. In the alleyways people selling their wooden crafted ornaments and suchlike from a makeshift sheet spread out over the pavement, always ready to scoop it up and move along when the Gendarmerie approached. The Promenade des Anglais stretched for miles, lined with shops, restaurants, and parks to one side and on the other an expanse of golden sand as far as the eye could see. Rollerbladers, cyclists and chic dog owners dressed in their finery with their well-groomed pooches paraded up and down the waterfront. At night the restaurants and bars came alive spilling out onto the paved areas with street artists, musicians and entertainers on every corner. With the Bay de Anglais decked out with tens of thousands of multi-coloured lights you just can't help but get drawn into the magic of the City. We would sit for hours outside the bars and restaurants soaking in the ambience and making the most of our favourite pastime – people watching!'

'Did you go to Monaco? I've heard it's stunning!' asked Maria.

'We did indeed!' Keri replied and went on to share her experience with her new friend of staying in this millionaire's playground.

'From experience the best place to people watch is Monaco. We would frequently spot Formula One motor racing stars walking with their entourage and immaculately turned-out girlfriends with their model looks, hanging onto their arms playing to the waiting press with camera-clicking in abundance. Women of advancing years walking in and out of restaurants bringing sheer elegance by virtue of being fashionable. One evening we had just enjoyed a meal in a fish restaurant on the harbour front and were relaxing in the seating area outside watching the world go by, when we were drawn to the raucous behaviour on one of the yachts nearby where five men, whose loud voices carried through the air, were drinking huge glasses of brandy. A couple of them had moved to the back of the yacht and were smoking what looked like large Cuban cigars…not that we were watching that closely of course!' she laughed as the memories came flooding back. 'Definitely worse for wear they decided it would be a good idea to hit the town and stumbled down the gangway onto the shore. As they got closer their English and French accents became clear. A couple of them were being especially annoying to passers-by; the sort of behaviour you'd expect from a group of lads on a stag weekend in Magaluf not well-dressed men who'd just stepped, albeit rather unsteadily, off a luxury yacht in Monte Carlo! Two of them were up to all sorts of shenanigans, embarrassing themselves beyond belief. It looked like they were heading towards the bar next to ours. One was already blowing kisses across to Carol who, along with Emma, was facing them. Julie and I had our backs to them luckily! The rowdier ones in the group dragged their conservatory style chairs back from the glass table and started shouting across to the waiter, clicking their fingers in the air for attention. *"I'd snap their fingers off if they did that to me!"* said Julie and I do believe she would! As the evening went on they got louder and louder and started bragging to each other about how many properties they'd got, frequently shouting *"bring us more of your finest champagne!"* Two of the group were discussing plans to build a hotel on a Greek island, well, trying to talk about it, but being constantly interrupted by the drunken antics of the others. Shame that. It sounded quite interesting!'

'Did you stay in Monaco very long?' Maria asked gripped by everything Keri was telling her.

'Just for a few days. It was really expensive, and we were on a tight budget. By the end of October we were in the ski resort of Chamonix in the French Alps working as chalet girls. It was hard work and very long hours, but we loved it. Our accommodation was a bit basic but it had everything we needed, and it was good to be in one place after all the travelling, to settle down into regular jobs for a while with pay packets at the end of each week. We only had one day off a week but had the evenings to ourselves and usually spent them in the bar in the alpine lodge where we were living. We got discounted meals and ski hire and often spent our day off on the slopes. As spring approached and our last few days in Chamonix were upon us we finalised our plans for the remainder of the journey which would take us through Italy. Julie decided that when the rest of us continued on our travels she would fly back to Ireland. She was missing Mark. He had only managed to come out for a few days after Christmas before going back home to study. Anyway, that's enough about me. Tell me about your life here in the bay. Have you visited many places?'

'Only Athens. Where do you need to go when you have all this on your doorstep?' Maria replied opening her arms wide and gesturing all around. 'Come on, let's go and collect Annys. My story's for another day.'

Chapter Nine

It was early afternoon and many stallholders were packing away their wares. Most of Manos' paintings had been sold. Maria suggested after collecting Annys, that they go to see Manos and give him the good news. She had a quick chat to his friend who was stacking together ceramic souvenir plates and wrapping them in bubble wrap – the kind of memento you'd buy on a whim, get them home in one piece and display proudly as a reminder of your holiday. Keri wished she knew what they were saying and made a mental note to learn Greek; something she had been thinking about for a while.

Outside the school gates they talked about Manos' paintings and Maria explained to Keri that he'd always had an artistic streak and how she used to wind him up saying he'd got paint running through his veins instead of blood. 'Some of the kids at school would torment him because he was always sitting somewhere in a quiet corner with pencils and paper locked away in a world of his own. I got into more fights looking out for him. I was an only child and Manos was like my baby brother. Our parents were very close, and we spent a lot of time together even though there's a few years between us. His older brother Yannis didn't really have much time for him. He was always off doing his own thing with his mates. When I started going out with Demetrius, Manos became our little chaperone. He idolised Demetrius who would often take him fishing on his father's boat. He'd even take his notepad with him and when he got fed up waiting for the fish to bite he'd be sketching away, capturing different parts of the cove from his viewpoint in the sea. He'd often draw caricatures of Demetrius with a fishing rod in his hand in different poses bringing a smile to everyone's faces when he returned to shore. I've still got some of his drawings in a scrapbook in the attic. I must dig them out.'

Maria looked at her watch. 'We can go in now. Mrs Kashiotis, her teacher, likes us to go into school to pick the younger ones up. She's really lovely. The children think the world of her. She's been here ever since I can remember. Would you like to come in with me? I'm sure Annys would love to show you some of her work.'

As soon as Annys saw Maria she rushed excitedly towards her wielding a creatively glued together stack of boxes in a variety of shapes and sizes painted in a concoction of bright pinks and oranges.

'Annys! That looks…interesting,' exclaimed Maria bending down to take a closer look.'

'Mrs Kashiotis said we could make anything we wanted so I made something to keep my hair slides and bobbles in. It's good isn't it? She said if the paint was dry I could take it home.'

'It's really good Annys. It will look lovely on your dressing table. We're going to walk back with Keri. I bet she'd like to see some more of your work. Do you want to show her whilst I just have a quick word with Mrs Kashiotis?'

'Okay mama. *Yassou* Keri. Look what I've made today!' she said holding her creation out to show her.

'*Yassou* Annys. Oh that's beautiful. I like the colours you've used.'

'I painted it pink because my bedroom is pink,' she said proudly. 'Will you come and see my bedroom Keri?'

'I'm sure I will one day,' she replied smiling.

Annys pointed to some of her work displayed on the walls and explained to Keri that they were doing a topic about wildflowers and trees. Underneath the dried flowers and pressed leaves were the children's names and a few words describing what kind of flower or leaf they were.

'Have you shown Keri some of your work darling?' asked Maria walking towards them.

'Yes, she really likes my flower picture!' Annys replied excitedly. Making their way outside into the bright sunshine she took hold of Keri's hand and Maria moved to the other side, and the three of them skipped along the pavement swinging Annys into the air.

Manos tied the small motorboat to the side of the jetty, shook hands with his customer and returned the deposit. Business was booming. Guiding another boat alongside he shouted to the passengers to take it slowly and steer it to the left. Perfect. Helping the two youngsters out of the vessel he asked them if they had enjoyed their trip and judging by their smiling faces they certainly had. A rather sunburnt father stepped off after them, his neck, and arms red raw from the sun's powerful rays. He removed his sunglasses to wipe his brow only to reveal what looked like another pair underneath. Oh dear! That's going to hurt thought Manos as he waved them off.

'Manos! Manos!' cried Annys running down the hill into his outstretched arms. He swung her around and around, lowering her gently to the ground.

'Go and get yourself a cold drink from the fridge in the studio,' he said as she danced off happily.

'Hi you two. I was just going to make coffee. Would you like one?' he called out to Maria and Keri as they reached the pathway leading down to the boatyard.

'You know me! I wouldn't say no,' replied Maria.

'Yes please. That would be lovely,' added Keri.

'Great. How do you take your coffee?'

'Milk, no sugar thanks,' Keri replied as he walked into the studio, filled the kettle and switched it on.

'Did you go to the market today?'

'Yes, it was really busy. I had to drag this one away from one of the jewellery stalls! I could see the stallholder looking her up and down as though she was going to run off at any minute with her precious gems,' she teased. 'Mind you, she did have some lovely pieces didn't she Keri?'

'Oh yes, some of them were beautiful…especially the tanzanite!' she said smiling at Maria.

'Then we had lunch in one of the cafes at the side of the Town Hall.'

'Sounds like you've had a good day then,' he said stirring the coffees.

Maria put Annys' cardboard model down on the low wall in front of the boatyard and took the drink from Manos. 'Nice model Maria…you have been busy!' he said cheekily.

'Why thank you…it's for my hair slides,' she replied smiling. 'Actually, we've got some good news for you!'

'That sounds interesting,' he said pushing his hair back over his ears revealing his strong jaw line.

'Most of your paintings have sold today at the market and you've got some orders! Alex is bringing them over to you this evening.'

'Wow! That is good news!'

'Well done you!' said Maria raising her mug of coffee in the air as if it were a glass of champagne.

Annys walked up the jetty with a handful of pebbles. 'Manos, can we skim these?'

'Of course darling. Should we have half each?' he said bending down to take some from her.

'Let's show your mama and Keri how good we are.'

They all made their way down to the water's edge. Annys bent down to skim the first pebble. Three bounces later it disappeared beneath the surface. Manos was next. One… two… three… four… they counted as it broke the surface of the water and slipped out of sight. The two of them took turns until all the pebbles were gone. Annys bent down to pick up some more but was distracted by a noise further along the beach.

'Kimba!' she squealed with delight. 'Kimba!'

Helenka watched her gambol as fast as her little legs would carry her towards Annys.

'Come on!' she yelled bending down patting her knees. She had seen Helenka do this and the dogs always came running. Kimba stopped just short of Annys looking back to make sure Helenka was following and dropped the soaking wet ball at her feet. Annys patted her head and picked up the ball throwing it into the air. Kimba ran to fetch it, this time dropping it in front of Keri, who knelt down to pick it up giving her a fuss.

'She'll have you doing that all day,' Helenka said laughing.

'She's gorgeous. How old is she?'

'Six years. She's just had a litter and is brilliant with them, but I know she likes to escape with me from time to time...for some adult company.'

'Coffee mama?'

'I've just had one with Theo so I'm alright thanks. Thought I'd have a stroll with Kimba. We're taking one of the bitches, Sophie, to Iona's tomorrow. Kimba's mum, Sheeba, belonged to Iona,' she explained to Keri. 'But she died just before she had the pups. There are five in the litter, three bitches and two males. The two boys are going to my friends in the next bay, they're sisters and run a little craft shop just over the brow of the hill.'

'Their names are Prince and Zeppo,' chipped in Annys. 'I'm having one of the girls. Her name is Tasha. I chose all their names didn't I Helenka?'

'Yes darling, you did.'

'They're lovely names. What's the other girl called?' asked Keri.

'Her name is Kayle,' replied Annys proudly. 'She's going to stay with Kimba.'

As she heard her name her ears pricked up. She had been walking around in circles trying to find a cool spot and ended up in a shady area underneath a tap on the wall that kept dripping onto her head giving Annys the giggles. The girls talked about their day at the market and how most of Manos' paintings had sold. Helenka was so pleased for him.

'Come on girl,' she called over to Kimba who stretched languorously and ambled slowly to her side.

'We'll walk back with you,' Maria said putting her empty mug down on the wall. 'Don't forget your model Annys.'

Manos and Keri were deep in conversation. 'I'm sure Manos can entertain you for a while Keri if that's alright. I want to get this one home. No doubt she's got some homework to do.'

'Thanks for a great day Maria. I really enjoyed it.'

'Me too,' replied Maria.

As they strolled home along the beach Maria glanced back and saw them both walking into the studio.

Surprisingly, it was much brighter than she imagined. A long narrow building with windows along one of the walls overlooking the sea with natural light flooding through. Running along the length of the studio paintings stood propped up against the wall, lined up like soldiers standing to attention. Seascapes, landscapes, paintings of cottages perched high on hillsides; her eyes moved from one to another captivating her. She smiled spotting a collection of caricatures at the far end of the studio. On the wall behind the sink he had painted a fresco of rolling waves in the most astonishing shades of greens and blues she had ever seen. She reached up to touch the foamy waves, like a string of white stallions galloping fiercely towards the shore, imagining them washing over her arms and cooling them with their refreshing spray. How could anyone capture such an image in their minds eye and bring it to life in such a way?

His eyes followed her around the room, the sunlight iridescent on her sun-kissed flawless skin. As she moved through the studio he watched, her eyes dancing trying to take it all in. She reminded him of a small child in a sweetshop enticed by all the different confectionery. A warm breeze brought the salty smell of the sea through the open window. She turned to face it. The sand such a golden colour. The water almost the same shade as the sky, melting into each other on the horizon. Birds hiding in the trees at the side of the studio called out to one another. A butterfly fluttered in through the window softly settling on one of the canvases; a pretty floral piece so realistic even Mother Nature thought it was real. She stood there utterly spellbound.

Lifting himself onto one of the workbenches with his burly arms he asked Keri what she thought of the studio.

'It's absolutely incredible. I'm speechless!' she declared turning around to face him. 'You've got some beautiful canvases. I love the frieze on the wall. The colours you've used just bring it to life and some of the shades as the sun catches them are awesome!'

'Thanks. Glad you like it. It's my little haven,' he said swinging his legs.

They talked for some time about his artwork and how he had started selling some at the local markets. She told him about her bespoke jewellery and how she had sold several pieces on her journey through Italy. He spotted through the open window one of his boats coming towards the shore.

'It looks like the last boat of the day is coming in. I just need to moor it up. Back in a minute,' he said jumping down from the bench and walking towards the door.

She followed him. After he had guided the motorboat to the side of the jetty and shook hands with his customers he tied it to the landing stage. His biceps tensed as he wound the rope around the rusty bar sticking out from the side wall. Bending down taking the keys from the ignition his shorts stretched tightly over his taut buttocks; his calf muscles flexed. The fitted white t-shirt clung to his pecks. On his left wrist he wore three brown leather plaited bands. He turned to walk back up the path and the light breeze lifted stray strands of hair off his face. Keri caught her breath.

Manos was aware she had been watching him secure the boat. 'How do you fancy dinner tonight? I know a lovely little taverna in the village on top of the hill,' he said pointing towards the hillside. 'The view is beautiful at night. You can see the whole of the bay lit up with strings of lights running along the coast road from one side to the other.'

'That would be lovely, thank you,' she replied eagerly.

'Alberto who owns the taverna specialises in fish dishes. He cooks the most amazing swordfish. Should I pick you up from the apartment?'

'Yes, that would be great, thanks.'

'What time suits you?'

'Anytime really.'

'Should we say 8 o'clock?'

'Perfect!'

'That's a date then!' he said winking at her.

Chapter Ten

Alex tapped rhythmically on the door and entered Manos' apartment, calling out to him as he walked through to the kitchen.

'I'm in the shower Alex,' he replied. 'Won't be a minute.'

It was a stone's throw away from the boatyard and studio, a first-floor apartment at the end of a block just off the main road. He had lived there for nearly three years. The kitchen-diner was basic: he didn't really bother much with cooking. Most evenings he ate at his mama's taverna and usually grabbed a quick snack at lunchtime from one of the local cafés, although he always made time to have dinner with Maria and Annys at least once a week. When he moved into the flat, the first place of his own, Maria proved to be very handy with a paintbrush and helped decorate all the rooms in a different shade. The living room was dove grey which led to the kitchen-diner, a fresh light green in colour. The hallway was white to brighten it up as there was no natural light there. The bedroom pale blue and the same colour in the bathroom contrasting the white suite. He had dressed each room with some of his own paintings. They had gone to a store in the City to buy most of the furniture and from viewing the flat, decorating and furnishing it, had taken only four weeks. It had been a difficult decision for him to move out of the home he had grown up in. Yannis had left to live in the City a number of years before and Manos felt it was his duty to look after mama. When he brought up the subject of moving out she was more than happy, and after all, it was only a stones throw down the road.

'Blimey! Aftershave!' said Alex cheekily sniffing the air. 'It must be a girl…I can't ever remember you going to all this trouble for me!'

'Ha! Ha! I'm going out for dinner actually.'

'You never dress up to go out for dinner. Who's the lucky lady?' he replied, his eyes falling on the clothes strewn all over the room.

'Yes I do.'

'When?' challenged Alex.

'Now and then…' he retorted.

'I rest my case! Come on, spill the beans. We've been mates for a long time. You know you can't hide anything from me!'

'Okay! Okay!' he gave in. 'Her name's Keri. She's from Ireland. You saw her today with Maria.'

'Oh yes. I remember…a pretty young lass, blonde hair. What on earth does she see in you?' he laughed.

'She's obviously got taste!'

'Where are you taking her? Don't worry, I'm not going to stalk you.'

'Yeah! You'd better not either. Thought we'd go to Alberto's place.'

'Good choice mate. I'd better let you get ready then. Oh, there you go, I nearly forgot,' he said handing him a folded piece of paper with a list of names and phone numbers.

'I didn't think there would be that many interested! I'll ring them in the morning and invite them to the studio. I've got quite a few canvases ready now. They might be interested in one of those. Cheers mate. I owe you one.'

Alex let himself out of the flat and Manos carried on getting ready dropping the damp towel onto the bathroom floor. *What to wear*? He pondered. Normally, he would just put the first thing on to hand. But not tonight. Tonight was different.

Keri stepped out of the shower refreshed, wrapped a towel around her wet hair piling it up onto the top of her head and swathed another around her body. She thought her mobile was ringing whilst she was in the shower and walked over to the dressing table. A missed call from her mammy. She would give her a ring when dressed, there was plenty of time. She bent down to pick up what she had chosen to wear; a crisp white linen pair of trousers with a light brown leather belt, and a white lacy blouse that showed her delicate suntan off. She would wear her hair loosely over her shoulders accessorising with a pale pink flowery necklace on a light brown suede strap, matching bracelet, and tan sandals and an over the shoulder small bag. Spot on!

Alberto was chalking the specials of the day onto the blackboard at the front of the taverna.

Lavraki ~
Fresh grilled seabass, aioli, lemon, and herbs served with couscous salad

14 Euros

Midia ~
Mussels in a creamy sauce with side dish of Greek potatoes

16 Euros

Stifado ~
Tender pieces of lamb with onions, tomatoes, and aromatic herbs served in a casserole pot

12 Euros

Albondigas ~
Meatballs in a spicy tomato sauce served with rice or Greek potatoes

10 Euros

Souvlaki ~
Chargrilled pieces of chicken on a bed of rice with a tzatziki dip

11 Euros

Sautéed Mushrooms ~
In lemon and garlic served with fried aubergines and aioli

9 Euros

He stood up, looked at his handiwork and turned to walk back inside. A car in the distance winding up the mountain track caught his eye. When it got closer he could see Manos with a passenger he didn't recognise.

Parking in front of the taverna Manos opened the door for Keri, partly being the gentleman he was, and partly because the door was a bit dodgy. Alberto greeted them with outstretched arms.

'Welcome my friends.'

'Thank you Alberto. This is Keri.'

'Welcome to my taverna Keri. Let me get you a table with the best view of the sunset,' he said walking over to the terraced area, pulling a chair out for her and offering the menu. 'The specials today are on the board at the side of the bar. Can I get you both a drink?' he asked leaning over to light the candle in the centre of the table.

'I'll have a Mythos please,' replied Manos.

'A dry white wine would be lovely please.' Keri replied opening the menu.

He made his way back to the bar to fetch the drinks.

'Didn't I say the view was spectacular?'

'It's breath-taking Manos.'

He loved the way she spoke his name in her silky Irish tones. Scanning his menu briefly he asked her what she fancied to eat.

'I'm not sure…either the lasagne or moussaka.'

'Alberto makes the best moussaka for miles.'

'Moussaka it is then!'

Alberto carried a tray of drinks over to their table with a dish of olives and some slices of warm garlic bread. 'Are you ready to order?'

'Yes, I think I'll have lamb stifado please Alberto.'

'And I'll have the moussaka. Thank you,' she said returning the menu.

Soft music floated through the air from the bar as the

eucalyptus trees and lemon groves surrounding the taverna released their subtle fragrance. On the horizon where the sea met the sky, a blazing orange ball slipped slowly into the sea leaving behind the fading colours of the day. She leaned back in the wicker chair and sighed.

'It's quite something isn't it?' he said breaking into her thoughts.

'Astonishing…' she murmured.

'Theo used to bring me up here when I was younger. He's a friend of Albertos. They grew up together. He had an old van and I'd join him on trips delivering provisions to the tavernas and cafés on the outskirts of the village. We would always finish the day off here just as the sun was setting. He would have a raki with Alberto before setting off back to the village. Even then I was fascinated by the views and would take my sketchbook along. Every day there was something new to sketch.'

They chat together relaxed in each other's company. He explained how he became interested in painting from a very young age and loved experimenting with different colours and textures. She listened intently as he described the works of various artists who influenced him. She told him briefly about her travels through Europe and how she first got involved in making jewellery and that her passion turned into quite a money spinner supporting her financially throughout her travels, particularly useful during the latter part of her journey through Italy where she worked in a large hotel in Rimini. It was thanks to the hotel porter, a lovely little old man with a shock of white hair and droopy moustache, whose wife was on the local council, and who pulled some strings to get her a regular spot at the local craft market.

Manos admired the jewellery she was wearing, and she moved her hand towards him showing off the intricate patterns on the bracelet. Their hands touched. Her heart began to race. Hearing Alberto's footsteps they moved their arms away from the table.

'Moussaka for the lady,' he said placing the steaming dish in front of her.

'Thank you Alberto,' she said as he reached across to put the bowl of stifado on the table in front of Manos.

'Can I get you anything else?'

'Can we have a jug of water please?' asked Keri.

'Yes of course,' he said turning to go back to the kitchen.

'Mmmm…it smells delicious,' she said picking up the cutlery.

'Wait until you taste it!' replied Manos.

They savoured every delicious mouthful, offering each other little tasters of their own meal. Unable to make up their minds what dessert to have they decided on a cheese and fruit platter. The night sky was now filled with a blanket of stars, their white points of light glistening in the cavernous expanse of darkness. Keri felt relaxed in his company and the evening flew by. He shared with her tales of the older folk in the village and antics of the younger ones. He loved how she threw her head back when she laughed revealing her slender neckline and how her cornflower blue eyes sparkled in the moonlight. Their faces were illuminated by the flickering candle casting its golden hue as they sipped their coffees.

After saying good night to Alberto they make their way back to the car pausing at the top of the track next to the car park to take in the magnificent views. Standing closely side by side their hands rested on the wooden railing as they looked down to the village below, the lights reflecting on the sea as the waves moved steadily back and forth. Manos pointed to the brightest star. Putting his hand back onto the railing it touched hers. She felt a rush of electricity between them. He turned his body towards her, taking her face gently into his hands and caressing her neck tenderly. She could feel the warmth of his breath on her lips. Looking deeply into her pale blue eyes as they slowly closed he brought his lips down to hers. They melted into each other's arms. She could feel his heart beating fast against her breast and wrapped her arms tighter around his shoulders taking in the musky scent of his aftershave. Parting their lips for a moment and opening her eyes she looked deeply into his with affection. And again their lips met, breathing their souls and love into each other. Resting her head on his shoulder, he moved her golden locks away from her face, like silk running through his fingers, breathing in the sweetness of her perfume. He wanted this moment to last forever.

Back in her apartment Keri opened the balcony doors and leaned on the railing. She looked up into the starry night sky and reflected on her evening with Manos. She would never forget this evening… the night she fell in love.

Chapter Eleven

Keri straightened up in the hard plastic chair, made even more uncomfortable by the clamminess of her skin on its rigid surface. Noticing the ceiling fans on high speed and thinking she might be able to escape the soaring temperatures, she had wandered into the café to log into their Wi-Fi and check her e-mails. Outside, waves of heat flickered up from the pavement and patches of tarmac melted on the uneven road, the distinct smell of hot asphalt crept in through the open door.

She took a mouthful of water from her bottle and went back to her e-mails. There were a handful of new ones; a couple from her parents, one from a cousin who she had kept in touch with throughout her travels, and the rest of them from Emma, Julie, and Carol. She tried to check them at least once a week, sometimes more often depending how easy it was to get a decent signal. It was lovely to hear all the gossip from back home. She worded her replies very carefully so as not to give anything away about her feelings for Manos. Keeping her cards close to her chest she wrote about the places she'd visited and generalised about the people she had met, describing the beautiful villages on the little Greek island, the spectacular sunsets, the current heatwave, and how some of the people in the village had taken her under their wing.

Her mind kept wandering back to the conversation with Helenka about the fishing boat disaster and before she knew it she had typed *"The Crimson Tide"* into a search engine which came up with several news reports. Clicking on the English translation she began to read the account of what they believed had happened on that fateful night.

Christophe climbed out of the taxi at the opposite end of the bay to Yannis' piece of land and looked all around him. Wearing black shorts and a plain white short-sleeved shirt he hoped to blend in with holidaymakers and locals alike but still stood out like a sore thumb. Walking through the village he realised it was a lot smaller than he initially thought. Passing a row of shops with apartments above he looked across the road and noticed a restaurant called Ellas. A middle-aged woman was setting tables and putting a vase of fresh flowers on each one. As he walked past unhurriedly he could feel someone watching him. He was aware of an elderly man moving away from a doorway of a shop. Continuing his journey he noticed someone approaching dressed in black trousers, white shirt, and black shoes. A waiter he thought. The waiter nodded to him. Christophe returned the compliment. He paused to look through the window of a gift shop taking a momentary look to his left and watched the young man disappear into the restaurant.

'Mark! Mark! Over here,' called Helenka. 'Did you see that man snooping around?'

'What man?' replied a puzzled Mark. 'And why are you standing on a stool?'

'Look! Over there!' she pointed nearly losing her balance. 'A taxi dropped him off. He doesn't look like he's on holiday does he?'

'I suppose not,' he said dreamily making his way towards the kitchen to start his shift.

'He looks up to no good if you ask me!' she said craning her neck to see where he was heading.

She moved to a new vantage point at the front of the taverna where she spotted George's wife Anna and dashed across the road to her. Anna had also observed the well-dressed stranger and was on the case too, much to George's amusement.

'I wondered how long it would take you two to get together for a gossip!' he joked with the pair of them. 'I knew Anna was up to something. She's been rearranging the window display for ages!'

Hearing a car coming towards him Christophe glanced around. Leaving a cloud of exhaust dust behind it the car ascended into the mountainous road ahead. Watching it disappear he carried on walking through the village.

Feeling he was still being watched Christophe walked past the boatyard and fishing shop and along the coastal path taking in the vista. Once at the top he started pacing the area checking the compass on his fancy watch, his thoughts turning to the build. With the gradient of the land the foundations would need to be deeper than he had originally considered. Taking a pen and paper out of his pocket he began drafting ideas and making quick sketches. Unbeknown to Christophe he had attracted the interest of someone else.

Curiosity getting the better of him, Manos made his way up the steep bank towards the stranger. As he got closer he could see it was the same man who was with Yannis the previous day.

'Hello. Can I help you at all? asked Manos as he reached the stranger.

'Hello!' he replied sharply.

'I'm afraid this is private land,' said Manos straight to the point.

'Yes I know. I'm working for Yannis Papadopoulous. His architect. Christophe Dafoe,' he said with his hand outstretched.

Shaking his hand Manos introduced himself. 'Manos Papadopoulous. His brother. Pleased to meet you. Yannis mentioned getting his architect to inspect the land.'

'Yes, there's quite a lot to take in.'

'He's been talking about the development for quite a while now. I never thought he'd actually do it!' Manos said light-heartedly.

'He's told you about it then?'

'Oh yeah. It's something he's been planning for a long time.'

'And you don't think the land might be a little on the small side?'

'No. Not at all,' he replied keeping an eye on the boatyard below.

'I saw you coming up from the yard down there,' he said pointing downhill.

'That's right. I own the boat yard and outbuildings. I've warned him not to make his villa too big. I don't want him blocking my sunlight!' Manos joked.

'Oh I'm sure that won't be the case.'

Christophe's mobile rang. Checking the caller on his screen he asked Manos to excuse him as he needed to take the call.

'No problem. Good to meet you. I must get back anyway,' he said turning to go back down the hillside to the boatyard.

Christophe walked in the opposite direction taking the call. After a short conversation he made his way back into the village turning left towards Lefko Bay, thinking about the strange conversation with Yannis' brother wondering why he had not told him about the hotel. Why the secrecy?

Keri left the coolness of the café and went back out into the heat of the City still feeling strangely emotional after reading about the tragedy that had happened to the people she had begun to care about, finding it incomprehensible what the families must have gone through. The busy streets radiated the heat of the day, with people pushing and shoving, and drivers honking their horns impatiently. The aroma coming from the coffee shops mixed with the fumes of the City. Stray dogs lazed around in dusty alleyways waiting for scraps of food to be thrown in their direction. She moved slowly through the streets, the air thick and oppressive. Pollution and confusion in every direction. Give me the serenity of the bay any day she thought. *I really need to get out of here.* Deciding against another nightmare journey on the bus she made her way to the nearest taxi rank.

'Galazios Bay please,' she said to the driver as she slid into the back seat.

'Okay,' he replied pulling away from the curbside. 'Have you had a good day in the City?'

'Yes thank you. It's terribly busy though. And so hot!'

'It is at the moment. No-one seems to have any idea when this heatwave will end. Hope you don't mind me asking, but are you staying in one of George's apartments?'

'I am indeed,' she replied.

'I thought so. I've seen you in the village. I'm Spiros by the way.'

'Pleased to meet you. My name's Keri,' she said leaning back on the cool leather seats looking through the side window as they sped away, leaving behind the commotion of the City for the quietness of the countryside, where sheep strayed into the roads and goats ambled around nibbling bark off the old trees.

Keri observed Spiros through the rear view mirror thinking what a good head of hair he had, which led her to ponder how old he might be. Possibly in his late fifties, difficult to tell with his dark leathery skin. A pair of glasses rested on the tip of his nose that he kept pushing upwards, only seconds later for them to slip down again.

Spiros watched Keri in his mirror thinking what a lovely girl she was. Come to think of it he had seen her with Manos in the village a few times. Nothing escaped his attention.

As they descended into the bay, passing Alberto's taverna, Keri took in the views, the memory of the previous evening still fresh in her mind. She smiled to herself.

'I see you're happy to be back in the bay.'

'Oh yes. It's just so beautiful isn't it?' she replied. 'And so peaceful.'

'It is. I don't know how people can live in the City. I've always been a country dweller myself. I've lived in the bay all my life, in the same house my parents lived in,' he said pointing to the peninsula between Galazios and Lefko Bay where a tiny house overgrown with shrubbery clung to the hillside. He went on to explain how his family had owned the land and ran a smallholding, working well into their eighties. He'd never really been that interested in farming and started his own taxi business when he was in his early twenties.

Pulling up outside George's apartments Keri got her purse from her handbag and paid Spiros his fare.

'Thanks very much. It was lovely to meet you,' she said.

'Thank you. Enjoy the rest of your stay. I'm sure I'll see you again.'

'No doubt you will. I'm here for a while,' she said climbing out of the car. 'Bye Spiros.'

'Goodbye Keri,' he said driving away.

At the end of the road heading back to the City he spotted a man signaling to him.

'Do you need a lift?' he asked.

'Yes please. To the City.'

As Spiros maneuvered the car back into the hillside he saw one of the elderly ladies from the next village tending to one of the roadside shrines. Her brother had been killed in a car accident many years ago and she and her sister took it in turns to look after the shrine. He slowed down as a mark of respect and acknowledged her.

Christophe watched the landscape rolling by at speed, knowing he would never get used to the erratic driving of the Greeks as he tried to focus on the notes he had made. Spiros broke the silence by asking his passenger if he was enjoying his trip to the island. When he didn't answer Spiros reminded him that he had picked him up from the airport a few days ago.

'I never forget a face,' he told him. 'Are you here on business?'

'Yes, business,' he replied abruptly.

'How long are you here for?'

'Another day or two.'

The conversation was stilted to say the least. Approaching the City Spiros asked his passenger where he would like to be dropped off. The taxi rank at the harbour he told him. Looking across to the apartment block where Yannis lived Spiros couldn't help wondering what he was up to with this man in his cab.

'Hi K. Would you like to meet up? M x' the text said.
'Yeah. In an hour? At your studio? K x'
'Perfect! x'

Closing her mobile she went through to the bedroom and placed it on the dressing table. She couldn't wait to jump into the shower and get the City fumes out of her hair.

Putting the phone back into his pocket Manos went outside to hose down the jetty. He couldn't get her out of his mind. He'd never felt like this about anyone and smiled to himself as he remembered his evening with her.

Maria leaned on the gate at the back of Helenka's and watched Annys playing in the garden with the pups. She heard a noise behind her and turned around.

'Oh hi Keri. How are you?'

'Hi Maria. I'm good thanks. And you?'

'Not bad at all. Are you off out somewhere?'

'I'm meeting Manos.'

'Are you…?' she said with a glint in her eye.

'I'm glad I bumped into you. I've been bursting to tell you. I went out for dinner last night…with Manos.'

'You kept that quiet!'

'It was a spur of the moment thing really. We went to the taverna in the hillside, Alberto's place, and had a lovely meal.'

'I bet you did. Come on. Spill the beans!'

'I don't know what you mean.'

'Was it a romantic meal? Candlelit and all that?'

'I'm afraid I couldn't possibly say.'

'Come on,' she said moving closer.

Keri smiled coyly. 'We had a great evening. Alberto fussed over us all night. We sat on the terrace and the views of the sunset were the most amazing I've ever seen. Alberto pampered to our every need…'

'I don't want to know about Alberto. I want the gossip on you two!' she interrupted.

Keri laughed as she told her that Manos was the perfect gentleman, they got on really well and had a lovely time. Keri didn't share their intimate moment. She wanted to keep it locked away in her heart for now.

'I knew you two would hit it off and he's certainly brought a sparkle to your eyes.'

'Thanks Maria. I think I'll be seeing a lot more of him and I'm hoping he feels the same way.'

'Oh, I'm sure he does. You make a lovely couple. Will I see you later? I'll be with Helenka this evening. We're having dinner together about five o'clock. Would you like to join us? Annys will be with us, that's why we're eating early.'

'Are you sure Helenka won't mind me gatecrashing?'

'No, of course not. She's taken a right shine to you and loves to hear tales of your travels too. She told me about knowing your parents and how she would sit for hours listening to stories of their travels.'

'Five o'clock it is then. And thanks Maria…for everything,' she said giving her a quick hug. 'Better get going. I'll see you later.'

And she walked towards the studio with a spring in her step humming a tune she'd heard in Alberto's that she just couldn't get out of her mind.

Standing the yard brush in the corner he saw Keri walking towards him, the breeze wafting through her golden hair. Smiling at him she lifted her sunglasses onto her head and followed him inside. Putting his arms gently around her tiny waist he breathed in her perfume.

'Mmmm…you smell gorgeous.'

She smiled up at him draping her arms around his neck as he leaned forward to kiss her and nestled into his chest.

'I couldn't wait to see you again,' he whispered.

Looking into his dark brown eyes she kissed him again with fervour.

Chapter Twelve

Christophe stepped out of the taxi and made his way through the paved streets to the hotel. As soon as he reached his room he poured a large whisky and sat down to look at his notes and drawings and weighed up the pros and cons of the project. It would certainly double the size of the bay, which probably wouldn't go down too well with the locals. The complex would definitely appeal to the guests and the location alone would be an attraction…but would the land be big enough? Certainly not without the boatyard and outbuildings. They would have to go. Interesting meeting the brother today, Christophe thought reaching for the bottle and pouring another drink. No wonder Yannis was on edge when he visited last. The land would without doubt suit a villa but not the sort of hotel he would be interested in investing in. Picking up the calculator he did some number crunching. With the underpinning and extensive foundation work alone even before the building work started it wouldn't be worth it. Sitting back in his chair and reaching for his mobile he planned his next move.

Dropping the keys into her handbag, Keri made her way down the steps and across the road to Ellas. She could hear the Town Hall clock in Lefko Bay chiming five o'clock. She was really looking forward to having dinner with Maria, Annys and Helenka and after talking to her parents about their pending visit she couldn't wait to give Helenka the good news. They had always planned to visit once Keri had arrived in Galazios Bay. She would have a word with George to see if they could stay in one of his apartments for a week or so. Walking up the wooden steps to the taverna she was greeted by a smiling Annys running towards her who started talking nineteen to the dozen about her day at pre-school.

'Annys! Let Keri get in. She was so excited when I told her you were having dinner with us.'

'She's fine aren't you darling,' said Keri bending down to listen to her.

Helenka hearing the commotion came out of the kitchen to greet Keri.

'Hi Helenka. Hope you don't mind me joining you.'

'No problem at all. It's lovely to see you. Did you have a good day in the City? Spiros popped in earlier and said he'd picked you up. You know what it's like here. You can't sneeze without someone knowing!' she laughed. 'What can I get you to drink my dear?'

'Could I have a frappe please? I can't get enough of them!'

'Of course you can.'

'Thanks Helenka,' she said sitting down at the table.

Annys settled herself on the chair next to Keri. She reached into her handbag and took out a tiny parcel and gave it to Annys.

'A little present for you – I thought you might like it,' she said smiling as the little girl's face lit up.

'Thank you Keri,' said Annys politely as she opened the gift wrap.

'Mummy look what I've got! she said lifting the silver pendant out of the box.

'Oh isn't that pretty,' exclaimed Maria.

'Can I wear it now Keri?'

'Of course you can,' she replied opening the little silver clasp and placing it gently round her neck.

'Thank you Keri,' she said giving her a big hug and skipping around the table to show Maria.

'Isn't it beautiful Annys. Aren't you a lucky girl?'

'I'm going to show Helenka and Theo,' she declared running off in the direction of the kitchen.

'It's lovely Keri, but you shouldn't have. It must have cost you a fortune.'

'I made it a few weeks ago just before I left Italy on my way to the island. I've got a few similar pieces. I was trying out a new style and thought Annys might like it. I hope you don't mind.'

'No. Not at all. It's a lovely thought. You do wear some beautiful jewellery Keri.'

'I think every piece I own at the moment is something I've made.'

Annys ran back to the table closely followed by Helenka with a tray of drinks. 'Annys has been showing us her pretty necklace haven't you darling.'

'It's gorgeous isn't it?' said Maria smiling.

'You are a very talented young lady,' praised Helenka. 'How long have you been making jewellery?'

'I've always loved designing pieces but took it more seriously when I was at college. I did an Art and Design course. A group of us decided to go travelling after college. The other girls would spend hours planning what clothes, shoes, and handbags they would take. I would be trying to work out how many craft tools and materials I could get into my case. They would torment me terribly about it!'

'And did you manage to bring many tools with you?'

'Oh yes, but I've been stopped at passport control a few times and when I open my case get some very strange looks indeed!'

'I bet you do!' laughed Helenka. 'Where have your travels taken you?'

Keri took a sip from her glass and began to recount her travels to Helenka and how she got most of her ideas and styles for a new range of jewellery whilst travelling through Italy.

Theo walked over from the kitchen carrying a steaming dish of lasagne.

'*Efharisto* Theo. I said to give me a shout when it was ready, and I'd have fetched it.'

'No problem. I could see you were busy and didn't like to interrupt!' he joked. 'Enjoy your meal ladies!'

'Thank you Theo.' Maria and Keri said in unison as he made his way back to the kitchen.

'I hope lasagne's okay for you Keri. I remember you having one the other day, so I guessed it was a safe bet.'

'Lovely thanks Helenka,' she replied taking the plate from her. 'It's so good of you to share your meal with me.'

'My pleasure. I'm pleased you could join us. Carry on with your story Keri,' encouraged Helenka.

Keri continued between mouthfuls of the tasty lasagne.

'Tuscany was so beautiful. We stayed in cheap bed and breakfasts as we travelled through the region. Vineyards rolled down the hills into the lush valleys and there were cypress trees as far as the eye could see. Enchanted castles and rust-coloured farmhouses covered in moss clung precariously to the hilltops with sandy roads snaking around them.' She took a sip from her drink and continued. 'Florence and Pisa were my favourites. Florence just oozed character with its impressive architectural history. Palaces and churches housed some of the greatest artistic treasures in the world. Art galleries and museums lined the oldest streets in the City. I remember spending a day in the San Lorenzo Library with its magnificent exhibition of Michelangelo's work. There was a church on top of a hill – I think it was called San Minato al Monte and the views of Florence were out of this world. And Pisa…now there's an elegant City! It's got a kind of majestic solitude about it. I was quite taken with the leaning tower of Pisa. Mind you, once you get away from the tourist trail and wander the peaceful streets you soak up the real atmosphere. It's a university town you know…'

Maria and Helenka stared at her taking in her every word.

'Oh God! Sorry. I'm going on and on aren't I?'

'No, not at all,' said Helenka. 'It's lovely listening to tales of your travels. It takes me right back to when your parents talked about their journey. You have the same knack as your mother for bringing the places to life. I remember the first time Dino and I went over to Italy. Yannis was a young lad, and I was expecting Manos. Dino had a cousin who had moved to Italy with his young family. They ran a smallholding and asked us to stay in their farmhouse. We spent a couple of weeks there and had a fabulous time. It was a few miles inland from Rimini and we spent a lot of time on the beach.'

'I loved Rimini,' chipped in Keri. 'I worked in a beach front hotel there. Harry, the porter, and his wife took me under their wing. It is a beautiful area isn't it?'

'Oh yes, it certainly is, especially when you move inland a few miles from the busy coastal resort. Dino loved to help them out on the farm. Yannis would collect the eggs and help look after the chickens and I spent a fair bit of time baking bread and cakes, then the boys would take the produce to market. They made quite a good living working the land. Don't get me wrong, it was hard work, but they weren't afraid of that. After Manos was born we still went over a couple of times a year and all the children used to play together on the farm. They'd often come over to the island with endless supplies of citrus fruits picked freshly from trees in the orchard. Dino's cousin was actually a carpenter by trade and he'd got a workshop on the farm where he would make the most amazing pieces of furniture which would be shipped over to his brother's shop in Lefko Bay. In fact, he made that dresser over there,' Helenka said pointing to it. 'You can't get pieces of furniture like that anywhere. He personalised it especially for us,' she said proudly.

'It's beautiful isn't it,' said Keri getting up to take a closer look.

'Would you like your drink topping up my dear?'

'Yes please,' she replied offering her glass to Helenka.

Annys ran in from the garden talking excitedly about the pups. 'Keri, would you come and look at them?'

'As long as it's okay with your mama and Helenka.'

'Yes, of course it is.'

'Come on Keri,' she said holding her hand and leading her through the kitchen and into the garden, followed by Maria and Helenka carrying the drinks.

Tails wagging eagerly, the pups clambered onto each other to get a better look at their visitor. Peering over the wooden door Keri saw Kimba straight away and leaned over to stroke her head. Annys unbolted the lower door and five pups tumbled out. Every time the door was opened it was as if it was their first taste of freedom and they rolled around haphazardly darting here and there. Last of all Kimba sauntered out lazily into the balmy early evening air and made her way to the shady tree at the end of the garden where she could loll around and watch the activities from afar.

Helenka plucked Tasha and Prince from the mayhem, hauling them up to her chest. Prince struggled to get away, legs circling in the air wanting to be back on the ground with his playmates. Keri lifted one of the pups from her.

'That's Tasha,' Annys explained, as the pup snuggled into her neck. 'She's mine and coming to live with us when she's big enough.'

'She's gorgeous, so soft and cuddly. I can see why you chose her. Her brothers and sisters are all lovely too,' she added quickly. 'Have they got homes to go to as well?'

'Oh yes,' replied an excited Annys who went on to tell Keri their names and where they were all going to live.

Keri listened intently as Tasha fidgeted in her arms. Kneeling down on the floor she placed the wriggling ball of fluff onto her knee and was soon bombarded by the others wanting some attention from the newcomer. They yapped away circling her and launching themselves onto her lap. She fussed them all equally whilst Annys fetched some toys from a basket in the corner.

'I hear you went to Alberto's last night,' said Helenka.

'I mentioned it to Helenka earlier. I knew you wouldn't mind,' said Maria with a twinkle in her eye.

'Of course I don't mind. We had a lovely time. Alberto is such a gentleman! He made me feel so welcome. The meal was beautiful, and the views of the whole bay are amazing.'

'I think I remember your parents going there a few times. It would have only been half the size though. He had it extended about ten years ago and doubled the size of the terrace. Alberto and his wife used to live in the cottage next door and decided to renovate the apartment above the taverna to make the most of the stunning views. Sadly, she passed away a week before they were due to move in. Alberto decided to stay in the cottage but after a couple of years moved into the apartment and had the cottage renovated, which he now rents out. The builders did a great job. It's always popular up there with tourists wanting a view with their meal. His food is absolutely amazing too! What did you have to eat?'

'I had moussaka and Manos chose stifado. He said it was the best moussaka for miles and he was right. It was so tasty…sorry Helenka! I shouldn't be saying such things to a fellow restaurateur!'

'No. No. Not at all my dear! It's true. It is the best! I've tried to replicate it…but don't even come a close second. And I've asked him for the recipe so many times you wouldn't believe, but he won't share it! Says it's got a secret ingredient passed down through the generations – so I just have to be happy to eat there every so often instead!' Helenka said smiling.

After a while they all went back inside and picked up where they had left off with their earlier conversation, with Keri explaining how her two friends returned home to Ireland after their stay in Rimini, and how she continued her journey to the little Greek island travelling south to take a ferry from the Port of Ancona on the Adriatic Coast. She described leaving Italy behind, and just visible on the horizon her first glimpse of the cluster of tiny islands, the largest of which would be her home for the next few months. The vista as they approached was just how her parents had portrayed it. One by one the lush emerald islands emerged through the azure waters reaching skywards, mystically drawing you to their unspoilt beauty.

Chapter Thirteen

'Annys darling. Can you get the door please?' Maria called from the kitchen.

Reaching up to unlatch it she squealed with delight upon seeing Keri and launched herself into her arms.

'Who is it Annys?' Maria asked wiping her hands on her apron.

'It's Keri! she replied taking her hand and pulling her into the kitchen.

'Hope you don't mind me popping in. I know the other day you said if I was passing by…and I was just walking along the headland. It's gorgeous isn't it?'

'Yes, beautiful. Would you like a cup of tea? I was going to put the kettle on after I'd got this last batch of cakes in the oven. I got roped into making cakes for Sunday School. One of the mums who usually does the baking isn't well, so I offered to help out. I think there'll be some spare ones though!' she said roguishly.

'Sounds good! I'd love a drink please.'

'What would you like? I'm having camomile. I've got lemon, raspberry and mint infusion.'

'Could I have lemon please?'

'Mama, can I show Keri my bedroom?'

'Of course you can if Keri would like to…'

'I'd love to!' Keri interrupted. 'Come on then, lead the way.' And off they went hand in hand up the narrow staircase.

'Close your eyes,' said Annys as they approached the bedroom door. 'Ta-da!' she exclaimed opening her arms like a magician's assistant.

Walking through the doorway a profusion of sheer pinkness met her, it was like stepping into a princess's bedroom in a fairy-tale castle. Swathes of fabric with silk ribbons and bows flowed from the ceiling resting softly on the edges of the bed. Pretty satin appliqués throughout enticed you into the fairy-tale. One wall was painted like the wall of a castle with a window looking out onto an enchanted forest. Throws and cushions adorned an old white ottoman and in the corner a dressing table with delicate gold stencilling, home to the newly created pink hair band box! It was like falling into a vat of sweet pink candyfloss transporting Keri right back to her childhood.

'Do you like it?' asked a wide-eyed Annys.

Keri blinked. 'It's beautiful. Like a princess's bedroom. 'I love the colours. It reminds me of my bedroom when I was a little girl. I called it my pink palace.'

'I picked all the colours myself and mummy made the curtains and everything. I helped her with the cushions,' she proudly declared showing Keri her handiwork.

'And your hair band box looks lovely on the dressing table.'

'Tea's ready!' came a voice from downstairs.

'Thanks, we're coming,' replied Keri.

'I'm going to call my bedroom the pink palace too! Let's go and tell mama!' said Annys skipping across the landing.

Keri gently closed the bedroom door taking another peek as she did so.

'Out here!' called Maria from the patio, setting the drinks down on the small stone wall looking out to sea. Annys jumped up onto the wall and swung her legs over to face the sea. Picking up the tumbler of squash and drinking it hurriedly she said how much Keri loved her bedroom and that it was like hers when she was a little girl. 'Where's my new skipping rope mama?'

'In the toy box under the stairs.'

'Katerina will be here soon and she's bringing hers. It's red...but mine is much nicer, and I want to show it to Keri,' she replied heading off to rummage around in the box.

Walking through the kitchen and out onto the patio Keri was dazzled by the bright sunshine and lowered her sunglasses from the top of her head to shield her eyes. A vision in pink resembling a whirlwind in a confused rush sped by, skipping rope in hand.

'Keri! Look at me!' she called breathlessly. *Mickey Mouse built a house. How many bricks did he use? One, two, three, four...*' she chanted gaining speed and declaring she can get up to twenty – her friend Katerina only managing ten! '...*five, six, seven, eight...*whoops! Watch me again. *One, two, three, four, five...sixteen, seventeen, eighteen...*'

'Well done!' cried Keri clapping her hands to the rhythm.

'You have a go,' she said offering Keri the skipping rope.

'Oh, I don't know. I've not skipped for years.'

'Please...please...' Annys said looking through the top of her eyes like a sad puppy.

'Okay! Okay! Go on then,' she replied taking the rope and starting to rotate it slowly. Getting the momentum going she began to sing the first skipping song that came into her mind.

'All together girls, never mind the weather girls. When I call your birthday, you must jump in...January, February, March...'

After a couple of verses and a quick explanation from Keri, Annys was ready to jump in.

'...April, May, June...' The first few attempts ended in a tangle of legs and rope, but after a while they got a rhythm going, and both sang along happily.

Maria heard the small wooden side gate creak open above the mayhem in the garden and turned around to be greeted by Katerina, a slight girl and very timid. Waving bye to her mama and hearing the commotion she clutched Maria's hand tightly as they walked through the maze of plant pots and garden ornaments.

'Katerina! Katerina! Look at us! Keri's taught me a new skipping dance.'

She stood at Maria's side reluctant to let go of her hand. Maria bent down encouraging her to join in but with little success. 'Do you want to come into the kitchen with me and we'll see if the cakes are ready to come out of the oven yet? When they're cool enough some of them will need decorating. Would you like to help? Annys has already got some of the decorations ready,' she said pointing to the collection of sparkly silver balls and rice paper shapes.

'I always help *yiayia* ice the cakes when we bake,' she said still clinging onto her skipping rope like a toddler clutching their security blanket. Maria smiled and lifted her up onto one of the breakfast bar stools while she removed the cakes from the oven placing them onto a wire cooling rack.

A breathless Annys burst into the kitchen a few minutes later, skipping rope in hand excitedly telling Katerina about it all. 'Come on Katerina. Let's go and play upstairs.'

She didn't need telling twice. Jumping down from the stool and running towards the staircase in hot pursuit of Annys they made it halfway upstairs before hearing a voice shout up from the kitchen. 'Leave your skipping ropes down here please!' Within seconds two ropes came tumbling downstairs landing in a tangle on the bottom step.

Maria made her way back outside to a rather breathless Keri.

'I'm so unfit! I haven't been to the gym in ages!' Keri said flopping into the nearest chair. 'It was good fun though. Can't remember the last time I picked up a skipping rope – and it'll probably be a while before I do it again! Annys' friend is terribly shy isn't she?'

'Yes, very. She's quite the opposite of Annys. It makes me wonder how they get on so well. Her parents live on the bend in the main road near Ellas, opposite George's apartments, above the dress shop. Her mama works there in the mornings and a couple of hours in the evenings during the summer, and her papa runs his father's butchers in the village.'

'Yes, I know the one. I've popped in a few times – the dress shop that is, not the butchers! The other day I bought a lovely cotton print pale blue skirt and a couple of t-shirts. The lady was really helpful. Her English was impeccable. I feel quite ashamed sometimes only being able to speak a smattering of Greek. Everyone I've met in the bay has a brilliant command of the English language.'

'For many it just comes naturally, there's always been a lot of English-speaking tourists visit during the summer months. The children are taught English at a very early age and pick it up quite easily,' she explained collecting the empty cups from the wall. 'Would you like a top-up and some cake?'

'Yes, please, that would be lovely. Or should I say *nai parakalo oti tha itan yperocho.*'

'*Bravo! Bravo! Efharisto.*' she replied encouragingly. 'That's great! If you want I don't mind helping you learn a bit more.'

'That would be fantastic, but only if you have the time of course.'

'I've got plenty of time,' she said walking towards the stairs and calling to the girls checking they were alright. Two voices could be heard shouting back in between fits of giggles. In the kitchen Keri rinsed the cups ready for another drink. Maria filled the kettle, clicked it on and offered Keri a pot containing different flavoured tea bags. Choosing a lemon one again she dropped it into one of the mugs. Maria popped a camomile into the other. Reaching into the cupboard for a plate she chose a selection of cakes and passed them to Keri who took them outside and put them onto the blue patio table.

'I'll be out in a minute with the drinks.'

'Okay.' Keri called over her shoulder as she walked towards the wall watching the activities in the bay. A handful of rowing boats and small motorboats moved slowly through the shallow waters. Kayaks bobbed unsteadily over the small waves left behind by the boats and a lonesome pedalo went round in circles, its passengers making very little headway in returning to the shore.

'There you go,' said Maria proffering a steaming mug of lemon tea.

'Thanks very much.' Keri said taking it from her cupping it in both hands and breathing in the gentle fragrance. 'I was just watching the boats. You've got a beautiful view. How long have you lived here?'

'It was my grandparent's house. When they passed away I inherited it. We left it as it was for a number of years just keeping it tidy with a coat of paint here and there. Then when Demetrius and I decided to get married we thought it would make a perfect home. It needed a lot of renovating and modernising, but both our families were on hand to help, and friends were roped in too. Within a few months we had turned it into a lovely home keeping the outside the same colours my grandparents had chosen all those years ago – blue and white. As far back as I can remember it's always been known as the little blue and white house. When we married and first moved in we loved nothing more than sitting on the terrace watching the boats coming and going. We'd sit for hours until the sun disappeared into the sea. Small waves would trickle over the rocks as the cruise ships glided majestically on the horizon. I used to dream about being on one of them one day…' she recalled with sadness in her eyes.

'Helenka told me about the accident. She explained everything to me. I'm so sorry Maria. I can't begin to image how awful it must have been for you and Annys.'

'It was. Sometimes I still can't believe it happened,' she said, a tear escaping and rolling down her cheek. 'It was the darkest time of my life. Demetrius and I had grown up together. We were childhood sweethearts. He was my soulmate. We were so happy and then in a blink of an eye… it was all gone. So many lives changed that day.'

Keri leaned over to comfort Maria. They stared out to sea in silence for what seemed like an eternity. Maria very rarely spoke of the tragedy but sitting on the wall holding Keri's hand she decided to share with her new friend her most precious memories leading up to that ill-fated day.

It was a couple of days before Theo's 60th birthday. Demetrius, Dino and Spiros had got together to finalise the arrangements for a surprise party at Ellas. They were sitting on the terrace of the little blue and white house in the early evening knocking back the ouzo. Maria had prepared some tapas with olives, feta, tzatziki and homemade bread still warm from the oven. It was all agreed. Spiros would collect the birthday cake from his cousin's bakery in the City. His speciality being celebratory cakes and he was more than happy to "*knock something together*" as he called it, in return for Spiros handing his customers business cards promoting the shop. Deal done! He was also working with George to source the balloons, banners and table decorations – obviously under the direct supervision of Anna guiding his every move. Dino had been put in charge of catering and under the ever-watchful eye of Helenka, he put together a list of food and drink which she then tweaked but somehow still managed to let Dino think it was all his idea. Demetrius was to arrange the entertainment and lighting. Of course, Annys and Maria were only too pleased to help him organise the music and dancing, leaving him with the sole responsibility of the twinkle lights – and splendid they looked too after a little fine-tuning from the ladies of the village! It had all come together like clockwork, and the men congratulated themselves on a job well done! Now all that remained was to get Theo to the taverna. He often helped out in the evenings, especially when it was busy. Helenka would give him a call to say she had taken a couple of last minute group bookings and that she might not be able to cope and would he mind helping out just for a couple of hours. And with the promise of a special birthday meal later in the evening when it quietened down he jumped at the chance! She told him she would invite Manos, Yannis and Spiros, George and Anna, Demetrius, Annys and Maria. He adored Annys. Just a nice quiet meal with friends. No fuss.

The whole village had turned out for the party. It was the best kept secret of all time. Surprised he certainly was and touched that his friends would go to the trouble of planning a special birthday celebration just for him. The singing and dancing went on until late in the evening. Drinks were flowing freely, and everyone was on top of the world. The cake, a wonderful creation in the shape of a chef's hat with the words '*Theo 60 today*' piped in blue icing around the edge, had been sliced and put into little cake boxes supplied by Spiros' cousin with the bakery's name embossed in gold letters and handed out to all the guests. An army of people worked their magic in the kitchen transferring the mountain of pots and pans back to the order that Theo expected in his domain. The table decorations had been handed out to the ladies of the village as a memento of the evening. Some of the youngsters had been put in charge of gathering the balloons. A task which had taken quite some time, thanks to the older children who had a great time tormenting the younger ones by punching the balloons high into the air out of reach, with most of them now blowing around the beach.

As the party drew to a close and the guests began to drift away, Theo poured himself, Demetrius, Dino, Spiros and George a nightcap, had their last celebratory cigar of the evening and raised their glasses to long-lasting friendships. On the horizon another storm was brewing. Thunder rumbled in the distance; flashes of light forking into the sea. Storms had been forecast for early evening, but the rain held off for the party. It had been an unsettled couple of days. Hot and humid. Maria remembered watching the lights on the branches of the trees dancing wildly as the wind whipped them up into a frenzy. Helenka and Anna cleared the tables unclipping the tablecloths, folding and returning them to their rightful place on the dresser. All that remained was for the coffee pot to be put on. Judging by the amount of alcohol consumed, coffee would unquestionably be most welcome. There would no doubt be a few sore heads in the morning. Everyone said their goodbyes, wished Theo well for the umpteenth time and made their way home zigzagging through the narrow streets still high from the evening celebrations. Demetrius scooped a sleepy Annys up into his arms, took hold of Maria's hand and walked slowly along the boardwalk with the stars shining down like diamonds against a moonlit velvet sky. Pulling Maria closer as they neared the little blue and white house he gently nuzzled her ear sending shivers down her spine despite the intense heat of the evening. Turning the key in the lock and opening the door quietly so as not to wake a now sleeping Annys, she unwound the balloons from her wrist and tied them to the banister. Demetrius made his way carefully up the stairs avoiding the creaky ones and moved steadily across the landing to Annys' bedroom, gently placing her in bed and tucking her favourite teddy under her arm. Moving her hair away from her face he bent down, kissed her forehead tenderly, and made his way slowly out of the room closing the door to behind him. Sashaying into their bedroom he kicked off his shoes, unbuttoned his shirt, not unlike the style of a male stripper cavorting around the room, dropping his clothes onto the floor in what he thought was a sexy dance. Finally he collapsed onto the bed with only his boxer shorts and socks on, which was a blessing! Moments later he was snoring peacefully.

The next morning they had breakfast together as usual, just a slice of lightly buttered toast and coffee. Annys still had a couple of hours sleep left but Maria used to like getting up early with Demetrius, having breakfast with him, then watching him walk down the boardwalk to the boatyard, collecting Dino on the way. She would wash the breakfast pots, jump in the shower and sit on the terrace with another coffee just in time to watch The Crimson Tide sail out of the bay. That morning was just like any other but by nightfall it had turned into a nightmare.

Keri squeezed her hand not knowing what to say. There was nothing to say. They both stared into the distance as a ship sailed silently by.

Manos, cloth in hand drying his brushes, stepped outside the studio squinting as the bright sunshine hit him. He'd been working for most of the afternoon on a seascape. To the forefront of the canvas soft grains of golden sand glistened as they reflected the sun's rays. Delicate ripples shimmered on the shoreline and farther out to sea white spray soared upwards into a crescendo crashing back down into the darker waters. The sun glowed with delight. Warm colours filled the sky, a profusion of pink grapefruits and waxy lemons. And for the final touch he added a small dark thick stroke with a dappled grey patch underneath breaking the clean line of the horizon, an afterthought as he watched the cruise liner moving majestically through the Straits.

Watching the ship fade away Maria turned to Keri catching her hand.

'Thank you so much for listening to me…I've never shared that with anyone. Everybody always seemed so wrapped up in their own sadness, dealing with their own grief, I didn't want to burden anyone and have them pitying me thinking I couldn't cope, so I just carried on. If I didn't talk about it, it hadn't really happened. I know it sounds ridiculous now but it's how I handled it. I concentrated all my efforts on Annys and protecting her. Don't get me wrong, my parents and friends, and of course Helenka, were all there for me, as we were for each other, but I found it easier to live in our little bubble – just me and Annys.'

'Oh Maria, I'm here if you ever want to talk or need a shoulder to cry on. I suppose it makes it easier opening up to me because I'm not directly involved,' she said holding Maria close in her arms, rocking her gently from side to side as the tears rolled freely down her face and the pent-up emotion racked through her body.

'Thanks…thanks…Keri,' she sniffled catching her breath. I'm so glad you came into my life.'

'Me too! I feel really at home here and I know we're going to be great friends!'

'We certainly are!' replied Maria as they hugged each other, Keri with tears welling up in her eyes too.

'What are we like? We're a right pair!' she said brushing her tears away with the back of her hand. 'Let me tell you some good news.'

'Go on then! Goodness knows we need some. I think I know what it is though,' she said with a smile creeping onto her tear-stained face. 'Your parents are coming to the bay?'

'Blimey! News does travel fast! I had a phone call from them during the afternoon. They'd booked their flights and were giving me the details so I could see George. I'd already spoken to him to check if one of his apartments was available. I just mentioned that a friend was enquiring. I wanted to tell Helenka myself. Anyway, I was at Ellas last night and just happened to drop into the conversation that they were planning to visit and before I could finish the sentence Helenka had shouted Theo over. The pair of them were over the moon to say the least. Theo couldn't wait to start planning a welcome party. Within a very short time of sharing the good news she'd flagged down Spiros in the middle of the road, returning from a fare in the next village, and then ran across to tell George and Anna! Moments later anyone who's anyone had heard the news about the visit. It really was quite amusing to watch unfold.'

'I love Helenka! She's such a character, phoned me first thing this morning to share the news. I've heard so much about them over the years it'll be lovely to actually meet them. How long will they be staying?'

'A couple of weeks. I can't wait to see them. It's been quite a while. When I was travelling with my friends we spoke at least once a week and e-mailed regularly.'

'It'll be great. I bet you can't wait.'

Tears welled up in her eyes again at the thought of seeing her parents. 'Oh God! I'm off again! Sorry Maria. I didn't realise how much I missed them until we started talking,' she said wiping her eyes.

'Come on! Let's shout the girls down to decorate the cakes,' and into the coolness of the kitchen they went arm in arm. 'Would you like to meet tonight for a few drinks? I can ask my parents to look after Annys then we can have a proper chat.'

'That would be lovely,' she replied punching Maria's number into her mobile.

Chapter Fourteen

Staring out to sea, sandals in hand, she walked leisurely along the boardwalk daydreaming. Her mobile rang, the familiar voice pulled her from the past and back into the present. *'Keri. Hi.'*

'Hi Manos.'
'I was just locking up the boatyard and saw you.
Stay where you are. I'll be with you in a minute.'
'Will do. See you soon.'

Looking around she spotted a fig tree on the edge of the beach. Dropping her sandals onto the ground she sat beneath it slightly shaded from the heat of the sun and watched him emerge from the side of the studio. Her heart raced as he walked towards her. He knelt down at the side of her pulling her gently into his arms and lifting her sun kissed face upwards. Waves of pure emotion consumed her as he tenderly brushed his lips against hers.

'I've missed you,' he whispered kissing her neck.

'Me too,' she said leaning against his muscular torso and

tracing her fingers over the contours of his face. Wrapped in each other's arms they dropped back onto the soft warm sand. Smiling into her sparkling blue eyes he lifted himself up onto his elbows kissing the tip of her nose. He stood up arms outstretched, and she pulled herself up brushing golden particles of sand off her clothes. She picked up her sandals and they made their way back onto the boardwalk hand in hand.

'What are the letters carved into the pathway for?' she asked.

Manos explained how the villagers had crafted and built it carving their initials into each piece of wood. As they walked slowly along he spoke their names in whispered tones explaining who each and every one of them was and giving her an insight into their lives.

'How beautiful. What a lovely idea. They'll be there forever.'

'Yes. It's a lasting memory of those who are no longer with us,' he reflected. Keri squeezed his hand tightly fighting back the tears once again.

'I've heard on the grapevine that your parents are coming over,' said Manos.

'Yes, I can't wait. It all happened so quickly,' she replied.

'Bet mama's really pleased.'

'Oh she was! Her and Theo are already planning a special evening.'

'When do they arrive?'

'Next Thursday afternoon and are staying for a couple of weeks.'

'Are you meeting them at the airport?'

'Yes, I was going to ask Spiros if he'd take me.'

'Would you mind if I did?'

'But won't you be working?'

'I can shut up shop for a couple of hours. I'm usually working in the studio in the afternoon. Anyway, Lukas will be in the boatyard to keep an eye on things. He works on a casual basis doing a few hours a day here and there to fit in with his evening bar work in the next bay.'

'That would be great if you're sure you don't mind.'

'That's sorted then. Just let me know what time you want picking up. Where are they staying?'

'In one of George's apartments.'

'Lovely, that'll be handy for you. Do they know about me?'

'I may have mentioned you,' she teased. 'That's why they're coming out. To drag me back to Ireland on the next plane!'

'Ha! Ha!' he said tickling her until she tumbled to the ground giggling. Pinning her arms above her head he brought his face down onto her bare neck and rubbed his stubbly chin against her making her squeal, legs kicking in the air ferociously. 'Am I going to get a serious answer from you young lady?'

'No! Never!'

'Well I may just have to tickle you some more then!'

'Stop! Stop! I give in…yes okay…I told them I'd met someone very special. They know you're Helenka and Dino's son and can't wait to meet you,' she said bringing her legs up to her chest and cradling them comfortably in her arms. 'They were really upset to hear about your papa.'

'Thanks Keri,' he said moving a wayward strand of hair from her face and stroking her cheek. She pulled him closer to her and side by side on the soft warm sand they watched the world go by, each lost in their own thoughts.

'Thanks for getting back to me…yes that's right…about 10 kilometres south of Galazios Bay…a much larger piece of headland but the same stunning views…okay…I'll collect you from the airport at 12.30…yes, we'll go straight there after dropping your bags off at the hotel. Oh, and by the way, it's bloody hot here – make sure you've suitable clothing! I got caught out with that one!'

Christophe sat back in the chair studying the map again. Much better, he thought. Far more appropriate.

'Go with the flow of the music Mark. Listen with your heart. Lose yourself. That's it,' encouraged Theo. 'Back to the beginning. Start off slowly. Increase the speed gently… toe, heel…toe, heel. You've got it. Keep the movement. Lift your right arm higher when you turn. That's it. Swoop and stretch. Great! Great!'

Mark took a swig of water from the bottle. 'That felt good. Cheers Theo!' Don't think I'll ever be as confident as Alex and Manos though. I don't want to let them down.'

'Don't forget Mark they've been dancing for years – since they were able to walk. It's in their blood. In all my years I've never seen a non-native pick up the steps so quickly and with such passion. Carry on like this mate and you'll soon be entertaining the customers with them!'

Helenka came out of the kitchen. 'Looking good Mark,' she praised. 'Theo knows what he's talking about. He was an expert in his day!'

'In his day! In his day!' he ranted moving into the middle

of the room where the tables and chairs had been pushed back to allow plenty of room for Mark to practise. Tapping his feet to the music he moved slowly, seductively, swooping and bending, feeling the rhythm. Faster and faster, he increased the pace. Helenka clapped to the beat, swaying her ample hips to the tempo.

'Okay! Okay! I take it all back. You're still the best! Now come and sit down before you fall down!' she pleaded pouring him a well-deserved cold drink. Taking it from her he wiped his brow with his handkerchief and sat down, somewhat breathlessly, not admitting he was getting a bit too old for this game. Even though he knew he should leave it to the younger ones he just couldn't help himself especially when Zorba the Greek was playing. It took him right back to his youth. His papa and elder brothers taught him all he knew. They travelled the island performing at weddings, birthday celebrations and in the latter years as tourism came to the island, in hotels and tavernas drawing in huge crowds. Sitting back in his chair he rubbed his arthritic knee, finished his drink and disappeared into his memories.

Sitting at the end of the harbour wall, Keri dipped her feet into the crystal-clear waters her legs cooling instantly. Manos joined her, legs moving in unison they watched the seagulls diving into the sea behind the returning fishing boats, fighting for the fish guts thrown back by the fishermen. The sound of music travelled through the air from Helenka's taverna. Distant laughter penetrating the quietness of the bay.

'What's it like here in the winter? Keri asked shielding the sun from her eyes. 'Bet its quiet when all the tourists have gone.'

'The village can still be quite busy with one thing and another. There's plenty of DIY to be done, repairs to shops, bars and tavernas – all the jobs that can't be done during the summer. Most people in the village can turn their hand to almost anything. Last year George and Mark, who works in mama's place, emptied the apartments and gave them a complete overall. This year he has plans to redecorate the shop and extend into the backyard. George's brother is a builder so he'll be doing most of the building work, with Mark and Alex doing the labouring. Ellas is usually pretty quiet during the winter so mama can take it a bit easier. She's got many friends and takes time out to go visiting while Theo holds the fort. She doesn't really stop though, usually ends up helping make jams, chutneys and preserves but it makes a welcome change for her. Spiros tends to be busy most of the time, running errands for everyone. And of course, everyone looks after him by supplying meals, fresh produce and suchlike so he gets by alright.'

'What do you get up to?'

'Well, the boatyard practically runs itself. Obviously people aren't taking the boats out so it's just general maintenance to keep things ticking over. Most of my time is spent in the studio painting and building up the stock for the coming season. The light can be so diverse in the winter and the paintings take on a totally different look. I've still got a handful from last year; you'll have to come and have a look and see what you think.'

'Yes, I'd like that,' she replied enthusiastically.

'The whole village gets involved in olive harvesting between November and February. Most of the people in the bay have families in nearby villages so quite a lot of time is spent olive picking. It's hard work and very long days but satisfying. The whole community comes together. There's plenty of eating, drinking and, of course, singing. You should know by now the Greeks never do anything without singing their way through it! If it's a decent harvest it can give the families a good living, which is definitely reason to celebrate. The olives in this region tend to be mainly for oil production and although most of the oil goes for export there's plenty kept behind on the island.'

'Sounds great. I might have to stick around for the next harvest.'

'I'd love nothing more,' said Manos smiling.

Stepping out of the shower Maria wrapped herself in the soft white towel and walked through to the bedroom. Opening the wardrobe door she chose an outfit for the evening – crisp white linen trousers, a pale blue t-shirt, matching jewellery and she was ready to go. Walking along the path at the side of the road she checked her watch. Plenty of time she thought humming a tune she'd just heard on the radio. With the sun disappearing like a bright orange ball into the sea, seagulls circled the rocky outcrop at the end of the breakwater. Approaching Ellas she spotted Felix hiding under a bush waiting for his moment to pounce on the unsuspecting birds. Clapping brusquely she startled them and off into the night sky they soared filling the air with the sound of frenetic flapping. Felix's eyes darted from tree to tree with the furore. Moving gracefully towards Maria he wrapped his lean feline body around her legs purring with delight. She bent down to pick him up.

'Oh Felix! You are a rogue!' she reprimanded as he nestled into the curves of her body. 'But you are such a handsome fella.' Hearing a door shut Maria turned to see Keri coming towards her.

'Hi Keri. I've got someone I'd like you to meet,' she said stroking his soft warm tortoiseshell coat. 'This is Felix. He's a little scoundrel, always up to no good.'

'He's gorgeous. What a lovely colour,' she said tickling him under the chin. In return he purred and closed his eyes tilting his head backwards for more of the same.

'He's a little devil. Always chasing the birds! It's a good job they're quicker than he is!'

'Felix. What are you like!' said Keri caressing him. 'Who does he belong to?'

'He's a stray but has many homes. He took a shine to Mark who started leaving saucers of milk out when he first came to the bay. They kind of adopted each other,' she said putting him back onto the ground gently.

'Where would you like to go for a drink?'

'Anywhere. I don't mind,' replied Keri.

'There's a little cocktail bar over there,' she said pointing in the direction of Lefko Bay. 'It's on the hillside and has a lovely view out to sea. Should we have one in there first?

'Yes, that sounds great.'

A gentle early evening breeze was refreshing after the heat of the day. They made their way to a table on the left of the terrace underneath a sprawling olive tree. The lights from the veranda reflected on the gentle undulation of the sea.

'Be with you in a minute,' called the waiter from the bar. Keri picked up the cocktail menu trying to work out what drink was what. She had picked up quite a few Greek words on her travels and was able to translate most of the menu.

'Oh, that one looks tasty,' she said trying to attract Maria's attention. 'What do you think?'

'Sorry Keri. I was miles away. Which one are you looking at?' Maria blushed.

'Well, I was looking at the menu. You seem to be transfixed by the barman!' she said laughing.

'I don't know what you mean,' she said putting on an innocent smile.

'You've not taken your eyes off him yet! A lovely view out to sea indeed! I don't think it's the sea view you're interested in!' Keri replied as they burst into fits of giggles.

'What can I get you ladies?'

'I'll have a *Pina Colada* and my friend would like *Sex on the Beach* please,' said Keri.

'Coming right up,' he replied with a cheeky smile and a glint in his eye.

'I love what you've done with Annys' bedroom. It's gorgeous,' Keri remarked.

'Thanks. It turned out much better than I thought it would.'

'Annys said you designed and decorated it.'

'Yes, that's right. I've always been interested in design and putting different colours and fabrics together. And, like yourself, I've made quite a few pieces of jewellery – not quite up to your standard though. I've never been to college or anything like that, but I really enjoy dabbling with pieces and have even sold some items of jewellery in Katerina's mama's shop.'

'I might have been trained but you've got a natural talent,' replied Keri as the drinks arrived. '*Efharisto.*'

'You're welcome,' replied the barman placing Keri's drink on the napkin.

'*Efharisto*,' said Maria blushing again taking the drink from him.

'You're welcome,' came the standard reply.

'Mmmm, that's lovely!' said Keri sipping her drink through the long yellow and white stripy straw, moving the decorative orange umbrella to one side.

'Yes, I know...' Maria replied dreamily, her eyes following him again.

'I meant the drink!'

'So did I,' she said smiling. 'When I was very young I remember sitting with my grandmama, helping her make clothes for babies to sell at the market in Lefko Bay. She taught me how to crochet and knit. I'd only be about Annys' age and would sit for hours on the terrace of the little blue and white house putting the most unlikely colours together, but it would work. I kind of got into the jewellery thing by mistake. Grandpapa bought me a make-your-own-jewellery set one Christmas and I was absolutely hooked and had made all the items by Boxing Day. I had some Christmas money and wanted to spend it on more materials, so grandpapa took me into the City. We came back with all sorts, and he treated me to a craft box to keep everything in. In fact, I've still got it.'

'I think it may come in very handy!'

'How do you mean?'

'Well, I was hoping to earn a bit of money by making some jewellery while I'm in the bay and thought about selling it at some of the local markets. It's something I'd planned to do, but I really need to build my stocks up first. What do you think about us working together on it? We'd make a great team!'

'What a brilliant idea! I'd love to help. We could use my spare room as a workshop. That's where I do my sewing and crafts.'

'That would be fantastic. Are you sure you wouldn't mind?'

'No, not at all. There's plenty of worktop and storage space.'

'If you're okay for time we can perhaps start putting a few ideas together over the next few days. I have plenty of designs and sketches I've been working on. I'll bring them round for you to look at. Then we can go into the City to stock up on everything. Don't worry though, I'll pay for the materials seeing as we're going to be using your place to work from. Would Annys like to help do you think? Some of the designs I've done are for youngsters – bracelets, hair bands, slides and that kind of thing. Bet she would really like choosing the colours. That's if it's alright with you of course. Sorry Maria. I do tend to get a bit carried away!'

'It's a great idea! I know Annys would love to help. She might be young but has some amazing ideas. I know I'm biased but she's really got an eye for design. There are a handful of very good suppliers in the City that I've used a number of times. We can start with them.'

'Can I get you another drink ladies?' asked the barman picking up the empty glasses from the table.

'Should we? Do you fancy another?' asked Keri.

'Sounds good to me. Can I have the same again please?' said Maria, the colour rising in her cheeks.

'Me too. Thanks.'

'I reckon Manos and Alex might be able to help with advertising. I'm sure they wouldn't mind displaying some pieces on their stall in Lefko. And they know people who regularly do the circuits on the island who are always looking out for stock to buy in bulk and sell on.'

'Hey that sounds great. Oh, I'm really excited. It's lovely having someone who shares my passion.'

Chapter Fifteen

Sometime later, and a few cocktails later, linking arms the girls made their way unsteadily to Ellas. Manos sat on the wooden steps leading down to the beach lager in hand taking in the panorama before him. The moonlight danced on the silvery ripples of the sea and small perfectly formed waves crept up onto the cool sand. Rhythmic. Smooth. Silent. The girls skipped along the boardwalk giggling. Catching sight of Manos they shouted out to him at the top of their voices. His response, a wolf whistle across the bay. Standing up he finished his drink and put the empty bottle on the table calling across to mama forewarning her that peace was about to be shattered. Helenka appeared in the doorway of the kitchen throwing the red and white checked tea towel over her shoulder and wiping her hands on its edge.

'Hey! Look at you pair!' she shouted to the girls. 'Good time?'

'Great thanks!' they replied in unison collapsing into one of the two-seater cane settees at the front of the terrace. Helenka pulled up a chair and sat with them.

'Could you get us some drinks please love?' she asked Manos as he stood behind Keri massaging her shoulders tenderly.

'Will do. Looks like you two have had a good evening!'

'We have. Maria took me to the cocktail bar on the hill. The views are amazing!'

'They are indeed! What would you all like to drink then?'

'Oh, can I have a gin and tonic please babe?' asked Keri leaning her head backwards. He reached down to kiss her forehead.

'Me too please Manos,' said Maria.

'Mama?'

'I think I'll have an orange juice and lemonade with ice, thanks.'

'Coming right up.' And he made his way over to the bar.

The girls shared their plans with Helenka. 'Sounds like a great idea,' she said enthusiastically.

'What idea's this then?' asked Manos as he balanced the round black plastic tray in one hand and placed the four drinks onto the table.

'We're going into business together!' replied Maria happily.

'Sounds intriguing. Tell me more.'

'Well, we both love designing and making jewellery. So, we've got a business plan. Well, sort of anyway,' explained a rather tipsy Keri.

'Okay. And how long have you had this plan?'

'A couple of hours I reckon,' Keri replied suppressing a giggle.

'Yes, it all came together nicely after a few cocktails… hiccup…oh…excuse me!' said Maria putting her hand up to her mouth.

Keri helped out. 'All the best partnerships are made over a few drinks!'

'That's right. We're going to work from my spare room. Keri's got the tools and plenty of designs to start us off. We're going to pick up some essen…essenals…essentiash… stuff over the next few days,' she sniggered.

Keri rescued Maria again. 'And we're hoping to sell some of the pieces at the local markets and see how it goes.'

'A very good plan indeed! I may be able to help you with advertising. Me and Alex can display some items on the stall.'

'That'll be great if you could. Alex won't mind, will he?'

'No, of course not Keri. He'll be only too pleased to help. I'll have a word with him tomorrow. He's got quite a few contacts around the island who'd be interested in buying bulk if you could get a few dozen pieces together. And…Alex has got a soft spot for Maria. He'll do anything for her!' he said winking in her direction.

'Stop it!' Stop it! You're making me blush!'

'Not for the first time tonight,' whispered Keri as they burst into fits of laughter again, like little school children trying to keep a secret.

'I think these two have had one too many cocktails tonight mama. What do you think?' he said roguishly.

'Ahhh…they're in high spirits. It's good to let your hair down every so often isn't it girls!' *Yamas*!' she said raising her glass into the air.

'*Yamas*!' said the girls together.

Pushing her chair back from the table Helenka stood up and made her way over to the bar. Filling a jug with iced water she grabbed some glasses and brought them back to the table.

The Little Blue and White House

'There you go. Help yourselves. I'll leave you three to it.'

'Thanks Helenka,' said Keri concentrating all her efforts on pouring a glass of water. Maria and Manos talked about the various markets where the jewellery would sell well. Keri listened intently. They talked about the variety of jewellery; styles and volume; the market they would aim for; overheads and profit margins. They would draw up a business plan to keep track of spending, sales and yield.

'Anyway, I'm going to get going now. It's been a long day,' said Maria getting out of her chair and stretching. 'Don't know about you but I'm shattered. Thanks for a lovely evening,' she said leaning over the table to hug Keri. We'll catch up tomorrow.'

'Yes. That'll be great. I'm so pleased we're gonna be working together. I can't wait. Goodnight.'

'Come on. I'll walk you home. Back in a few minutes,' he called over his shoulder.

Helenka kissed Maria once on both cheeks. 'I'm really pleased you and Keri get on so well,' she whispered gently into her ear.

'Me too,' replied Maria as she started to make her way down the wooden steps on the veranda and along the boardwalk towards the little blue and white house.

'Can I get you another drink Keri?'

'Oh, yes please Helenka. I'll have another gin and tonic,' she said following her to the bar. Isn't Maria a lovely girl? We hit it off straight away. I think we're going to be great friends, and of course, great business partners!'

'She is lovely. Like a daughter to me. It's been a difficult couple of years for her and it's smashing to see a smile back on her face again. You've brought some sunshine back into her life…into all our lives!'

'Bless you Helenka.' And with tears prickling in her eyes, not for the first time today, she wrapped her arms around Helenka's ample waist and took a deep breath swallowing hard.

'Here he is love. You go and sit down with your drink. I'll bring him a Mythos over. Would you like anything to eat?'

'No thanks. I'm okay.'

On the horizon the moon dangled from the dark blue sky. A beautiful night. Tiny lights from the lamps along the coastal path reflected on the sea like emerging stars. Talk and laughter floated through the air from nearby bars. Conversation drifted easily between them from one topic to another – how her parents travelled through Europe and ended their journey on the little Greek island; how she grew up listening to tales of their travels; why she was named after one of the bays. He caressed the nape of her neck, sharing in the excitement of her parent's forthcoming visit. He couldn't wait to meet them. To think they knew his papa all those years ago – where their paths had crossed they shared the same history – thousands of miles apart and they would be together again. If only his papa was here to share it…

'Earth calling Manos!'

'Sorry, I was miles away.'

'I know. Where did you go?'

'It's silly really. I was just thinking about our parents and how their past has brought us together.'

'No, it's not silly at all. I think it's lovely that our families have this special bond, and at least they know each other so there won't be any awkward silences when they meet,' she said squeezing his hand. 'If I could have one wish it would be that I could have met your papa.'

'I know love. He would have adored you!'

Shivering slightly in the now cool evening air Keri finished her drink. Hand in hand they made their way back to her apartment. Overhanging bougainvillea filled the air with its sweet fragrance. Turning the key in the lock and pausing for a moment in the doorway, two silhouettes barely distinguishable in the darkness. Tracing the outline of his face she reached upwards, her lips finding his, his hand on the back of her head pulling her towards him. Her pert breasts pressed against his muscular chest, hearts beating faster with anticipation. Stepping backwards and guiding him through the open door with a sense of urgency she took his hand and led him towards the bedroom...

'We will be making our decent in approximately ten minutes. Please fasten your seat belts and make sure your trays are clear and in an upright position. Please do not leave your seat until the plane stops. Thank you for flying with us and may we wish you an enjoyable onward journey.'

Tilting slightly to the left the aircraft began a slow and steady turn. Through the wispy clouds everything began to come into view. The ground looked like a tiny map emphasising the mountainous tracks snaking to little houses of different colours, shapes and sizes. Cars resembled small toys and barely visible animals grazed in the hillside. A sudden bump and the landing gear was released. Feeling his ears pop, he swallowed in an attempt to release the pressure. Trees and rooftops whizzed by at speed as the aircraft made its final decent onto the runway. Seconds later, a groaning and rumbling as the tyres met the tarmac, then coming to a juddering halt and taxiing slowly to the arrival gate.

Waiting in the arrivals hall Christophe stood impatiently chewing his already short fingernails. Walking towards him a dubious character with a long scar on his cheek only showing up in a certain light.

'Good morning,' said Christophe shaking his hand. 'Did you have a pleasant journey?'

'Bit of a bumpy landing. You forget how little tarmac these back of beyond airports have!' he grumbled.

'Let's get you a coffee – you look like you could do with one.'

'You drag me all the way out here and you offer me coffee!' he said in a low gravelly voice. 'A scotch would go down much better!'

'Okay. Come on,' he said making his way through the masses of holidaymakers. Why three planes have to land at the same time then none for the rest of the day he would never understand.

Running her hand along his arm Manos twitched then turned towards her. She curved her body against him watching his chest rise and fall in a steady gentle rhythm. Flashes of a future she'd dreamt about, hoped for, wished for. She kissed his bristly chin, his skin warm and salty.

'Coffee? 'she asked reaching for her wrap from the chair at the side of the bed and tying it loosely around her.

'Mmmm…please…' he replied sleepily.

Picking up a hair band from the dressing table she lifted her hair up off her neck into a topknot and made her way through to the kitchenette flicking on the kettle as she headed towards the balcony doors, throwing them open and securing the wooden shutters on their hooks. She breathed in the fresh cool air; the early morning sunshine already burning its way through the mist. Another hot day she thought.

Manos stretched his arms above his head and propped the pillow up behind him. 'Thanks love,' he said taking the mug of steaming coffee from her. Walking to the other side of the bed she placed her coffee onto the bedside table and slid back into bed snuggling up closely to him.

Maria sat on the terrace of the little blue and white house daydreaming. A trickle of waves washed over the pebbles relaxing her mind. After her revelations the previous day to Keri, she'd had a sleepless night drifting in and out of consciousness with Demetrius at the forefront of her mind, finally falling into a peaceful deep sleep around dawn, not waking until after 9 o'clock. A lie-in a luxury only afforded when Annys was with her grandparents. Picking up her mobile she sent a WhatsApp to Keri.

On the bedside table the mobile buzzed. Keri picked up her phone. 'It's from Maria, wondering if I'd like to go into the City today.'

'I can drop you both off before lunch if you like. I've got to pick some parts up I ordered for one of the boats.'

'That would be great if you don't mind. What time's best for you?'

'Should we say 12 noon?'

'Thanks babe,' she replied planting a kiss on his cheek and firing off a quick reply to Maria.

Pulling her closer she melted into his arms. Resting her head on his chest she ran her fingers slowly over his muscular thighs, running her tongue sensuously down his torso, feeling his pectorals tighten with every breath. Releasing her hair from the hair band and teasing it over her shoulders he massaged her long slender neck as they slid back under the covers.

Chapter Sixteen

The hotel bar was a modern contemporary design with a polished black Italian marble floor throughout. On one wall a rich purple wallpaper with swirls of silver; subtle grey walls to either side and a black and chrome bar along the far end with floor to ceiling mirrors. Simple monochrome pictures with spotlights above of the City adorned the walls. Christophe held the heavy glass door open for Jon to make his way through. Resting his suitcase against the wall he sat down on one of the ivory suede chairs, dropping his phone and sunglasses onto the small glass table. Christophe beckoned to the bar tender.

'Two scotch on the rocks please.'

'Certainly sir,' he said placing two coasters and a dish of assorted nuts onto the table.

Jon reached for his iPad. 'I'm assuming there's internet connection here?'

'There is indeed. It's a bit hit and miss in the City but tends to be fairly reliable in the hotel,' replied Christophe fidgeting slightly. 'At least it's a bit cooler in here with the air-con don't you think?'

'Quite. Quite.' he replied half listening as he checked his e-mails. 'Show me on the map where the proposed development is.'

Christophe removed his pen from his shirt pocket and pointed to the relevant area on the screen.

'And where's the alternative?' Christophe pointed again. 'Okay. Well, I've already had a look at your initial calculations and produced projected budgets for both areas and the figures speak for themselves. Your first choice will be far too expensive to develop. The second option looks much more promising. I'll be interested to see both pieces of land though before making my final decision.'

'Yes of course.' Christophe replied as the bar tender placed the drinks onto the respective coasters.

'I just hope I'm not wasting my time here!'

'When you see the extent of what I've got planned I'm sure you'll agree it's financially viable for both of us,' replied Christophe relaxing slightly as his whisky hit the spot.

'Indeed. I'll study the architectural drawings later. I note the planned airport expansion is still moving forward.'

'Yes. I've collated all the information you requested from the airport governing body, a record of their data for the last five years, projected statistics and predictive analytics.'

'Let me have the information this afternoon.'

'No problem,' he replied. 'We'll check you into your room and I'll bring everything to you then. I've got an appointment early afternoon, so it'll give you chance to look through it all. I'll only be an hour or so.'

'Okay. Fine,' he said draining the last drop of whisky from his glass.

Christophe and Jon had come a long way since boarding school where they first met. Jon was there for him when his parents were killed. His own father had died when he was young, and his mother decided the best thing for him would be to send him away to boarding school. He'd always been a very demanding child. During their teenage years they'd spend hours hatching deals and creating business plans. With so much ambition and drive they just couldn't fail. By the time they'd gone onto Higher Education and attained First Class Honours Degrees in Business Management and Accountancy, and each sailing through their Masters, they were raring to put all their plans into action in the big wide world. With two astute business heads, plenty of contacts in the right places and an abundance of confidence they made a good team. Both had inherited their parents' fortunes and business effects and could now move forward into the business world they were born into. For the last ten years they'd worked hard and played equally hard, their paths crossing on occasion. Jon was the more ruthless of the two. He was a shrewd businessman and would do whatever it took to pull off the right deal. Christophe tried to live up to his expectations when they worked together but somehow always felt second-best. This time Christophe was the major stakeholder in this particular project pulling all the strings. It felt good. It had to work. He had to make it work.

Checking all the documentation was in order he closed the file, picked up his keys, wallet and phone and made his way to Jon's room.

'Come in!' barked Jon.

'Here's the paperwork you wanted. I'll see you later this afternoon. Give me a call if you need anything.'

'Will do. We'll catch up later,' he replied taking the proffered documents.

The girls flopped down into a double patio seat on the terrace of a pavement café opposite the harbour, their bags brimming with supplies.

'Oh that's nice!' exclaimed Keri kicking off her sandals and stretching her long golden legs.

'I never expected us to get the majority of stuff so quickly,' said Maria. 'I thought we'd have to shop around quite a bit more. We did really well!'

'That first shop had a terrific selection – all the colours under the sun in gemstones and not too expensive either!'

The waitress came over to take their drinks order and placed two white coasters onto the table in front of them. Keri lowered her sunglasses shielding her eyes and leaned back into the comfortable seat to watch the world go by. A gecko slithered up the side wall making Keri jump. 'I don't think I'll ever get used to them!' she shrieked. 'One ran out in front of me on the balcony the other night. Frightened me to death!'

'We get loads of them in the bay. They come down from the mountains and hide under the rocks. We've got one that lives at the bottom of the garden. He darts in and out of the tiniest crevice. Annys calls him her pet. He comes quite close to her now but won't have anything to do with me. Wonder how he'll react when we've got the pup!'

The drinks arrived and the girls settled back into their seats watching the activities in the harbour. Vessels unloading their goods, reloading and refuelling. Dusty trucks filled to the brim with wares heading all over the island. Port workers shouting animatedly to one another, arms flailing to make themselves heard. Passengers on a ferry disembarking from one of the neighbouring islands. Day-trippers queuing for the return journey with their souvenirs, carefully gift-wrapped in the unique island paper – light brown and blue stripes with outlines of seashells. Keri sipped her chilled drink, her eyes drawn to a group of school children having a picnic at the side of the beach in a sheltered area, chatting excitedly to one another, with teachers fussing over them making sure they'd all got their sunhats on.

'Maria. You'll never guess who stayed over last night…' said Keri grinning from ear to ear.

'Did he? Oh! How exciting!' exclaimed Maria giving Keri her full attention. 'Come on…spill the beans!'

'It wasn't planned. Just kind of happened. One minute we were standing in the doorway, then the next, well, we were in bed! What more can I say!'

'Plenty!' said Maria smiling broadly. 'No, seriously, you two are made for each other!'

'Thanks Maria. I feel wonderful when I'm with him. He makes me feel so special. He's just one in a million. I'm so happy!'

'I know. You really suit each other. Both of you are meant to be together. Don't tell him I told you but when I bumped into him the other day we got talking and he was saying he never thought he'd ever meet anyone like you!'

'That's so lovely. Don't worry Maria I won't say a word. Whatever we talk about is between us – never to be shared with anyone.'

'He's had a rough couple of years coming to terms with losing his papa, and three good friends. He deserves some happiness and you've certainly put the sparkle back in his eyes!'

'I've never felt this way about anyone before. When I first came to the island I just knew something magical was about to happen, I'd no idea I would fall in love not only with the island but the man of my dreams!'

Leaning forward and reaching for her drink Maria noticed Yannis across the road with a smartly overdressed stranger. 'Hey Keri! Look who's over there! I wonder what he's up to.'

'Manos said his brother had been showing someone around the land at the back of the studio the other day. Then he spotted him snooping around on his own and introduced himself as Yannis' architect. Hark at me! I'm starting to sound all protective about the bay!'

'That's no bad thing!'

They watched Yannis and the stranger exchanging conversation briefly then parting with a shake of their hands. Maria wondering what he was up to. Keri thinking the stranger looked familiar but couldn't quite place him.

By the time Christophe returned to the hotel Jon had worked his way through all the necessary documentation, had made some notes and was eager to visit the plots of land.

'I've ordered a taxi to Galazios Bay for 3 o'clock. We'll have a quick look at the land there then go straight onto the area south of the bay.' Christophe said assertively. 'I'll meet you in the foyer in fifteen minutes.'

'Okay.' Jon replied checking his watch and closing his black leather briefcase.

On the way to the bay Jon and Christophe exchanged conversation, recalling their trip around the South of France on the yacht six months or so ago. Jon's business was on the up, half a dozen new branches had opened establishing his consultancy in some major European Cities. Christophe had a strong and capable team working with him on some corporate projects enabling him to diversify into the hospitality business, recently acquiring land for retail and residential developments in mainland Spain and the Balearic Islands. Spreading his wings further afield he had moved into the Italian and Greek markets using local tradesmen wherever possible on all of his projects. He was building quite a portfolio and was a major stakeholder in a number of companies throughout Europe enabling him to reinvest heavily in new ventures.

The taxi pulled up at the side of the road next to the land in Galazios Bay. Jon and Christophe got out, Jon taking in the surrounding area. Walking up the hillside at the side of the plot Christophe explained his initial thoughts for the hotel complex. After a short discussion both agreed that without the boatyard it just wouldn't work.

Back in the taxi they looked at the plans for the piece of land in a resort a few kilometres south. Winding through the mountainous region they were treated to glimpses of the resort through tall blue ice cypress trees, row upon row, stretching upward towards a pure blue sky. Ruins of an imposing Venetian fortress watched over the town. The scent of eucalyptus trees carried on the breeze through the open windows. In the distance sleepy hamlets nestled in the hillside with pastel painted houses clinging to the slopes. The road snaked down towards the sea, a lively harbour coming into view with small yachts anchored off the shore, and flotillas of colourful fishing boats further afield. The beach, pristine, with broad sweeps of pale sand shelving gently into semi-transparent waters flanked either side by small caves and pebble coves. To the north dazzling white sands seemingly only accessible by boat. To the south a scenic peninsula with picture postcard views. As they neared the centre of the town music from the bars merged into one sound. Bustling with holidaymakers the main street was a hive of activity, a particular favourite with young people and couples. Side roads were dotted with boutique shops, tavernas and a plethora of bars.

Christophe asked the taxi driver to pull over at the side of a piece of wasteland where some old buildings had been razed to the ground. Jon's first impressions were good, very good in fact. Holding a commanding position in the centre of the town, the gradient of the land rising steeply upwards into the hillside offered spectacular views across the whole bay. The two men paced the land, taking in the cosmopolitan atmosphere of this bustling town. Much busier than its neighbours an established resort with plentiful amenities. A holiday hotspot. Formerly a fishing port it had managed to retain its character whilst moving with the times and giving the holidaymakers what they craved. Each morning in the harbour the fishermen would bring in their haul still using traditional techniques always attracting a small crowd. Along the main street an array of tavernas cooking the catch of the day seafood dishes and local cuisine. The same fishermen could be found mid-morning with a glass or two of chilled Retsina outside the cafes lining the harbour wall playing the Greek backgammon game *tavli*.

Surveying the compass app on his phone, Jon turned to the left, then the right, looking at the panorama in front of him, making some notes on the architectural drawings.

'What do you think?' inquired Christophe.

'Much better than the other area. Has there been any other interest?'

'A little but they weren't prepared to pay the full asking price,' he said by way of an explanation.

'That's good then. I think we might have to move quickly on this one,' he said taking one last look around. 'Okay. I think we're done here.'

Back in the comfort of the air-conditioned hotel bar they pored over the plans making slight modifications here and there, maximising the panoramic views. Planning permission was already in place for a development and the hotel would fit the bill perfectly. A modest hotel, with a classic design decorated in the typical pastel shades familiar to the area. All 32 bedrooms with private balconies would have sea views, eight double rooms over four levels. On the ground floor a modern reception with beige marble floors, seating to one side and a small stage in the corner enticing passers-by with live music in the evenings. The fifth floor would be home to the restaurant and a lounge area with floor to ceiling windows taking in the vista. Guests would be able to enjoy their dining experience in the evening whilst watching the sun slip into the sea. An infinity pool sunk into the sixth floor with plentiful sun loungers and a bar serving snacks and refreshments. To the rear, overlooking the mountains, for the more active guests, a well-equipped gym and a personal trainer on-hand – for a small fee. Landscaped gardens with tiered terraces and narrow pathways paved in stone would weave through the hillside at the back of the hotel, a cool shaded area to escape the heat of the day. With its position in the bay it would almost certainly appeal to a younger clientele, more than happy with a short walk to the nightlife they yearned for.

'Thanks very much Spiros,' said Keri stepping out of his taxi, the sound of bouzouki and clapping coming from Ellas.

'*Efharisto* Spiros. See you later.' Maria called to him as she retrieved the rest of the shopping bags from the back seat.

He pulled away slowly navigating his way around a couple of stray cats lazing in the sunshine. The girls were drawn to the joviality floating through the air.

'Fancy a drink Keri?'

'Sounds like a good idea.'

'I've got time for a quick one before I pick Annys up from her grandparents – and I'm intrigued to see what's going off at Helenka's. She was expecting a quiet afternoon.'

Once inside they were greeted with Mark practising his Greek dancing with Theo sitting tapping his right foot to keep the beat. They stood for a while watching. Helenka beckoned the girls over to the bar.

'Hello you two. Looks like you had a good shopping trip. Can I get you a drink?'

'Yes please,' replied Maria leaning the bags against the bar, not taking her eyes off Mark. He's brilliant isn't he!'

'Yes, he's certainly got the gift! Theo said he'll be able to perform at the next Greek evening – which looks like it might be for your parents Keri.' Helenka went on to explain that he'd been teaching him a range of traditional folk dances. 'He's outstanding at Tamikos. It's one of the oldest dances in this region passed down through generations. Over time each generation have added their own uniqueness to the dance.'

The three of them stood by the bar sipping their refreshing ouzo and lemonade, mesmerised by the fast pace of Mark's dance; graceful yet flirtatious, bordering erotic with each swaying movement.

'Okay Mark! That's it for now! Looks like you have a captive audience over there,' Theo called over to Mark gesturing towards the bar. 'Come and get a drink.'

'That felt good!' said a breathless Mark.

'It was absolute perfection!'

'It's harder than a workout in the gym…but much more rewarding!'

'What can I get you boys?' asked Helenka.

'The usual for me and a well-deserved Mythos for the talented Mark!' replied Theo slapping him firmly on the back. 'Put it there young man,' he said extending his arm to shake his hand. My work here is done. I cannot teach you anymore. You make me very proud! You are a natural!'

'*Sas efharisto para poli* Theo! You are a wonderful teacher!'

'You're now ready for your first public engagement. Please raise your glasses to Mark! *Yamas*!'

'*Yamas*!' They all chorused together.

Christophe sat back in his chair satisfied with his final version of the plans. Folding the cover back on his iPad he prepared an e-mail to his lawyers to enable them to start working on the legalities of the project. A whole manner of things would have to be taken into account – Greek building rules and regulations, construction policies, upgraded planning permission and a structural analysis of the site. Greek building law was particularly stringent with all building specifications having to meet anti-seismic building standards. Yannis had supplied lists of companies based on the island; structural engineers, architects, plumbers, electricians and a plethora of local tradesmen – very useful contacts indeed. It would give his legal representative a couple of day's head-start before his return to France.

Chapter Seventeen

In a cloudless sky the sun, bright orange and perfectly round, glowed. White capped curling waves tossed themselves onto the shore. Maria said goodbye to everyone in Ellas and made her way up the winding road to her parents to collect Annys. Keri and Mark sat on the veranda steps looking out to sea discussing the weather back home and the impending visit the whole bay seemed to be gearing up for.

'My parents are so looking forward to coming to the island. I haven't seen them for months. It'll be great catching up,' she shared with Mark. 'They were here years ago.'

'Yes, Theo was telling me all about it,' Mark replied.

'Who's talking about me?' asked Theo pulling a chair up at the side of the steps.

'Keri was just telling me about her parents.'

'They'll be over the moon to see everyone again after all these years,' she said easily.

'Looks like the whole village will be out to greet them!' replied Theo. 'We'll have a grand time on Thursday night. We've got the musicians in place; Helenka's in charge of food and drink; Mark, Manos and Alex will start the dancing off – speak of the devil! I was just talking about you young man. Sit down and join us.'

Alex dropped the keys to his pick-up onto a nearby table. 'I hope it was all good Theo!' said Alex laughing. 'Where's Maria?'

'She's gone to pick Annys up from her parents. We've been into the City to get some supplies. We're going to work together on some pieces of jewellery. She's got some great ideas,' replied Keri. 'We're hoping to sell some of the items at the local craft markets.'

'Maria mentioned the two of you were going into business together. If there's anything at all I can help with just give me a shout.'

'Thanks very much Alex, that's great,' replied Keri.

'*Herete* Alex!' called Helenka as she walked steadily over to the small group with an assortment of cold drinks.

Alex stood up to take the drinks from her and placed them onto the table. 'I've got the pick-up whenever you're ready Helenka.'

'Should we make a move as soon as we've had this?' she suggested.

'I've got everything ready for them. Kimba was having a good rummage around earlier wondering what was happening but Prince, Zeppo and Kayle were just leaping around as usual oblivious to everything. I reckon the Romano sisters will have their work cut out with Prince and Zeppo! Kayle seems the calmer one. Agethe Lambros is really looking forward to having Kayle around – she's been lost since losing her dog. Is it okay if we drop Kayle off last?'

'Of course, whichever way you want to do it is fine with me,' replied Alex.

'Kimba will get some well-earned rest and time together with her two lasses. Annys is picking Tasha up at the weekend and Sophie is staying with me.'

Alex picked up his keys and put the empty glass on the table. 'Let's get this show on the road then!' he said walking towards Helenka's kitchen and through to the garden. 'See you all later!'

Two of the dogs were rolling around frantically in the long grass chasing colourful butterflies. The other three were exploring the contents of the courtyard which they had managed in a very short time to strew across the terrace. Kimba stretched out in the late afternoon sunshine watching from afar.

'What are you lot up to? said Alex picking a couple of them up by the scruff of their necks, legs flailing in the air. 'Come to Uncle Alex!' he said lifting them higher, his muscular shoulders thickening, then lowering them closer to his chest where they stole the chance to lick his face with unconditional affection.

Helenka joined him and began gathering everything together once again. 'I heard the fracas out here. What are those two scamps up to now?'

'They're just fooling around aren't you fellas!' he said lowering them to the ground and making his way towards the gate.

'Come here!' said Helenka sternly to the brood as they darted after him. 'Prince! Zeppo! Here!'

The red truck had an open body with low sides and a hinged tailgate which Alex lowered and jumped up onto with ease and unlocked the crates secured by belts to the side of the pick-up. One by one they were lifted into the crates under the suspicious eye of Kimba who was aware something big was about to happen. The dogs looked around inquisitively with this new activity and change to their daily routine. Helenka ushered Kimba and her two bitches into the outbuildings and settled them down. After loading the remaining bits and pieces into the truck they set off on their journey to the next bay where the boys would begin their new adventure. Not used to the motion they tried desperately to remain upright during the journey; noses poking through the wires of the cages they sniffed in the cool salty air, sneezing episodically.

Eagerly awaiting their arrival were the Romano sisters – each one had made up their mind well in advance which dog they would like and had visited them a few times over the last couple of weeks. Excitement was in the air.

Keri's mobile rang.

'Excuse me Theo, I must take this call. It's my daddy.'

'Okay, see you later,' he called as she gathered her shopping bags together, answered her phone and skipped lightly down the wooden steps onto the boardwalk below.

Mark was in the yard bringing the sacks of fresh fruit and vegetables through to the kitchen where Theo joined him. With youth on his side and his athletic build and strong physique he had taken over some of the heavier jobs in the taverna previously done by Theo.

'*Efaristo* Mark. That's great. I can take over here now. We've got a couple of hours or so before we need to set up for the evening. Why don't you get off home and be back here about 5 o'clock?'

'Will do. See you then. You've got my number if you need anything.'

Keri reflected on the conversation with her daddy. They were looking forward to seeing her so much and meeting Manos. Mammy had started packing days ago. Everything but the kitchen sink had gone into the cases – most of it at least twice! *"She wants it all to be perfect..."* he had whispered. Smiling to herself, she looked through the wardrobe for something to wear for the evening and was distracted by a ping on her mobile. It was Manos. Her smile grew broader. She replied telling him she'd meet him in the bar on the corner near his studio in an hour.

The day melted into evening. Helenka and Alex made their way back to the bay after settling Kayle in with Agethe. Agethe, better with animals than people, lived an isolated life high in the hillside overlooking the bay. Her villa, small and square in need of a coat of paint, had been in her family for a number of generations.

Helenka turned to Alex. He squinted as the sunlight glistened through the trees on the mountainous track, his long eyelashes framing large dark brown eyes. His rugged olive skin scorched from many hours working outdoors under the powerful heat of the sun.

'There's no rush to get back Alex. Theo's preparing the evening meals and Mark's setting up. Do you want to pop to see Maria's parents while we're nearby? I've not seen them for a while. We can see if they need anything taking down to the bay. And if Maria and Annys need a lift back...'

'Good idea,' he replied turning into the side road leading to their house.

'There's Annys in the garden,' said Helenka pointing through the open window, the refreshing scent of lemon wafting in from the groves alongside the driveway. As they neared the house Maria and her papa could be seen gathering fruit from the fig trees at the far end of the terrace. Mama, watching Annys playing from her position in the loggia whilst shelling pods of peas for dinner, raised a hand to acknowledge them. Walking towards them the air was thick with sweetness from the clusters of lavender alongside the path.

'*Kalisperia!*' she called. 'Welcome! How are you both?'

'*Kalisperia!*' Helenka replied reaching out to kiss her on each cheek. 'I'm very well indeed. We've just dropped three of the dogs off at their new homes and thought we'd pop in to see you on the way back. How are you keeping?'

'Not bad thanks, a few aches and pains – the heat gets to me terribly! I'll be glad when it cools down a bit,' she said picking up the folded tea towel from the chair at the side of her and wafting it with vigour. 'Come and have a sit down. I'll get us all some cold drinks. Back in a minute.'

Alex waved. '*Herete* mama!' he called over to her as he made his way towards the orchard where Maria and her papa were.

Annys spotted him and ran full speed with her arms in the air. 'Spin me round Alex! Spin me round!' she squealed excitedly. He bent down scooping her up into the air and swinging her around in circles before lifting her onto his broad shoulders.

Sitting on the bar stool gazing out to sea Keri sipped her cool lemonade through the pink and white stripy straw that kept floating up to the top of the glass, fascinated by the way the sea was almost the same blue as the sky. It was difficult to tell where one ended and the other began.

A voice broke into her thoughts.

'Hi darling!'

'Hi Manos!' she replied reaching up to kiss him.

'You look miles away,' he said catching his breath from his sprint to the bar.

'I seem to be doing that a lot lately,' she said smiling. 'I was wondering if it had changed much since my parents were here last.'

'Mama reckons it's not really changed since she was a little girl – and that was quite a while ago!' he said grinning. 'The church records can trace many of the families back hundreds of years.'

'I bet that's fascinating to look through.'

He pulled up a stool at the side of her taking her soft warm hands in his. Talking for a while they enjoyed a couple of drinks then made their way hand in hand along the pathway snaking up through the hillside towards Alberto's taverna, music and chatter drifting upwards from the bars below on the early evening breeze. By the time they had reached Alberto's the sun was disappearing into the sea and the evening sky turning into a deep tranquil blue.

'Mammy and daddy, Pat and Moya as they are known to their friends, can't wait to meet you and see all the old faces again. We spoke earlier to finalise the arrangements. It seems ages ago since I was with them,' she said squeezing his hand. With the fresher mountain air bringing some respite from the heat of the day they walked into Alberto's choosing a quiet table in the corner with views overlooking the bay.

The morning advanced. Helenka swept the tiled floor of the taverna. George and Anna stacked shelves pricing the items as they went along. Spiros dropped Theo off in the village on his way into the City. Maria sat on the terrace of the little blue and white house with Annys colouring the pictures in her book. Alex worked in the boatyard catching glimpses of Maria across the bay. Mark took delivery of the fresh fruit, vegetables and meat for the taverna. Business as usual in Galazios Bay.

Manos and Keri left the bay behind. The small dark blue and yellow motorboat powered towards the secluded cove Manos had told her about the previous evening. The waves crashed against the rugged shore in the distance. Many miles away a cruise ship balanced as if on the edge of the world. Approaching the cove he slowed the speed down. The sun glistened on the smooth surface of the sea. Shoals of colourful fish darted around beneath them. Keri dangled her fingers in the clear cool water. 'It's beautiful Manos!' she said as they neared the shoreline.

Switching the engine off he stood up and stepped off the boat into the shallow waters, turning to Keri and lifting her gently onto the beach, catching her sweet perfume on the zephyr. Her feet felt the soft warm sand beneath. He turned to drag the small boat out of the sea onto the untouched golden sand. The tiny horseshoe shaped cove fashioned by the constant movement of the sea was flanked by lush palm trees with long verdant grasses creeping onto the edge of the beach. Keri bent down to pick up a pearlescent shell, shimmering in the strong sunlight, brittle looking but so very strong. Kneeling down she collected more shells, such colours as she had never seen before – pale pinks and blues, delicate peaches and apricots. Irregular shapes – an open fan, a small fish, a perfectly formed cone. Manos joined her.

'It's beautiful isn't it,' he said.

'Yes, it's paradise. So peaceful. So quiet,' she replied dreamily.

'I like to think of it as my secret cove. I've been coming here for as long as I can remember. Papa used to bring us when we were younger, then when we were old enough me and Yannis would come on our own, or sometimes with Alex and Demetrius. The last couple of years if I feel I need to escape I come to the cove to take time out and think.'

'It's a really special place Manos,' she said gazing into his smiling eyes. 'Thank you for sharing it with me.'

As he drew her into his arms, she slid hers around his neck. Her body moulded into his; their hearts beating to the same rhythm. Closing her eyes she could taste the scent of him. Strands of dark hair fell onto his forehead as he reached down to kiss her. The only sounds were the seabirds calling to each other high above in the cloudless sky and the gentle swishing of the small wavelets as they danced on the shore.

Letting go of his hand she suddenly shot off in the direction of the promontory at the far end of the beach. 'Come on! Race you!' she called over her shoulder. He gave chase. Reaching the end of the cove they both slowed down, and with his arms around her waist he lifted her gently onto a large rock.

'There's something I've been wanting to say to you Keri…' he said cupping her face in his hands. '*S'agapo*…my darling…*s'agapo*.' Pulling him towards her she whispered in his ear '*S'agapo* too Manos!' Her feelings enveloped her as he leaned forward gently brushing his lips against hers. She loved him with every fibre of her being – heart, soul, body and mind.

They made their way hand in hand back to the boat; their feet sinking into the soft sand leaving two pairs of perfect imprints behind. An array of pink shades scorched the sky as the sun slipped gracefully into the sea.

'There's something I need to tell you Manos,' she said coquettishly.

'What's that my darling?' he asked puzzled.

'*S'agapo perissotero apo sokolate*!' she teased.

'You love me more than chocolate do you?' he replied falling about laughing.

Chapter Eighteen

Toolbox in hand Alex made his way down the path to the side gate of the little blue and white house. Annys circled around the garden on her bicycle whilst Maria pegged the washing out. He whistled a tune that had been playing in his head all morning, tapped on the gate and let himself in.

'Hi Maria. I was just passing. Hope you don't mind me popping by. Helenka mentioned your gate was catching. Should I take a look?' Alex questioned.

'Hi Alex. Oh yes please, that would be great if you have time,' she replied, her heart giving a little flutter.

'Alex! Alex!' called Annys peddling towards him as fast as her little legs would go.

Putting his toolbox on the ground he knelt down, arms outstretched to catch the careering Annys as she came towards him.

'Careful darling!' Maria called out. 'Don't knock Alex over! Would you like a cold drink? I was just going to mix some squash.'

'That'd be lovely and whilst you do that Annys can help me mend the gate,' he replied opening his toolbox and showing Annys what tools he would need. Maria walked towards the kitchen door, leaving Annys chatting excitedly to Alex, telling him all about school and Mrs Kashiotis, how she had let them paint what they'd been doing the previous weekend and that she'd painted a picture of Tasha.

As Maria returned with a tray of drinks and placed them on the low wall overlooking the sea Alex was just finishing oiling the gate hinges. 'There we go. Job done!' he declared snapping the toolbox shut. 'Couldn't have done it without my little helper though.'

'Thanks ever so much.' Maria said walking towards the gate. 'That's great! I've been meaning to get it sorted for ages.'

'No problem. While I'm here is there anything else needs doing?' he asked gulping the refreshing squash.

'There's just one more thing if you really don't mind. The curtain track in the dining room is a bit loose at the end. I'd sort it myself but it's a bit out of my reach,' she explained as they made their way towards the house.

'Me and my apprentice will have it done in a jiffy!'

Maria busied herself in the kitchen. On the window ledge was the painting Annys had done, she moved it onto the table. Annys ran up to her whispering into her ear. 'That would be lovely darling,' said Maria.

'That should do it,' declared Alex tightening the screw.

'Close your eyes!' Annys told Alex. 'Hold your hands out – no peeping.'

Alex did just so, and she proudly placed the painting into his hands.

'You can open your eyes now,' she instructed.

'Oh Annys, that's a beautiful picture.'

'You can keep it forever.'

'Thank you. I shall put it on the kitchen wall as soon as I get home. The colours are lovely.'

'That's because I wanted it to be the same colour as Tasha and she's lovely too!'

'It won't be long now until she comes to live with you. Bet you're very excited.'

'I am. Mummy said we can go shopping for all her things soon.'

'Who's hungry?' Maria asked as she made her way into the dining room. 'Let's have a spot of lunch at Helenka's. Have you got time Alex? My treat. Call it a thank you.'

'I have indeed! I'll just tidy my stuff up and pop it in the van.'

Minutes later they were strolling happily along the boardwalk towards Ellas, Annys on his shoulders, giggling as she reached up to touch the overhanging trees.

The heat reflected off the tarmac as they stepped onto the staircase and were greeted with the faint smell of aviation fuel. The terminal building hadn't changed at all; still resembling a large olive green shed with faded welcome posters in a variety of different languages pasted onto wooden pallets. Inside a cacophony of excited noises. A sea of faces all around them, eyes darting back and forth as people claimed their luggage off the only carousel as it juddered around the over-sized shed. With no air conditioning the blazing sun soon penetrated through the curved corrugated iron roof. A handful of cases and a rather sad-looking parasol remained unclaimed on their umpteenth journey around the conveyor belt. A second plane thundered towards the shed. Despite all the commotion Patrick and Moya were over the moon to be back.

Resting his arm on the back of her chair Manos reversed into a parking space, handbrake on he turned the engine off and leaned over to kiss Keri on the tip of her nose.

'Come on! Let's do this!' said Manos with a wry smile.

'I'm so excited!' she replied happily.

Manos put his arm around her shoulders as they made their way to the terminal building. She spotted them straightaway and ran over.

'Mammy! Daddy! Over here!' she shouted.

'Keri! Keri!' echoed her mammy's voice, as they ran into each other's arms, completely oblivious to everyone around them. They hugged swaying to and fro. Manos and Patrick walked towards each other offering a handshake and a slightly uncomfortable pat on the back.

'Daddy! Come here!' Keri said running into his arms.

'How's my little girl?' he asked stepping back to take a good look at her. 'Look at you! All grown up!'

'It seems such a long time since we saw you!' her mammy chipped in hugging Keri by the waist and pulling her close again.

'You both look so well,' Keri said. 'Mammy. Daddy. I'd like you to meet Manos, Helenka's son.'

'Very pleased to meet you both,' said Manos leaning forward to reciprocate Moya's embrace. 'Keri's told me so much about you. All good of course!'

'We're pleased to meet you too aren't we Patrick,' she said smiling.

They made their way towards the exit, the girls at the front chattering non-stop. The boys following with most of the luggage.

Lifting the last of the cases into the boot, Manos caught

a glimpse in the distance of Yannis shaking hands with the dubious Christophe as he bid farewell and walked towards the terminal. He got into the car contemplating what he'd just seen.

Leaving the airport behind he steered his way around the perilous potholes, bumping along the mountain road, the terrain tumbling gently downwards offering glimpses of olive groves and whitewashed houses through the trees. The sun shone its best bright yellow rays onto the sea turning it into a dazzling display of aquamarine with silver undertones, as if offering its warmest welcome to the visitors.

Bringing the car to a halt outside George's apartments he switched off the engine.

'We're here!' declared Keri excitedly.

'Oh look Patrick. Nothing's changed! Everything looks so familiar,' Moya declared as she got out of the car.

'I can't wait to show you around mammy!'

Patrick stretched his legs, taking everything in, and made his way to the back of the car to help Manos with the luggage. Keri and Moya were already on their way up the stone steps leading to the apartment. Manos and Patrick caught them up. Unbeknown to Keri, Manos had arranged with George to have a bouquet of fresh flowers on the table for their arrival; a fusion of pinks, lilacs and wildflowers welcomed them. Moya read the gift card propped up against the vase:

"Wishing you a happy stay on the island.
With love and happiness from Keri and Manos xx"

'Oh that's such a lovely surprise! Thank you both of you, they're beautiful!' she said embracing them.

A confused Keri looked over her shoulder at Manos who winked cheekily at her.

Patrick wandered over to the balcony, opening the door to reveal the most spectacular vista over the terracotta rooftops and right down to the sea. It didn't seem two minutes since they were here last – but it really was a lifetime ago. Moya joined him, took his hand gently and smiled into his loving eyes.

Keri waved her parents a cheery goodbye as she closed the apartment door behind her. Manos had already left a while before and headed for the boatyard. They settled down into their surroundings, unpacked, and had a coffee on the balcony taking in everything around them and reminisced about their last visit many years ago.

'I think I'll shower and freshen up love,' she said to Patrick planting a kiss gently on the top of his balding scalp, his hairline had receded rapidly over the last couple of years. Long gone were the days when he used to have his shoulder length blonde streaked hair tied back in a ponytail. His face gained more softness with every passing year. She touched his shoulder and he turned to kiss her hand.

'Okay love,' he replied. 'Can't wait to get out there and explore.'

Moya chose a fresh cotton dress, a blue and pink flowered print, a powder blue scarf, so as not to burn her neck, flat pink sandals and matching small hessian handbag that she would wear across her. Sunglasses on her head, she was ready to go. Patrick wore beige chino style trousers with a pale blue short sleeved shirt for the occasion, soft leather footwear, as you never knew quite how far you might be walking and it always paid to be comfortable.

Keri's footsteps clip-clopped on the concrete staircase,

a quick rap on the door, and she entered the room smiling from ear to ear as her parents stood in front of her as if on some sort of military inspection!

'Will we do love? Don't want to let you down.'

'Oh mammy! Don't be silly. You could never let me down!' she laughed. 'You both look lovely. That's a very pretty dress.'

'Thanks love. I thought it would be nice and light to wear this afternoon.'

Arm in arm, the three of them made their way from the apartment.

'I thought we could go and see George and Anna first. They've really looked after me.'

'I remember them so well,' said Moya. 'Such a lovely couple. Anna used to keep George on his toes!'

'Sounds like they've not changed a bit!' Keri said smiling.

The door opened. George looked up slowly from his newspaper.

'*Herete* Keri!' he smiled getting off his chair and walking towards her. 'And you have your lovely family with you. Patrick. Moya. Welcome!'

'*Kalimera* George!' she replied stepping aside so he could greet them.

'Anna! Anna!' he called through to the back of the shop. 'We have visitors!'

Anna bustled through the shop recognising them straight away. Moya hurried towards her, arms outstretched, and they hugged each other warmly rocking from side to side. Behind them a lot of handshaking and back-patting.

'How was your journey?' asked George as he leaned over to kiss Moya on both cheeks.

'Very good,' replied Patrick reaching over to greet Anna. 'Was good of Manos to pick us up. Lovely chap.'

'Yes, I think so daddy!' chipped in a smiling Keri. 'We're meeting up later at Helenka's if you'd like to join us.'

'You just try and stop us!' said Anna clinging onto Moya. 'Where are you off to now?'

'Thought I'd show mammy and daddy around the bay then have a spot of lunch at the taverna on the hill.'

'Good choice Keri. See you all later.'

'We shall look forward to it,' said Moya turning to wave goodbye to them both.

On their walk around the bay her parents pointed out the shops and houses that hadn't changed at all. They ambled through the maze of narrow streets, untouched by the usual hustle and bustle of many places you return to years later only to find they have changed beyond recognition, and more often than not with fast food restaurants dotted on every corner. It was as if time had stood still in this little paradise.

As they reached the café Keri pointed out where Manos' boatyard and art studio were.

'I'm looking forward to seeing the yard again. I remember Dino showing me around all those years ago,' said Patrick.

The door was wedged open with a thick piece of cardboard. They walked straight in and chose a table near the window; a welcome breeze rolled down from the hillside. Inside, the walls were painted in cheery citrus colours with soft lighting in the darkest corners. Square tables spilt out onto the pavement; blue and white checked tablecloths covered the sun-bleached pine beneath. A basket of condiments on each table – oils, vinaigrette, salad dressings, as well as a napkin holder, menu, a single flower in a clear vase and a well-used glass ashtray. The typically blue wooden chairs with hessian seats worn down from years of use positioned at each side of the table. Welcoming smells drifted across from the far corner of the long thin room, an indication of where the kitchen was located. From behind a flyscreen of faded wooden beads a woman appeared wearing a full-length apron with marks down the front from wiping her hands constantly. A middle-aged woman with a friendly round face, rosy cheeks and large brown eyes greeted them. Her thick dark hair tied up in an untidy bun perched on top of her head with a pencil running through the middle of it. She made her way over to them taking the pencil out of her hair, licking the end and lifting the notepad from her pocket.

'*Kalimera* Keri,' she said approaching the table and nodding to the three of them. 'What can I get you today?'

'*Kalimera*,' replied Keri. 'I'll have my usual feta salad please. A Greek salad with chicken for mammy, and chicken souvlaki for daddy please. Oh, and a side order of tzatziki. Thanks.'

'Any drinks at all?' she asked.

'A soda water, lemonade and a cappuccino please,' replied Keri.

'Okay. It shouldn't be too long. Pleased to meet you both. Is it your first day in the bay?'

'Yes, it is. We flew in this morning. We're here for a couple of weeks,' said Moya.

'Have a lovely stay,' she said before returning to the kitchen with their order.

Chapter Nineteen

With the humming of the radio in the background Manos went about his work at the boatyard whistling as he swept the sand off the pathway leading down to the jetty. Waves crashed onto the rocks sending salty sea spray soaring high into the air. The last boat back for the day had been tethered securely to the seawall alongside the other boats, all creaking in harmony with the movement of the tide. A small shoal of silvery fish moved together in the shallow turquoise waters as the mid-afternoon sunlight glistened on the surface.

Hearing a noise behind him he turned to look. Felix!

'Come here fella!' he said bending down to scoop him up. 'What are you up to?' Felix lay in Manos' arms curled up like a baby and purring with delight, his eyes bright and playful.

'Let's get you a saucer of milk,' he said making his way over to the studio.

Through the tall cypress trees he could just about make out the three figures in the distance.

'We've got visitors Felix! Better get the kettle on.'

Walking down the path through the lush green hillside towards the boatyard and back into the heart of the village Keri and her parents talked excitedly. They stopped to admire the view. Where the sea met the sky seagulls squawked chaotically in the distance, diving frenziedly into the water in search of their catch.

'Nearly there,' declared Keri pointing to the boatyard and studio.

'Oh yes,' said Patrick. 'I can see the boatyard – doesn't look like it's altered all that much. Boats lined up on the left, still the same little shed at the side. Dino always kept a bottle of something hidden on a shelf behind his engine oils and tools! Wonder if Manos has kept the tradition on?' he mused.

'Is that the art studio at the side?' asked Moya as they got closer.

'It is mammy. He's such a natural artist. Over the last couple of years he's built up quite a portfolio of paintings and has got some beautiful pieces.'

'How does he manage to do both?' Moya asked. 'He must be run off his feet!'

'He's got some hired help in the boatyard now, which gives him plenty of time to paint,' replied Keri waving to Manos as they got nearer.

Patrick had always shown an interest in all sorts of watercraft and was fascinated by their workings, so as soon as they reached the boatyard he made his way straight down to the jetty to give the boats the once-over.

'You'll have to excuse him Manos.' Keri said laughing as Patrick strode down the path. 'He can't wait to see your boats!'

'They are, how you say…boy's toys!' Manos informed

Keri much to the amusement of Moya. 'You must not come between a man and his boat!' And with a glint in his eye he joined Patrick to show him around.

Hearing voices, Felix appeared rubbing up against Keri and Moya's ankles, back arched and purring with satisfaction. They fussed him for a while then sat on the wall taking in the uninterrupted views, a welcome breeze every now and then off the sea. Coming towards them Manos and Patrick chatted away like old friends. Patrick beguiled by it all, pointed to the old shed.

'Come!' said Manos steering him towards the shed. 'I want to show you something.'

Opening the creaky door, specks of dust danced in the sunlight, and a spider scurried into a corner behind an old dusty cobweb. Manos reached onto the top shelf behind an old rusty tin and took down two small dusty glasses and shared with Patrick the story of his papa's secret stash of Metaxa brandy, and how he used to partake in a swift one with his papa, recalling how the first time it had made him cough, but how grown up he thought he was!'

'I remember those glasses! Dino snuck them out of the taverna when Helenka wasn't looking…and the brandy! He used to invite me for a quick drink when I popped down to the boatyard to see him. We had such great times together! Such a terrible tragedy. I bet you miss him very much.'

'I do. Every day. I like to think we had a very close bond, the two of us…' he said replacing the glasses in exactly the same spot on the shelf and closing the door behind him. 'Come on, best get back to the ladies!'

Seeing the boys making their way over Keri and Moya stood up to join them. On entering the studio Moya was blown away by the kaleidoscope of colours that greeted her. Canvases and paintings festooned the room. Her face lit up as she moved through the artwork propped up against every available space. Her eyes drawn to the far end where the wall was painted with a plethora of every shade imaginable where Manos had mixed colours and tried new ideas before putting them onto canvas. Moya took in the beautifully framed view through the side window, with the backdrop of lush green hills and dark foliage. The scent of olives and the sound of music floated through the air. Dreamily she made her way back to the others visibly moved by the vista before her. One particular painting brought a tear to her eye: A sunset. Mellow, tranquil, and so very peaceful. Keri put her arms around her mammy's shoulders kissing her cheek softly.

'They're beautiful aren't they!' said Keri.

'Absolutely magnificent!' proclaimed Moya. 'In all my years, I've never seen such stunning artwork. It really does take your breath away.'

'I knew you'd feel like that mammy,' she replied taking her by the hand and strolling back to the boys.

Theo looked up from his newspaper seeing a figure he recognised walking towards him.

'Patrick!' he exclaimed. 'How wonderful it is to see you after all these years.'

'You're looking well Theo,' he replied outstretching his hand.

'All the better for seeing you!' said Theo pulling Patrick towards him. 'Moya! Come! Join me!' he said excitedly leaning over to greet her. 'Manos! Fetch your mama. She's in the yard,' he said moving some chairs up to his table.

'*Herete* Keri. So good to see you all!'

'*Herete* Theo,' she replied kissing him on each cheek.

Helenka returned with an armful of fresh flowers picked from the garden. 'I've got just the place for these!' she said bustling towards the small crowd that had gathered on the veranda. Placing the flowers carefully onto a nearby table she made her way over.

'Moya. Patrick. Good to see you both! I've been so looking forward to your visit,' she said embracing them. 'Where did the time go?'

'I know!' replied Moya. 'It only seems like yesterday.'

Manos brought over a selection of drinks and placed them onto the middle of the table. Taking one of the glasses he leaned on the wooden railing of the veranda enjoying the chatter and listening to the stories he'd heard his mama tell over the years, never tiring of them, always taking him straight back to the happy family times spent with his papa and Yannis and all the fun they'd had growing up. Helenka's eyes sparkled as she told tale after tale, bridging the time they'd all spent apart and filling in the lost years.

Over the next couple of hours, the VIPs had gathered quite a crowd. By the time George and Anna joined them Ellas was brimming with raucous laughter. Anna's radar had been pierced by the sounds carrying across the road and with minimal persuasion George closed earlier than usual so they could join in the fun!

Spiros parked up outside Ellas and made his way down the pathway bumping into Maria at the foot of the veranda. Together they walked up the wooden steps towards everyone.

'Looks like quite a crowd,' said Maria to Spiros.

'It does!' he replied. 'I've just finished for the day, knew Keri's parents were in town so thought I'd drop by.'

'Me too. Annys has gone to mamas for a few hours so I'm at a bit of a loose end,' she said, catching a glimpse of Alex over Spiros' shoulder. 'You go on in Spiros, I just need to have a word with Alex.'

The hours flew by with much laughter and a handful of tears. Having moved on from the soft drinks they were now drinking copious amounts of ouzo and raki with the occasional '*Yamas*!' to be heard and glasses raised. And inevitably the hideous vase had made another appearance!

From his vantage point on the veranda Manos watched Keri. Catching her eye he winked cheekily gesturing to meet him on the boardwalk. Her heart gave a little flutter as she moved through the crowd. Minutes later she was in his arms, leaning into him, reaching upwards until their lips met, soft and warm. His thumb caressing her cheek. Her fingertips running down his spine. Their hearts beating as one. In the distance the joyous sounds from Ellas, intermingled with the whisper of the waves creeping up onto the beach and disappearing within moments into the golden sand leaving behind a slight saltiness in the air.

'Well, you've made a lasting impression on my parents. They couldn't sing your praises enough!' she teased, the soft Irish lilt more apparent in her voice since her parents arrival. 'Manos this! Manos that! I reckon you tick all their boxes as a perfect partner for their daughter!'

'But of course!' he countered light-heartedly kissing her forehead. 'They're really lovely, and your papa's got such a dry wit. I can see why mama and papa got on so well with them.'

'It's such a shame your papa's not here,' she said tenderly. 'I would have loved to have met him.'

'He would have loved you Keri!' he replied stroking the side of her face gently as they made their way back along the boardwalk to the get-together.

Christophe settled into his seat, a window seat, not of his choosing, as it seemed there had been some kind of mix up with his airline booking. Generally speaking, he always travelled business class, unless forced otherwise, and chose aisle seats so as to make a quick exit on landing. He rubbed his chin and absorbed himself in the documents in front of him. Jon had sent over the revised drawings they had been working on for the preferred plot of land south of Galazios Bay. Before making his final decision, he would seek the advice of his trusted accountant whom he worked with on all his projects and would meet with their architect. He wanted to make absolutely certain this was a money spinner and not a money pit before asking Yannis to join Jon and himself. It would be good to have him on board to overcome the language barrier and with all his local knowledge who better as a hands-on project manager. As the plane soared higher it banked to the right, Christophe caught a glimpse of the resort below that would soon be getting a new hotel.

The big day had arrived. Ellas was a hive of activity. Balloons inflated; banners strung around the room; fairy lights swathed from the ceiling; party poppers scattered around the tables. Final preparations had been made to the dishes to be served throughout the evening and notices prepared well in advance informing customers of the private party taking place that evening.

'How does that look?' asked Alex as he wrestled with the last string of twinkle lights on the veranda.

'Looking good Alex,' replied Maria. 'A little more to the left. Perfect!'

Helenka rummaged around in one of the boxes of decorations and happened upon Theo's 60th birthday banners, stopping her in her tracks. She sighed lightly. Maria put a comforting arm around her shoulder.

'Oh Maria. Why did we have to lose them?' she questioned, a solitary tear rolling down her cheek.

'I know,' replied Maria lovingly. 'It's still so very hard.'

Helenka placed the banners neatly back into the box, wiped her cheeks on her apron and turned to Maria. 'Come on!' she said sniffing 'Help me get some drinks together. I think we all deserve one!'

Keri, Patrick and Moya had spent the day in Lefko Bay. After a late lunch in one of Keri's favourite tavernas they went their separate ways. Patrick made his way towards the harbour whilst Keri and Moya strolled through the alleyways leading up the steep hillside from the village centre, along uneven lanes and well-worn flights of stone steps. They walked past the tiny old houses with their colourful wooden shutters serving two purposes – to keep the inside warm in the winter and cool in the summer. They admired the brightly coloured doorways and breathed in the aromatic scent of the flora around them. Reaching the boutiques high above the village they were rewarded with the sun's golden rays sparkling on the azure sea far below. Entering the first shop Moya gasped. She remembered going there on her first trip to the island all those years ago. Once inside, the girls chose some outfits to try on for the party. Moya picked a burnt orange chiffon dress with matching flowing scarf. Keri opted for one she'd spotted a few days earlier, an aquamarine lace cocktail dress in the same shade as a hair slide and earrings that she had made when first arriving in the bay.

Patrick's stroll had taken him to a small café bar on the harbourfront. Settling himself down he watched the boats coming and going, from tiny colourful fishing boats to the pleasure cruisers and water taxis the visitors took to nearby islands. Mythos in hand, he was thumbing through a well-read newspaper that had been left on the table and, as luck would have it, it was a British tabloid, as the girls joined him. Lifting their shopping bags onto a spare chair they ordered two frappes.

'Looks like you've had a good afternoon!' he said eyeing up their bags.

'Yes, it was lovely,' replied Moya. 'Do you remember that little dress shop at the top of the hill? Well, it's not changed a bit! The two ladies that ran it both left a few years ago and the owner's daughter has taken it over, but inside nothing's changed. It's as charming as ever!'

'Can't say I do really. I do remember lots of clothes shops though!' he said rolling his eyes.

'Cheeky!' replied Moya as she took her drink from the waiter.

'I'm going to get off now,' said Alex to Maria. 'I'll see you tonight. It'll be a good evening. See you later Helenka!'

'Thanks Alex for all your help,' she replied waving from the kitchen.

As he walked down the side of the taverna to the main road Maria couldn't help watching him until he was out of sight.

'Right then. What else needs doing before I go and pick Annys up?'

'I think that's about it Maria. Decorations all done. Tables are ready. Do you think there'll be enough room for dancing over there?' Helenka said pointing to the centre of the room. 'I don't think we can move the chairs back anymore.'

'That looks fine,' replied Maria. 'And there's plenty of room over at the right side of the bar for all the instruments.'

'Food's all prepared: Salads, pasta dishes, cheeses and cold food are in the tall fridge as well as the desserts. All the fish dishes are in the small fridge, and the beef steaks, lamb and chicken are marinating nicely ready to put onto the grill. The stifado is on a low heat on the hob and the bakery have just delivered all the fresh bread. Looks like we're ready to roll!' said Helenka wiping her hands on her apron.

'We just need the guests of honour now!' Maria replied making her way down the steps to the boardwalk and blowing a kiss over her shoulder.

Chapter Twenty

Brushing her hair to one side Keri clipped the slide into place, tweaked her earrings and added a couple more sprays of her favourite perfume, standing back to take in her reflection in the full-length mirror.

Manos buttoned his shirt, ran his fingers through freshly washed hair, splashed some aftershave on his clean-shaven skin, picked up his wallet and keys and headed for Ellas.

'You look beautiful mummy!' said Annys.
'Thank you darling,' she replied fastening the strap on her sandals and scooping Annys up into her arms. 'Have you got everything in your bag for mama and papas?'
'Yes. I like having sleepovers with them!' she squealed dancing around the room.
'Come on then darling,' Maria said picking up her handbag, phone and keys from the dresser in the corner.

Alex closed the window shutters, locked the door behind him and made his way into the still night air through the maze of narrow alleyways and onto the main road leading down to the village. He ran his fingers through his still damp hair pushing it back from his eyes and whistled happily. Hearing a car slowing down he glanced sideways.

'You off to Ellas?' the voice cried out through the open window.

'I am. You too?' he replied as Spiros slowed right down.

'Hop in.'

'Cheers!' said Alex moving the newspaper off the passenger seat and shutting the car door behind him.

'Thought I'd drive down. I'm not working tomorrow so can leave the car down there and pick it up in the morning.'

'Sounds like a good plan!'

Helenka removed her apron, had a quick wash and a change of clothes, and took the grips out of her hair, before brushing it vigorously and arranging it into a loose chignon. She applied her favourite deep red lipstick, added some beads and matching bracelet, a dab of perfume and she was ready to greet her guests.

Theo had arrived early. He helped himself to a Metaxa, perched his large frame on one of the bar stools and was steadily working his way through a bowl of olives, under a strict warning from Helenka not to touch the *mezedes*!

Mark and Katrina chatted excitedly as they walked lightly up the wooden steps. He made his way over to the makeshift stage whilst she put her bag under the counter and reached around the kitchen door taking a clean apron off the hook.

'*Kalispera*!' she greeted as Helenka walked into the kitchen. 'What would you like me to do this evening?'

'*Kalispera* Katrina,' she replied kissing her on both cheeks. 'Everything is set up. Could you start with the drinks? On arrival make sure everyone gets a glass of champagne. There's a dozen bottles on that shelf,' she said pointing to the left-hand side of the bar. 'If you can keep their glasses topped up until those bottles are gone. After that they'll be ordering and paying for their own drinks. We prepared as much of the food as we could this afternoon, so about 7 o'clock when everyone is here, Manos and Alex will put the meats on the grill. At the same time, with Marks help, we'll put a selection of savoury dishes on each table. We'll get the desserts out later in the evening after some dancing.'

George and Anna strolled across the road to Ellas.

'It'll be good us all getting together,' Anna smiled at George.

'Yes. I'm famished. Hope we don't have to wait too long for food. I didn't have much lunch!' said George patting his stomach animatedly.

'Oh George!' scowled Anna playfully punching his arm.

'Only joking Anna!' he laughed. Some way behind them, a figure Anna recognised…Yannis! Hope he doesn't cause any trouble tonight, she thought.

'Theo!' Maria's papa called as he raised a hand into the air.

'Come. Join me,' Theo replied above the music.

'How's it going? Are you keeping well?' asked Maria's mama pulling out another bar stool.

'Very well thanks. And you?'

'Good thanks. It does look lovely in here! Where's Helenka?' she asked looking around the room.

'She'll be back soon. Just finishing getting ready.'

By 6.30 people had started to arrive to the sound of traditional Greek music and a very welcome glass of bubbly. An assortment of *mezedes* and *pikilia* to accompany the drinks were dotted around the tables and bar area. Helenka, as host, greeted each one of her guests with boundless enthusiasm. By 6.45 all the guests were chatting away happily with each other. Helenka glanced around the room, checking everyone had a drink in their hand. Picking up a spoon off a nearby table she tapped the side of her glass. A gradual hush descended upon the room and the music was lowered.

'*Kalispera*! I just wanted to say thank you to everyone for coming and for all your help in putting this wonderful evening together,' said Helenka with a smile. 'It's lovely to see so many friends and family together again and to welcome back to the bay our special friends Patrick and Moya. No doubt everyone has got a lot to catch up on. So without further ado I would like you all to raise your glasses to Patrick and Moya. Health and happiness always! Have a wonderful evening!'

Rapturous applause and the sound of glasses clinking resounded around the room. Patrick put his arm around Moya's shoulders, as she mouthed a thank you across the room to Helenka. The music started up again and Helenka began rallying the troops to bring the food from the kitchen.

The music grew louder and louder and rang out into

the night. People clapped to the beat. With tables now laden with a selection of food the mouth-watering smells enticed everyone to fill up their plates. From Helenka's special recipe *keftedes*, tasty meatballs in herby tomato sauce with a secret ingredient that had been passed down through the generations, to a firm favourite, her take on the hearty Greek stew beef *stifado* brimming with pearl onions and orzo served with chunks of olive bread. Half of the cold platters had been brought out from the kitchen; the remaining salvers of food would be used later in the evening when everyone needed a second wind.

The drinks were flowing, and the dancing had begun.

In the far corner of the room Keri and Manos shared their food with each other. Manos had a small plate of *keftedes* with a creamy *tzatziki* dip; Keri was already on her second bowlful of the tasty *stifado*, relishing every mouthful. They broke hunks of bread off a large piece that he had brought over for them, and shared mouthfuls of the delicious food.

'Mmmm!' said Keri wiping the last of the sauce off her dish with a piece of crusty bread. 'That was delicious! Are you not having any more Manos?'

'I'll have something else later. Don't want to fill up too much before my solo,' he replied. 'I'm on after Mark. Alex is going first.'

'Everyone is having such a wonderful time. My parents look so happy!'

'Do you want a drink of anything? I'm just going to get a glass of water before I go on.'

'No, I'm fine thanks. I might go and have a word with Helenka before the serious dancing starts!' she said following Manos and taking their plates into the kitchen. 'Enjoy!'

Alex moved athletically through the crowd making his way towards the dancefloor, hands above his head clapping to the music, encouraging everyone to join in. Theo had moved to the edge of the bar nearest the dancefloor and was tapping the counter in time with the music. Alex's lithe, supple body moved seductively.

'Come on!' he shouted as he swooped and twisted, feeling the rhythm of the music in his blood. Everyone was cheering and clapping to the cadence.

A nod from Theo and a few welcome words of encouragement from Manos, and Mark was dancing his way to the front. Alex raised his right arm into the air and high fived Mark before flopping into a chair at the side of where Manos was standing.

'That was great mate!' he said as he handed him some iced water.

'Cheers!' he said breathlessly between gulps.

Maria's papa was nearby holding Annys on his shoulders. 'Good one Alex!' he said as he wiped beads of perspiration off his forehead.

'Did you hear me and papa cheering?' put in a delighted Annys.

'I did. I could hear you above everyone else!' he said ruffling her hair.

Mark slowly twisted and turned with the music, like a seagull diving for food on the crest of a wave. As the music got faster and louder everyone clapped and cheered. Manos joined him as he reached a crescendo.

All eyes were then on Manos as he began to dance, with Mark retreating to the side of the room relieved it had all gone so well, and a thumbs up from a delighted

Theo. The mandolin player took centre stage with Manos and the pace quickened once again, everyone stamping their feet to the distinctive beat. Sweeping his hair from his eyes and with his arms reaching high up into the air he delicately plucked at imaginary butterflies. Everyone was mesmerised by the hypnotic moves before them. With his years of experience, from boy to man, Manos had a gift for captivating his audience. The music quickened, building up to a crescendo. His biceps gleamed with a thin sheen of sweat as he brought his arms steadily down by his side and tapped his feet to the rhythm, calling for everyone to join in. Breathing steadily to bring his pulse rate down he turned to the musician, taking a bow towards him in gratitude. Then turning to the audience he welcomed Alex and Mark back to the floor for the last part of their routine. With arms around each other's shoulders and legs kicking and crossing they moved in unison rising and falling to the beat, circling the room, and taking an accentuated bow at the end to thunderous applause.

Stepping forward Theo turned to the musician signalling for him to take a break for some well-deserved refreshment, he picked up the microphone and tapped it, clearing his throat. '*Kyries kai Kyrioi*! Ladies and Gentlemen! Welcome!' A hush descended right through the room. 'I will keep this short as I know you all want to get on with dancing, eating and drinking! We welcome our friends from near and far. Today is a magical day with smiles to smile, dances to dance, love to share and without a doubt some tears to cry. Please raise your glasses to Patrick and Moya who return to our village after a number of years, but what only seems like yesterday. Can we also please say a big thank you to Helenka and everyone who had a hand in helping to put on this spectacular evening! *Yamas! Yamas!*'

In between the dancing Patrick and Moya caught up with everyone and shared one another's stories from over the years. It was almost as if they'd never been away. Mobile numbers were exchanged and countless photos taken for posterity.

The ouzo was flowing and everyone was on their feet dancing. From across the room Alex picked Maria out in the crowd, their eyes met and held each other's gaze for a few moments before she spotted Keri watching, blushed and looked away shyly. Alex made his way over to where they were standing and lifted Annys up onto his shoulders in one swift movement.

'Would you two ladies like to dance with me?' he said smiling.

'Yes! Yes!' squealed a very excited Annys, arms waving in the air.

'Okay darling. One last dance before mama and papa take you home.' Maria said as she took Alex's outstretched hand. The happy threesome made their way into the throng of the dancefloor. The last time Maria had danced like this was at Theo's 60th party, with a much younger Annys on Demetrius' shoulders.

In the kitchen Helenka was putting the final touches to the desserts while Katrina started clearing away some of the empty serving dishes and platters to make room for them. A selection of *baklava* – honey and orange blossom flavour; lemon with orange syrup; and cinnamon and walnut. A tray of *loukomadies*, Greek doughnuts, and a large bowl of watermelon in honey syrup with a cool cinnamon yogurt dip.

'These are ready to go out now please Katrina,' said Helenka pushing them forward on the counter. She followed on with the plates, napkins and cutlery. In the distance the setting sun was ablaze with colour, vibrant oranges and deep pinks with the sea lustrous like pure gold. A speck of light winked from a tiny fishing boat. Placing the items onto the table she made her way out to the veranda to watch the sun disappear on the horizon, offering up a little prayer to keep the fishermen safe. The night sky lit up with a million stars. Cicadas, happy with their lot, chorused their sweet chirping as they clung on to the branches of the nearby trees. Helenka was reflective. So many times she'd stood on this very spot, under the old olive tree that she used to climb in her younger days, pondering life's twists and turns, never taking anything for granted as it can be so cruelly snatched away in the blink of an eye. She shuddered. Wisps of hair fell from her bun and swayed in the warm breeze.

Brushing the crumbs from his grey droopy moustache and smoothing down his nearly white t-shirt Theo ambled over to Helenka, picking two drinks up on the way. So as not to startle her as she seemed deep in thought he whistled along to the tune playing in the background. She turned to see his friendly face and his warm hazel eyes with their weathered laughter lines, so familiar to her, and smiled.

'Thought you'd like a drink,' he said offering her one of the glasses. 'What a great evening! Everyone's really enjoying themselves.'

'I was just thinking about all the parties we used to have when we were all together.'

'There certainly have been plenty!' replied Theo. 'Never been a party like this for quite some time though.'

'It feels good!' she said nodding and raising her glass. '*Yamas* Theo! And for everything.'

'And to you too my dear,' he smiled warmly raising his glass to hers.

Helenka turned back to the room. In the midst of all the dancing she spotted Moya waving across to her.

'Looks like the desserts are a hit Theo. Go and get some before they all disappear!' she laughed. 'I'm just going to have a word with Moya.'

'Think I will.' And he made his way over to the table pausing briefly to refill his glass.

'Oh Helenka! What can I say! What a fabulous evening! Thank you so much,' said Moya catching her breath and taking Helenka's hands in hers.

'Glad you're having such a lovely time!' she replied kissing her hands. 'Didn't the boys do well with the dancing. It was Marks debut performance too.'

'It looked like he's been doing it for years!'

'I know! Theo's been mentoring him and he's been practising as much as he can. Tonight was the perfect opportunity for him to shine. He's always such a quiet lad, great to see him come out of his shell a bit.'

On the far side of the room Keri took Manos' outstretched hand and they swayed to the music. There was a tenderness in the way Manos smiled at Keri that caught Moya's eye.

'Looks like they get on really well Helenka,' she said.

'Oh yes. Such a lovely girl. We got talking soon after Keri

arrived in the bay and she seemed so familiar. She's your double Moya when you were her age! I've sort of taken her under my wing. Hope you don't mind.'

'Of course not! I was a bit worried at first when she went off on her travels but then once she'd arrived on the island and said she was staying in the bay I was really pleased.'

'We had quite a few chats, still do in fact, usually over a glass or two!' chuckled Helenka. 'Just like her mother!'

'I don't know what you mean Helenka!' she said emptying her glass. And they both burst into fits of laughter. Glasses topped up, they carried on reminiscing.

'Night night darling! Be good for mama and papa,' said Maria blowing kisses to them as they made their way across the road and up the hill.

Inside Alex was helping Katrina and Mark clear a few tables and wash some glasses.

'You did well Mark!' Alex praised. 'Keep it up and I'm sure you'll get a few regular slots in some of the bars. I'll put the word out.'

'Cheers mate!' replied Mark.

As they went out of sight, Maria turned to go back to Ellas and thought she saw Yannis sitting on a tall bar stool outside a taverna down the road. Wonder what he's up to she thought. Alex was sitting on the wooden steps with two bottles of beer. He offered her one, chinking the sides of the bottles together as she took it and sat down beside him. The soft evening breeze wrapped itself around her and the ivory candles in their tall glass jars along the boardwalk flickered softly. Above them the lemon and fig trees interwoven with twinkle lights moved gently in the zephyr. Tethered boats rocked to and fro like a baby's cradle, soothing, reassuring. In the distance, the silvery moon lit up Maria's sugar-cube white house, the surrounding trees casting shadows over the cornflower blue shutters. They both gazed out to sea, each lost in their own thoughts, comfortable in each other's company.

Spiros, Theo, George and Patrick had taken themselves outside and were discussing the finer points of car engines. How special their first cars were, even though they spent more time off the road being tinkered with than on the road. They had all agreed that it didn't matter how old you were but the deep growl of a car engine and smell of diesel was the best ever!

"Probably why I've spent most of my life in my car!" chuckled Spiros. "Can't beat being out on the open road, all this wonderful scenery, and to top it off being my own boss to come and go as I please!"

The party was in full flow. Mark took his place behind the bar, with Manos helping out when it got busy. Katrina was emptying and reloading the dishwasher with crockery and glasses. Anna, not one for sitting around, took it upon herself to help Katrina, who was happy to have an extra pair of hands.

Chapter Twenty One

In a quiet bar on the main road into Galazios Bay sat a lonely Yannis, cigarette in one hand and a pint in the other, watching the comings and goings in Ellas. One day, he would win them over with his plans. They would come round to his way of thinking. The hotel complex would bring the village much needed employment right from the very start – from building it to staffing it, not to mention the income it would bring to the bay. Why are they all so blinkered? The sooner this place caught up with the 21st century the better! He would put Galazios Bay well and truly on the map. Finishing his drink he made his way up the hill, walking past the brightly painted houses with their window boxes brimming with garish geraniums and suchlike. He followed the steep winding path leading up to the cliffs above Lefko Bay, and past the small church that stood proudly over both bays.

Memories came flooding back of walking to church early every Sunday morning en masse, through the creaky imposing black wrought iron gates which seemed far too big to have such a small church behind them. The children in their Sunday best. The boys in plain crisp cotton shirts and shorts handed down from various cousins over the years, much too big and held up with a belt. The girls in their best dresses falling below the knee. Children altogether. Adults altogether. The tiny old stone Orthodox Church sat in the middle of the cemetery with its crooked grey headstones where generations of his family before him were laid to rest. It was overgrown with wildflowers in the main. Some graves were still regularly tended with fresh flowers and small shrine-like memorials adorning them, others covered in moss and lichen. His eyes followed the yews and cypress trees stretching upwards to the sky. He remembered the well-worn stone steps leading you inside the church with its encaustic tiled floor polished to within an inch of its life by an army of women volunteers from the nearby villages. No matter how much they scrubbed they could never get rid of the stench of stale tobacco which hung in the air at the narthex. The imposing nave with its whitewashed walls leading to the sanctuary over which shone a colourful stained-glass window with icons of the prophets and apostles. The air tinged with the scent of incense as if trying to hide the musty hymn books.

He shuddered and continued on his way, the forested area to the right of him plunging downwards to the white sandy coves beneath. This little hideaway was the place he'd first learnt to swim, and when he was much older would dive with his friends off the white cliffs into the turquoise waters below. Most evenings in the summer months, when his papa wasn't fishing the next day, they would go with Manos and spend a few hours swimming in the clear warm waters and sunbathe on the rocky outcrop. He stared at the inky sea on the horizon as it merged with the sky seamlessly creating one dark chasm as the moon disappeared behind a solitary cloud.

The noises from the village broke his reverie. From his vantage point high above Galazios Bay he could see the party in full swing spilling out onto the terrace. The music troubled him. He stood for a while taking it all in then slowly made his way down the overgrown path towards Lefko Bay and hailed a taxi back into the City.

As the evening drew to a close the girls danced on into the night. Moya's chiffon scarf had been long since abandoned over one of the chair backs, and they were all holding hands, dancing in one large circle, coming together with their arms rising high above their heads and then recoiling like the waves on the seashore, reminiscent to a much loved hokey-cokey but with a smattering of Greek dancing thrown in for good measure. The girls bubbled over with excitement, dancing like they were on hot coals and singing their hearts out! The menfolk stood around in small groups drinking copious amounts and polishing off the remnants of whatever happened to be left on the buffet table.

The pace slowed. Couples started forming on the dancefloor, moving together and shuffling side to side. Alex led Maria up the wooden steps under the clusters of old grapevines with their roots firmly in the ground, their lush grapes hanging down in deep purple bunches. As they began to dance she felt his warm comforting hand gently on her back and let her head rest upon his chest, relaxing into his arms. Swaying together to the soft flow of the music she felt at peace and allowed herself to savour every moment. Alex wrapped his arms closely around her not wanting to ever let go, drinking in her scent as a tumble of hair fell over her closed eyes.

Since losing his best friend, Alex vowed to take care of Maria and Annys as best he could. They'd all grown up together and were always there for one another – Demetrius, the younger brother Alex never had.

The evening flew by. As the last of the party goers made their way home Helenka flopped into a chair, exhausted but elated. Theo came out of the kitchen, tea towel over his shoulder.

'Well that was some special evening!' he declared, his reddened face beaming. 'And as for the dancing, didn't the boys do a great job! Mark was on-form, top class. He'll go far that lad.'

'Oh it was!' replied Helenka sipping from her glass of water and fanning herself with a napkin. 'Patrick and Moya had a lovely time catching up with everybody too. It was certainly an evening to remember.'

He pulled up a chair to join her.

'Thanks for everything my friend,' she said reaching over the table to cup his hands in hers. 'I couldn't have done it without you.'

'We all worked together, just like we've always done,' he said gently covering her hand with his large, tanned hands. The same hands that reassured her that her world was safe again.

'There's not been a party like that for quite some time. I think that's all about to change.'

'I think you're right Theo!' she replied happily.

With her sandals swinging over her shoulder she took each bare footstep slowly along the boardwalk never tiring of the feeling of millions of silky grains of sand between her toes.

Maria took Alex's hand in hers as he turned to her kissing away the last traces of her soft pink lip-gloss, behind them the twinkling lights at Ellas gradually getting smaller. Walking along further towards the little blue and white house the fading light caught the contours of his face. Such a friendly face. Her heart skipped a beat, and not for the first time tonight. She'd toyed a lot lately with her feelings…about her and Annys… moving on with their life…her soulmate Demetrius…

As if he could see into her thoughts he stopped and turned to face her.

'I just need to say something, but don't know quite where to start,' he said taking a deep breath.

'Please don't ever think I would take Demetrius' place. He will always be with me. With us. In here,' he whispered, his voice quivering slightly, lifting his hand to his chest, a solitary tear escaping the corner of his eye.

His soothing words carried a reassuring thread through her heart, like sunshine weaving through the clouds.

'Oh Alex I know how you feel. We can't change the past and believe me I've wished for that so much,' she said brushing away the tear from his cheek.

'The passage of time might dull the pain and we learn how to live with it by putting on a brave face every day and just getting on with things. I'm so blessed to have Annys. For such a long time she was my only reason for getting up every day.'

'I miss him so much Maria. I just don't know how you've coped,' he sighed.

'I cope for Annys' sake. We talk about him all the time as if he's still in the room. I see him in her eyes every day, in her mannerisms, her character, her infectious laughter, and how she dances to his favourite music when she thinks no-one is looking. It's the little things that keep me going. What about you? Four of your friends gone in the blink of an eye. It can't have been easy for you.'

They sat down on the edge of the boardwalk looking out to sea, Maria tracing her fingers through the engraved initials, brushing gently aside the grains of sand.

'I was lost for a while, like I'd lost my way in life. It was such a dark time. I felt like a robot trudging through everything, just going through the motions,' he sighed.

'I'd sit on the rocks at the end of the bay drinking myself into a stupor to numb the pain. It felt like the world was dissolving around me. I didn't belong anywhere. Then one night I'd reached my lowest point.'

He hesitated and gathered his thoughts before continuing.

'I remember sitting there feeling the cliff edge drawing me nearer then out of nowhere felt a hand on my shoulder, calming, warm, reassuring. I looked around but no-one was there, nothing but echoes of our childhood laughter. A voice told me to snap out of it. Life is for the living…do it for all of us. At that moment I knew I had to start living again – for all those who had lost their lives, and I vowed not to waste another minute on my own self-pity. I take nothing for granted anymore. The trauma of that night might lessen over time, but it'll always be there to remind us that everything can change in a heartbeat.'

She squeezed his hand swallowing back her tears as they set off again.

'I've never shared that with anyone before. You're so easy to talk to. When I'm with you I feel I'm not alone. I look into your eyes and it feels like everything belongs in the right place again.'

'It's good to open up about your feelings Alex. It does you no good bottling everything up. I've learnt that. I'll always be here for you. You know that don't you?' she said placing his hand on her heart and covering it with her own. 'We keep our precious memories safe in here. For Annys I keep our memories alive and we make new ones. The three of us will make new memories together. It doesn't mean we forget the old ones, but we just add to them and to the rich tapestry of our lives.'

'We'll look to the future together Maria, the three of us. I'll take care of you and Annys through the good times and the bad. I'll always be here for both of you.'

As they stood together watching the top sphere of the moon vanish seamlessly into the sea, she let her rainbow tears trickle down her face for all she had lost.

Reaching the terrace of the little blue and white house Alex turned to Maria with open arms and she walked straight into them feeling a huge sense of belonging that she'd not felt for quite some time.

Chapter Twenty Two

Felix jumped off the wall and trotted cautiously with purpose, his tail aloft, in the direction of the fishing boats docking in the tiny harbour of Lefko Bay. Mmmm…dinner, he thought. If I can just get there before those pesky birds!

'Maria! Keri! Over here,' called Helenka waving from a table at the front of one of the colourful tavernas along the harbour wall. Moving her shopping basket off the chair next to her she stood up to greet the girls. There was a gentle breeze in the air and the green tablecloths wafted lightly at the edges. Keri removed her sunhat and placed it onto the spare chair.

'I was just watching Felix eyeing up the fishermen's haul. Quite a character isn't he. Thinks the old fishermen can't see what he's up to! He'd always loiter around our boys when they came back with their catch,' she said moving a stray lock of hair away from her eyes.

The girls sat down and ordered some drinks.

'Yes, he's always been a cheeky chappie!' replied Maria.

The early afternoon sunshine sparkled on the surface of

the sea emphasising the crystal-clear waters beneath. Beyond the harbour clinging to the cliff edge was a row of brightly painted houses with their black wrought iron Juliet balconies at each of the upstairs windows to take in the far-reaching views across the bay. The smell of fresh fish permeated the air around them and the lines of the boat masts clinked rhythmically in the breeze, their flags flapping in unison. The girls kicked off their sandals simultaneously.

'You pair are like two peas in a pod!' said Helenka smiling.

'I heard from my parents earlier,' Keri told Helenka sipping her drink.

'I can't believe it's a couple of weeks since they returned home,' she replied.

Keri reached into her handbag for her phone.

'Look at these,' she said proffering her phone to Helenka. 'Daddy's put the painting Manos did for them in pride of place on the wall above the mantlepiece. Mammy said she can't take her eyes off it. Only has to look at it and it brings her right back to the sunsets on the island.'

'He did a great job capturing the early evening atmosphere on that painting,' said Helenka looking proudly at the photos.

Maria picked up the menu. 'Are we having a snack?' she asked.

'Good idea,' replied Keri.

'Can do,' said Helenka. 'I've got a couple of hours before I need to be back.'

They made their choices and ordered.

'I've just been to see my friends who had two of the pups last week, the sisters who own the craft shop on the hill.

They're settling down lovely and up to mischief as usual – the pups that is, not the sisters!'

'A bit like Tasha. She's only been with us a week but is a mischievous little madam! Has taken over the place. Annys plays with her from morning till night, they've developed quite a bond.'

'Kimba is happy with just Sophie around, I think she's glad of the rest, and now Sophie's got her mum all to herself she keeps snuggling up to her.'

Patrick walked in from the kitchen coffees in hand and offered one to Moya.

'There you go love.'

'Thanks Patrick,' she replied dreamily, her eyes moving from the painting to the mug of steaming coffee. 'I was just thinking about our time away. It's lovely to be home but I do miss the bay and everyone.'

'Yes, me too,' he said picking up the newspaper off the side table and settling down to read the sports pages.

'Wasn't it good of Manos to take some time off and show us around the island. There were so many places I'd not even heard of and I loved going to see the old familiar ones too,' she said thoughtfully. 'What was that little taverna called on the top of the hill?'

'Taverna? No idea,' replied Patrick.

'You do know. The one we went to on the last night with Keri and Manos, and Helenka and Theo. It had a beautiful view over the bay.'

'Oh yes. Very nice…'

'Patrick! Are you listening to anything I'm saying?'

'Indeed my love.'

'Well? What was it called?'

'What was what called?'

'The taverna!' she replied shaking her head.

'What taverna?' he asked lowering his newspaper and peering over the top.

'The one on the hillside with the yellow shutters. You liked their terraced garden with the pots of geraniums... Apollo! No, wait that's not it! Oh it's on the tip of my tongue...Agnios?' she said sipping her hot coffee.

'Taverna Apostolis,' he replied nonchalantly disappearing back into his newspaper.

'That's the one Patrick! I'd quite like a terrace like that at the end of our garden. There's that paved area on the left. We could have some Mediterranean style pots with the same kind of plants in them, and one of those round tiled bistro table and chairs. That'd finish it off nicely. What do you think?' she said moving towards the window cradling her mug.

'Whatever you want my love,' came his casual reply, ideas racing through her mind to bring a little bit of Greek magic into their garden.

Keri's mobile rang.

'Hi Manos.'

'Hey! Can you talk?'

'Yes. I'm with Maria and your mama. We've just left the harbour front.'

'Lovely. Can I meet you at the apartment in an hour? I've got some good news!'

'Of course. Can't wait!'

'See you then!' she replied slipping her mobile back into her pocket and catching up with the girls.

From his now familiar hotel room in the City Christophe took in the views over the rooftops, particularly hazy and dry today, very much different to the view from his office in France. Surprisingly though he seemed to be drawn to this place more and more with each visit. Swirling the glass of whisky in his hand and holding it up to the light, a habit he'd got into at university, he breathed in the sharp aroma and took a large swig feeling it dominate his senses and burn its way down his throat, soothing his mind. He recalled the first time he met Yannis in his tiny, stuffy office, seeing something of himself in him, all that ambition burning in his eyes. He just needed his big break.

Yannis disconnected the call and replaced his mobile on the desk next to a pile of papers. Nothing in Christophe's voice gave away what he needed to see him about. Soon enough he would find out what his plans were.

Hearing the sound of Keri's flip flops on the stone steps Manos looked up from his phone. He smiled to himself as her mellifluous voice called up to him as he sat outside her apartment.
'Hi Manos!'
'Hey!' he replied standing up to greet her, his arms open wide. She ran into them. He brought his face down to hers kissing her passionately. Their breaths mingled. Running her fingers down his spine she pulled him closer, his broad chest resting against her soft breast. Fumbling in her pocket for the keys she unlocked the door and they both shuffled into the cool apartment, kicking the door to behind them.

'Come on then!' said Keri as she made her way into the kitchen to get some cold drinks. 'What's your good news?'

'All in good time,' he teased.

'I'm bursting here Manos!' she replied throwing ice cubes at him.

'Okay! Okay!' he shouted shielding himself with his arms from the barrage coming his way.

'You know I said I'd look into having a stall on Lefko craft market…' now he had her attention. 'Well, with Alex's help we've managed to secure a much larger stall in a prime position.'

Her face lit up.

'The only thing is it's in four days' time! I know you said not before next weekend, but it was too good a chance to miss – and that's not all. They want you to have the stall three days a week until the end of next month at least.'

'Oh wow Manos! That's great news! Me and Maria better get our act together! How did you manage all that?' she asked flinging her arms around him.

'Well, the guy in charge of the market knows me well and owes me a favour and said if I wanted to sell some of my paintings on the same stall he would let us have it at discount as there were no smaller ones available. So I snapped his hand off!'

'I can't believe it!' she said excitedly.

'I showed him some photos of your work and he was well impressed.'

She leaned on the balcony railing, drink in hand.

'Thanks Manos. I can't wait to tell Maria. How will I ever repay you?' she replied with a twinkle in her eye.

'I'm sure we'll think of something,' he winked playfully.

Yannis took a deep breath and knocked firmly on the door.

'Enter!' called Christophe. He closed the door behind him and walked through the dark narrow hallway over to where Christophe was standing by the window.

'Good afternoon Yannis,' he said pouring two drinks and offering a glass to his guest.

'Thank you,' he replied taking the proffered drink, beads of perspiration forming on his forehead.

'As I said on the phone earlier, if you are free for a couple of hours I'd like to involve you in a project I'm looking at.'

'Yes, I've cleared my diary for the afternoon.'

Christophe gestured for his guest to take a seat.

'I'll get straight to the point. After extensive discussions with my business partner Jon, and our accountant, we've decided not to go ahead with a development in Galazios Bay. In short, the financial gain on the build, not to mention the costs once up and running, would be of no benefit to the investors, staff, and community and that's not what I'm trying to achieve here.'

Yannis shifted awkwardly in his chair as Christophe continued.

'There's some land a few kilometres south ripe for development, in an established resort. We've already purchased the land with planning permission in place for a 32-room hotel and spa, with four master suites for our more discerning customers. Most of the balconies will overlook the sea. There'll be an infinity pool built into the top of the building, a restaurant and bar reserved for hotel residents and a bar area to the front of the hotel which will be open to non-residents.'

Christophe settled himself into a chair opposite. Unclipping his well-worn black leather briefcase he placed the architect's drawings on the table. 'Take a look at these. See what you think.'

Yannis focused on the paperwork in front of him thinking this wasn't quite how he thought the meeting with Christophe would go today but at the same time feeling strangely relieved. Christophe returned with drinks refreshed.

'They look really good, but I'm not quite sure where I come into this if you're not going to use my land?' replied a somewhat puzzled Yannis.

'Let me explain,' said Christophe. 'My proposition to you is that of Project Manager. I want you on our team. You would be the eyes and ears on the ground, overseeing the day to day running of the build. We want to use local tradespeople and you have the contacts and can break the language barrier down. You'll get a regular salary with plenty of perks which we can discuss later.'

'Sounds good. I'm certainly very interested,' replied Yannis shuffling the papers in front of him.

'Very good. Would you like to go and see the land now? Get a feel for what we want to realise with the development.' Christophe asked.

'Yeah that would be great thanks,' he replied feeling more relaxed. Could be the drink, he thought, together with a strange sense of relief that it was moving away from the bay.

Christophe rang for a taxi as they headed off to the hotel foyer, pleased it was going so well.

The taxi pulled over and stopped at the side of the road directly in front of the piece of land. They both got out and walked over to inspect it. Christophe opened up the drawings and balanced them on the side wall. After much pointing and pacing around the site Christophe's vision was coming to life. Worked into the designs ancient architectural details mixed with modern touches. He explained that many of the original stones had been salvaged, dismantled carefully, cleaned, and stacked at the back of the land ready to be woven into the new build. After an hour or so they returned to the car and headed back to the City.

Shaking hands on the steps of the hotel foyer they went their separate ways agreeing to meet up later for dinner and to discuss the finer points. Spiros watched this exchange from a nearby taxi rank with a feeling of unease.

Parking up outside his house at the end of his shift Spiros got out of the car, stretched and walked over to his rickety fence and leaned on it to take in the views that had guided him from boy to man – views he never tired of. He caught a glimpse of Manos through the trees walking up the hill and lifted his arm to wave. Manos returned the greeting making a slight detour towards Spiros.

'Just the man!' he exclaimed. 'Have you got a minute Spiros?'

'All the time in the world. Just finished a shift. Come on up!' He went inside to boil the kettle and picked two mugs up off the draining board. 'Time for a brew?'

'Always got time mate.'

They settled down on the terrace with their mugs of tea.

'How's business?' asked Manos.

'It's good. Quietening down a bit now. I've no complaints though. Not picked up quite as many fares over the last couple of weeks, but it's a welcome change after the busy summer to be honest,' replied Spiros.

'How's it going at the boatyard?'

'Yeah, not bad at all, it does seem quieter this season – no idea why, but it's given me more time to paint,' said Manos. 'I'm happy with that though.'

'Wanted to let you know the good news. I've got Keri a stall on Lefko market. Her and Maria are making handcrafted jewellery. She's been looking to set up a small business now she's come to the end of her travels, so thought I'd give her a helping hand. I'm going to display some of my paintings there too.'

'That's good news! Anything I can do to help, just give me a shout. Why don't you get some business cards printed and I can hand them out to my customers, maybe drop some off in the City too.'

'That'd be great Spiros! Thank you my friend. I'll get onto it. In return I can put some of your taxi cards on the stall. People often want a ride back up the hill after visiting the market. A lot only intend wandering through the market, then end up laden down with shopping and waiting forever at the taxi rank in the square.'

'Sounds like a plan!' Spiros replied raising his mug in gratitude.

They sat companionably in the late afternoon sunshine.

'Saw your brother in the City today with that jumped-up Frenchman, you know, the builder with his big ideas! The French one…not your brother,' clarified Spiros.

'Oh Yannis can be quite rude too! Believe you me!'

'I reckon he's up to no good. Keeps sniffing around! Yannis wants to watch his back with that one!'

Spiros went on to tell Manos that he thinks he's worked out that he's after the land at the back of the boatyard to develop it.

'It's not what we want in the bay! I've been watching him swan about the City with his cronies like he owns the place. There's another chap he's been in cahoots with! Wouldn't trust either of them!' barked Spiros.

'Yeah, I've seen them around and met one of them, introduced himself as Christophe Dafoe. I reckon he's Yannis' architect for the villa he's been on about building for years now.'

'Has Yannis told you that?'

'Well, not directly. I guess I just put two and two together.'

'Word is that he's after the land to build a monstrous hotel. I think you need to talk to that brother of yours, before we lose all this!' he said bluntly looking over the bay with arms extended.

'Leave it with me,' replied Manos as he made his way down Spiros' driveway. 'He won't get away with this!'

'You be careful lad!' shouted Spiros after him.

Chapter Twenty Three

The waterfront teemed with life. Pavement cafes full of people enjoying their early evening drinks. The façades of the old buildings painted in bold blues and greens, garish oranges, and yellows. At the far end of the harbour they arrived at a taverna specialising in seafood, segregated from their neighbours with rows of multicoloured geraniums in rectangular pots. The air was thick with the smell of garlic and herbs. With noisy chatter all around they took their seats next to each other looking out to sea. The sun began its slow descent giving a hazy glow all around. With waves moving in harmony like a metronome, reflections of the harbour lights glimmered on the sea.

Orders placed. Down to business. Yannis pushed the wedge of lime into the bottle and took a refreshing mouthful. 'Nice taverna this. Best seafood in the City.'

'Yes, I believe so. It came highly recommended by the concierge of the hotel. It's his cousins place,' replied Christophe. 'So, tell me, what are your thoughts about the development?'

Yannis took a deep breath. 'I agree with you. I can see

now that my land wouldn't have worked. Galazios Bay isn't the right area for such a development. Whereas the land you have chosen is just right for the kind of hotel you're looking to build. All the services are in place for a start and it's already in a tourist hot spot. It all makes sense.'

Christophe nodded in agreement. Yannis continued.

'The architect's drawings are something special. It'll fit in with the nearby buildings and won't look out of place at all. I particularly like that they've intertwined the old stonework with the new. It feels like it's honouring the past whilst looking to the future. Local people will appreciate that touch. What will also go down well is using local tradesmen on the build. Most of their work is seasonal so any extra income is always a bonus,' he said taking another swig of beer.

Christophe raised his hand to get the attention of the waitress and gestured for two more beers.

'I'm glad you've realised your village isn't the right choice. To be honest with you Yannis, I'm actually quite pleased you're not disappointed. You've got too much invested in the place – family and friends – your past and your future.'

Yannis removed his cutlery from the rolled-up serviette as their meals and more beers arrived. The aroma of the fresh seafood platter drifted upwards. Side dishes of Greek salad, and *horiatiko psomi*, together with a selection of dips were placed before them. Christophe lifted some of the delicious seafood onto his plate and took a wedge of lemon.

'I remember mama teaching me how to bake *horiatiko* in the wood burning oven. I'd be about eight or nine. The smell of it always takes me right back to happier times with my parents and grandparents,' he said offering the basket of the rustic bread to Christophe. 'Here, you must try some.'

'Thanks,' he replied taking a slice of the dense crusty bread and ripping it in two. 'It does smell good. Are you from a large family Yannis?'

'All Greek families are large!' he joked. 'I was lucky to grow up with both sets of grandparents close by too. There's only mama and my brother now though. Lost my father a couple of years ago in a fishing boat accident as well as three friends.'

'Sorry to hear that. I did read about it, the storms and everything. It must have been dreadful for you all. Terrible losing a parent like that,' said Christophe empathetically.

'Yeah. Turned our world upside down. It's a very close-knit community – you've probably picked up on that! I don't think you ever get over something as big as that, you just learn to live with it. It affected both our bay and the next village where two of the young lads came from. We all went to school and hung around together, inseparable we were as kids. Maria who lives in the blue and white house at the far end of Galazios Bay lost her husband, Demetrius. He was the same age as us. They've got a little girl; she must be about five years old now.

'Oh that's dreadful,' Christophe replied. 'Children can be quite resilient though. I speak from experience. Lost both my parents in an accident. I was just a bit older than her. Sounds like she's got a loving family and friends around her. Unfortunately, I had neither.'

Yannis, taken aback by Christophe's revelation, wiped his hands on his napkin and took a drink from his bottle.

'How awful for you. Sorry, I had no idea.'

'It's okay. It was a lifetime ago. I was at boarding school when they were killed, hardly ever saw them. Always felt

I was in their way, a liability if you like,' said Christophe despondently. 'When they were around I was always being palmed off somewhere! You're lucky to have such memories Yannis. Treasure them.'

The waitress cleared the plates away and left the dessert menu on the table. The sky was now a neon blue in colour threaded with silver and the evening air was much cooler.

'It's not been easy. I think I lost my way a bit afterwards and shut everyone out. I was always the troublesome one growing up. Must have drove them all mad at times when I look back! I've upset a lot of people over the years and I reckon I've got some bridges to build,' shared Yannis with his newfound companion.

They both stared into the distance lost in their own thoughts. The waitress took their dessert orders, placed two more bottles on the table and made her way back to the kitchen.

'Anyway, down to business,' Christophe said clearing his throat. 'Anything else you'd like to add to our earlier conversation?'

'Not really, save to say I do have a few ideas of my own,' replied Yannis.

'That's what I was hoping for. Go on.'

'If you don't mind me saying, I think you might be missing a trick by not putting wrap-around balconies on the side elevation to take in the views of both the mountains and glimpses of the sea through the tall trees along the promenade.'

'Do you know, that would work well, and we can charge more for those rooms. Most people will pay extra for a bit of a sea view!'

'Exactly!' replied Yannis. 'And I've got some people in mind already for the build – experienced tradesmen who will bring the building to life.'

'Sounds good Yannis,' replied Christophe picking the spoon up to tuck into his dessert. 'Oh that's tasty!'

'It's the best Greek sweet in these parts!'

'What's in *halva*?' asked Christophe taking another mouthful, savouring the taste.

'Well, there are three different types from different regions but in my opinion this one has the edge over them all. It's a semolina base flavoured with cinnamon, lemon, nuts, and raisins, soaked in honey. I said it was good!'

'I reckon we'll put you in charge of catering when the hotel's up and running! Which brings me to my next question. I'd like you to oversee the employment of the hotel staff, local people of course. I'll need a small team putting together, from reception and housekeeping, to kitchen, restaurant, and bar staff. You'll obviously get all the training you need to fulfil the role. When everything's in place the team will be answerable to you in the first instance. How do you feel about that?'

Yannis put his spoon down on the empty plate and dabbed the sides of his mouth with the napkin.

'I'd be only too pleased to be involved in the build, getting the staff in place and being hands on,' he replied.

'That's what I was hoping. I'll make it worth your while. You'd be the best person on the ground. These are your people, and they will respect your decisions, other than bringing an outsider in.'

'That would make sense,' replied Yannis taking another drink from his bottle.

Christophe went on to explain there would be the prospect of more similar developments in the future on the island and other neighbouring islands that are crying out for what his company have to offer.

'I won't expect you to manage other hotels though Yannis. You will put managers in place for them. I want you to be on hand with the management of this hotel only for the time being.'

'Can I get you anything else?' asked the waitress as she cleared the dishes away and replaced the burnt out candle.

'Should we have coffee?' said Christophe to Yannis.

'Yes, that'd be good. A *sketos* for me please,' he replied pushing his empty bottle towards the side of the table.

'That's strong black without sugar,' he clarified looking across at Christophe.

'Same for me but with sugar please,' Christophe told the waitress.

'Okay. One *sketos* and one *metrios* it is,' she replied turning back to the kitchen.

Christophe continued.

'There'll be plenty of perks with the job, such as travelling, all expenses paid when on site, a decent commission as each property is completed and up and running.'

'Well, it certainly sounds too good an opportunity to turn down. So, in answer to your question, yes I would be pleased to accept your offer!' he replied with absolute certainty.

'Shall we shake on it?' asked Christophe proffering his hand.

'Indeed!' replied Yannis, his arm outstretched.

'Welcome aboard! You won't regret it!'

'Thanks for the opportunity Christophe. I won't let you down.'

Keri crossed over the road towards the boardwalk. Her blonde hair tied back in a ponytail with a light blue ribbon. The gentle evening breeze caught the hem of her pastel blue floral cotton dress lifting it from the side as she walked. She could see Manos leaning on a fig tree on the edge of the beach and tip-toed up behind him putting her hands over his eyes.

'Guess who?' she said in a high-pitched voice trying to disguise her Irish accent.

'I have no idea. Perhaps if you could wrap your arms around my waist?' he replied comically.

'How's this?' she obliged.

Turning to face her he laughed 'Oh it's you!' She released her hold and pushed him backwards. 'Come here,' he said opening his arms for her to walk right into them. He pulled her closer and wrapped his bronzed arms around her in an embrace which soothed him in a way he hadn't expected. He inhaled her perfume; the same one she had worn the first time they met. She looked up into those dark brown, now familiar, eyes and reached up to kiss him. He reciprocated. His heart beating faster, rooted in the moment. She was the only person he'd ever known who could make his heart skip. Nothing else existed. Their lips parted. With hands intertwined they turned to look towards the sea. Across the shimmering blue waters golden hues from the fading sun danced on the horizon. Honey coloured pillars of sunlight reached down and bounced off the sea heaven-bound again as they walked steadily hand in hand along the boardwalk towards Lefko Bay.

'Fancy a drink in the cocktail bar?' Manos asked.

'Sounds good,' she replied as they crossed over the road making their way slowly up the hill to the bar.

Taking their seats, they ordered two Mythos beers and watched the last of the sun fall slowly into the water leaving everywhere aglow, painting the sky fiery oranges and hot reds. Within moments, wispy grey clouds took over the skyline.

'I wish I could capture that vista,' she said dreamily to Manos.

'I will capture it for you my darling. Look! Over there!' he pointed with excitement.

She followed his gaze. In the distance a pod of dolphins played together, frolicking in the breakwater near the rocks.

'Aren't they beautiful,' she said taking photos on her mobile. 'Such free spirits!'

No sooner had they arrived, and they were gone again, far beneath the waves, the sea tranquil once more.

'They often play near the rocks at the far end of the bay. When the bigger ships sail through they love nothing more than swimming alongside and putting on their acrobatic display in the ship's wake. I've seen them quite close up when I've been taking the boats out. Beautiful creatures!' said Manos settling back into his wicker chair.

'Did you go back to the boatyard this afternoon?' asked Keri.

'Yeah. The yard was pretty quiet, but it gave me chance to have a tidy up and sort some canvases out for the craft fair. I've got about a dozen together so far. I saw Spiros earlier, told him about the market and he's going to spread the word.'

'That's great news! I'd better get down to some serious work now then!' she replied smiling.

'We might be able to put some work his way too by having some of his business cards on the table,' Manos said. 'He also told me, which I must admit I did have my suspicions about, that Yannis has got himself involved with a developer calling himself Christophe Dafoe. Spiros said rumours are going around that he's after building a massive hotel at the back of the boatyard on Yannis' land. I wouldn't put it past him to pull a stunt like that!'

'Oh my god! That's terrible! Surely he can't get away with it. It would take over the bay! Yes, I know who you mean. I've seen Yannis knocking around with him when I've been in the City.'

Leaving the taverna Yannis and Christophe walked along the harbour front before going their separate ways and agreeing to meet up the next morning at the hotel to sign the contracts. Christophe turned into the street his hotel was on, each stride along the dusty pavement taking him closer to solitude. He turned, not ready to go back, and made his way back down into the throng of the City. It was the first time he had really noticed it in all its glory. Geometric streets all running off the main square with tall, crooked buildings defying gravity itself. Ahead of him one of the oldest buildings on the island, so the plaque nailed to the wall said. A faded flag fluttered in the late evening breeze. Before long he had reached the paved area of the old quarter. Music blared out from the bars resonating around the buildings, bringing them to life once more. As his journey took him further along the road, the atmosphere changed, becoming calmer, almost hedonistic.

The Little Blue and White House

A distinctive sweet aroma wafted through the air and took him right back to the first time he'd partaken. He'd be about fourteen. A single skinny, rough looking joint handed around his dorm at boarding school. He'd watched the others before him and waited patiently in anticipation for his turn, taking a slow drag on it and passing it on, then the windows thrown open to disperse the evidence into the night air for fear of getting caught.

At the far end of the pavement he stopped at one of the quieter café bars, sat down outside and ordered a drink taking in the atmosphere. Mainly locals, all very much more laid back than from his own neck of the woods, acting like they didn't have a care in the world. He'd never really noticed before how much more relaxed everyone looked in these parts. They've probably never lost a night's sleep wondering whether a deal would go through or not, he thought slightly envious.

Leaning back in his chair he stared up into the midnight blue sky. A million stars flickered behind the shadow of the lacelike wispy grey clouds. Mesmerised, he let the ambience wash over him. It seemed this little Greek island was working its magic even on the likes of Christophe.

Chapter Twenty Four

With a little detective work and some reluctant help from Spiros, Keri found herself outside Christophe's hotel room. She'd had a close call as Yannis exited the building, darting to the side of the entrance and examining far too closely the balustrade and stonework until he was well out of sight. She knocked firmly on the door.

'Hello. Can I help you?' he asked.

'I hope so,' she replied abruptly, and most out of character for her. 'You don't know me, but I know who you are and what you're up to!'

'Okay…and what's that then?' he questioned.

'The hotel you want to build in Galazios Bay!' she snapped back.

'I think you've got your wires crossed somewhere,' he replied calmly.

'I don't think so!' she said with her heart thumping in her rib cage.

'Let's discuss this inside,' he said walking away from the doorway and along the hallway, which infuriated her even more.

She followed him, slamming the door behind her, and continued with her rant.

'I can't believe you have the audacity to come to this island with your ruthless ideas without any consideration to the harm you would be doing to the area, not to mention the upset to the residents in the bay. I've met your sort before! In fact, I've met you before, but you wouldn't remember that! You and your yacht friends fooling around. You think you can trample over everyone, but not this time!'

And with a sharp intake of breath she had said her piece.

He turned to face her. She fidgeted uneasily. What on earth was she thinking?

'I take it you've finished your rather impassioned speech?' he replied smirking. 'Although you may be surprised to learn that I do remember seeing you in the South of France with your three friends. My colleagues were somewhat rude and for that I apologise. They were a little worse for wear, but that's no excuse for their behaviour. Should we start again? My name is Christophe Dafoe, and you are?'

'My name is Keri Doyle,' she replied reluctantly shaking his outstretched hand and feeling a little embarrassed with her outburst.

'Keri. If I may call you by your first name?' she nodded in acceptance. 'Yes, you are partly right. I did initially come to the island with the sole purpose of building a luxury hotel. I had been approached by someone here on the island with an offer of buying some land in Galazios Bay, but after extensive investigations my company felt it would not be appropriate to build there. Instead we purchased a plot of land in an established resort on the island with planning permission already in place.'

'Oh. I see,' she replied feeling somewhat awkward. 'I may have spoken out of place.'

'It's fine. I can understand how it must have looked seeing strange faces wandering around taking much too close an interest in the bay.'

'Indeed, very unsettling. From one outsider to another, they've been through enough already, they don't need any more distress.'

'You have no worries there,' he said, and surprising himself, actually meant it. 'I didn't realise you were an *outsider*…like me. I assumed you lived here.'

Feeling more at ease and her heart rate slowing to a near normal rate she replied.

'It's a long story but I do have a lot of history on the island, as do my parents. When you saw me and my friends in France we were travelling through Europe. We each had a different destination, mine being this beautiful island. I've become very close to the villagers as did my parents before me. They made friends here to last a lifetime and to me it now feels like home, like I belong here…'

The words rattled around in her head. I belong here! I belong here! Saying it out loud she realised that for the first time in a long while she actually felt she did belong somewhere. It was almost like coming home. She smiled to herself.

He broke into her thoughts.

'I do understand you know. If you'd have told me somewhere could get into your soul, I would have dismissed it as madness. But there's something about this place…it draws you in. Anyway, rest assured my company will do the right thing. In the short time I've been here I've grown to respect the island and its people.'

'Thank you Christophe,' she said looking at her watch. 'I better get off, I've got somewhere I have to be, and…erm… sorry about earlier with my little outburst.'

'It's fine. I think I deserved it!' he replied showing her to the door.

Walking out of the hotel and into the heat of the City she made her way over to where Spiros was waiting feeling satisfied that Christophe would come good and do the right thing.

'Thanks for waiting Spiros,' she said. 'There's nothing to worry about.'

She recounted her visit to an eager Spiros.

'Thanks again for being here. I couldn't have done this without you.'

'No problem at all Keri. I was only giving you five more minutes than coming to see what was happening!' he replied.

'I did cut it a bit fine didn't I. Sorry about that. Once he'd started to explain everything time ran away with me.'

'All sounds very plausible though,' he nodded. 'What are your thoughts?'

'Do you know Spiros; I do believe him. He's got no reason to lie.'

'Yes, that's true, particularly if he told you about the other resort. One of the taxi drivers mentioned a French company had bought some land south of the bay where an old hotel once stood.'

'It all makes sense now,' she replied smiling.

'Would you like a lift back to the bay? I've got my last pick up for the day there in a couple of hours. Just gives me enough time to grab a snack and coffee at home first.'

'That would be lovely thank you Spiros,' she replied as he

opened the passenger door that had been his leaning post for the past 20 minutes as he stared at the hotel doorway.

As Spiros wound his way through the familiar mountain roads Keri relaxed taking in the spectacular vista from her window reflecting on the realisation that this place was now her world. Her love. Her life. Her heart fluttered like a butterfly. Through the open window she could hear the cicadas in the trees calling out to each other in their high-pitched musical performance. She remembered reading somewhere that the spirituality of their shrill sound symbolised change and rebirth. Never more had she felt it than at this moment. Glimpses of the sea and the golden sands of Galazios Bay flashed past. Through the labyrinth of dusty tracks descending the mountain the car travelled gaining speed. Greenery giving way to pretty buildings on either side. Her new life. Her new home. Coming into the village the houses either side painted in soft pastel shades with their facades smothered with bougainvillea in full bloom welcomed her. The tiny front gardens and balconies a riot of colour with lanky geraniums spilling from well-loved hanging baskets. The car slowed as it turned the corner in front of George's apartments. Keri alighted and Spiros was back on his way, but not before agreeing not to say anything to Manos about today's events. Keri would explain everything to him later.

Anna waved enthusiastically from the shop doorway, after nearly tripping over some boxes in her haste to see who was getting out of Spiros' taxi.

'Been into the City?' she called over to Keri through the open door.

Keri turned around.

'*Herete* Anna. Yes, it was very busy and hot there today. I'll be glad to get out of the sunshine for a while. You and George both ok?' she replied racing up the stone steps before Anna could ask any more questions.

'We're good thanks…' Anna replied craning her neck to see Keri disappear into her apartment.

Helenka finished her coffee and placed the empty china cup back onto the saucer, reached down to caress the pups' ears once again, pleased they were both settling down nicely, and bid farewell to the sisters. Her weekly coffee and cake catch-up had taken an unusual twist when the conversation turned to rumours of a hotel complex being built on the headland. She had listened intently to what they had to say, putting two and two together and realising the land they were talking about was owned by Yannis. Keeping this well and truly to herself she made her way back home feeling rather unsettled.

'Helenka! Helenka! Over here!' shouted Theo from across the road.

'*Yasas!*' she responded raising a hand to him.

He crossed over and caught up with her reaching out to take her bags. Ever the gentleman she thought.

'*Se efcharisto file mou*,' she thanked him giving him the heavier of the two bags. 'I've just been for coffee with my friends in Lefko. Thought I'd pick up a few bits and bobs on the way home, always end up getting too much. Where are you off to Theo?'

'Was just stretching my legs, didn't realise it was as hot as this outside! Might have to stop off at yours for refreshments,' he said wiping his brow with his free hand.

'Good idea,' she replied walking steadily and staring straight ahead.

Theo noticed that Helenka didn't seem her usual bubbly self. Following her into the kitchen and dropping the bag onto the counter he asked if she was alright.

Taking a deep breath, she replied. 'I'm fine thanks Theo.'

He took her by the shoulders and led her towards one of the tables near the bar.

'Now sit down. I'm going to get us some drinks.'

He had not known her for all these years without realising something was wrong. She did as she was told, again this was most unlike Helenka.

'There you go! One orange soda with a splash of lime and ice. Just how you like it,' he said placing the drink onto a napkin in front of her and taking the seat opposite. 'I don't want to pry my dear, and you can tell me to go away, but you look like you've got the weight of the world on your shoulders.'

'Oh Theo, my friend, where do I start?' she replied with a sigh.

'Take your time. I'm not going anywhere,' he said leaning back in his chair.

She explained the conversation with the sisters.

'I know Yannis can be thoughtless sometimes but to pull a stunt like this right under our noses…I just feel so let down. I gave him that land after Dino passed away. For years he had wanted to build himself a villa to live in, so I stupidly gave the land to him. What does he think he's playing at? Has he no respect? Does he really hate me that much Theo?'

'No Helenka, of course he doesn't hate you,' he reassured her gently, keeping to himself that he would quite happily wring his bloody neck! 'He's just lost his way that's all. I'm sure when he's thought about it properly he'll realise it's not the right place for a hotel.'

They sat in silence for a while.

'We were doing alright weren't we Theo?' she questioned. 'The last few years have been hard for us all, but we're getting there aren't we? I miss the boys so much, it's an ache that never goes away,' she said softly, wiping a tear from her eye. 'Why has he cut himself off from us all?'

'It's probably his way of coping. Everyone grieves differently. He's a good lad deep down. Always did get himself into scrapes mind! The stories Dino used to tell me over the years.' He remembered fondly their late-night drinking sessions and putting the world to rights. 'It'll all sort itself out my dear. Try not to worry too much.'

'Yes, he was a force to be reckoned with when something wasn't going his way. Dino had the knack of talking him around and smoothing things over. I hope he hasn't got in over his head this time,' she said with concern.

'Do you want me to have a quiet word with him?' he asked.

'Perhaps – it can't do any harm I suppose,' she replied.

'Have a think about it and let me know,' said Theo finishing his drink.

Manos stepped out of his van and walked over to where Yannis was sitting on the harbour wall at the far end of the City.

'Yannis!' said Manos as he approached. 'How are you?'

'Manos!' he replied turning his head to greet him. 'I'm okay thanks. And you?'

'Yeah, good. Should we walk along the promenade?'

'Okay,' he replied swinging his legs over the wall and catching up with a retreating Manos. 'How's it going at the boatyard?'

'Ticking over nicely,' Manos replied swiftly.

'Do you still have time for your artwork?' asked Yannis.

'I do. Got quite a collection together now. How about you? Been busy?' he asked.

'Oh, you know, not too bad,' he replied guardedly.

An awkward silence sat between them with stilted conversation until they reached the end of the seafront.

'Fancy a beer?' asked Manos nodding towards a quiet bar on the seafront away from the main street.

'Sounds good,' agreed Yannis. 'It's a bit hot. Be nice to get out of the sun for a while.'

Spiros closed his gate and walked steadily down the hillside towards the shore to clear his head. Reaching up into the foliage of an overhanging fig tree he yanked a piece of fruit from its branches, cleaned it on his sleeve and bit into it, still warm from the heat of the sun. Ever since he could remember he'd been plucking fruit from the trees and bushes all around him. As a young lad his papa had encouraged him to forage in the woods on the hillside, always plentiful with juicy oranges and lemons, not to mention an abundance of sweet nectarines and apricots from the orchards at the edge of the village. An only child to his more mature parents he would work the land with his papa making sure his mama had enough fresh food for the delicious soups and tasty stews she made each day for their return. The harrowing stories of generations before him had always stayed with him – the struggles to put food on the table and the famine all around them. His mama would be down at the harbour at the crack of dawn waiting for the fishermen to return with their catch every Friday without fail. He smiled to himself. Weaving in and out of the backstreets the smell of lavender threaded through the air reminding him so much of his beloved mama. She would always have bunches of the stuff hanging all over the house and would make lavender pouches in netting tied up with cream silk ribbon for birthdays and celebrations, thanks to the rows of lavender bushes in the garden. When his mama's hands became twisted and cruelly deformed by the arthritis, he would sit patiently at her side on the small hand-carved stool by the fireside, helping her cutting the stems and tying them into bunches.

On the day his mama passed away, Spiros and his papa had been working in the fields. Spiros had picked some wildflowers and lavender on the way back to the house to put into a vase by her bedside, not knowing she had drifted away that afternoon. From that day forward he had always had the heady fragrant flower in the house, whether it be fresh from the overgrown purple bushes in the garden, or dried hanging from the beams, tied into the fabric of the building. After his mama's passing he and his papa continued to work the land, and to make ends meet Spiros took a part time job with the local taxi company. Not even a year later his papa had gone too, died of a broken heart many had said. Spiros was completely lost and threw himself into the taxi business; after a few years affording his own car and working for himself. The land had become overgrown over the years, but still the row of lavender bushes flourished year after year.

Chapter Twenty Five

Manos took a mouthful of the cool blonde lager and a handful of roasted nuts from the dish in the centre of the table.

'I think we need to talk about your land behind my boatyard!' Manos said straight to the point. 'I hear you're thinking of selling it to a company to build a hotel on. And you think that's a good idea do you?'

'It's something I've looked into,' replied Yannis.

'And when were you going to share this with us?' said Manos sharply.

'There's nothing set in stone. It was just an idea…'

'And let me guess…you were just about to tell us! Or were you waiting until the bulldozers moved in!'

'I would have talked to everyone about it first.'

'Really?' questioned Manos. 'Come on Yannis! I know you better than that! You had no intention of telling anyone. Do you think we're all stupid or something and haven't seen strangers wandering about the village for weeks now sizing everything up?' Yannis looked down at the floor. 'You can't even look me in the eye can you! This is a new low even by your standards!'

'It's not happening anyway!' Yannis announced.

'Have you just decided that then?' asked Manos.

'No!' he snapped back fixing his eyes on the floor again.

'Sure about that? Changed your mind because you've been caught out!' Is that it Yannis?'

'No! Not at all. Let me explain.'

'Go on then. Let's hear it.'

'Yes, I was looking into building on the land…'

'We know that!' interrupted Manos. 'You said it would be a small villa! Not a bloody great hotel!'

'You've every right to be angry!'

'Angry! Angry! That doesn't even cut it!'

'As I said – I was investigating developing the land but after looking into it, it wouldn't be the right thing to do having such a large hotel in the bay. And contrary to what you might think I do agree with you. I should have been upfront with what I was planning.'

'Down to price was it? If the price was right you'd still go ahead?' challenged Manos.

'No, not at all. It was nothing to do with price. If you'd asked me that a few months ago I would have said yes! But no, not now.'

'What's changed then?' Manos pushed.

'Everything really. I thought that's what I wanted – selling the land and moving on. I didn't feel part of it anymore. Like I didn't belong.'

'Of course you belong!' said Manos realising for the first time that his brother seemed to be struggling and probably had been since the accident. 'Did you not stop to think what this would do to mama – you selling up and clearing out?'

'I'm ashamed to say I didn't. Everyone seemed to be getting on with their lives. I didn't know what to do so started spending more and more time in the City. If I moved away the nightmare just didn't seem real. I got talking one day to some property investors who I'd been working with on a hotel insurance matter. They were looking at developing their spa hotel business on the island and I mentioned having some land in Galazios Bay, of which they seemed particularly interested. Before I knew it I was showing them around the land in the hope they would buy it.'

'I see. Can't say I understand why you would want to see a monstrosity of a hotel there though,' replied Manos.

'Yes, I realise that now. I got a bit carried away with it all…'

'It seems like it. So, where do you go from here?' asked Manos.

'Well, I've seen the other plot of land the company have bought. There was an old hotel on the site that was crumbling, which has since been demolished, and the land has planning permission in place. Christophe's company have already purchased it and are building a boutique hotel and spa in its place. The plans are in keeping with the area, using as much of the original stonework as possible. The photos of other developments his company have done on nearby islands are stunning. They always build sympathetically for whatever area they are in and use local workmen and local products. All the staff are from the area and have a passion for the region,' he explained. 'In fact, Christophe has asked me to join the company as Project Manager overseeing the build, sourcing local tradespeople, and looking after the employment of all the staff to run the hotel afterwards. And I've accepted!'

'Oh I see. Are you happy with that?' asked Manos.

'Yes I am. Very much so,' he replied. 'If all goes well there will be similar developments on other islands to project manage too. To be honest Manos I'm looking forward to a new challenge. Something I can really throw myself into.'

'I'm pleased for you Yannis. I really am. But what about your business in the City?'

'I've decided to sell. My colleague's been wanting to buy me out for quite a while now so I'm going to take him up on the offer.'

'Sure you're not rushing into anything?' asked Manos.

'Not at all. I've had plenty of time to look into everything and to check out Christophe's company. I've got a reasonable price for my share of the business too. I've not been happy in the City for a while so it's the right time to move on.'

'Where will you go?' Manos asked.

'I'm thinking of moving back to Galazios, rent first to see how it goes,' Yannis explained feeling more at ease now.

The brothers talked into the afternoon, with much to catch up on. Yannis shared photos of Christophe's other hotels scattered throughout the Mediterranean. He was impressed by what he saw. They made their way back along the promenade to the centre of the City. Some bridges had been mended; old wounds closed up; a lot of issues resolved that had divided them in the past. Yannis opened up to Manos how much he had missed family and friends in the village, knowing it was all his own doing. He wanted the chance to start afresh, to put everything behind him. He had a lot of friendships to repair. But before all that he must go to see his mama to apologise for his behaviour of late.

'See mama sooner rather than later, she's been beside herself worrying about you. When you've got yourself settled do you think you might build that villa you've always talked about on the headland?' asked Manos.

'That's something I wanted to talk to you about,' replied Yannis.

'Go on. I'm intrigued,' said a curious Manos.

'As long as mama is happy for me to do this, I'd like to ask if you would be interested in buying my land behind the boatyard.'

'Okay. That's not what I was expecting you to say. Why do you want to sell?'

'I've been looking into purchasing some land on the hillside between Galazios and Lefko Bay to build a villa. I can use the proceeds from selling my half of the business to buy the land, but I'll need to raise some more capital to develop it, and to cover the building costs. I know you've always wanted to extend the boatyard to have a separate art studio at the back, and it seems the perfect solution for both of us.'

'I can see that would make sense. It keeps the land in the family too, always a good thing. Have you got a figure in mind?' asked Manos.

'I have indeed. I had it valued not so long ago, with and without planning permission, and I've got the paperwork back at the flat. Would you like to pop in and have a look? It's only round the corner from here,' he said pointing to the tall apartment block down the road.

Manos looked at his watch. 'I think I would, then I must get back. I thought you lived the other side of the City.'

'I did. This is just a temporary move to tide me over,' replied Yannis.

Together they climbed the grey stone stairwell two steps at a time avoiding the broken glass bottles strewn around the ground floor. Their footsteps echoed in the dark dank corridor leading to Yannis' flat. Manos looked around him at the paint peeling off the damp walls on either side as Yannis put his key into the lock and turned the rusty doorknob. He was glad to step inside away from the stench of stale urine that hung in the air, much like one would find in the stairwell of a municipal car park. The apartment wasn't much better Manos noticed, stuffy and sparsely furnished with only the essentials.

'Have you been here long Yannis?' he asked curiously.

'I moved in a few weeks ago. It's nearer to work and a lot cheaper,' he replied, his face reddening slightly. 'It's just a place to rest my head. I tend to spend most of my time at work and then eat out afterwards. The rent's half as much as in the cultural quarter.'

'Right,' replied Manos slightly taken aback by the squalor his brother was now living in. 'Are you okay for money Yannis?'

'Yeah, fine now. Had a few customers didn't pay their bills and a bit of a lull last winter. It all took its toll on the business to be honest. Everything's unpredictable in this line of work. That's part of my reason for wanting a change.'

'Very true. I completely understand now,' agreed Manos.

Yannis sifted through some papers spread out over the old, stained dining table. 'There you go. The valuation papers,' he said handing them to Manos to read through. 'And here's the ones with planning permission attached,' he said walking over to the open window where Manos was studying them closely.

'Thank you. Are you happy with both the figures?' he asked.

'I am. Very much so. What are your thoughts?' Yannis replied.

'Both seem a good price,' Manos remarked.

'The figure with the planning is for a four bedroomed villa on two levels with the front elevation overlooking the sea.' Yannis explained. Manos nodded.

'I'm very interested Yannis. As long as mama is happy with our agreement,' he replied offering the papers back to him. 'I'd be delighted to take it off your hands, so to speak.'

'I'd really like you to have it. Like you say, it keeps it in the family, and you'd probably appreciate the land a lot more than me. I'll be much happier living at the top of the village, still got great sea views, but from a distance which suits me just fine,' Yannis declared taking the papers from him.

Manos' mind was in overdrive with what he could do with all the extra land. 'Go on then! Let's make a deal now Yannis!' he said offering him the figure he had in mind.

'Yes. That sounds good to me!' Yannis replied with a sense of relief that his brother wanted to buy the land from him.

'Should we shake on it? Obviously with the proviso mama is on board with it all, which I'm sure she will be, particularly knowing you'll be moving back from the City,' said Manos.

They shook hands, patting each other's backs in an impromptu bear hug.

'I'll go to see mama in the morning,' said Yannis.

'Good news! I'll be in the boatyard if you want to drop by afterwards.'

'Thanks Manos. Will do,' he replied feeling reassured.

'Anyway, I really must be on my way. See you tomorrow mate,' he said checking his watch again and drawing a huge breath that he hoped would sustain him as he sprinted down the malodorous stairs and exited the building into the fresh air.

Chapter Twenty Six

Maria walked to the gate with Alex.

'See you tomorrow after school,' he called to Annys who was absorbed in lining up the watercolour paintings on the patio to dry. The three of them had spent the afternoon creating their very own masterpieces under strict instructions from Annys on who was painting what! 'She seems quite excited about starting school tomorrow.'

'Yes, she does. It's me who's nervous about it. I know she's moving up with all her friends, but she still seems so young.'

'Come here love,' he said gently opening his arms for her. 'She'll be fine, don't you worry.'

'I know you're right,' she sniveled into his chest. 'I don't want her to see me upset when I drop her off.'

'You'll be alright Maria. You're bound to be a bit anxious, but she'll be that pre-occupied with all the excitement and her friends she probably won't even notice.'

'Thanks Alex,' she replied blowing her nose on a tissue from her pocket.

'You know where I am if you need me,' he said wiping a stray tear from her eye. 'Happy tears! Yeah?'

'Happy tears indeed!' she smiled reaching up to kiss him.

Spiros walked up the wooden steps into Ellas, turning to acknowledge Alex in the distance.

'*Yassou!*' he called over to Helenka and Theo as he made his way towards them.

'*Yassou* my friend,' replied Theo. 'Come! Join us!'

'There you go!' said Helenka offering her chair to him. 'I'll fetch us some drinks.'

'It's a warm one!' said a weary Spiros as he sat down and wiped his brow.

'Certainly is!' replied Theo.

Helenka came over with a tray of drinks and the three friends chatted for a while. She brought up the subject of the proposed hotel build and shared her concerns with Spiros too.

'I'm sure there's nothing to worry about Helenka.' Spiros replied not divulging all he had learnt from Keri's visit to the Frenchman. 'I had heard the rumours too, but am sure that's all they are, just rumours. There'll be no building of any such hotel in the bay!'

'You seem quite sure about that my friend,' said Theo.

'Well, you know, I hear all sorts of gossip, usually just pie in the sky ideas – this being one of them!' Spiros assured them without revealing his source of the information and steered the conversation onto safer ground. 'Anyway, tell me, how are the sisters getting on with their new arrivals?'

Keri heard Manos' car before she saw it turn the corner. It had been a knack she'd picked up from her childhood. Living at the end of a long lane, whenever a car had travelled down the track she would close her eyes and listen to the sound of the engine as it approached. Waving to Manos as he slowed down, she smiled to herself upon recognising the purr of his car's engine as it came into sight. She got into the passenger seat and reached over to kiss him. Pulling her closer, he ran his fingers through her silky hair breathing in the sweet scent of her favourite perfume. Moments later they were weaving their way through the mountainous road to Alberto's, Keri's hand resting lightly on his leg.

'How's your day been?' she asked.

'Good thanks. Met up with Yannis today,' he said negotiating a particularly tight bend just before the sharp turn into the car park. 'And what have you been doing?'

'Oh this and that,' she replied unbuckling her seatbelt and stepping out of the car.

They walked hand in hand to the edge of the car park and leaned on the fence taking in the views. Tightly packed clusters of silvery eucalyptus trees before them leaned towards the fading rays of the sun and swayed in harmony with each other releasing their delicate minty fragrance into the air as if dancing to the music from the taverna as it floated tunefully on the breeze.

A familiar figure walked slowly towards them.

'Alberto, my friend,' said Manos, his hand outstretched to greet him.

'Manos! How are you?' he replied accepting his hand and pulling him into an embrace.

'Keri! So lovely to see you beautiful lady!' he said reaching for her hand and placing a kiss on the back of it.

'And lovely to see you too Alberto!' she replied.

'Would you like your usual table?' he asked as they made their way over to the raised terrace.

'Yes please Alberto,' replied Manos.

'There you go,' he said pulling one of the chairs back from the table for Keri to be seated.

'Thank you very much,' she said politely, as he brushed away imaginary crumbs from the already immaculate white tablecloth.

'Would you like to order drinks now?' he asked.

'Yes please Alberto. I'll have a Mythos and Keri?'

'Same for me please,' she replied taking the menu from him.

'I'll be back for your order shortly,' he said disappearing inside to fetch the drinks.

They studied the menus, both lost in their own thoughts after the events of the day.

'Manos?' said Keri quietly. 'There's something I need to tell you.'

He closed his menu, placing it in front of him.

'What's wrong Keri?' he asked reaching across the table and taking her hand in his.

'Where do I start?' she questioned as Alberto came back with the drinks and took their food order.

'Go on,' he said.

She took a sip of the refreshingly cool beer and began telling him about her meeting with Christophe.

'I had to do something,' she finished.

'You should have told me where you were going, it might have turned nasty,' he replied with concern.

'In hindsight, yes perhaps. But I'm used to sorting things out for myself, and Spiros was keeping an eye on things from outside. He wanted to tell you, but I insisted I would tell you tonight.'

'I see,' he replied. 'It all makes sense now.' Manos went on to explain about his meeting with Yannis, his struggles over the past few years and what his brother's plans were for the future.

'That all sounds good doesn't it. I'm glad he's going to see Helenka tomorrow. She'll be really pleased to have both her sons back in the bay,' said Keri.

'That's true I suppose,' he replied considering everything.

Alberto placed the food down in front of them. Grilled seabass for Keri, and roasted lamb *kleftiko* for Manos.

'Can I get you anything else?' he asked.

'That looks lovely thank you. No nothing else for me,' replied Keri squeezing the wedge of lemon over the fish which sizzled as its juice trickled onto the steaming dish.

'Nor for me Alberto, *efharisto*,' replied Manos picking up his cutlery and lifting some salad from the shared bowl.

'*Parakalo*, you're welcome. Enjoy your meal.'

The sun dipped into the deep Prussian blue sea leaving behind streaks of burnt orange and copper throughout the sky as the birds sang their evening chorus all around them.

'He's asked me if I would like to buy his land at the back of the boatyard,' Manos said stirring sugar into his strong black coffee. 'I've accepted and agreed a price with him. He was going to sell it anyway, so I'm happy to buy it from him.'

'That's great news Manos!' Keri said sipping her coffee.

'At least I know it's not going to get into the hands of any greedy developers now!'

'That's true! I'm really pleased for you. Have you any idea what you'll do with it?' she asked.

'I've got a few thoughts racing around in here,' he replied tapping his forehead. 'I'd love to extend the boatyard and have an art studio at the back and possibly a small villa overlooking the sea on the higher ground,' he said pointing to the clearing in the distance.

'That sounds perfect. The views would be amazing!' replied Keri drinking the last of her coffee and dabbing her lips on the napkin.

'We'll drive down past the yard on the way back and have a closer look before it gets too dark, if that's okay with you,' he replied putting some cash onto the silver dish together with a generous tip for Alberto.

'We're off now my friend,' he called over to his host. 'We shall see you again very soon.'

'Thanks Alberto. It was a lovely meal,' Keri said as they started walking towards the car.

'Thank you very much. See you both soon,' he replied clearing the table.

Manos saw the land in a different light now. As he stood hand in hand with Keri looking out to sea the waves crashed against the rocks on the headland noisily, curling as they hit land before dissolving into white foam. Then silence until the next wave reached the cliffs.

'I'll never tire of the sound of the sea,' he said squeezing Keri's hand.

'I know what you mean. It's such a beautiful place too. It's like coming home for me!' she smiled.

He turned to face her. 'I know it's crazy...but stay! Stay

here in the bay with me! Share my dream!' he blurted out taking both her hands in his.

'W-what?' she said trying to take it all in, her eyes wide with both wonder and confusion.

'Sorry…I didn't mean it to come out like that and put you on the spot,' he said blushing slightly. 'The words just tumbled out!'

'I like the words that tumbled out! I like them very much!' she replied, a smile creeping onto her lips. 'Do you mean it Manos?'

'I've never been so sure about anything in my life!' he replied gazing lovingly into her sparkling blue eyes.

'Let's do it!' she cried falling into his arms. 'Why not!'

He picked her up high into the air, both of them in a state of euphoria. She squealed with excitement until they both dropped to the ground in joyous laughter. Beneath them the earth felt warm and soft as they snuggled up together under the blanket of stars twinkling high above in the clear night sky, lost in their own world.

Annys' first day at school had arrived. Maria tried to keep busy preparing sandwiches for lunch for her daughter. Her favourite fillings had been purposely chosen the previous day. A piece of fruit and a homemade cupcake the last things to go into the lunchbox. Drinks would be supplied by the school throughout the day.

Her mobile bleeped.

Sending love and lots of hugs to my two favourite girls xx

Her heart skipped a beat. She typed her reply.

Thanks Alex. Annys is so excited! I'll pop by after dropping her off at school if that's still okay? xx

Of course it's okay. I'll have the kettle on xx

She placed the phone in the back pocket of her jeans. 'Are you ready to go Annys?' she shouted upstairs.

'Coming mummy!' she replied flying down the stairs, pigtails swishing side to side, held in place by two bright blue silk ribbons. As she landed on the bottom step she did an impromptu twirl for Maria, who scooped her up into her arms.

'How did my little girl get so grown up! You look beautiful,' she smiled spinning her around in the air.

'I love my dress mummy!' Annys declared proudly. 'Can we go now?'

'Yes. I'll just get my keys,' she said turning around quickly so Annys couldn't see her moist eyes. It didn't seem two minutes since she herself was dressed in the same blue and white pinafore dress, white ankle socks and shiny black shoes, being waved off at the school gates by her mama.

They reached the school in plenty of time before the bell would signal the start of the new school day. Any anxieties Maria might have had were soon gone when Annys met up with her friends in the playground. Prompted by the teachers, the older children began forming a friendship arch leading to the main entrance. The head teacher clapped her hands together to get everyone's attention. The excited chatter quietened somewhat. Within minutes the older children were lined up in two rows facing each other, their hands linked together in the air to greet the new starters. A short speech from the head to the younger children welcoming them into their school family, and they were soon skipping through the arch and into the school with cheers and clapping from their audience at the school gates.

Chapter Twenty Seven

Keri cradled her coffee as she watched Manos doing his magic in the kitchen. He'd promised his special pancakes and the smells drifting towards her were mouth-wateringly delicious. As she walked towards the balcony the morning sun shone its golden rays into her eyes. Lifting her free hand to shield them from the brightness she caught a glimpse of Maria walking down the hill towards the village, making a mental note to give her a call as it was Annys' first day at school.

Manos placed their breakfast onto the table with a 'ta-da'! Steam snaked upwards from the stack of pancakes as the golden syrup flowed down the sides and over the blueberries onto the plate.

'Mmmm…they look amazing!' said Keri walking over to take her seat at the table.

'Told you they were my specialty!' replied Manos putting the cutlery down in front of them, together with a fresh pot of coffee. Keri delved in scooping up some of the sauce and adding a spoonful of blueberries onto her plate.

'They smell so sweet,' she declared putting a forkful into her mouth. 'Oh wow! They're scrumptious!'

'Yep! Nice and healthy too – with the fruit!' he winked, not wasting any time joining her.

Keri placed her cutlery onto the now empty plate. 'That'll certainly keep me going for a while. Thanks Manos,' she said pouring them both another coffee. 'Before we go to see Helenka I just want to pop back to the apartment to get showered and changed.'

'Okay, no problem. I've got to drop in at the boatyard this morning anyway, I've got a delivery coming. Meet you at Ellas, say, about eleven?'

'Perfect!' she said finishing her coffee and reaching under the sofa for her brown leather sandals discarded in haste the previous night.

Maria stood at the doorway to Alex's apartment listening to his welcoming footsteps from inside getting louder and louder on the tiled floor. He opened the door wide, and she ran into his arms sobbing her heart out.

'Hey come on!' Dry those tears,' he whispered gently stroking the back of her neck. Reaching behind her to close the door he guided her into the living room.

'I'm sorry Alex…I've been holding it all in…' she said between sobs. 'I was fine until I got here…then it just came over me like a wave…I'm sorry…'

'Don't be sorry. I understand. Couldn't get you and Annys out of my mind earlier. How was she?' he asked softly.

'Oh she was fine. Just like you said she would be,' replied Maria.

'Well that's good. I bet she'll be having a lovely time,' he reassured her holding her hands tightly in his.

'I know you're right Alex. She looked so grown up.'

'Have you got time for a coffee?'

'Yes please,' she replied letting go of his hand and following him into the small kitchen. 'What are you doing this afternoon?'

'Nothing I can't change. Why?' he asked stirring their coffees and offering one to her.

'I was wondering – and you can say no – but would you like to come with me later to pick Annys up?'

'I'd love to!' he replied without hesitation. 'What time?'

'She finishes at 3:20. I'll be leaving home just before 3 o'clock. I can meet you on the way.'

'Sounds good to me!' he replied happily. 'What are your plans for the rest of the day?'

'I told Helenka I'd drop in after taking Annys to school, then I'm meeting up with Keri to talk about how we're going to market the jewellery.'

'Busy day for you then,' he said. 'It'll certainly go quickly.'

'That's what I'm hoping,' she replied putting her empty coffee mug onto the draining board. 'Thanks for letting this crazy woman in!'

'My pleasure!' he said pulling her closer towards him. 'The more time I spend with my crazy lady is no bad thing!'

Keri checked her watch and looked up to see Manos walking towards Ellas from the boatyard. She waved. Helenka walked onto the veranda.

'*Kalimera. Pos eisai?* How are you?' she called down to her.

'*Kalimera Helenka!*' she said looking up. '*Poli kala, efharisto.* Very good, thanks. We were just coming to see you,' she replied as Manos joined them.

The Little Blue and White House

'Lovely, come and sit down and I'll get us some refreshments. Do you want the usual?' asked Helenka heading towards the bar.

'Yes please,' she replied touched that she knew her well enough now to know her favourite drink, and for that matter, her favourite food too.

They all sat happily together. Helenka occasionally popping into the kitchen to check the lunchtime food was coming together. They talked about the news for the craft markets, how they were planning for them, and Maria's involvement. Manos' hand caught Keri's leg under the table. She smiled at him and nodded.

'We've got some good news mama!' he announced taking hold of Keri's free hand resting on the table. 'Keri's going to be staying a bit longer than she'd planned!' he said grinning.

'That's great news Keri!' she replied. 'How long are you looking at?'

'Well…I'm actually going to make the island my home!' she said beaming.

'Keri! That's wonderful news! I'm so thrilled for you!' said Helenka reaching across to embrace her. 'Can you stay on at George's apartment?'

'I'm hoping so for a few more weeks…' replied Keri looking over to Manos.

'Then Keri's moving in with me!' he shared with a most joyful Helenka.

'Wonderful! I am very happy for you both! You really have made my day!' she said clasping her hands together. 'It's about time we had some good news! Have you told your parents yet?' she asked as she refreshed their drinks.

'We're going to call them this afternoon. We wanted you to be the first to know,' she replied.

'That's so lovely of you both. Thank you,' she said wiping a stray tear from the corner of her eye.

They chatted for much of the morning. Yannis' name cropped up in conversation and Helenka shared what she had learnt from her friends about the building work. Manos put her mind at rest and told her to expect a visit from him very soon, whilst reassuring her that no such hotel would be built in the bay, and that he too was bringing good news!

Making her way along the sandy boardwalk towards Ellas, Maria reflected on the last few hours and smiled to herself. The shadows of the fig trees alongside danced playfully in the slight breeze as she walked lightly along the familiar route she had taken with Annys many times before; her daughter skipping over the shadows. Now the only shadow was hers. Voices in the distance broke into her musing. She looked up. On the terrace stood her three friends. She swallowed the lump that had found its way back up into her throat again and waved. Quickening her pace and taking a deep breath she continued along the path reaching them moments later.

'How did it go? Was Annys alright?' asked Helenka.

'Yes, she was absolutely fine. Don't know what I was worried about,' replied Maria far braver than she actually felt.

'That's good!' said Helenka holding both hands out to Maria. She took them, feeling safe instantly and smiling a watery smile. Keri leaned over to hug her friend, whispering into her ear that she would see her later and would text.

Manos and Keri made their way across the road and back to Keri's apartment.

'I hope mammy and daddy are as happy as Helenka when I break the news to them,' she said.

'I'm sure they will be,' replied Manos squeezing her hand.

Maria followed Helenka into the kitchen and recounted what had happened at the school gates, how the older children had formed an arch for the younger ones to go through.

'She was amazing Helenka! Far better than me!'

'I'm sure you were brilliant. It's all credit to you my love. You have given her the confidence to do anything. You and Demetrius gave her the roots to grow and you, my darling, have given her wings to fly and to follow her dreams.'

'Thank you. I couldn't have done it without you though,' she said embracing Helenka once more.

The screen on Keri's mobile lit up with two very familiar faces.

'Hi mammy. Hi daddy. You both okay?' asked Keri.

'We are indeed! And you?' said Moya fiddling with her screen to level it up on the surface in front of them. *'Can you see us both alright?'*

'Yes, that's it.' replied Keri smiling.

Keri turned the screen towards Manos. He waved and asked how they were, giving his mama's love to them both.

'It was so lovely to see her and catch up with everyone.' said Moya still adjusting the angle of her phone.

'She's already talking about your next visit – so you'd better get planning!' he joked.

'We can't wait, can we Patrick!'

'That's right!' he joined in, always feeling a bit uncomfortable on Facetime, and much preferring to talk face to face.

'Mammy. Daddy. I've got something to tell you.' Keri said grinning.

'I'm guessing it's good news judging by the look on your face. You never could hide your excitement Keri!' replied Moya.

'Let her speak woman!' interrupted Patrick as they all burst into fits of laughter.

'You know how settled I feel here, well, I've decided I'm going to be staying on the island for a while, quite a while actually...' she said holding hands tightly with Manos.

After sending much love, albeit virtually, she clicked the red disconnect button.

'I'm so excited Manos. It all seems real now! They were really pleased for us weren't they!'

'They were my love!' he replied planting a kiss on her forehead as he walked past her towards the balcony. She joined him, her head in a joyous whirl of excitement. Leaning against him she watched the rhythm of the sea washing up on the shore knowing without a doubt that this was where she was always meant to be.

Maria carefully unwrapped the three pieces of honey cake, a new recipe Helenka had been experimenting with, and placed them on the patio table.

'That smells good!' papa professed taking the largest portion from the napkin as her mama shook her head at him.

'How was Annys this morning love?' she asked.

'She was really good. No problem at all. As soon as she saw her friends, she was off,' replied Maria feeling more positive as the day went on.

'That's good. She'll be like her mum and love her schooldays. You were always so happy there,' she said hugging her shoulders as she walked around the table pouring the tea.

'This cake is really good!' said papa eyeing up the two remaining pieces.

'Don't even think about it!' mama said rapping his knuckles as Maria filled them in on her day so far.

Chapter Twenty Eight

'*Yassou* mama!' said a rather tentative Yannis.

Helenka turned to see her son walking towards her.

'Yannis! How are you?' she replied wiping her hands purposefully on her apron.

'I'm very well mama,' he replied.

'Sit down. I'll get us some coffees,' she said delighted her son had come.

He did as instructed. She placed the drinks on the table and took the seat opposite him. For a while they sat looking out to sea making small talk.

'Can I get you anything to eat?' she asked.

'No thanks mama. I'm fine. I must say though the smells coming from the kitchen are as delicious as ever!' he remarked.

'It's probably the lamb stifado. Your favourite! I'll send you home with some to reheat for your supper if you like.'

'That'd be lovely thanks,' he replied fidgeting slightly.

Observing her son's body language she fell silent and waited for him to open up with what he was really there for. He took a deep breath and began to share his story.

The Little Blue and White House

She listened intently to everything, stood up slowly walking around the table taking both his hands in hers, and bent down to kiss the top of his head gently. No words were needed. He stood up in front of her, turned and she wrapped her arms protectively around his thin frame, his unshed tears trickled from his closed eyes. Hugging him tightly she whispered how proud his papa would have been of him and that he had just lost his path for a while. He sighed with relief. He had so much to look forward to and felt a sense of peace to be back where he belonged.

Maria made her way along the twisty track down the hillside back into the village. Along the boardwalk she spotted Keri and Manos walking in opposite directions. She supposed he was off to the boatyard, and Keri looked as if she was heading to the little blue and white house.

'Keri!' she shouted quickening her step.

She turned and raised her hand in acknowledgment, slowing down while her friend caught up.

'Hi Maria! How's it going?'

'Hi! Good thanks,' she replied greeting her with an embrace. 'The day's going so quickly! I thought it would drag!'

'That's good then. Are you okay for time?' Keri asked following her through the side gate and onto the terrace.

'Yes, I've got an hour before setting off to pick Annys up. Have a seat,' she said pointing to the two deckchairs at the end of the patio. 'Would you mind putting the parasol up? It's a bit of a suntrap here, but it catches a lovely breeze off the sea. I'll fetch us some cold drinks,' she said disappearing into the house.

Keri settled herself down and watched the motion of the waves washing up onto the rocks below. She smiled to herself as she thought about the previous evening with Manos. She was roused from her reverie by the sound of Maria's footsteps coming towards her.

'Penny for them…?' she remarked putting the drinks onto the low stone wall.

Keri giggled. 'Where do I start? I've got so much to tell you – I don't think we'll get any planning done today!' And with that she recounted the last 24 hours to a thrilled Maria.

Keri's story told, Maria began to share with her friend how things were going with Alex, with a twinkle in her eye, Keri noticed.

'I'm really happy for you both! And he absolutely adores Annys! Anyone can see that!'

'She worships the ground he walks on, follows him around like a puppy!'

'Oh that reminds me, how's Tasha doing? Is she settling down alright?'

'She's gorgeous. I'll go and fetch her; she can have a run about. It gets a bit hot out here for her sometimes. I took her for a short walk earlier before going to mama and papas, but she's better inside where it's cooler during the day. She's got the whole of the kitchen to play in. To be honest, she spends most of her time sleeping at the moment.'

Maria leaned over the kitchen stable door and scooped up the little wriggling ball of fluff, holding her to her breast as she walked across to Keri.

'Look at you!' Keri exclaimed and caressed her fluffy face and ears.

Maria bent down and placed the writhing pup gently

onto the floor. With her soft paws eager to explore and her tail wagging ferociously she raced around the terrace sniffing the ground and investigating the open space with much energy. A soft white feather falling to the ground from a seabird flying high above caught the pups attention. She stopped in her tracks, head to one side with this new phenomenon, watching it fixedly as it floated through the air and came to rest in front of her. Gamboling towards it she sniffed up, lifting her head as it stuck to her wet nose. Keri knelt down in front of her and removed it gently. Tasha jumped onto her lap and started climbing up her clothes, sharp nails piercing into her skin as she made her way upwards to check out her new playmate. Reaching her destination she licked Keri's face with unconditional love. Keri breathed in the sweet puppy scent as she snuggled into her neck, inhaling deeply, relishing the strangely intoxicating aroma. She lifted her into the air and Tasha reached out with one of her paws in an attempt to make contact with one of Keri's earrings.

'No you don't!' she said throwing back her head. 'You're a little monkey! But so adorable!' She kissed her black shiny nose and popped her back onto the floor. Tasha scurried off as soon as her paws touched the ground onto her next adventure which involved chasing some leaves that had blown into the corner.

'She's gorgeous Maria!'

'She is indeed! A little rascal at times but so cute! Her and Annys are inseparable,' she replied as the pup happily scampered around the terrace.

Manos slapped Alex on the back as he turned to make his way home.

'I'm really pleased for you mate! You make a lovely couple and Annys loves you to bits! It's about time you got together…and don't worry, Demetrius would be happy with everything. I know he would. Believe me!'

'Cheers mate! It means a lot to me that does!' Alex replied smiling. 'Great news about you and Keri too! We've got some celebrating to do!'

Helenka divided the steaming pan of remaining *stifado*, after dishing up a plateful for Yannis earlier, into two casserole dishes – one for Maria, Alex, and herself for their early tea, and the larger of the two for the evening service. For Annys she would prepare her favourite pizza with double pepperoni on top. She busied herself in the kitchen singing happily as she peeled vegetables for the evening meals. Katrina would be with her soon to take over the preparations. Mark would be back from his break in England next week, but Katrina had been more than happy to take on a few extra hours here and there. Maria helping out now and again when Annys was at school had been very welcome. And as for Theo, she thought fondly, giving her a hand in the bar, making sure everything was in order at the end of the day, and always there to share a nightcap with her. She had a lot to be thankful for and plenty to smile about today, thrilled with the news that Keri was staying on the island and moving in with Manos. Yannis' return to the bay and his new venture pleased her beyond words. She pondered how easy it was to lose your way in the rich tapestry of life.

At the school gates Maria waited patiently for the bell to sound.

'I hope she's had a good day,' she said not taking her eyes off the main entrance.

'Bet she's loved it!' Alex reassured her squeezing her hand tightly.

'Here they come!' she cried at the sound of the bell and the door opening wide moments later. 'There she is!'

'Mummy! Alex!' yelled a very excited Annys as she ran towards them.

'Come here my darling!' said Maria kneeling down and wrapping her arms around her daughter.

'Alex! You came too!' Annys squealed and pulled the three of them into a massive hug.

Annys skipped along the boardwalk towards Ellas sharing the experience of her first day at school.

'Look mummy and Alex! Over there!' she exclaimed pointing to a large cruise ship gliding majestically along in the distance. 'We learnt all about different kinds of holidays today. I told the teacher about how people go on holiday on a big ship like that one and how it goes past our house!'

'That sounds super darling!' said Maria proudly.

'Let's lift you up onto my shoulders Annys, then we can wave to the people onboard,' Alex said bending down for her to climb up.

'Look! They're waving back!' announced an ecstatic Annys.

Helenka hummed along to one of her favourite songs on the radio whilst putting the finishing touches to the pizza, when Annys ran up behind her jolting her out of her daydreams.

'Helenka! I liked school. We told stories! I did mine

about a ship and we just saw it over there. It was the same colours, and the people on holiday waved to me!'

Smiling down to a breathless Annys she wiped her hands on her apron and kissed her cheek.

'That sounds great my darling! Did you have lots of fun?'

'I did! I can't wait for tomorrow to see all my friends again,' she replied racing back out of the kitchen like a whirlwind.

'Mummy, can I play on the beach? Alex can help me build sandcastles.'

'Fine by me!' declared Alex turning around to make his way back down the steps to the beach with a very excited Annys leading the way.

'Come on Alex! Quickly!' she shouted grabbing his hand to hurry him along.

'Looks like you've got no choice on that one!' Maria called after him. 'Annys! Fifteen minutes please! No longer! Helenka is making your favourite pizza.'

'Okay mummy!' she called from the edge of the sand as she took off her shoes and socks. 'Alex will tell me when it's time!'

He gave a thumbs up over his shoulder.

Sandcastles built, moats to guard them, waiting for the seawater to creep up steadily, they all watched from the taverna's terrace as they tucked into Helenka's specially prepared meal. Annys polished off the last piece of her pizza.

'Can I go now and see if the water has come up to my sandcastle yet?' she asked.

'You can. What do you say to Helenka for dinner?' prompted Maria.

'Thank you for my pizza and my drink.'

'That's my pleasure darling. I'm glad you liked it,' said Helenka clearing the plates away.

'Here, let me help you,' said Alex as he moved everything else off the table.

Maria stood up and watched Annys make her way confidently back down to the beach. Alex came up behind her and placed his hand gently over hers on the wooden railing.

'You okay love?' he asked.

'Yes, fine thanks. I was just thinking how she takes everything in her stride,' she replied dreamily.

'She is one very happy little lady. She's a credit to you my love!' he said warmly.

'Thanks,' she replied squeezing his hand.

Helenka refreshed their drinks and took them over to where they were standing at the far end of the veranda.

'Thanks very much for our dinner,' she said taking the drinks from Helenka and placing them carefully on the wider part of the railing. Helenka put the empty tray on a nearby table and joined them.

'Sounds like she's had a great first day!' said Helenka.

'She really has. It's been a good day all round. It was lovely of you to do a special meal for us all. Annys loves your pizzas.'

'My pleasure! She does indeed,' replied Helenka.

'We've got something to tell you,' said Maria still holding Alex's hand. 'Me and Alex are going to make a go of it. We've not gone into this lightly. It just feels so right.'

'Oh my darling! That's such wonderful news! I've seen the twinkle in your eyes for a while now. Congratulations both of you.' Helenka said happily. 'Do you know, that's the third bit of good news I've had today!'

Helenka recalled her day to them as they stood together under the dappled shade of the lemon tree watching Annys playing on the beach in front of them.

Keri took a step back to admire their efforts. Most of her stock was now neatly displayed on the white silk cloth draped over the upturned empty storage boxes of varying sizes on the trestle table. Just the finishing touches to be done, she thought, pleased with the display and well worth the crack of dawn early start. It had been a busy week for Maria and herself, culminating with plentiful stock and a good selection of jewellery for the customers to either buy or view before placing an order for bespoke items. Alex was helping Manos with the final heavier pieces of artwork.

'Looking good mate! I didn't realise you had so many paintings!' said Alex.

'There's still some back at the studio, but that's it for today though,' Manos said stowing the empty packaging under the table. 'Thanks for this Alex.'

'Yes, thank you Alex,' said Keri as he made his way past the front of the stall.

'It's the least I could do. Looks great by the way! I'm off to pick Annys up, we're going to the beach with a picnic this morning. Maria will be with you soon. Hope it all goes well.'

Keri took a swig of water from her bottle and popped her wide-brimmed straw hat on her head.

'We did it my love!' Manos whispered into her ear.

'I know! I wasn't sure we could pull it off in such a short time, but we did!'

Throughout the square a cacophony of sounds filled the air as the traders dragged their old wooden barrows, passed down through the generations, over the cobbles. Children played in the narrow streets around the square knowing they'd be in line for a piece of fresh fruit, expertly thrown over to them from the stallholders, their cheeky little faces full of gratitude. Rosy cheeks all around!

Keri reached forward to tweak a few pieces, pleased with how the early morning light was reflecting on them.

'I can't believe how word has got around about our stuff! How far away are the other two markets who want us to join them?' Keri asked.

'One's only a few kilometers away. The other is on the far side of the mountain. There's no direct route but it draws in the crowds, mainly holidaymakers looking for a keepsake to take back home,' he replied pointing up the hillside beyond the top of the village. It's about an hour away, but definitely worth it. Stalls on that market are hard to come by.'

Alex and Annys settled down on the blanket under the shade of the rocky outcrop at the end of the beach, scattered around them buckets and spades, bats and balls, and a fishing net for the rockpools. Alex opened the picnic prepared by Maria with a selection of their favourite foods as the seagulls swooped down from the burnt orange cliffs to investigate what they might be able to scavenge.

'Hope you've left me some lunch!' Maria called as she walked towards them.

'Mummy! Come and sit here with us!' Annys called out with a mouthful of tuna and cheese pita bread.

'Hi love!' said Alex as she knelt down to kiss them both.

'Good timing! We couldn't wait any longer. How did it go today?'

She took a sandwich from the cool bag. 'Yes, really good! We sold over 40 items and took another dozen orders for personalised pieces. Keri and Manos are finishing up, and I've just dropped some boxes off at home. Can't believe it's only been a week since our first stall. It's really taken off!'

'That's great news Maria!'

'And what have you two been up to then? I could see your amazing sandcastle from over the other side of the beach!'

'It's a princess castle! That's why it's got a big tower of course,' explained Annys.

'That makes sense,' she replied. 'It is very tall. I like the shell windows.'

'That's what princesses have on their castles!' Annys said proudly 'Alex said so!'

'True story,' he said with a cheeky wink.

'That's the last of the things from the van,' Manos said shutting the doors and making his way into the boatyard.

'Lovely!' replied Keri stacking up the boxes neatly against the wall at the back of the studio. 'I just need to take this box to Maria's later, so we can make the rest of the orders up tomorrow,' she said placing it on the worktop nearest to the doorway.

'We did well today,' he said pulling her towards him.

'It was fantastic! We've both had so many enquiries. We make a good team!' she replied as he drew her closer sliding his hands into her back pockets with ease and reaching down to kiss her. The sweetness of his lips pressing firmly on hers made her heart skip a beat. She reciprocated, wrapping her arms around his waist bringing him closer. She could feel his heart beating faster. They separated slowly.

'Being with you is so magical,' he said breathlessly. 'I love you so much.'

She gazed into his eyes, twisting a strand of his dark brown hair that had fallen in front of his face and tucked it behind his ear. She loved this man to the core.

'And I love you too,' she said closing her eyes and leaning against him breathing in his musky scent. The hairs on her neck danced with delight, images passing by of their time spent together and their adventures yet to come.

They reached the little blue and white house and dropped the sandy bags and towels onto the patio. Annys raced over to the wall waving frantically at the massive ship on the horizon.

'Do you think they can see us mummy?'

'I'm sure they can darling! Let's all wave!' she said lifting both arms high into the air.

Alex joined them picking one of the towels up off the floor and shaking it from left to right as you would a flag on a stick.

As if on cue the ship's horn signaled loudly and reverberated throughout the bay. Annys squealed with excitement.

'They saw us! They saw us!' she shouted skipping around the terrace.

'I think they did!' declared Alex scooping her up and spinning her around high up off the ground.

Moments later the ship disappeared from view sailing slowly along towards its next port of call.

'I'd love to go on a cruise!' said Maria to Alex. 'Demetrius never fancied it. He always said he spent enough time working on the sea in his fishing boat without spending his downtime on one!'

'That makes sense. I can understand his reasoning,' he said helping Maria shake and fold the beach towels. 'I've got a cousin who works the ships. He was always trying to get me to join him, but to be honest I'd rather be on one as a guest, other than working on one!'

'I love the romance of it all, sailing away into the sunset with a glass of champagne after a day ashore exploring exotic places and looking forward to waking up in a different port the next morning,' she said happily.

'I'm sold! he announced. 'There's loads to do on board you know. All the food and entertainment, I hear the shows are really good. There're shops, swimming pools, spas and plenty of bars and lounges.'

'It's something we could look at in the future,' replied Maria, realising it was the first time she had dared to dream of a future without Demetrius.

Chapter Twenty Nine

Helenka busied herself in the taverna placing lunchtime menus on each table, attaching white plastic clips to the edges to hold the cloths in place, and folding the crisp linen napkins absentmindedly. She stopped and looked out to sea. How different to the dreadful rolling seas that took away the lives of their loved ones, she thought. A white butterfly with black veins and golden hues rested softly on the back of one of the blue wooden chairs – ironically, Dino's favourite seat on the veranda. She watched it, captivated by its beauty. She could see him now, drink in one hand, smooth worry beads the colour of rich earth in the other, looking out to sea, watching the comings and goings in the bay.

'Come on! Snap out of it!' she admonished herself and continued with her preparations for the midday service.

George passed Anna the last pieces of jewellery for the window display. She had made it her job over the years to reorganise it regularly and loved nothing more than people watching, perfecting the art of stocking shelves whilst keeping a close eye on what was happening in the street outside!

'George! Quick! Look! Who's that with Yannis?'

'It's probably a customer walking into Ellas at the same time!' George replied tutting at his wife's nosiness. 'Come away from the window. We've done now!'

She reversed slowly out of the window vestibule, taking one last look across the road.

'He looks familiar. Wait! I know! We saw him the other week. I don't trust him one bit. He's got shifty eyes!'

She took a cloth from her apron pocket and moved outside with haste, wiping imaginary marks off the already gleaming windows.

'Yannis!' she bellowed across the road. 'Not seen you for a while. How are you?'

He turned, saying something she couldn't quite catch to his co-conspirator.

'I'm good thank you for asking. You and George alright?' he replied continuing on his way.

'We are. Just trying to get these marks off the window…' she said into the air as they had already made their escape down the path at the side of Ellas.

She turned to George who was standing in the open doorway.

'He's hiding something. Couldn't get away quick enough if you ask me!'

'No-one is asking you Anna,' he replied casually, quite used to her overcurious mind. 'Keri's jewellery is selling like hot cakes. I think we should increase the order. I'll talk to her when she gets back from Ireland.'

'Such a lovely girl. I'm glad she's going to be moving in with Manos. I just wish that brother of his would sort himself out!'

And with that she disappeared into the stockroom at the back of the shop with the empty packaging. George sighed, shook his head, and followed her steadily.

'Sorry about that Christophe. She's neighbourhood watch!' Yannis said rolling his eyes.

'No worries!' he replied dismissively.

'Mama. I'd like to introduce you to Christophe Dafoe,' he said as they walked up the wooden steps onto the terrace. 'Christophe, this is Helenka Papadopoulous.'

'Very pleased to meet you Mrs Papadopoulous,' he said shaking her hand firmly.

'And you too Christophe,' she replied politely. 'Please, call me Helenka.'

'It's a lovely place you have here…Helenka,' he said taking it all in.

'Thank you. It's been in the family for many years,' she said walking towards the bar. 'Can I get you a drink? Hot or cold?'

'May I have a black coffee please?'

'Of course. Yannis, coffee too?'

'Please mama,' he replied giving Christophe a short tour of the taverna, pointing out photos of his ancestors adorning the walls, many faded with the passage of time.

She placed the drinks onto the table. 'There you go. Help yourself to sugar.'

'Thank you very much,' Christophe said taking the cup nearest to him. 'The views are spectacular over the bay.'

'They certainly are. We are very blessed.'

Over coffee they had quite a chat, with Helenka talking about their family; the boys when they were growing up;

Dino's tragic death; and how the villagers had come together over the years for many a celebration at Ellas.

'Anyway, that's enough about me,' she said to Christophe refreshing their coffees. 'Tell me about yourself and what brings you here.'

'There's not that much to tell really,' he replied.

'Come on. Don't be shy!' she said encouragingly.

Before long he found himself sharing details of his life that he had never shared with anyone – not even his psychiatrist! Colourful memories as a young child rushed to the forefront of his mind, things he thought had been lost forever. Shadows from the past came forward as if somehow unlocked, relieving him of this heavy burden he had carried with him from boy to man. He leaned back in his chair and sighed. Helenka was like the mother he'd never had. A feeling of calm came over him as he fixed his eyes on the golden sand, still moist from the retreating tide.

'Sorry about that...' he said regaining his composure. 'I don't know where all that came from.'

'It's fine Christophe. I do understand you know. Grief can be a strange thing and rears its head many years later. We try to bury things out of sight but when the time is right it all comes flooding to the surface. Today is your day.'

Yannis placed the empty cups back onto the tray and took them into the kitchen, emerging moments later with a jug of water and three glasses.

'I was telling mama yesterday about my new venture into the world of hospitality,' he said pouring an iced water for each of them.

'Yes, it all sounds just the job,' said Helenka.

'It'll be a good partnership. With my head for business

and Yannis' roots in hospitality we'll be learning from each other throughout the build, and then with Yannis in place to manage the hotel afterwards it should work well.'

'The hotel designs are wonderful mama! All the mod-cons you expect nowadays, but the building will look like an authentic Greek hotel that's been there for years.'

'Indeed,' interjected Christophe. 'Your son's had some brilliant ideas for the build too. He's far more in touch than I am with what is needed in such a development.'

'It sounds like you two will make a good team!' she said raising her glass of water to toast them both. 'Here's to the future! *Yamas!*'

The three of them clinked glasses in the air in celebration.

Keri propped her mobile up against the pile of coasters on the coffee table and settled back into her chair. Within seconds her best friend's face filled the screen.

'Hi Emma! It's so lovely to see you!'

'Keri! And you too! Look at your golden tan! It suits you!'

'Thanks. To be honest I've not had much time lately for sunbathing. I've been busy...erm...working...'

'Working? Intriguing! What's been happening then since we last spoke?'

An hour later, and after a much-needed catch-up, Keri disconnected the call, their conversation racing through her mind, pleased her friend was happy with the news that she was staying on the island and moving in with Manos. Equally good news that Emma had met *'the love of her life, Chris. It's early days, but he's the one!'* she recalled her friend saying excitedly. They had arranged to meet up when Keri and Manos returned from their trip to Ireland, as she would be joining him on a business trip at the end of the month.

Humming happily to herself Keri continued packing for their trip.

Mark dropped his bags onto the floor of the apartment and flung the balcony doors wide open in the hope of lessening the stuffiness within. He stood quietly on the balcony, his eyes closed, feeling the warmth of the late afternoon sunshine prickling his face. He'd only been away for a couple of weeks, but oh how he'd missed this place! As pleased as he was to go back to England to see family and friends, this was where he belonged. Turning to go back inside to unpack he heard a rustling sound coming from the bushes at the side of the window and went to investigate.

'Felix! Come here my boy! Did you miss me?' he said lifting him carefully out of the shrubs. 'Let's get you a saucer of water. You been waiting for me?'

He placed him gently onto the floor along with a drink and started unpacking. Felix joined him after quenching his thirst, weaving in and out of his legs, rubbing his body with determination and purring with pleasure as he did so. Mark knelt down on the floor to tickle his ears.

'Do you know…I thought I'd missed the hills and valleys at home, stone walls and cottages…but nah! Give me these views any day! Don't you agree Felix?'

'You talking to yourself again?' joked Theo as he sauntered past the apartment catching the tail end of his conversation with the cat. Mark lifted him up.

'He's happy listening to me jabbering on! And he doesn't answer back!'

'Ha! Ha! Welcome back. We've all missed you – it's been very quiet!' Theo laughed out loud again.

'Cheers mate! It's good to be back. I'll pop down to Ellas later.'

'See you there! I'll leave you two to carry on with your catch-up!'

They dashed through the car park in the torrential rain dragging their suitcases behind them. Keri frantically pressed random buttons on the key fob to unlock the hire car. Throwing the luggage into the boot they clambered in, soaked to the skin.

'Welcome to sunny Ireland!' she declared starting the engine.

'At least in Greece the rain is warm!' Manos countered shivering.

'Mammy's doing special hot chocolate topped with marshmallows. That'll soon warm you up!'

'Is that really a thing? he questioned pulling a face.

'It most certainly is!' she replied leaving the airport behind them.

Moya emptied the last few plates from the dishwasher, dried her hands and looked through the kitchen window again. The rain lashed against it and the wind howled around the guttering.

'They're here Patrick!' she called out hurrying towards the front door.

'Bet they're drenched!' said Patrick as he joined her in the hallway.

Running across the driveway to the porch they were

greeted with the smell of warm soda bread. Keri kicked off her wet sandals and stepped onto the welcome mat, the same mat that had welcomed many visitors over the years.

'Come on it! Let's get you both dried off,' said Patrick taking their cases off them and putting them at the side of the radiator. 'Terrible weather!'

Hugs exchanged, they all moved into the warmth of the living room.

'How was the flight?' asked Patrick, while Moya went to get towels for them. 'There's been quite a few cancelled today with the poor weather.'

'Bit rough for the last hour, and not the best of landings,' replied Manos taking one of the towels from Moya.

'That's an understatement! It was throwing us around all over the place!'

'You get yourselves dried off and I'll make some drinks to warm you up. Do you like hot chocolate Manos?'

'That would be lovely thanks Moya,' he replied.

'Marshmallows on the top?' she said disappearing into the kitchen.

'Perfect!' he said trying not to make eye contact with Keri who he could see smirking in the corner.

'*Kalispera* Helenka!' said Mark as he climbed the steps two at a time.

'*Kalispera! Kalos orises piso!*' Welcome back!' she replied walking over to greet him. 'Did you have a good break? How was England?'

'Oh you know…very wet! It was nice to see the family again though. What's been happening while I've been away?'

'Take a seat and I'll fill you in,' she replied heading over to the bar for refreshments and the rota for the next few weeks. 'Theo said you were back.'

She handed him the rota and picked up the drinks from the bar.

'Thanks Helenka,' he said taking one from her. 'The shifts look good.'

'Well I knew you said you would like some more. Hope that's okay.'

'They're perfect!' he replied typing them into his mobile. 'Has it been busy?'

'Yes, very much so, but that's no bad thing,' she replied taking the seat opposite. 'With Manos and Keri in Ireland, Alex has been keeping an eye on things at the boatyard with the new lad, and Maria's working hard on the jewellery for the craft fairs.'

'Yes, Alex sent me a text and mentioned it was all hands to the deck.'

'Yannis is back in the bay. He's started work with Christophe, the Frenchman, on the hotel development in the south. He's also working with Manos on the plans for the boatyard extension and villa on the land at the back,' she said.

He nodded sipping his drink not wanting to interrupt her with the fact that he already knew all this thanks to Alex's regular updates. He could see that she was pleased Yannis had sorted himself out but would never share with her that he knew a lot more about the situation than she thought he did.

'How's Annys getting on at school?' he asked.

'Absolutely loving it she is!' she replied beaming. 'Settled down straight away.'

'That's good news. Anyway, I'd better get off and leave you to it. I'll see you in the morning,' he said finishing his drink.

'It's great to have you back Mark,' she said clearing the table and replacing the rota under the bar.

'Thanks again for the shifts. Much appreciated,' he called over his shoulder.

Yannis studied the plans, turning them this way and that. Everything seemed in order. The builders were in place, made up of local companies and a couple of Christophe's established construction workers from his team who had been with him for a number of years and familiar with how he worked. All the foundations were in, and the structure was taking shape. The materials for the first part of the build were now on site and it was a hive of activity. True to his word Christophe had taken a step back and let him get on with managing the project on the ground. He trusted him to do a good job and so far was pleased with what he saw.

In his spare time he was helping to clear the land at the back of the boatyard and keeping things ticking over until Manos and Keri returned. The plans for the extended art studio and the villa had been approved before their trip so it was all moving forward.

Helenka took Kimba for her early evening stroll along the boardwalk heading towards the boatyard. In the distance she could see her son in the overgrown brambles on the land at the back. Heading towards her was Theo.

'Helenka!' he called out raising his hand.

'Theo, my friend!' she replied smiling.

'Yannis is cracking on with clearing that land,' he observed.

'He is indeed. Looks like it's going really well,' she said slowing down and unclipping Kimba's lead so she could have a wander and a good sniff around.

'He seems much happier,' he said bending down to pat Kimba's head.

'Oh he does Theo! I'm so pleased. His new job's doing him good. He's back to his old self again. I don't mind telling you I was quite worried about him, but I think we're going to be alright.'

'He'll be fine now,' he agreed.

'Yes, I think so. Dino would be so proud of the boys,' she said reflectively.

'He would my dear,' he replied putting a comforting arm on her shoulders. 'Right. I'll see you back at Ellas after your stroll. Take your time. There's no rush.'

They continued on their way, Helenka heading for the rocky outcrop where the chiseled cliffs dropped down into the emerald sea.

Upon reaching the taverna Theo looked back to see Yannis wending his way down the hillside to his mama. He sighed contentedly.

'I don't think I'd ever get used to driving on the left,' joked Manos as Keri negotiated a particularly tight bend at the foot of the Galtees on the way to Limerick for some essential clothes shopping.

'At least the roads here are tarmacked!' she sniggered.

'That's true,' he laughed. 'How much further is it?'

'About half an hour,' she replied 'We'll get some lunch

before we hit the shops. Walking around the foothills has given me quite an appetite. What about you?'

'Sounds like a good idea,' he said taking in the lush green scenery as they sped along the winding country lanes. 'Think we've walked off Moya's full Irish breakfast; if that's even possible!' he exclaimed patting his stomach.

'I'm pleased with this car,' she remarked. 'It's not bad at all, a bit bigger than my old one, but comfier and much more economical.'

'What did you have before?' he asked.

'A Peugeot 208. I sold it before I went travelling. The money came in very handy.'

'That makes sense, saves it just sitting there too,' he said as she pulled into another layby so Manos could take more photos on his phone. He was hoping to capture some of the views on canvas and create some artwork for their new home to remind Keri of Ireland. He'd done quite a few sketches in his art pad too which was never far from his side.

'Look how quickly the mist comes down over the mountains. Two minutes ago those mountain tops were as clear as a bell,' he said snapping away. 'And the autumn colours are just something else.'

'It is beautiful isn't it,' she replied wrapping her arms around him and breathing in his familiar scent.

Leaving the mountains behind they reached their destination of Limerick, a typically southern Irish City on the Shannon estuary. King John's castle stood proudly on the banks of the river, another photo opportunity thought Manos as he recalled Patrick mentioning it the previous day as one of Keri's favourite places to visit when she was a young girl. Walking from the car park into town Keri explained

The Little Blue and White House

that it was the third largest City and held the title of National City of Culture in 2014, putting the place well and truly on the map. Today it boasted three shopping centres, the largest of which they were heading.

After a light lunch in one of Keri's favourite riverside cafes they hit the shops. The shopping mall was a typical 1970s concrete structure with high cathedral like ceilings and walkways shooting off in all directions, with music following shoppers from one store to another. Top end designer shops worthy of catwalk status rubbed shoulders with charity shops with their wares spilling out into the mall.

'I think that's everything,' said Keri looking around to make sure no shop had gone untouched. 'How about you? Do you need anything else?'

'No, I think I'm done. I didn't expect buying all these winter clothes, but I suppose they'll come in handy on those cold wintry evenings back home!' he teased.

They placed their bags into the boot of the car and made their way home.

'If I forget to tell you later, I've had a lovely day! Not been on a proper shopping trip for a long while,' she said. 'And we've both got new clothes for tomorrow's party.'

'True, but what was wrong with my black trousers and white shirt?'

'Nothing, unless you want folk to mistake you for a member of staff!' she joked. 'At the pub we're going to for the Ceili evening all the staff wear black trousers and white shirts! It's a jeans and baggy jumper kind of place for customers.'

Moya finished setting the dining table. She checked her watch, expecting them to arrive shortly, and made her way into the kitchen to put the finishing touches to the meal, a hearty Irish stew with side dish of colcannon.

'We're home!' Keri called as she unlocked the front door. 'Oh that smells lovely!'

Manos followed behind laden with the heavier bags.

'I don't need to ask if you had a good day – not with all those bags!' she said. 'Dinner will be an hour or so. Would you both like a cup of tea, we were just about to have one?'

'Yes please Moya,' Manos replied as Keri made her way into the lounge where Patrick was sitting reading his evening paper. Keri planted a kiss on top of his head.

'Hi daddy! You both had a good day?' she asked taking the seat to the side of him.

'Very good thanks. Looks like you've been busy!' he replied eyeing up the bags in the hallway.

Manos joined them with a tray of tea followed closely by Moya.

'I had another look at your villa and boatyard drawings, hope you don't mind. They really are quite something,' commented Patrick.

'Of course, no problem. I'm really pleased with them. They're not a million miles away from my initial sketches. The architect's done a great job,' replied Manos. 'Glad you like them. I'm going to ring Yannis later to check all is okay. He's overseeing everything for us.'

'What did you buy today?' asked Moya curiously.

They both burst into fits of laughter.

'We'll put it this way mammy…if it was left to Manos he'd look like one of the waiters at the pub!'

Faraway the pearlescent moon lit up the serene navy sea spreading shimmers of light like shards of glass on its surface. Yannis sat on the old grey stone steps, polished to a shine by generations of inhabitants before him, sipping his beer straight from the bottle, his hands calloused by the manual work he was unaccustomed to. It was good to be back in the village, he thought. He'd certainly missed these views and the calmness of the bay. The ground floor apartment he was renting might be a bit rough around the edges, and in need of a coat of paint, but to Yannis it was home, and he hadn't felt like that about anywhere for quite some time. Placing his empty bottle onto the ground at the side of him he stretched his legs over the steps, the sea creeping gently up the harbour wall just feet away. Tasting the saltiness in the air he licked his lips, his musings interrupted by his mobile ringing in his pocket.

'*Yasas Manos!*' he answered looking at the screen and making his way inside.

Manos joined the others in the living room for a nightcap, taking the proffered tumbler of Irish whiskey from Patrick.

'Thank you,' he said sitting in the seat next to Keri. 'That was Yannis. It's all going really well with the land clearance for the villa, and the foundations are already in at the back of the boatyard.'

'That was quick!' she exclaimed as he shared the photos Yannis had just sent. 'It's really taking shape!'

'Yeah, Christophe's got some of his builders on it too, in between working on that hotel build. Mama can't praise him enough!'

'Helenka is a good judge of character!' said Keri.

'She certainly is!' Moya added. 'Always sees the good in everyone.'

They took their seats, fastened the seatbelts, and listened to the cabin crew giving their safety instructions. To the side of them the engines roared loudly fighting against the wind. Seconds later they were bumping along the runway gaining speed before taking flight and pushing through the clouds. A ding throughout the cabin instructed the attendants that the plane had reached its cruising altitude. Stowing their seats away they sprang into action with much efficiency engaging with customers as they passed through the narrow aisle with refreshments, perfumes and aftershaves, and an abundance of souvenirs of the flight.

Keri looked out of the small oval window as the plane gained altitude, mesmerised by the cloud formations beneath them. Manos took her hand.

'You alright love?' he asked softly.

She rested her head on his shoulder and smiled up at him with watery eyes.

'I'm fine thanks. I've had such a lovely time with mammy and daddy. It just brought home to me how much I missed them when I was travelling. Clearing my room and packing everything up to be shipped out made it all seem so real. I'm not just moving home, down the road, but to a new country, and a new life,' she shared with her soulmate. 'Don't get me wrong, I can't wait to move to the island, to move in with you, and for us to start our new adventure. It's just… sometimes I realise how much I miss them…'

'Come here,' he said wrapping his arms around her. 'It's a massive change for you, but I'll be with you every step of

The Little Blue and White House

the way. Yes, you're bound to miss them, but it's only a short flight away. We can go back and forth as much as you like... now I've got my woolly jumpers! And they can come to Galazios as often as they want to. It'll be like a second home for them. Don't forget we're having a guest room, and it's got their name on it.'

'What did I do to deserve you,' she said reaching up to kiss him.

'Can I get you some drinks?' asked the air hostess.

'Oh yes, two glasses of champagne please,' Manos replied letting go of Keri's hand and reaching into his pocket for his debit card. He swiped the machine and took the two small plastic bottles and glasses off her and placed them onto the tray in front of Keri.

'*Slainte* my darling!' he said raising his glass to hers. 'To our future.'

'*Slainte!*' she replied, her Irish accent stronger than ever. 'New beginnings.'

'Bit smaller bottles than the ones at the party!' he joked emptying the remaining champagne into their glasses.

'Yes, just a bit. I have no idea where Emma got that Methuselah bottle from. She mentioned her partner had contacts in the business and had sent it over. It was a lovely surprise she was able to fly back for the party and really good to catch up with everyone.'

'It was a fantastic evening, great learning some Irish dancing too. I loved the sounds from the bodhrans and fiddles. Mind you, those pipes had a life of their own!' he laughed.

'We had some good craic! I'd no idea mammy and daddy were getting everyone together like that. It was quite a party! I love a Ceilidh evening with the old Irish music, dancing, and the folklore. Hey, we ought to have one at Ellas if Helenka's up for it.'

'She'd love it! You know mama! To be fair, some of the instruments and music aren't dissimilar,' he said. 'We could turn the taverna into an Irish pub for a night for some toe-tapping and a singalong, replace Mythos with Guinness and make sure there's some Irish Whiskey. I'm sure that would go down well.'

'And I've got some great Irish recipes Helenka might like to try,' she added happily.

Making its final approach the plane banked sharply to the left treating its passengers to glimpses of small scattered golden islands sitting in a cerulean blue sea. Manos pointed out and named all the different islands and as their altitude dropped further, the one Keri would call home.

'Look Manos! There's Maria's little blue and white house on the headland,' she said excitedly.

'That's it. If you follow the coastline along to the rocky outcrop before the next bay, you can just about make out the boatyard and the land at the side where the villa will be,' he explained to a fascinated Keri.

'Oh yes! I can see it!' she said with delight.

The plane gracefully tilted one final time before moving inland on its descent to the runway. Keri squeezed Manos' hand tighter.

'We're home Manos…I'm finally home…' she whispered happily as its wheels gently kissed the runway.

Chapter Thirty

~ One Year Later ~

'The transformation from the rundown outbuilding with its leaky roof and damp peeling walls to what stands here today is all down to you my friends,' said Maria from her podium on the narrow sea wall. 'It's now a thing of beauty… and no leaks!'

Everyone laughed in agreement.

'We wanted to get you all together as a thank you for your hard work. Each and every one of you have been part of this journey. Keri and I are thrilled to bits with our new workshop. It'll be so much easier working from here with our growing business and certainly a lot more spacious than the spare room!'

She turned to face Alex.

'You made this happen Alex. Without you it wouldn't even have got off the ground.'

'Teamwork my darling!' he said lifting her down from her platform. 'Let's get this party started!'

As the meat sizzled on the barbecue all the other food

was brought out from the kitchen and placed onto the trestle table in the shaded corner of the terrace. The door of the refurbished outbuilding remained open, and people drifted in and out exclaiming their surprise at how bright it now was.

'What a grand job!' declared Theo.

'Much bigger than I remember from when I used to come down here with my parents and it was overflowing with Maria's grandpapa's fishing tackle,' Spiros commented.

The room itself was long and narrow with whitewashed walls, spotlights along the ceiling and wall lights for the intricate work that the nature of the job demanded. A bench ran the length of the building with two leather stools tucked neatly underneath. Floor to ceiling storage cupboards at the far end housed the larger equipment and materials, with smaller drawers and baskets covering the wall above the worktop. Either side of the window overlooking the sea, nooks and crannies filled with an array of boxes containing gemstones and beads, clasps and wires, and a whole manner of delicate components needed to create their exquisite pieces. An Aladdin's cave of precious jewels ready for the picking.

'Maria, my darling,' said Helenka taking her hand. 'It looks absolutely wonderful. What an amazing job you've all done!'

'Thank you. I couldn't have done it without your help. Everything you do for me and Annys, we appreciate it so very much,' Maria replied hugging her tightly.

'I love spending time with Annys, and she loves nothing more than our walks together with Tasha, Kimba, and Kayle. It's worked out really well with Theo moving into the taverna too. It's company for me and, bless him, he's taken on such a lot of the workload so that I can spend more time doing the things I love; walking with the dogs, and meeting my friends for coffee without having to rush back. And he looks out for Mark like he's his own son!'

Spiros was in deep conversation with Maria's parents about his memories of coming to see her grandparents at the little blue and white house, recalling how he would sit on the wall, legs dangling, eating fresh warm bread straight from the oven whilst his papa would help mend the nets.

Annys and Katerina skipped around the terrace giggling happily. Now in their second year at school they were inseparable, and very much the best of friends.

Yannis and Manos turned the food over on the barbecue with practised ease, a bottle in one hand and tongs in the other.

Alex and Lela poured the champagne into glasses, gave one to Manos and started handing them out to the guests. He jumped up onto the wall and tapped the side of his glass with a spoon.

'I would like to make a toast to the girls,' said Manos. 'They've come such a long way from the cocktail fuelled evening where the seeds of their new venture were first planted to what you see today – a successful business, built on hard work and determination! Both of them have put their heart and soul into it. A few weeks ago, over more cocktails…erm…there seems to be a theme here…they were batting about some names for their business and this one was the front runner,' he said taking a small brass door plaque from his pocket. 'Please everyone, raise your glasses to the girls and *Kermar Bespoke Jewellery. Yamas*!'

With lots of cheering and whooping Keri and Maria took the plaque from Manos and held it up for all to see. He hopped off the wall and hugged them both.

'Alex and I thought it would finish off your new workshop.'

'It's fabulous!' replied Keri.

'Absolutely perfect!' said Maria as they made their way over to Alex.

'Now let's eat!' shouted Manos above the noise.

After the blackness of the night the dawn presented itself with soft golden and copper hues flooding through the open balcony window and resting upon the bedroom walls, illuminating everything in its path with calm gentle tones.

Keri stretched, swung her legs off the bed feeling the coolness of the marble floor beneath her feet, and walked slowly over to the terrace, her eyes drawn to the vista before her. She breathed in deeply filling her lungs with the fresh morning air. Birds soared high above with their balletic performance before swooping like darts, wings tucked tightly by their side piercing the smooth surface of the sea with precision on the hunt for food. Time after time they persevered until rewarded with their catch, then set off in the direction of the cliffs to gorge themselves. Her eyes settled on a small fishing boat in the distance where the sky met the sea. She watched it approach steadily towards the harbour with a trail of seabirds squawking alongside vying for the best position to retrieve the smaller fish being thrown back into the sea by the fisherman. Tearing herself away she headed for the kitchen following the smell of freshly ground coffee as it drifted along the hallway.

Up since the crack of dawn, Manos had been for a run through the village as it slept, showered, and made them some freshly squeezed orange juice. He hummed quietly as he poached the eggs and popped two slices of bread into the toaster as Keri joined him.

'Happy one month anniversary in our new home!' he said smiling.

'And to you too! I can't believe it's been a month already!' she replied wrapping her arms around his waist.

He turned to kiss her, his lips meeting hers as she melted into his arms, their bodies pressed tightly against each other.

Pop! 'That's the toast done,' he said pulling away reluctantly. 'Do you want to take the coffees onto the terrace? I'll be out in a minute with breakfast.'

Picking the mugs up from the counter she made her way back through the villa fascinated with how the early morning light brought the artwork on the walls to life. The floor to ceiling windows running along the front of the building flooded the ground floor with sunlight throughout the day. It still stopped her in her tracks when she walked through and each time treated to a whole new palette. If only she could encapsulate the colours and bottle them like a favourite perfume to keep the memory of that moment alive forever. Her eyes were drawn to Manos' paintings of Ireland – a montage of her favourite places from her childhood capturing the myths and legends of her homeland. She turned to go outside, Manos joining her moments later with two steaming plates.

'Mmmm…that's delicious!' she said between mouthfuls. 'I can never get the eggs quite right!'

'Years of practise,' he joked.

'Yesterday was great fun wasn't it.'

'It sure was,' he said finishing his last drop of coffee.

Keri took the empty plates back into the kitchen and returned with the cafetiere.

'Everyone had a good time. I think they were quite surprised with the workshop. Most of them spent the afternoon reminiscing what it was like when Maria's grandpapa kept his fishing nets in it,' said Keri topping up their mugs.

'They did indeed! It's going to be perfect for you to both work from.'

Alex and Maria walked hand in hand along the boardwalk after dropping Annys off at school.

'Do you need anything picking up in the City?' he asked. 'I've a few things to do there today.'

'I don't think so thanks. We've got everything we need to start in the workshop this morning. We're going through the order book first. Then I'm going to begin fashioning my bracelet for the wedding. I'm so excited!' she replied touching her necklace dreamily.

'Me too!' he said squeezing her hand. 'I'll put the plaque on the door this morning, then you'll be officially open for business!'

'That'll be great Alex,' she replied opening the gate. 'The party was fantastic wasn't it! Reckon everyone enjoyed themselves.'

'They certainly did my darling!' he said as they made their way over to the workshop.

'*Geia sou file mou!*' Keri called over to them from the open door.

'*Kalimera!*' replied Maria hugging her tightly.

'I hope you don't mind me letting myself in. I was a bit early, couldn't wait to get started!'

'Of course not! It's our workshop now, and spectacular it looks too!'

'And here's the finishing touch,' added Alex walking towards them with some tools.

'I'll put the kettle on,' said Maria once they'd decided on the position of the sign.

As the yacht slipped gracefully from its mooring leaving the bustle of the port behind, Christophe joined Emma at the stern taking two champagne flutes from the steward on the way. The Captain and First Officer were now in full command of the yacht as it started its journey south, with Christophe stepping down from the bridge after navigating their way through the busy harbour. A journey that would take them to the little Greek island he now thought of as home.

'Thanks Chris,' said Emma taking the proffered glass. 'Isn't it a touch early for champagne?'

'Never too early! It's five o'clock somewhere!' he winked, clinking glasses together and taking a seat at the side of her on the plush cream leather sofa that wrapped around the deck to the aft.

Moving further away from land they were treated to spectacular views of the French Riviera. The sweeping Bay of Angels with its majestic crisp white hotels adorning the grandiose promenade. To the portside, narrow buildings climbed up into the mountainous region beyond taking on warmer tones of burnt oranges, ochres, and cinnamon. Ropes and lines stored securely away they gathered speed staying close to the shoreline in the direction of Monte Carlo for lunch, before heading down to Corsica in the early evening.

The morning progressed. Over tea the girls planned a timeline for their orders. They worked well together, side by side, radio on in the background and always plenty to talk about.

'I'll get us some lunch,' said Maria. 'I've some fresh crusty bread, cheese, hummus, and tomatoes, if you fancy that.'

'Oh lovely! I'll bring lunch tomorrow,' Keri said stretching her legs.

'We can eat on the patio,' suggested Maria.

'Sounds good to me,' she replied following Maria into the kitchen. 'I'll sort some drinks out.'

'Thanks. There're some cold ones already in the fridge.'

Keri poured the drinks, dropped in some ice, and took them outside placing them on the low wall. Pulling two chairs closer together so they could easily share the platter, she sat on one and took the plates and cutlery from Maria.

'I can't wait to see Emma,' said Keri between mouthfuls. 'She said they were sailing from Monaco tonight, via Corsica, Sicily, and Malta. It should take them a couple of weeks, so they'll have a week in the bay before the wedding.'

'Eek! It's coming up so quickly! I'm going to start putting the bracelet together this afternoon. The shell's polished up beautifully and the silver hearts arrived the other day. They match this perfectly,' she said touching her necklace tenderly. 'I've made Annys and Katerina a bracelet each using silver hearts and some small beads to match the colours in their dresses.'

'They'll love that!' replied Keri wiping the last of the hummus from her plate with a chunk of bread. 'Thanks Maria, that was delicious. Lunch with a view! I can definitely get used to this.'

'My pleasure,' she replied taking the empty plates into the kitchen. Keri followed with the glasses.

'Lela's popping by soon,' Maria said smiling. 'She's back today from visiting her cousin in Athens. It's a shame she couldn't get yesterday, but with her flight delayed, she wasn't expected back until about midnight.'

'It'll be lovely to see her. I got on with Lela the first time I met her. She reminds me very much of Emma. I don't see her for months, but then we just pick up where we left off. I'm so pleased she's got together with Christophe; they make such a lovely couple!'

'Helenka loves it when they visit,' she said as they made their way back to the workshop. 'She took Christophe under her wing the first time she met him. Said he told her they were the family he never had. He loves staying in your old apartment with Anna fussing over him – you know what she's like. I'm really glad that he and Yannis have become firm friends too. He really looked out for him and guided him through managing the hotel project. I can't wait for the grand opening.'

'Yes, it should be good! All the jewellery is boxed up ready for the display unit in the hotel reception now. I reckon there'll be a lot of work coming our way once they're open. It'll be fine as long as we keep ahead of ourselves with the best sellers,' she said as they settled back down to work. 'Manos was thrilled to get the commission for the hotel artwork. He's also given him the contract for any future hotels as well as replacing some of the paintings in his already established ones. It's the break he needed. I'm so proud of him!'

'He's going to be really busy, but at least with the two lads helping out at the boatyard it'll free him up some more time for painting,' replied Maria.

'Yes, that's true. Mind you, he does love dipping in and out of the boatyard. That's where it all started, and it'll always be in his blood.' Keri replied.

Lela made her way to the little blue and white house with a spring in her step, her basket of fresh fruit from the market in Lefko hooked over her arm. It had been good to catch up with her cousin's family, she thought fondly, a twice yearly trip that she looked forward to with much excitement. Nine times out of ten they visited the same places, ate in the same tavernas, and had coffee in the same kafenios. And there was always a trip to the Acropolis and the Temple of Olympian Zeus, followed by a picnic in the national gardens. But she loved it, nonetheless.

Through the side gate she made her way along the path to the workshop where she could see Maria and Keri hard at work.

'*Kalispera!*' she called to them.

'Lela! *Kalispera!*' replied Maria getting off her stool to greet her friend. 'I'm so pleased you could make it.'

'Lovely to see you. It's nice to be back home,' she said sharing with them tales of her holiday.

'Right you two!' said Maria. 'I have something for you both. I just need to pop inside – back in a minute.'

Keri and Lela exchanged puzzled glances as Maria instructed them to stay where they were. Moments later she emerged with two small ivory coloured boxes tied up with gold ribbon.

'My gift to you for being my bridesmaids,' she said offering a box to each of them.

They opened them in unison, undoing the ribbon carefully and taking out the delicately crafted silver bracelets with matching earrings and gasped with wonder.

'Wow! Maria! They're absolutely beautiful!' remarked Lela holding the bracelet over her wrist.

'Oh Maria!' exclaimed Keri taking the earrings from the case first and holding them up to the light to look more closely. Tiny silver hearts on the stud at the top, a long curved olive leaf in the middle and sitting at the bottom a beautifully crafted scallop shell with dainty embossed colorations. 'I've never seen anything so stunning. The design is exquisite!'

Maria fastened the clasp on the bracelet. Lela turned her arm this way and that, admiring the delicate figaro chain. On one of the links was a heart, an olive leaf, and an intricate shell to match the earrings.

'They're so pretty Maria. I can't wait to wear them. Thank you,' said Lela hugging her tightly. Keri joined in the embrace.

'Yes, thank you so much! They're gorgeous. I absolutely love them.'

'I'm really pleased with how they've turned out. I wanted them to match my jewellery. I've made Annys and Katerina bracelets too, theirs have silver hearts and daisies on to reflect that they are flower girls. I'll go and fetch them. Won't be a minute,' she said running back into the house as the girls admired their special gift.

Yannis stood in what would soon be his tiered terrace, not the building site it looked today. Another couple of months and his villa would be finished, well, enough to move into anyway. It might not have any paint on the walls yet, but doors, windows, and a fully functioning bathroom and kitchen were all he needed to move in. Maria and Keri had been fussing over him with their mood boards for the décor and furnishings, his only request being that he didn't want it too girly! He laughed out loud as he remembered their shocked faces. *'As if we would!'*

He made his way back into the village to meet Manos and Alex for drinks, glancing over his shoulder as he walked to see his villa sitting proudly amongst the lemon groves high up on the hillside.

Alex tucked Annys up in bed after reading a bedtime story which had turned into *'just one more pleeeease…'* followed by *'promise this will be the last one…'*

He made his way downstairs blowing kisses into the air for Annys to catch.

'You're a glutton for punishment!' joked Maria. 'She knows you won't stop at the one book. That's why she prefers you reading to her than me!'

'And there was me thinking it was my animated voices she loved!'

'No. You're just a pushover!' she laughed as he scooped her up into his arms and swung her around in their kitchen.

'See you later,' he said kissing her tenderly.

'Have a good night. Give my love to Manos and Yannis.'

'Thanks, won't be late. Will do,' he replied grabbing his keys, wallet and mobile from the sideboard.

She moved into the living room and watched him walking towards the village centre, butterflies still dancing in her tummy, overwhelmed with the happiness and love they shared for one another.

Emma made her way to the top deck to take in the early morning views. Always an early riser she was showered, dressed and in search of coffee. A crew member on watch walked slowly over to her in the semi light of dawn.

'Good morning. Can I get you a coffee?' he asked.

'You must have read my mind! That would be lovely thank you,' she replied. 'What a beautiful morning. The dot on the horizon, what is it?'

'That'll be Corsica. We should arrive mid-afternoon,' he explained before heading off in the direction of the galley.

She leaned against the railing breathing in the salty sea air, hypnotised by the movement of the sea as the yacht sliced its way through, propelling white foam to either side like a parade of galloping white horses.

The first port of call was the picturesque marina of Saint-Florent to the north of the island. Emma stepped onto dry land glancing down at the turquoise waters below as she took Christophe's hand to steady herself. Once in the village centre with its maze of narrow streets they strolled towards the Citadella di San Fiurenzu, an ancient fortress from the fifteenth century. Upon climbing the old stone steps they were rewarded with the most incredible panoramic views.

'Christophe. It's beautiful. Just like you described it.'

'Fabulous isn't it,' he replied indicating the various

landmarks as they walked around the ramparts. 'I've been here a few times. It's a perfect spot to get away from it all and to think.'

'It's so peaceful,' she whispered squeezing his hand.

'It is indeed. And just down there…' he said pointing to the hillside on the left. '…is a tiny café where we can go for lunch. They only serve local traditional food, which is absolutely amazing.'

'Sounds perfect.'

Keri reread the e-mail from Emma describing her journey so far. They had island hopped through the Mediterranean, visiting a couple of ports in Sicily, and had left Malta the previous day, now well on their way to the island. She couldn't wait to see her friend and smiled to herself as she scrolled through the many photos of the beautiful places they'd visited. It took her back to the girls travels through Europe which seemed like a lifetime ago. Christophe had invited Keri, Manos, Yannis, Alex, Maria and a very excited Annys to join them on a jaunt around the island. She hit the reply button on the keyboard to accept on behalf of them all with suggestions for some coves to visit where the water was crystal clear for swimming.

She closed the laptop, tied her hair up loosely and set off down to the village popping into George and Anna's before heading to Ellas for lunch. When she arrived at the taverna Yannis was in deep conversation with Helenka and Manos about the forthcoming champagne reception.

'*Kalispera!*' she called to them and pulled up a chair.

Manos stood up and kissed her before pouring her a drink.

'Yannis was just telling us about the grand hotel opening next week.'

Recapping everything for her, from the schedule of events to what canopies would be served; the guest list and invited dignitaries to the musical performance by an up and coming band from Athens, he then went on to explain that all the glass display cabinets in the reception area were now in place and ready to be filled with the jewellery and glassware.

'It'll be spectacular,' said Keri. 'I'm going to pop in this week to set up the jewellery displays.

'The company producing the glassware are setting up on Tuesday. If you want I can give you their number so you can sort out with them if you want to be there at the same time or separately.'

'That would be good thanks Yannis,' she replied.

'I think Christophe's back a couple of days before the opening,' he added.

'Yes, that's right. They're hoping to arrive mid-week. I've had an e-mail from Emma today and told them we're all looking forward to our day on the yacht.

Alex and Maria settled down at the kitchen table with a glass of wine. Annys was snuggled up in bed after another mammoth bedtime story.

'So much for a quiet affair!' she joked picking through the RSVPs. 'Everyone's accepted! I can't believe it. So that makes seventy adults and eighteen children.'

'It's great everyone can come,' he said topping up their glasses.

'Right, we better get on with all the final preparations then,' she added picking up her wedding notebook and pen.

'*Yamas* my love! To our special day!' he said as they chinked glasses.

The crew secured the yacht alongside the harbour wall and Christophe and Emma stepped ashore. A row of cafes and small tavernas greeted them on the quayside. Hand in hand they made their way up the winding path into the hillside, the warmth of the afternoon sun on their backs. Before long they had arrived at their destination – Christophe's hotel.

'Good afternoon Mr Dafoe. The room is ready for you,' said the receptionist handing him the key card to the honeymoon suite. 'Would you like drinks on the terrace?' she added.

'We'll see the room first, drinks afterwards,' he replied taking the lift to the penthouse.

He slid the card into the handle and pushed the heavy oak door open. She walked into the room and gasped, her eyes drawn to the spectacular view through the concertina floor to ceiling window stretching along the length of the wall. The room had been refurbished to the highest standard, with a fresh modern look in pale blues and soft greens with threads of cream and gold throughout. The colours mirrored the shades of the sea beyond, with flashes of sunlight reflecting on the ivory walls bringing the paintings to life. She ran her hand along the back of the chaise longue positioned to the right of the window. The super king size bed with its crisp white Egyptian cotton sheets was covered with a plethora of cushions in all shapes and sizes in flowery prints. Along the corridor leading to the sumptuous bathroom stood a row of fitted wardrobes in light oak with a dressing room to the side. She made her way dreamily onto the balcony with Christophe following closely behind.

'What do you think?' he asked.

'It's absolutely beautiful,' she replied. 'Maria and Alex will love it!'

'I hope so. Yannis has booked the water taxi, just for the two of them the morning after the wedding. They're staying here for two nights, then being chauffeur driven to the harbour to pick up the ship's tender for the five night cruise.'

'They'll love it Chris! Keri and Manos are looking forward so much to having Annys, and I know Annys is really excited too.'

'You can see their house from here,' he said pointing to the dots on the nearby island. That tall building is the church on the periphery between the two bays of Lefko and Galazios, and if you follow the bay round on the right, that blue speck is their house.'

'Oh yes! I can just about make it out,' she said squinting.

'I think Manos is getting a telescope so Annys can watch the ship sail by,' he said as they made their way back downstairs to the terrace for drinks.

The day of the hotel's grand opening had arrived. A crimson ribbon of pure silk was stretched across the main entrance and quite a crowd had gathered outside.

'*Kalimera oloi. Kalos irthate.*' Christophe said with confidence as he welcomed the guests. 'It is a privilege to be with you all today to celebrate the opening of our first hotel on this beautiful island. My right hand man on this build, Yannis Papadopoulous, has worked tirelessly and the results speak for themselves. The workmanship is exceptional and I'm sure you will agree that the hotel sits spectacularly amongst its neighbours as if it has always been there. Enjoy looking around the hotel, help yourselves to refreshments and if anyone has any questions please feel free to speak to either Yannis or myself. So, without further ado, I now declare the Dionysos Palace Hotel open!'

As the ribbon was cut and floated to the ground the crowd applauded loudly and moved forward climbing the gleaming marble steps into the foyer collecting a glass of champagne on the way. Christophe stepped aside and took a glass off the silver tray as the waitress passed by, making his way over to Emma, Keri, and Manos.

'That was lovely Chris,' Emma said reaching up to kiss him.

'Well done mate!' said Manos patting his back.

'Good job there's plenty of food, they all seem to be heading for it!' added Keri waving to Helenka as she made her way over to them.

Christophe handed her a glass of champagne and kissed her lightly on each cheek. 'Lovely to see you mama H.'

'I wouldn't have missed it for the world,' she replied. 'Yannis said it was something special, and he wasn't wrong!'

'We're really pleased with how it's turned out. Would you like to come with me, and I'll show you behind the scenes, the areas we've not opened to the general public today.'

'Oh yes please. I'd love that. I wouldn't mind seeing the kitchen,' she replied eagerly.

He took her arm in his and they walked slowly towards the rear of the hotel chatting like old friends.

'He has so much respect for Helenka,' said Keri.

'Never stops talking about her. Love how he calls her mama H,' replied Emma.

'Yes, she's certainly taken him under her wing. She was thrilled to bits he'd asked for her help on the Greek menu for the hotel,' added Keri. 'It's given her a new lease of life!'

The last guests had left, glasses and empty food platters had been taken through to the kitchen. Yannis helped his staff tidy away the poseur tables and bar stools into the storeroom in the basement. It was a hive of activity as they prepared to receive the first paying guests later that afternoon.

A light lunch had been arranged by Christophe and Emma for their friends – Helenka, Manos and Keri, Alex, Maria and Annys. Making their way up to the terrace they were soon joined by their hosts and Yannis.

The food arrived. As their glasses were filled Yannis stood up.

'I just wanted to say a big thank you to you all for supporting me on this venture. Christophe for believing in me; Manos for never giving up on me; and mama for always being there for me.'

Helenka wiped away a stray tear and sniffed.

'*Yamas* bro!' said Manos patting his back and raising his glass.

'*Yamas* everyone!' said Christophe as they took their seats for lunch. 'Please enjoy!'

'I can't believe it's been a week since the hotel opening!' said Emma to Christophe as they welcomed their guests on board.

'It's flown by!' he replied lifting Annys safely onto the

yacht. The ropes untethered and they were on their way for a day sailing around the island.

Anna placed a vase of fresh flowers onto the sideboard and a small basket of provisions in the kitchen for their guests and made her way back downstairs to the shop.

'All done love?' asked George as he emptied some bags of coins into the cash register.

'Yes, it looks lovely,' she replied looking at her watch. 'Spiros should be at the airport now. Their flight's due in any minute. Can't wait to see them again!'

'Over here!' Spiros shouted across the car park as he opened the car boot.

'Good to see you again mate!' Patrick said reaching over to shake hands.

'Hello Spiros!' said Moya as he took the last of the bags from her and kissed her hand.

'Good journey?' he asked as he drove away from the airport.

'Yes, not bad at all thanks,' replied Patrick from the passenger seat. Moya sat comfortably in the back marvelling at the beautiful scenery as they made their way through the mountainous roads and down into the village.

'I spoke to Helenka last night,' she said. 'Keri still has no idea we're arriving early – thinks we're coming the day before the wedding!'

'I know. She's asked me to pick you up in a couple of days!' he replied laughing. 'Anna's got the apartment ready, so you'll be able to freshen up before we meet at Ellas for lunch. George is closing the shop early so they can join us, and Maria's parents are coming too. Christophe's under strict instructions not to be back before 5 o'clock, so that'll give us plenty of time for a catch up and help them prepare for later.

White lacy clouds floated slowly through the pale blue sky changing shape high above them.

'Look!' declared Emma. 'That one looks like a horse!'

'Strange shaped horse! It's more like a cat.' said Maria shielding the sun from her eyes.

'No idea what you two are looking at…all I can see is a spoon!' added Keri, as they all burst into fits of laughter.

Maria swung her legs off the side of the sun lounger and stretched.

'I think that's the cove we're heading for,' she said pointing to the tall grey cliffs in the distance with an abundance of caves carved out by the sea. The entrance to one of the larger caves bore weathered rock formations to either side. The three of them made their way from the top deck and down the spiral staircase to join the others as the engines slowed. Clearly visible was the seabed where the anchor had been dropped. The ladder was lowered at the rear and a small dingy launched over the side for Annys to use. Christophe checked her life jacket was fitted correctly and helped her down the ladder into the dingy where Manos was waiting. Yannis bobbed about in the water at the side of it.

'Come on in girls! The water's lovely,' he shouted up to them.

'We don't need asking twice!' Maria yelled as they all jumped in together.

'Helenka! Theo!' called Moya as she made her way over to the bar.

'Come here love!' replied Helenka hugging her friend. 'So pleased you were able to make it.'

'Thanks for sorting everything. Look – there's Anna and George,' she said excitedly walking over to greet them.

'*Kalimera!*' said Anna squeezing Moya tightly. 'Is the room alright for you?'

'It's perfect! Thank you so much for the flowers and hamper.'

'Our pleasure,' Anna replied as they wandered over to the others arm in arm.

'Spiros will be here shortly,' said Theo. 'Let me get everyone a drink. Lunch won't be long.'

All back on board they gathered on the deck for lunch as the anchor was raised. The yacht moved gently away from the rocks and headed for a tiny hamlet on the west of the island with a small port, a smattering of pastel painted houses and a long stretch of golden sand, for an afternoon of ball games on the beach.

'Yummy!' said a very excited Annys tucking into a bowlful of creamy chocolate ice cream.

'This is my favourite flavour too!' said Manos.

'Can I have some more please?' she asked politely.

'You most certainly can!' he replied topping her dish up and pouring a generous helping of chocolate sauce over the top. 'You definitely deserve seconds after all that swimming!'

'Thank you for lunch,' said Moya as she helped Helenka clear away the pots.

The Little Blue and White House

'It's been lovely catching up,' she replied stacking the dishwasher.

Anna joined them with a tray of cups and glasses as the men moved the tables into a large rectangle in the centre of the room for the dinner party and arranged seventeen chairs around it. Theo emptied the box of decorations whilst Maria's papa helped Spiros bring in the buckets of pink and cream flowers from the cool outbuildings. Moya, Anna, and Maria's mama lined the three tall clear vases on the bar and started to work their magic. Helenka set the white china dinner plates, side plates and cutlery onto the crisp white linen tablecloth, adding a pink napkin to each one. Theo polished the crystal stemmed glasses, whilst Patrick put the small cream candles into their holders dotting them around the table for Helenka to tweak once the flowers were all in place, and then helped Spiros thread the pink and cream fairly lights through the beams above the table. The final touch, thousands of tiny crystals were sprinkled over the table. Perfect!

'Who's for a game of cricket?' shouted Alex as he hammered the stumps into the sand.

'Me! Me!' cried Annys discarding her bucket and spade. 'Can I hit first?'

'I'm sure you can bat first,' replied Alex as everyone positioned themselves in a large circle.

Sometime later and with the heat of the afternoon sun beating down, Annys was declared the winner! Gathering all their belongings they made their way back to the coolness of the yacht and some very welcome refreshments.

Gaining speed on the return to Galazios Bay the breeze came in waves coating the skin in a light mist of bitter saltiness. Manos pointed out to a fascinated Annys her little blue and white house as they neared the bay.

'Look mummy! It's our house! Over there!' she said eagerly.

'Oh yes darling!' Maria replied thinking this would have been what Demetrius saw twice a day when he was on the fishing boat. She sighed. Alex joined them and hugged Maria tightly as if he knew where her thoughts had drifted off to.

'Action stations everyone!' screeched Helenka as she spotted the yacht navigating the headland and entering the bay. 'I reckon they'll be here in about fifteen minutes.'

All the hot food was ladled into casserole dishes and bowls full of vegetables put onto the hotplate to keep warm. Baskets with rolls and breads were covered with tea towels to stop the flies having a feast. Theo, Spiros, and George hovered around the bar whilst Helenka waited on the terrace to welcome the day trippers.

Annys was first to arrive racing along the boardwalk towards Helenka.

'It was fantastic on the boat! We swam in the sea at the caves and played games on the beach. I had chocolate ice-cream!' she gabbled breathlessly.

'Welcome back everyone!' said Helenka as they filed into the taverna.

'What's going off here?' asked Maria taking in the scene before her. 'Have you got guests?'

'Yes my darling…you are our guests!' replied Helenka moving to the side. 'We thought we'd have a special pre-wedding celebration.'

'It's beautiful. Thank you so much. Just as I thought the

day couldn't get any better,' she replied pulling Helenka in her arms.

'Thank you so much,' added Alex taking Maria's hand.

All the guests gathered round as Theo and Spiros handed out the drinks.

'Perfect timing Christophe!' said Helenka with a smile.

'Are they here?' he whispered.

'Yes, in the kitchen,' she chuckled.

Helenka made her way over to Keri to ask about their day.

'Oh I forgot to light the candles. Would you mind popping into the kitchen for the lighter please? It's on the shelf at the side.'

'Of course,' she replied weaving in and out of everyone. She pushed the door open.

'Surprise!' shouted Moya and Patrick at the same time.

Keri jumped backwards, her face blank with confusion.

'Mammy! Daddy! What are you doing here?' she yelled running up to them. 'I don't believe it! When did you get here? I had no idea!'

The three of them hugged tightly as Manos joined them.

'You made it then!' he said grinning. 'Great to see you both!'

'Were you in on this too?' asked Keri not wanting to let them go in case they were just a figment of her imagination and would disappear before her very eyes.

'Maybe…' he winked as the four of them made their way into the dining area to an abundance of cheering.

'I now pronounce you husband and wife,' declared the priest proudly. 'You may now kiss the bride!'

'*Na zisete!*' echoed throughout the congregation as the newlyweds made their way out of the church on the hill and into the bright sunshine. Emerging from the darkness they were treated to an unbroken rainbow rising out of the sea arching high up into a cloudless sky before falling back down again. Underneath its midpoint a dark red fishing boat disappeared into the distance. Maria's eyes sparkled like sunbeams dancing on the sea as she held Alex's hand tightly and touched her heart-shaped locket feeling a wave of peace and happiness overwhelm her. On her wrist Demetrius' pink shell shimmered on the bracelet as the sunlight caught the silver hearts on either side. Before long the happy couple were joined by their bridesmaids Keri and Lela, and flower girls Annys and Katerina.

The wedding guests made their way down the hillside and along the boardwalk towards Ellas. Fresh flowers interwoven with cream twinkle lights adorned the handrail on the wooden staircase leading up into the taverna. Ivory and soft pink swathes of tulle embellished with flickering lights draped over the balustrades encompassing the room, with matching tulle bows prettifying the backs of the wooden chairs. Three long tables ran parallel to the top table dressed in white cotton tablecloths embroidered with delicate rose quartz flowers along the edges, and fresh fragrant pink rose petals scattered over the tables. As the guests found their place settings the alabaster coloured candles shone warm and welcoming.

Manos picked up the microphone and stood at the side of the steps.

'May I have your attention,' he said as a hush descended throughout the room. 'It is my great honour to introduce you to the new Mr and Mrs Galanis. Please join me in congratulating the happy couple!'

The music started as they stepped forward hand in hand to rapturous applause from their family and friends. They took their seats with the rest of the room following suit. The wedding reception was soon in full swing, with the hired caterers doing a grand job, even if Helenka had been on tenterhooks all week about allowing them to take over her taverna, in particular her precious kitchen! Alex and Maria sipped champagne as they watched their guests chatting happily.

Evening fell and the atmosphere in the room changed with the pretty glow from thousands of glistening lights. The music slowed and the guests mingled eagerly awaiting the announcement of the wedding dance. Lela took the silk sash and arranged it carefully over Maria's Chantilly ivory lace dress, whilst Alex unfolded the large white cotton handkerchief.

'Please put your hands together for the bride and groom as they dance the *Kalamatianos*.' said Manos into the microphone. 'You are invited to pin your monetary gift to Maria during the dance.'

Annys and Katerina ran up to them to be the first ones to do so with a little help from Keri and Lela who had the job of handing out the pins, along with small envelopes. Before long the sash was laden with an array of notes, envelopes, and handmade pouches from their very generous guests. The heavy sash was removed and placed into the box with the wedding cards behind the top table.

As the evening drew to a close, the last of the guests

started making their way home singing and dancing as they went. The caterers had long gone, with a promise of returning in the morning to collect their wares. The wedding party, Helenka and Theo, Christophe and Emma, the only ones left.

'Who's ready for a coffee?' asked Helenka kicking off her shoes.

It was a resounding yes all round.

Christophe joined Helenka in the kitchen to help bring the coffees out onto the terrace. He slipped a folder under his arm which had been hidden earlier and popped it under his chair. When everyone was seated he whispered to Annys that it was time to give them their wedding present. Annys jumped enthusiastically onto Emma's knee as Christophe tapped the side of a glass with a knife.

'I just wanted to say what a pleasure it has been to help you celebrate your special day. You have wonderful family and friends who have made me…us…feel so welcome. I am thankful to call you my friends and that our paths are now woven together. You have shown me what true friendship is,' he said retrieving the folder and taking Emma's hand. 'Our gift to you is for a few days away. Keri and Manos are going to look after Annys, and I'm sure they're going to have a great time, as are you!'

'Yes we are!' shouted Annys as she hopped off Emma's lap to take the folder from Christophe and danced over to Maria and Alex with it.

'We are indeed! We've got lots of things planned haven't we darling,' Keri added as Annys hugged her on her way past.

Annys perched on Alex's knee as Maria carefully opened the wallet and gasped with astonishment. She took out the top sheet and read the words out loud:

Mr and Mrs Alex Galanis are
warmly invited to spend a two night
spa hotel break on our neighbouring island,
before boarding a cruise ship for five nights,
stopping off at three Cyclades Islands,
and disembarking in Athens for a flight home.
All onboard food, drink, and entertainment included
and hire of a tuxedo and evening gown with accessories
for the formal evening, where you will be the Captain's guests.

'Oh my God! I can't believe it!' squealed Maria as she handed the letter to Alex and took the documents from the envelope. 'Christophe! Emma! I can't take it all in! I don't know what to say!'

'It's only what you both deserve,' he replied as she made her way over to thank them properly. Alex joined her.

'Thank you so much! You've no idea what this means to us both. I really can't thank you enough…and I've never actually seen Maria speechless before!' he joked.

Annys ran up to join in with the celebrations.

'I can't wait for you to go on holiday! Manos and Keri are moving into our house to look after me. And Tasha is going on holiday too, to Helenkas. Manos said you'll be able to wave to us from the ship!' she declared, her words tumbling out with excitement.

Maria scooped her daughter up into her arms.

'I love you so much my darling. Have you had a lovely day?'

'Oh yes mummy. The best day ever! I love you too, and my new daddy Alex.'

Maria held her a little tighter and breathed in her sweet scent.

Manos took the cover off the telescope lens and set the focus whilst Annys helped Keri bring the drinks from the kitchen, placing them onto the patio table.

'It's all ready to go,' he said to Annys lifting her up onto his shoulders.

Keri's mobile pinged.

'*We're on our way! Can just about see the house. We're on deck ten, the second balcony cabin from the front.*' she read out loud.

Manos carried Annys over to the stool behind the telescope.

'There they are!' shouted Keri. 'Look! I can see them waving!'

Sure enough, in the distance two very small familiar figures waving their arms frantically as the ship glided majestically by. Annys was captivated seeing them through the telescope.

'Mummy and daddy Alex saw me waving!' she said happily.

'They certainly did darling,' replied Keri as the ship moved slowly out of the Straits, its horn resounding around the bay.

The island, now only a speck, soon disappeared from view, the only sound to be heard was the crashing of the waves against the bow as it changed course. Lost in her thoughts Maria closed her eyes feeling the last of the sunshine kissing her face as she leant against the balcony railing.

'Mrs Galanis…' whispered Alex quietly, not wanting to startle his wife. He wrapped his arms around her waist. 'You have made me the happiest man in the world. I love you so much. You are my best friend. I will always be here for you… for you and Annys. We'll have so many adventures together.'

She turned to face her husband, her radiant smile full of joy, her eyes sparkling illuminating her soul. Taking his hands in hers she led him inside, kissing him with fervour.

'Mr Galanis…you are my love, my life. I am the happiest woman on earth. I feel so safe in your arms my darling Alex,' she breathed caressing the nape of his neck. 'I love you with all my heart, and always will.'

Telescope neatly stored, they made their way inside, Annys eager to finish her painting.

'Would you like to go and see Tasha later darling, and we can have some tea with Helenka and Theo?' Keri asked.

'Oh yes please! Can I have pizza?' replied Annys concentrating on the job in hand.

'Of course you can!'

Annys finished her picture, put the lid on her paints and took her pot of water and brushes over to the sink to rinse. Her artwork entitled *My Family* left to dry on the kitchen table with each character carefully labelled with love – *Angel Daddy; Mummy; Daddy Alex; Annys and Tasha.*

This book is printed on paper from sustainable sources managed under the Forest Stewardship Council (FSC) scheme.

It has been printed in the UK to reduce transportation miles and their impact upon the environment.

For every new title that Troubador publishes, we plant a tree to offset CO_2, partnering with the More Trees scheme.

For more about how Troubador offsets its environmental impact, see www.troubador.co.uk/sustainability-and-community